THE FLORENTINE ENTANGLEMENT

A NOVEL OF THE COLD WAR

PAMELA NORSWORTHY

Black Rose Writing | Texas

ISBN: 978-1-68513-694-9
LIBRARY OF CONGRESS CONTROL NUMBER:
PUBLISHED BY BLACK ROSE WRITING
www.blackrosewriting.com

Printed in the United States of America
Suggested Retail Price (SRP) $21.95

The Florentine Entanglement is printed in Book Antiqua

*As a planet-friendly publisher, Black Rose Writing does its best to eliminate unnecessary waste to reduce paper usage and energy costs, while never compromising the reading experience. As a result, the final word count vs. page count may not meet common expectations.

PRAISE FOR PAMELA NORSWORTHY

"Sharp prose. An incessant undercurrent of suspicion. *The Florentine Entanglement* by Pamela Norsworthy is an edge-of-your seat Cold War espionage thriller, deftly weaving political intrigue with personal betrayal. Norsworthy's novel keeps readers on edge until the last page. Classic spy fiction fans will appreciate this story's authenticity, its morally complex characters, and the theme of loyalty—in both marriage and intelligence work."
–Cam Torrens, bestselling author of *The Tyler Zahn suspense* series

"Spies and lies abound in the rocky political climate following World War II. Will love prevail, or will this entanglement bring only regrets? *The Florentine Entanglement* is a lush historical novel brimming with Pamela Norsworthy's elegant prose and rich details. This gripping tale of espionage is one not to miss."
–Anna Daugherty, award winning author of *The Grace Church* series

"A *Kirkus Reviews* 'Get It' Selection: The fates of two extended families are intertwined during World War II in Norsworthy's stirring historical novel [*War Bonds*]. Norsworthy masterfully captures the action on two fronts: home and battlefield. Her thorough research lends an immediacy to the narrative that makes the reader feel present for each scene."
–Kirkus Reviews

"In her debut novel, *War Bonds*, Pamela Norsworthy takes readers on a gut-wrenching journey through love and loss in World War II Europe. She tells the sweeping epic through the eyes of British and American POWs, a foster child forced to mature beyond his years, a Nazi commandant and his wife, and others. The story made me sob as I contemplated fidelity to spouse and country, moral boundaries loosening in the face of war, personal and patriotic sacrifice, evil, grace, and the drive to find beauty in an often-ugly world."
–Chris Lancette, for the Washington Independent Review of Books

"Readers looking for an engrossing, often poignant story to touch their hearts will find it here. Well-written and rigorously researched, *War Bonds* is a stirring novel and a welcome addition to the World War II genre."
–Historical Novel Society

THE FLORENTINE ENTANGLEMENT

For Gray, who breathes a special sort of kindness
that sweetens the world.

"It is inconceivable that a secret arm of the government has to comply with all the overt orders of the government."
–James Jesus Angleton, Former Chief of Counterintelligence, CIA

Following is cover plan to be implemented immediately:

"U-2 aircraft was on weather mission originating Adana, Turkey.

Purpose was study of clear air turbulence.

During flight in Southeast Turkey, pilot reported he had

oxygen difficulties. This last word heard at 0700Z over emergency

frequency. U-2 aircraft did not land Adana as planned and it can

only be assumed is now down. A search effort is under way in

Lake Van area. "

FYI normal procedures for search for aircraft will be

initiated by Adana Base Commander and initial press release will

be from Adana. Pilot's name being withheld pending notification

of next of kin.

PART ONE

CHAPTER
ONE

Saturday, April 30, 1960
Washington, DC

When Eleanor turned forty, Talbot staged an awkward little surprise party meant to lend credence to the idea that he was a loving husband and theirs a happy union, an ordinary marriage like those of their neighbors and work friends and so on. He meant well, Eleanor could give him that, so she resolved to respond with conspicuous enthusiasm. After all, she had a little actress in her.

Entering the airless back room at a little Italian place off Dupont Circle, Eleanor extended her arms in manufactured delight to greet the gathered guests. And here we are, she thought, clasping her hands and drawing them to her chest, nodding and offering a little bow of gratitude, the air of formality a vestige of her upbringing. Her eyes swept over the group in their cocktail dresses and pearls, sport coats and club ties. Members of the ensemble cast, tonight appearing in the role of Friend of the Principal. People from the neighborhood and the club, colleagues from the library who answered the bell when Talbot had called—probably at the eleventh hour. But they turned up on cue, each of them, reliable and dependable in that uniquely American way, souls who kept their church clothes clean and in good repair so they could, at a moment's notice, attend the funerals of even the less popular members of St. John's Episcopal Church, filling the pews for the ceremony of consecration less because the deceased was a person they would miss, more out of a sturdy sense of obligation. Or possibly because in a town like Washington, DC, there was always a chance of running into somebody important at the reception afterwards. These dutiful guests would be pleased, in upcoming weeks, to pepper conversations with mentions of how they'd been in the room that night for Eleanor Bentley's fortieth birthday party. Many would note, eyebrows raised, that Talbot himself had invited them. Yes, that Talbot Bentley.

Talbot left her side and circulated through the room, radiating a mission-accomplished satisfaction. He'd been out of the house the better part of the day, presumably seeing to final details of this little party. Flower arrangements on both the center table and the bar (dahlias—Caroline's favorite, she observed) seemed evidence of that. Swirling his bourbon in his glass—Jim Beam always—he moved about in that direct way of his, standing a hair too close in the habit of many Southern-born men, communicating earnest attention and challenging the person he was speaking with to step back, to create a hair's breadth of space. His fit physique, his handsome face, his solid confidence earned him wide permission to do this. In a man less attractive, this closeness would irritate. He clapped the men on the back, saying a few words as he reached for their women. Eleanor watched as he leaned in to kiss their cheeks, seeing how often he took just the slightest extra second to exhale, his breath warm on their scented necks, leaving the women to wonder if they'd imagined the intimacy—had he paused when lips brushed skin? Talbot Bentley worked for the government, after all. He couldn't be making a pass. Could he? The recipients of his breathy kisses would rationalize that one bourbon too many explained it. He was approaching the line, perhaps, but hadn't crossed it.

He stopped to visit with each couple—there were no singletons—letting them know how grateful he was they came, choosing a question for each that demonstrated his interest in their lives and welfare, collecting bits of information from them, sorting it, filing it away. *How are the kids? You getting all the appreciation you deserve at that new firm? Y'all moved out to Fairfax? How's the new house?* It did not cross the mind of a single guest that Talbot's interest in the comings and goings in their lives, the progress of their careers, the maturing intellects and skills of their children stemmed from a calculated or inauthentic place. The tilt of his head, the elegant, coordinated movement of dozens of tiny muscles in his face masked that this was less about getting to know his guests and more about his ceaseless drive to gather intelligence, whatever the setting. He laughed loudly with Leslie Grant, the rector at St. John's, who smiled as he sipped his Glenfiddich, the choice of Scotch practically a sacrament among Episcopal clergymen.

Talbot's quite pleased with himself, Eleanor observed, thinking he pulled off this little operation and surprised me.

As her guests began casting about for a second or third cocktail, servers began their ceremonial march from the kitchen, bearing plates of the restaurant's signature chicken parmesan. Talbot settled in beside Eleanor at the table, accepting the guests' praise of the deliciously flavored food as if he himself were the sous chef. Conversation traversed the moment's hot topics—the ghastly state of politics—Ike's dour VP whom nobody seemed to like and a Massachusetts senator who seemed far too young likely to face off in the presidential election; the disquieting noises out of Cuba, once a favorite playground among the Bentleys' circle. The summit between President Eisenhower and Soviet Leader Khrushchev was just weeks away, those around the table wondering if that meeting might lead to a clearing away of the persistent nuclear shadow they now lived beneath. Anxiety was high that the Soviets had more missiles and were building bombers so fast the United States would never catch up. The women whispered about the juicier subjects too: marriages teetering, teenage girls who'd suddenly departed town for a six-month visit with relatives, college boys drummed out of their dream schools for drinking or grades, one for having been discovered liking another college boy more than university rules permitted.

One by one, the diners relinquished their knives and forks and leaned back in their chairs, sated, but for a few more sips of this or that. A post-entrée lull overspread the room, infiltrating the thick cigarette smoke and the heavy perfume some of the women wore. On cue, the waitstaff swept in to clear the plates, replenish cocktails, then present an oversized platter with a birthday cake ablaze with candles.

"Hummingbird cake!" Talbot proclaimed as a waiter placed it in front of Eleanor.

Ah, Eleanor thought, Helen's doing. She forced her eyes wide with apparent delight.

Plucky Helen, Eleanor called her, because of her irritatingly can-do attitude. Whenever Eleanor went to see Tal at work, she first had to get past Helen, his secretary, who stood guard at the reception desk outside his private office. The woman was so cheerful, so positive, so *in charge*, that Eleanor wanted to poke an eye out. Either Helen's or her own. Helen had been with Talbot since last summer and like many in a long line of his secretaries, she always seemed so eager to go above and beyond for the boss. Some of these girls, Eleanor learned, did it because they wanted to ascend the ladder at CIA—break the mold and move into an intelligence officer job usually reserved for men. Others did it for the opposite reason; they wanted to find a man and being helpful and compliant, they believed, was the best way to secure one. If the pattern held, Eleanor figured Helen would be either promoted or engaged before too much longer.

Despite her contribution to the evening, Helen was not among the invited guests who would soon be pushing morsels of hummingbird cake around their plates. In fact, few women in the room would actually taste the cake, most of them waving off the little dessert plates, passing them on with a surge of virtuousness even as they murmured to their husbands they were ready for more alcohol. The plates orbited the table as the Auclairs arrived, Caroline rushing to Eleanor to apologize—the kids! the sitter!—while Rémy worked his way over to Talbot, offering a handshake and a sheepish shrug.

"Birthday girl! How's your night been?" asked Caroline, pulling up a chair and waving down the waiter for a drink. She looked at Eleanor, expectantly, eyes intense, a crease between her brows. Eleanor concluded something dramatic was at the root of their late arrival.

Eleanor lifted her wineglass, holding it in front of her lips as she spoke. "Tal probably invited them all this morning," she said under her breath, then more loudly, "So, where have you two been?"

"Oh, you know, everything."

On this, her fortieth birthday, a day presumably centered on her, Eleanor felt entitled to specifics. She waited placidly until the dead air compelled Caroline to speak.

"Rémy put a few hours in at the office this morning, then he golfed. Then he waltzes in about the time I expect to leave, but he has to shower and dress and Rémy being Rémy, he does not rush. So here we are. I drank three cocktails waiting for him, which was probably not the best idea since I haven't eaten anything since lunch. And we exchanged a few words over that. So. I'm sorry. Blame him. Have you enjoyed your night?"

"Feels a bit improvised," Eleanor confided, an over-bright smile on her face. "Talbot practically had to tell me what was happening to get me out of the house. Sorta spoils the surprise. Said he needed me to run an errand with him, then made me change into this dress—said we were going to grab a bite. Not even a milestone birthday that marks his wife as very, very old was enough to cause him to come up with a good cover story and work out the sticky details. He knows better than most that covert operations require planning." She took a long pull of her Chablis, scanning the room to make sure only Caroline was within earshot of her whispered rant. "Seems to me, he always thinks through things for work, or planning his fishing trips, the golf weekends. Even makes his staff help. For the important stuff." She paused again, this time for a pointed drag on her cigarette. "Some things must not be important enough for him to tap all his resources."

Caroline patted her hand. "Well, this is a bit unlike you. You're usually pretty sanguine about the mess that comes with marriage. But listen, that's men, right? They don't listen. They don't plan. We juggle work and home. They juggle themselves, and that's about all they can handle."

"Well, I won't be juggling him tonight, I can tell you that," Eleanor confided. Caroline lifted her gin and tonic in affirmation and salute, her eyes scanning for Talbot, who waved when he spotted her.

•   •   •

After he settled the bill on a table laden with full ashtrays and empty highball glasses, lipstick-stained napkins in crumpled heaps, Talbot stood and reached his arm around Eleanor, tucking her to his side—a gesture she usually appreciated but that tonight felt too possessive. She cast a last look at the cake— over half remained—and felt a ping of satisfaction at leaving it behind.

Eleanor inhaled the balmy air as they made their way to the car, waiting for the question she knew he'd wanted to ask all night.

"Did you enjoy your surprise party?" he asked, his hand massaging just above her hip. She resisted the urge to pull away. He had gone to all this trouble, after all.

"I did," she lied. "How were you able to pull all that together without me knowing?"

"I had a little help." They reached the car, Talbot leaning back on the passenger door, reaching for her and pulling her to him. "Happy birthday, my love." He ducked his head into the warm space at her neck, breath sharp with bourbon, his hands finding the hem of her dress, working their way up her thigh. He kissed her, long and slow. A precursor, she knew.

"Ok, tiger. Get in the car. I'll drive. It would not do for you to smash up your Corvette on my birthday."

His hands continued their work. "I'm fine, Ellie. It's just that you feel mighty good tonight. And this is good for us. We need to do more of this to keep us…you know…" he trailed off, then repeated himself as drunken people do, proving a point with recycled assertions.

Eleanor took his face between her palms. "Of course, you're fine. We always have sex standing up on the street at two in the morning. Not the least bit unusual. Get in the car if you'd like to finish what you seem to want to start."

Talbot smiled and obliged, crawling into the low-slung sports car, thudding into the bucket seat.

Eleanor did not enjoy driving Tal's car, not just the mechanics of it, but its conspicuousness—the screaming red color, the roaring engine. Corvettes begged for attention, especially in DC's sea of black sedans. Eleanor turned the key and shifted into gear, steering the car eastward. Despite the hour, there was traffic on the streets, mostly government employees, she imagined, heading to and from offices and conference rooms to manage countless crises the country would never even know about.

Talbot's eyes closed within minutes, his chest rising and falling as his breathing slowed. Eleanor moved through the adopted city she had never expected to know so well. She had practically memorized the street grid as L'Enfant designed it, including the traffic circles that confounded visitors, the neat way the National Mall tied the federal district together.

Her route took her onto Massachusetts Avenue and Wisconsin, along Embassy Row where the Soviet Embassy perched so near the center of things. In DC, she had learned, information—not celebrity or wealth—was the currency that opened doors to power. Talbot was a creature of all of it, but Eleanor still felt like an interloper. She knew her way around, certainly, and had her favorite cafes and boutiques—most of them in Georgetown. She'd gotten to know a group at St. John's Church and felt fairly comfortable when she and Tal attended, despite her lack of church background. But this Washington way of life differed so dramatically from how she'd been raised, when she'd owned few material things but had been rich in family—family she missed so deeply that she simply walled off her memories of them as disconnected from her, like characters in a movie she watched long ago.

She took Key Bridge over the Potomac, leaving DC for Virginia, where multitudes of government employees lived, including the Bentleys. Their Arlington townhouse was situated just a few blocks from the library where Eleanor worked, giving Talbot an easy commute to his office downtown. He and other intelligence officers were dispersed among buildings throughout the area. Next year, the new CIA headquarters was scheduled to open at Langley. By all accounts, this would be a state-of-the-art spy station with sophisticated technology that would ensure no contraband could be smuggled in nor secrets smuggled out. It was a standard hard to meet with the current set up, the hodgepodge of office buildings currently in use, adjacent to businesses and enterprises one assumed were legitimate—but might provide security holes the country's enemies could exploit. The Bentleys had once planned to relocate closer to the new headquarters, perhaps in McLean or Vienna, to a home with more bedrooms and a yard. But when no children arrived, there was no reason to find more space.

Eleanor pulled into the garage then came around to help Talbot heave himself out of the car. He stood, rocked unsteadily, and offered a small, apologetic smile. Leaning heavily on the car, he reached for her hand and drew it to his lips. "My beautiful wife. You are, you know. Beautiful. But man, I'm kinda tired all the sudden."

His little nap had sobered him up a bit, dampened his ardor.

"I know, Talbot. You've had a long day. Okay, let's get inside and get you into bed," said Eleanor, relieved she would not have to demonstrate her gratitude for the surprise party on this particular night.

"What time is it?" he asked suddenly, working to focus bleary eyes on his watch.

"A little after two-thirty. What—you have an appointment?"

"Can you do me a favor, Ellie? I'm gonna sleep just a little more, but I gotta make a call in an hour or so. Just a check-in. Can you make sure I'm up and moving?"

"I can do that, Talbot. I'll set my alarm and have some coffee ready."

He slipped his arm around her as they made their way to their bedroom. "I'm a lucky man, Ellie," he proclaimed. "You know what I need, and you give it to me, you support me, and I hope you saw that tonight with the party…"

"We're both lucky, Talbot," she interrupted. "Lucky we found each other." She helped him wrestle out of his shoes, his pants. "Amid all that chaos, the Fates brought us together."

CHAPTER
TWO

Eight months earlier, September, 1959
Cabin John, MD

Helen Sizemore waited in a booth at the back of the diner, silk scarf knotted under her chin, face half-hidden by oversized sunglasses, weighing whether she had time to order another Coke as cocktails, unfortunately, were not on the menu. She ran her palm across the sticky Formica table, brushing crumbs from someone else's meal onto the floor, noting a spill of salt near the napkin dispenser. She'd leave that for the waitress to clean up. A pair of women perched at the counter, hunched over midafternoon milkshakes, talking, giggling like girls between slurps, enjoying their freedom, perhaps, now that the school year had resumed. They seemed flighty, insubstantial to Helen, who felt fortunate she held a responsible job, a serious position, one that required her discretion and judgment. One customer, then another stopped in to pick up an order but it was mostly quiet — too early for the dinner rush.

Outside the window, Helen saw nothing out of the ordinary — no one settled on a bench, fixated on a single page of the newspaper, nobody having an extended conversation in the phone booth on the corner, no car circling and recircling the block. Just schoolchildren, stepping exuberantly from their bus, sweaters slung around necks and waists in deference to the warm September afternoon. Helen wondered if Indian-summer days like this made the students harder to wrangle. "Perhaps I should have listened to my mother and become a teacher," she mused, not for the first time. "It would have to be less stressful."

At lunch, Helen had left two sheets of paper—a carbon slipped in between—in the carriage of her IBM Electromatic typewriter. He had placed a single crumpled tissue in his trash can to confirm. A single sheet in the carriage would designate their meeting point at an inn south on Route 123, farther from the city, at the cusp of Virginia's horse country. No time for that today. The diner was only a few miles from DC in Cabin John, Maryland. She'd discovered it over the summer after this whole thing began. Small and verging on seedy, it was not a place their colleagues would wander into.

Helen had been recruited to CIA out of the College of William and Mary. A double-major in foreign affairs and romance languages, she was fluent in French and Spanish, managed pretty well in Italian, got by in Portuguese. It baffled her that Talbot had served overseas and met his wife in Italy but never cultivated much beyond the rudiments of a second language. She had already inquired at the Defense Language Institute about beginning a course of study in Russian. Helen hoped her linguistic facility would help propel her beyond the secretarial pool. She'd met women who worked as reports officers at CIA, and she hoped securing that role might launch her into the agent ranks. The personnel officer she consulted told her that perhaps after a year in Washington, she would be eligible to apply for clerk-typist jobs overseas.

"These days, there aren't many foreign postings for female agents who look like you," he had insisted. "We need women with Asian features for work in Indochina."

There was no hint of that in Helen's round green eyes and light brown hair. Given that the CIA personnel office wasn't always transparent about such things, Helen stayed attuned to movement around the office, openings that could lead to a new assignment. If she'd been old enough during Second World War, she often said, she would have forced her way into the Office of Strategic Services or maybe the British Special Operations Executive and been willing to employ whatever ruse was needed — sexual coercion, blackmail — to help win the war. Once she became fluent in Russian, she'd gladly take a placement behind the Iron Curtain.

But her assignment to Talbot's office had complicated her picture of what the future might hold. Barely a week into the job, when she was still finding her way around the building and still getting to know her boss, Talbot had asked her to retrieve lunch from the cafeteria for the both of them, so they could continue work reviewing a set of files. She brought up trays of meatloaf and salad, Talbot rushing to help her lay it out on the table in the conference room attached to his office, asking if he could pour her a coffee from the office pot.

They sat, finally, Talbot at the head of the table and Helen to his left. He reached a hand and clasped her wrist, locked his dark eyes on hers. "Dressed or undressed?" he asked, waiting a beat before he pointed to his green salad.

"Undressed," she responded.

"Excellent, Helen. Undressed is what I prefer. Always."

She looked away, hands fluttering to her hair then fussing over her meal as she considered how to respond. It took a moment for her to gather her courage to look him in the eye. "Good then. Glad I did it the way you like it," she said, shocking herself with her eagerness to play out this flirtation.

His hand slid from her wrist up her arm, stopping just below her shoulder, where he squeezed. "I'd say you're batting 1000, Helen. You're gonna do just fine here."

Settling happily into her role, Helen watched Tal deploy his smooth magnetism throughout their workplace — not just with her but with receptionists and cafeteria workers, with the girl who brought the briefing pouch each morning, with his male colleagues. Helen marveled at the connections he made and the trust he developed. Like most in his orbit, she was captivated by the athleticism in Tal's movement, the relaxed way he stood, mature and boyish at the same time. There was something both compelling and disarming about Talbot that made others want to move in his sphere. His role overseeing a top-secret project that had him reporting directly to Director Dulles added to his allure. But as far as Helen observed, it was only with her that Talbot fully exercised his skill at innuendo, patiently drawing her in, waiting for her to absorb a suggestive comment. This was evidence, she believed, the two of them were moving towards a unique, intimate connection.

When he emerged from his office into the reception area where she sat, to bring her a document or make a request, it took discipline for her to stay focused on the topic at hand. He had a habit of looking directly in her eyes and holding her gaze, daring her to be the first to look away. She liked to think of it as their private little contest. They developed a habit of lunch together in the conference room, where they chatted about his wartime service and her years at William and Mary, eventually nibbling around the edges of his marriage, of her career ambitions. A month into her tenure, Helen engrossed in her typing, Talbot drifted to her desk and placed a hand on her neck. He squeezed and left it there, his thumb massaging. Helen held her breath, leaning into the pressure on her skin.

"I need the notes on the folks in Adana," he said, extending an arm around her, presumably to reach her desk top to look for it. His Old Spice aftershave wafted around her head, earthy and male. She closed her eyes as she breathed in the scent then wheeled her chair around to face him. His eyes locked on hers, and instead of continuing to reach for the file he claimed to need, he reached for her chin, pulling her mouth to his, pressing softly before opening his mouth and inviting her to do the same.

"I've never met anybody like you, Miss Helen Sizemore," he murmured into her hair. And she believed him.

In subsequent weeks, through hand signs and scribbled notes, they established the signals needed to arrange their assignations, which began with coffee together, then cocktails, then much more. An uncrumpled tissue in his trash can meant no meeting that day. A red pen left aside his coffee cup meant he wished her to find a new meeting place. In response, she would hand him a *Life* or *Time* magazine article ostensibly related to their work, key words underscored to direct him to an upcoming rendezvous point. *The Washington Post,* folded in half with the Local section on top, left in her chair when he was in a meeting, was her cue to enter his office with an immediate need to review his schedule with him, all to create the impression for whomever he was meeting with that Helen irritated him with her efficient but myopic focus on her list of to-do's. When the *Post* was folded in quarters, he had left it there for her to read.

Having met his wife several times, Helen didn't feel particularly guilty about stepping into the Bentley marriage. They didn't have children, for one thing, and Eleanor's attentiveness to her husband seemed to come and go. From what he described, she wasn't the type to meet him at the door in the evenings, cocktail in hand, décolletage on view. More than once, he'd mentioned arriving home to an empty house and a cold stove, Eleanor blustering in later, apologizing for getting caught up in some project or another at her job at the Arlington Public Library. Episodes like these made Helen feel competent, superior, and affirmed. She interpreted Talbot's sharing of such stories as de facto praise of her, that he knew Helen would never lose track of time in such a messy, thoughtless way. But perhaps what he really meant was that he didn't foresee Helen losing her focus on him, situated as he now was, at the center of her life.

Infrequently, Eleanor came to the office for a lunch date with Talbot—something Helen hated. She usually greeted Eleanor with appropriate warmth, made a bit of circular small talk, then retreated to Talbot's office to let him know the wife had arrived. While Eleanor waited in the reception area, Helen and Talbot sometimes groped and grabbed at each other—the proof Helen needed before he headed out the door that he was devoted more to his secretary than his wedded wife. These intense interludes gave Helen the wherewithal to wave and smile at the couple as they departed for their lunch—but she still resented Eleanor's incursion into space she saw as hers and Talbot's.

When he traveled, Eleanor never phoned Helen for schedule updates or to inquire where he was staying, unlike many CIA wives, Helen heard, tended to do. To Helen, this was proof of Eleanor's basic, disqualifying disinterest in her husband and fueled Helen's own efforts to support and love Talbot because of what he didn't get at home. Even men having affairs expected their wives to inquire occasionally as to their whereabouts when they were traveling, didn't they? Only fleetingly did Helen allow herself to consider that the dearth of phone calls might be because Eleanor trusted her husband and believed in the strength and surety of their marriage.

Twice, Helen and Talbot had the good fortune to be dispatched on a business trip together. The first took them to a testing ground north of Las Vegas, Talbot overseeing its decommissioning and insisting he needed her with him to handle documentation. The second was a trip to London where she did little more than bring coffee during several days of meetings. On both trips, Talbot had requested adjoining rooms when they got to the hotel, loudly explaining they would be up half the night preparing for the next day's meetings. And they were up half the night. But not for that. After Talbot swept for listening devices and cameras in both their rooms, they commenced with their private festivities. The sex, the travel, the prospect that she, one day, might be an intelligence officer with her own portfolio of assignments—her own assistant at her elbow — left her exhilarated, in a persistent state of anticipation of the thrilling things ahead of her. That they were permitted to travel together, unchaperoned and unquestioned, led Helen to wonder if the spy factory recognized that CIA officers who took the kinds of risks the country needed them to take were also inclined to take sexual risks too — that it was better for all this to take place within the family, so to speak, with women who had passed background checks, instead of outside-the-bubble extracurriculars.

Helen had not gone looking for this. Had one of her friends been involved in an affair with a married man, Helen would have been scandalized and counseled her to quit it immediately, to recognize that she was being taken advantage of. But what had begun with a surreptitious kiss and spilled over into rushed, overheated trysts, had now become something wholly different in Helen's mind — redeemed because Helen was deeply in love. The physical encounters with her older, handsome, and sexually adept boss, created inside Helen a deep attachment and a need she wanted only Talbot to satisfy. Like every young woman who fell into bed with a married boss, Helen believed they would be together someday because it was meant to be. She craved him when she couldn't have him, even making up a phantom boyfriend (unmarried, of course) named Walter so she could share little vignettes of their conversations with her girlfriends.

Their meeting at the diner now was something she would not have tried to shoehorn into his schedule even two months earlier. They had slipped away together only last week. Talbot preferred they not meet in back-to-back weeks, and Helen was careful to avoid creating discernible patterns of travel or unaccounted for blocks of time within his schedule. But a suddenly canceled staff meeting opened his calendar for the afternoon, and Helen seized the opportunity, succumbing to her pervasive, accelerating need to see him alone, if only to feel his fully clothed body pressed up against her in the front seat of his car. The crumpled tissue he left in his trash indicated in Helen's mind that he felt the same. That it was sprinkled with pencil shavings indicated he would meet her near the diner.

Helen looked around to flag down the waitress to refill her Coke. Does this diner have a basement? she wondered—a question she now regularly asked herself. Bomb shelters were now de rigueur in DC—everyone was building one, stocking it with canned goods and water—accelerated by the Sputnik launch and the vast array of missiles the Soviets paraded through Red Square last May Day. Her duplex in Bethesda had a basement and the landlord had already moved supplies in, even if it wasn't yet properly sealed. Signs were going up all over the city to apprise visitors of the closest fallout shelter. Helen found the signs ticked up her anxiety, with their harsh black and yellow design and the stark typeface. She had learned they would soon be posted in every public building, so if the Soviets attacked, at least some Americans would survive. Helen was acutely proud to be serving her country in this perilous moment, helping navigate the high-wire tension, especially because she was doing it alongside Talbot.

Her Coke replenished, Helen reached into her pocketbook to withdraw her pack of Salems. Searching the depths of her bag for her lighter, her hand clasped the tiny Minox camera Talbot had used during the war. She gripped it, loving how the smooth metal felt in her palm. She'd found it several months earlier when she was loading office supplies into Talbot's desk—legal pads, pens, paper clips. She'd opened a drawer to neaten it, and there was this shiny, silver gadget. She'd pulled it out and held it up to him.

"What is this? A lighter?"

"Not quite." He'd smiled. "That's my little Minox. Used it all over Europe during the war. It's a camera, Helen. They issued me that when I served in OSS. Took some pretty important photographs—people turning up where they weren't supposed to be, meeting with people they weren't supposed to know, and documents that contradicted what the Nazis were saying publicly. Forgot I still had it. I haven't seen it since I moved into this office. But boy, that little gem did the job when I needed it." He reached to take it from Helen's hand.

"Does it still work?"

Talbot examined the miniature camera, turning it over and using his shirtsleeve to give it a polish. "Yeah. I think so. There's still film in there, and these things were pretty sturdy. No reason to think it wouldn't work."

"Why don't you put it on your console to show it off? You can put it next to the commendation plaque, the Churchill victory ashtray, that photo of you in Turkey."

"Nah. Just put it back in the drawer. I don't want to advertise that I still have it. They might make me turn it in." Helen gave the thing a bit more buffing then did as he had asked.

She could not have explained why she went back later and took it, why she dutifully placed new legal pads into the drawer, straightening them into neat stacks, before plucking the camera out and slipping it into her pocket while he was busy at his file cabinet. She just liked the idea of having something he seemed so attached to in her possession, liked the idea that she was close enough to him to know what it meant to him. She didn't need it—but neither did he. He hadn't even noticed it was gone.

Helen slid the Minox back in her purse, retrieved her lighter, and as she put a cigarette to her lips, his car rounded the corner. She rose, dropping the unlit cigarette into the ashtray and cash on the table. She turned down a short hall to the restrooms and, after a quick look around, stepped noiselessly out the service door of the diner and cut across the parking lot to intercept Talbot at the intersection a block away. Climbing into his Corvette in her pencil skirt while trying not to flash passersby was a bit of a losing proposition, Talbot noting the show of garter and lace, sliding a hand up her leg in approval.

"Cabin John Park?" he asked as he put the car in gear.

"Anywhere," Helen responded. "How much time? A few hours?"

"Easily. I told Knox I was knocking off early since staff meeting was rescheduled and *my secretary* was out with a doctor's appointment. Eleanor took the train to New York last night. She's up there with women she knew from Smith—something they do a few times a year. So, Miss Helen, I'm yours if you'll have me."

Helen could not hide her delight. How could he even ask if she'd have him? She relaxed into the rich red leather of the Corvette's bucket seat, closed her eyes, and breathed the smell of him. She wanted this always. Exactly this. To be next to Talbot with that look of longing on his face, bound, she believed, by their passion for one another and the work they shared.

"Well, I suppose, Talbot, if you're the best I can do…"

He looked at her in mock surprise, reaching for her thigh. "Oh, so I'll have to earn it, is that it? I'll have to prove to you that you're not settling for second-rate."

"So, I'm thinking," she smiled as she stroked his hand on her leg, "if Eleanor's away, do we really have to… I mean, what if we go to your townhouse?"

Talbot considered her proposal.

"Well, she'll be gone 'til Sunday night, so I'd have time to straighten up."

"You will. I'll help. And we can sleep in and I can cook. And of course, socks."

"Indeed. It's always better when we can stretch out," he said, his hand drifting under her skirt, "without socks on." Helen laughed.

When they couldn't carve out time to check into the inn in Warrenton — it was an hour outside the city — they went to Cabin John Park. Sometimes, Helen waited at the diner and he picked her up here. More often, she took a series of buses, threading her way into the woods to wait for him. Talbot would cruise in the back entrance, past the main parking lot and do a sweep to assess how many people were around and whether any vehicles looked familiar. He would park, then retrieve the blanket he kept for this very purpose from his trunk, along with a prop picnic basket which rarely contained a picnic. Then he'd walk from the open meadow down the hiking trail to their favorite tree, a beech with a nice, smooth bark where Helen would be waiting. And here, he would lean and hoist her to his waist to enjoy her, her full skirt draping their legs and the dense underbrush offering a measure of camouflage. "Dirty and dangerous," he had called it the first time they did it, but he said it in a way that told her he liked it, that it enlivened him. He said it reminded him of how he felt in high-stakes situations during the war, his pulse beating in his ears, every nerve ending activated. Helen's own pulse had raced during their first open-air encounter, scared they'd be seen and astonished at her inability to resist him. In subsequent months at work, she would learn the term "counterphobic," which described many intelligence officers at CIA. They were men who vigorously embraced risk, who sought it out and were attracted, not repelled, by it. Talbot, she learned, was one of these.

"No tree-leaning for us today and that's a good thing," Helen smiled, gesturing at her slim skirt, "because I wore the wrong thing." Sinking deeper into her seat, she turned toward him and lifted one stockinged foot to the dash, a position that showed off the delicate V of lace between her legs. She posed, taking her time to pull out a Salem, light it, and take a long slow drag. "But fair warning: I don't have an overnight bag—just my travel toothbrush in my pocketbook. I have nothing…NOTHING…to wear all weekend."

Talbot shook his head and sighed, slamming the car into gear and quickly crossing two lanes of traffic to turn towards his Arlington townhouse.

CHAPTER THREE

Eleanor

Fifteen years earlier, it had been Eleanor Halsey who'd drawn Talbot's intense, unrelenting interest. Their happenstance meeting in Italy, just after the war, came about because of Eleanor's devotion to the arts, her wish to develop her talent as best she could. The way she told the story, Eleanor was barely 19 when she learned about a program that invited international students to study Renaissance-style sculpture in Florence. And that was it; she absolutely knew she had to enroll.

As she would later tell Talbot, Eleanor grew up in faculty housing on the campus of Smith College where her father taught economics. The college was the artistic center of Northampton, with near-weekly concerts and recitals, art shows and lectures. As she explained it, a rotating roster of working artists came in from Boston and New York and Philadelphia each term as artists-in-residence, teaching a class or two and exhibiting their work either on stage in the case of the dance and music faculty, or in the campus art gallery. Eleanor found the visual artists the most compelling, the synthesis of the creative and the cerebral. She described many happy hours lurking about the gallery watching the installations go in, eavesdropping on always-tense conversations between artist and administrator as they debated optimal lighting and the best placement for certain paintings and pieces.

The college hosted opening receptions and farewell dinners for their faculty guests, which Eleanor attended in the company of her parents. Eavesdropping on conversations, observing semester after semester, Eleanor recognized these artists occupied their own realms. These were not open-faced people-pleasers interested in gathering more fans to their work; they seemed to her to have deeply interior lives, accessible only to themselves. They bristled at convention, finding it difficult to do the real-world things the college required — engage in cocktail party chitchat, grade student assignments, or turn up on time to teach. It was like they needed to hold back essential parts of themselves that could only be revealed through the art they produced. The sculptors, especially, spoke to her, teasing images out of stone or clay or metal to crystalize moments of pain or joy that resonated with Eleanor deep in her bones. By high school, she devoted hours to emulating them — in art class, in weeks-long summer programs, even managing to audit a college sculpting course — discovering, painfully, that she might not possess the technical gifts she'd seen in those who came to campus.

Then came the jarring loss of her father. Eleanor and her family were grateful to remain in their campus home, but felt his absence acutely, everywhere. After beginning college classes at Smith, Eleanor was eager for something new and when she discovered the sculpture program in Florence, it seemed ideal. Perhaps under the tutelage of highly-accomplished sculptors and art scholars, she could progress. If her talent could not carry her, an Italian education would prepare her to run a gallery somewhere, perhaps work as a curator or a docent. Anything that put her in the artistic ether, with people who saw life in shade and color amid shifting perspectives.

If her mother openly worried about her daughter wading into the political turmoil of 1938 Italy, Eleanor could not recall it. They shared the belief that the University of Florence would not extend a program to foreign students if there were a genuine threat. Both of them, Eleanor would later recount, were so focused on gathering the clothes and supplies Eleanor needed and making the somewhat complicated travel arrangements, that they failed to weave together threads in plain view, threads that soon came together to create a dangerous Europe.

September found Eleanor in morning lectures alongside her new classmates, flipping furiously through her Italian-English dictionary to track down words she didn't understand, her earnestness and naïveté drawing the indulgent notice of her advisor. Professor Gilberto Cossutta was esteemed in some quarters for his classical approach to sculpture, derided elsewhere as derivative and imitative, criticism leveled at every Italian sculptor since Michelangelo. Cossutta was responsible for directing Eleanor's course of study and would ultimately adjudge her talent and suitability to stay in the program. Each afternoon in the sunlit studio, he observed her in a bemused way, her striving to catch up to more advanced students, working to glean all she could from them through her questions and intense scrutiny of the way they worked. For her part, Eleanor wondered which of her gloriously talented classmates would become famous and how she might leverage that for a career for herself someday.

Even with the relentless pace of daily coursework and long hours in the studio, her evenings proved most formative. After they tidied up and closed the studio, she and her classmates loaded their straw totes with bottles of chianti and packages of bread and cheese and carried them to the Piazza della Signoria to hold forth. Here, at the city's political center, Eleanor learned the news of the day, as her tiny artist colony sorted through what was happening around them. Draped over the well-worn benches of the plaza, the Fountain of Neptune splashing gently nearby, evening shadows sliding up the side of the Palazzo Vecchio, the ancient town hall, the boys in the class—Italians,

Germans, a few French and Spanish — took the lead in discussing the current moment. Their declarations careened from a professor's pointed criticism of an assignment to an appraisal of the Italian campaign in Ethiopia. In both regards, Eleanor felt ill-equipped and out of her depth. She listened quietly, her brain furiously working to translate the unfamiliar words she heard, even as she tried to follow the political rationale across the unfamiliar geography.

Patrizio usually opened the discussion, his defense of the Italian military's sweep through Africa growing more passionate the more wine he consumed. Most in the group nodded along, not wishing to spoil these magical evenings with conflict, evenings that made them feel like proper adults, intellectuals even, with consequential opinions that mattered. The women in the class seemed especially open to Patrizio's viewpoint, nodding assents, lifting their cups of wine in approval. Eleanor suspected it was Patrizio's deep brown eyes, the dark curls that fell beyond his shirt collar so unlike the short-haired soldiers on the streets, the way he rolled the sleeves of his white shirt to reveal the taut musculature of his forearms, that compelled the women of their group to believe his argument was righteous.

"The new laws that finally rein in the Jews will break Italy's economic depression," he declared one night, soon after word came that Jews could no longer hold assets as they once had, pursue education, or travel freely in Italy.

"But what of Giovanni?" asked Remigius, a Frenchman from Lille. "He was with us in September and now he's withdrawn from university. He was a good man. Who was he hurting? Il Duce has always said the Mediterranean cultures, all of them including the Jews, share a common bond. What of that? What changed his mind?"

"Hitler did," laughed Antonia. "Mussolini just wants to be more like his little German friend, to make Europe more, I don't know… orderly."

"Stable," offered Patrizio.

"We'll see," said Remigius, pointing. As if summoned, a brigade of Black Shirts made their way through the plaza, prompting the men to sit up a bit straighter, lest their slouching be interpreted as insolence.

Eleanor's classmates supported the government, despite random concerns whispered and repeated among students. The Black Shirts could be reactive and capricious, hauling someone to jail for a gesture they interpreted as threatening or a look deemed vaguely hostile. So her friends did their best to present themselves as cooperative and passive, disengaged from the intensity of the political moment. In this, they were often derided by another group of students who opposed the Fascist regime. This second group was behind the printing and circulation of anti-fascist leaflets at the university, materials that urged Italians to rise up with the Communists to oppose Mussolini. The students in Eleanor's circle were aware of their illegal network and kept their distance so they could not be even remotely associated with their activities. And since these were their classmates, they did not want to be responsible for betraying them should a small detail float up to them, information they could be forced to disclose under pressure.

The soldiers marched across the pavement at a diagonal, families and couples skittering and hopping out of the way so as not to be caught in the irregular route. They are babies, Eleanor thought, so many with the thin frames of adolescence, yet to sprout a whisker. But they were well-trained, having already cultivated the menace needed to keep their countrymen in line. Schoolyard bullies, that's what they seemed like to Eleanor, a presence she believed had little consequence in her life.

•   •   •

As the new school term opened in January, 1939, Eleanor began to fret that she would not be asked back for the summer. Her comparatively primitive artistic technique had been exposed, prompting her to conclude that the only reason she'd been invited to matriculate at the university was because there were so few students with the means and desire to study in Italy with Europe on a knife's edge. She was a seat-filler who otherwise would not have been admitted. She made an appointment with her advisor to plead her case, hoping he could see her potential, her absolute dedication to her art.

Professor Cossutta sympathized with the girl; her struggles with her assignments were made more complicated by her limited Italian. Her language skills improved every day but nuance and subtlety were still beyond her. More than once, she had written a paper or half-completed a studio assignment before realizing it was not at all what her professors had asked for. The time she spent revising her work to satisfy the assignment cut in to her opportunities to improve her technique. And so it went. Cossutta had seen it many, many times among his variously skilled students; it helped him winnow, to separate the wheat from the chaff. When Eleanor approached him to discuss it, he suggested they meet at a tavern near campus.

Eleanor arrived at Trattoria Sergio Gozzi, finding the professor already ensconced in a corner booth, sipping a glass of red wine. He waved her over, patting the seat next to him. He poured a healthy splash of wine into the glass in front of her, not pausing to ask if she wished to have some.

"So," he began. "How is it going for you?"

She sighed. "In so many ways, I love it here — more than I can even say. There are so many things I had no idea about — no idea whatsoever — and I'm not just talking about sculpture and my class work."

"You're learning about the world, then, becoming an educated woman."

Eleanor nodded.

"So, tell me, what has Florence taught you?"

Eleanor reached for her glass and took a quick, nervous sip. She had expected a more perfunctory conversation on why she would not continue in the program or what she needed to do to stay. The professor's more personal interest in her took her by surprise.

"About the world. Europe. About the wisdom behind the fascist system. About the corrective laws the government has had to enact because of how the Jews have hurt the economy."

"Have they now?" asked Cossutta. "How so?"

And here she was lost, casting about for phrases, trying to articulate the rationale Patrizio had outlined during their many evenings on the Piazza della Signoria.

"Well, the property and business they own, the large percentage of assets that they hold…"

"This is a myth, my dear," said Cossutta, leaning in to speak quietly, reaching first to pat her hand, then to tuck a stray blonde tendril behind her ear. "This is merely how leaders consolidate power, blaming. Finding scapegoats to justify their actions, to keep capital for themselves as they oppress others who can't fight back."

At this, Eleanor gave an obedient little nod, mortified at how the professor would view her now, so callow that she took someone else's viewpoint as fact because she lacked the perspective to test it, to examine it. Her eyes dropped to her lap and she waited.

He continued, an elbow propped on the table, his mouth obscured by his wine glass, to ensure his next comment was a private one. "Italy could take a healthier path, one more fair to everybody. But now that we are aligned with the Germans, it will become much harder. But mine is an unpopular viewpoint in Italy in this moment, so you must keep it to yourself. Understand? Better to talk about this in a more private place. Now. About your studies." Again, he reached for her hand and she gave it to him, preparing herself for the words she feared most, that she would need to withdraw from the university and return home.

"You are raw. Very, very raw."

The way he said it made her feel exposed and vulnerable in a way she did not like. As if she should be ashamed of her undeveloped skill, embarrassed that the world could see it.

Cossutta continued. "You would benefit greatly if you spent more time simply working with the media, to try and fail, to try and test. You cannot skip over these stages of the process. Do you understand? Your determination—and it is admirable—cannot cause you to shortcut the work of building your skill. That takes time. Lots of time."

This did not sound like dismissal. She lifted her head and found Cossutta's eyes locked on her own, a kind smile on his face.

"Then what shall I do? Am I enrolled in the wrong courses?"

Cossutta squeezed her hand and drew it slowly into his lap. Eleanor held her breath.

"We must spend more time in the studio," he said, lifting his shoulders in a small shrug. "That is it. You must dedicate more time. I will supervise you and believe you will develop quickly if you are willing to put in the time and the work. With me."

•   •   •

In late summer, just as Eleanor began to believe the hours she'd spent with Cossutta in the studio were truly developing her eye and refining her technique; just as she was formulating her course of study for the fall term based on Cossutta's advice and guidance, Germany's push into Poland upended the course of life in Italy.

Eleanor reported to the registrar's office on the first Monday in September, clutching a list of desired courses, only to find students gathered around a shuttered door. She spotted Antonia leaning forlornly against the reception desk.

"The University has closed," Antonia said through tears. "No classes. And the boys are gone. They have been ordered to report to the draft board."

"Drafted?" Eleanor echoed. "By the military?"

"Yes, by the military. The government. A mobilization. Because of what happened in Poland on Friday. They're just—

gone. All of them. Back to their hometowns to prepare." She leaned in to whisper. "And Remigius has fled. They say he went home to France, cursing Mussolini every kilometer of the way, no doubt."

Eleanor had no frame of reference to make sense of what Antonia was telling her. Her world was her art classes, hours in the studio, picnics in the piazza with these friends, this community that revolved around shape and form and beauty.

"Surely this is temporary," Eleanor offered.

"Who knows? But I will have to return to Bologna, to my family. You need to decide what you're going to do, see if you can get home. There is nothing for us here, at least for the time being. Not even our friends."

Eleanor nodded, still working to grasp the enormity of what had happened.

"Cossutta," she said to Antonia. "I'll find him and see what he recommends."

Antonia nodded, offering a tearful hug. "Yes. He'll know. He'll make sure you stay safe."

•   •   •

Eleanor found him in his office, packing up his books, tearing up papers in files he said he no longer had use for.

"Is this real?" she asked him. "Can they really close the university? What are all the students supposed to do?"

Cossutta smiled ruefully. "They can and they have, my dear. Italy and Germany have formed the Pact of Steel, so all of Italy's resources must support the Reich, now that it has begun the war with Poland. Italian men are being ordered into military service and every industry must offer whatever help it can. That includes universities."

"But, professor, where does that leave me? Maybe it will be short-lived. Maybe I can wait it out."

"It will not be quick. These grievances will take years to settle and who knows how long the university will stay closed."

"What about you, professor? What will you do?"

"Depends on what the government has in mind for me, my dear. Depends on if it's something I wish to take part in. But you—I will help you as I can. It may no longer be safe for you here."

France closed its border with Italy within days and the Swiss allowed only those with diplomatic clearance to cross northward, leaving Eleanor with limited options to get out of Italy. Cossutta attempted to help her find passage across the Ionian Sea to Greece, quickly learning he lacked the pull and connections to get her a confirmed ticket; the passenger manifests were overtaken by wealthy Italians who had seen enough and were willing to pay and do whatever was necessary to get out from under the current regime. After a number of anxious weeks, Eleanor stopped pushing, resigned to the fact that for the moment, anyway, she would have to make a life in Florence. Miraculously, Cossutta found her a position at the Uffizi Gallery, Mussolini deciding Italy's museums would stay open and protected by paramilitary to ensure Hitler would not expand his art collection at Italy's expense. The whole thing was a bit of a sham: the museum was open sporadically and much of the collection had been moved underground. But for the next several years, her paycheck covered the rent on her small apartment and Eleanor had access to the gallery's exquisite collection any time she liked. She had hours to wander, to sit, to gaze.

When Rome fell to the Allies, her world shifted again. Her apartment ceased to be a haven and the streets became perilous—for blonde foreigners most especially—to navigate alone. Eleanor moved in with the few students she knew from the university who remained in Florence. Professor Cossutta took her in after that, Eleanor ultimately finding sanctuary at the city's convent. That's where she was when Germany surrendered. Despite the upheaval she'd endured—being cut off from her family, persistent food shortages, university friends scattered, some killed in the war—she believed she'd been given an incalculable gift: a years-long political education she would have never grasped had she stayed home. She developed a perspective that would shape her entire life.

A year after the war ended, Talbot arrived in Florence on assignment for the U.S. Army. When he turned up at the Uffizi for a private tour arranged for American military officers, he seemed to Eleanor to be exactly the man she'd been waiting for — a man, finally, with the power to open doors too long closed to her, who would help her emerge from her stalled life. She never completed her art degree and somewhere along the way, lost her once-avid desire to do so. Years later, as she shared details of her life story with friends and neighbors, she could neatly attribute her lack of a degree to the war, not to any deficiency of talent.

CHAPTER FOUR

Talbot

Alongside millions of patriotic Americans, Talbot enlisted in the army after Pearl Harbor fully expecting to take his turn on the line, clear-eyed that he might not survive the endeavor. At thirty-one, working for an established law firm in Atlanta, he could have avoided military service entirely or as his mother quietly urged, leveraged family connections to secure a posting stateside. But able-bodied and unmarried, he told her he'd feel like a coward for the rest of his life if he didn't step forward when his country needed him.

Unexpectedly, his University of Georgia law degree quickly moved him into a new pool of draftees. After basic training, he was plucked from his platoon and transported to Prince Edward Island, Canada where British security officers introduced him to the spy game. So rudimentary was the U.S. military espionage infrastructure in the opening days of the war, it was left up to the Brits and Canadians to train Talbot and other American recruits. By the end of 1942, Talbot was posted in Turkey, station chief for the fledgling Office of Strategic Services. Posing as a portfolio manager in a respected international bank in Istanbul, he and the cell he oversaw helped get cash in the hands of Resistance fighters in Europe while keeping an eye on the assortment of spies that traversed the Black Sea and the Mediterranean. The OSS bestowed on him the code name

Thrasher, the state bird of Georgia—an homage to his roots—and circulated the rumor that Talbot was in fact trading in illegal arms, a useful fiction that made adversaries wary, unsure of the length of his power and influence. His dark eyes and dark hair kept them guessing as to his nationality and his loyalties.

At the intersection of eastern and western cultures, Turkey grappled to retain its neutrality in the war, and was in fact the nexus of Axis and Allied intelligence-gathering. In a city crawling with spies, Talbot and his team quietly conducted a range of operations. Some were complex and sweeping, like engaging a string of couriers to drop supplies to saboteurs, who fanned out to the north to intercept and derail German trains. Daily, they worked to validate a perpetual if ragged stream of information, bits and pieces that filtered into their offices either accidentally or on purpose. Rumors, allegations, musings. A bank customer—an Austrian who arrived in Turkey soon after the Anschluss—was overheard lamenting the contents of the latest letter from her son, a private in the German army. Reading between the lines, she believed her boy's account ran counter to the Reich's glowing reports of success on the Eastern front. Talbot and his group pursued corroboration through human assets—bribery, pillow talk—and soon, an intercepted cable between low-level German communications officers who should have known better revealed that their compatriots were dying in the snow for want of warm clothes and ammunition. These early but accurate insights presaged the massive German defeat at Stalingrad, clarifying for the Allied command that after his costly miscalculation, Hitler might have limited resources to defend his Atlantic Wall. Talbot was pleased to have contributed a small piece of intel that helped the good guys see the whole field.

His work required him to cultivate an intense internal control of gestures grand and subtle, to master his facial muscles so that an eye blink, an involuntary tensing of his neck, his voice, would not betray him in a hard moment. As news arrived of the Allied invasion of France, he feigned such indifference that some of his colleagues questioned his loyalty, fearing he'd been turned. Coded messages went up to OSS handlers who responded, in so many words, that Talbot's response was apt for someone of unclear origin, rumored to be dealing arms out the back door of a Turkish bank; the Yanks' arrival on French shores could hurt business.

By V-J Day, Talbot and his colleagues were shredding documents and packing up their tools, most of the team more than ready to return home. Talbot's deputy, for one, was counting down the days. New Yorker Harold Warren was the sole member of the Istanbul cell with an actual background in banking. He was eager to resume his civilian career because the 1950s, he predicted, would be boom years and he wanted to be right in the middle of it. Talbot, however, was less ready to relinquish the broader sense of purpose—and successive high-stakes challenges—that had infused their work in Turkey.

"So, Tal," Harold began one night as they lingered over drinks, their office vacated, their personal effects packed for shipment. They were seated on the patio of a small bar, ringed by palm trees and open to the Sea of Marmara. The place was loud and raucous, with soldiers, refugees, citizens of the world, celebrating a world at peace. "What's next for you?"

Talbot, slightly drunk and completely content, studied the undulating waves just meters from the patio, their reliable rhythm reinforcing his sense of requiescence. That the war was over, that he was free to sit here with Harold and envision a future, a safe future in which he would no longer worry that an Axis assassin's bullet would find him on the street, seemed almost too great a gift.

"Well, Berlin, first, for the debrief, and then I plan to get into a little trouble in France. If I can get down there. You know, see the Riviera and just take it in and hell, not worry about anything for a few weeks."

"And check out a French girl or two, maybe, because I hear they are *zo hahpy to be free zhat when zey see an Amerh-e-cahn...*" this he said with the worst kind of French accent, "they'll do anything, *any-zing,* so Tal, maybe you want to pull your uniform out of your footlocker to get on their good side. Or their bad side. Just get on 'em however you can."

They laughed, heads thrown back, Harold slapping the table, drawing attention that no longer put them at risk.

"And after that, you going back to law? Back to Atlanta?" Harold pressed.

"I don't think so. I think I want…I don't know, to be a part of putting Europe back together. As I understand it, the occupation forces will be advising the provisional governments, which will have tremendous problems to solve. I think I could help with the work of sorting through some of the legal issues. But I don't know. I'll see what they say in Berlin."

"Better you than me, Thrasher. I'm leaving this mess in your hands."

•   •   •

Berlin proved a grim echo of the city it had been, Allied bombs having reduced block after block of the city to dust and rubble. Defeated German soldiers returned to find food scarce, abandoned cafes that would never reopen, limited running water and sanitation, and the few buildings yet to collapse teetering, many missing roofs and entire facades. This destruction, so brutal and evident across Germany, was precisely as the Allied command had designed it, lest anyone at some later point, contend that Germany had not lost the war. Hitler himself had promulgated the lie that Germany had not been defeated in the first world war but had been betrayed somehow in the signing of the peace. But now, the millions of people living on the streets begging for food put to rest, finally, the myth of the thousand-year Reich.

At the outset of his meeting at headquarters, his briefer informed Talbot that President Truman planned to dissolve OSS within days.

"Where does that leave me?" Talbot asked. "Looking for a bunk on a troop ship home?"

"Depends, sir," said the young army officer, a major, who went on to explain that Washington envisioned a new agency to eventually take the place of OSS. "For now, intelligence-gathering will be divided between the military and the State Department. You can keep your commission and transfer into the new operation, once it's up and running, if that sounds alright. The other option is to head back to civilian life—an honorable discharge and the thanks of a grateful nation for your service."

"What would I be doing before this new agency is operational?" he asked.

The major smiled.

"So glad you asked. We have a placement for a lawyer within our groups conducting damage assessments in cities across Europe. Washington wants a full picture of what it's gonna take to get Europe back on its feet. Not just the infrastructure damage. We need a better understanding of the strength of the various political entities still in play. Your skills would be useful—and you can do the grand tour of Europe on Uncle Sam's nickel, even though the place is a little pockmarked, shall we say, after six years of war."

While the contours of his work and of the new agency he would ultimately work for remained vague, it appealed far more to Talbot than returning to a law practice in Atlanta. So, much to his mother's disappointment, he accepted the major's offer, which came with three weeks of R&R folded neatly into the schedule.

The obliging major helped arrange Talbot's vacation travel, cobbling together transportation to the South of France. After a flight from Berlin to Paris, Talbot rode what rails he could in the general direction of the French southern coast. U.S. Army engineers were rebuilding rail lines the Germans had destroyed in their retreat but the job was massive, patchwork, and unpredictable. When the train abruptly stopped outside Dijon, his sanguine fellow passengers simply exited with their things and began to walk. Talbot hopped a farm wagon, the farmer more than happy to ferry the American with cash the fifteen kilometers past a burned-out station to one still receiving passengers. A Canadian army convoy mustering at the coast to exit the country picked him up to take him the final few kilometers.

Arriving, finally, at his small room in a little seaside inn in Nice, Talbot dropped his duffle and collapsed on the bed. He had intended to find a cocktail and take in the scenery. But once he was alone, the window open to the smell and sound of the sea, his body demanded he stop and sleep. The adrenaline that had kept him awake and alive amid years of dangerous duty had done its job. It could now recede and allow Talbot to recover his natural rhythms for resting, for eating, for sex. For the first five days, he slept twelve, fourteen hours a day. He awoke sometimes before noon, sometimes at midday, at which point he ate, read, then lazed in the sand where he promptly fell asleep again. His nap usually lasted until he sensed himself alone on the beach, the other holiday makers having made their way inside to dress for the evening meal. He drank lots of artesian water and very little alcohol, because he wanted to fully feel the world around him in all its emerging vividness; to shed the carapace that had protected and shrouded him during his wartime duty.

Seven days into his stay, the first morning he managed to awaken early enough, Talbot found an American newspaper — a week old — and made his way to the breakfast room. As he sat over his pastry and coffee, a woman approached and asked if she could join him, there being no other tables free. He obliged and they shared their stories, or parts of them anyway. Talbot said he was an American soldier on R&R (mostly true) and would be returning to the States soon (not exactly true). The woman said her name was Marie-Claire and that she was a widow from the Loire Valley, her husband killed in the earliest days of the war. She came to the coast to find members of his family and to begin to rebuild her life.

"Children?" Talbot asked, and after an almost imperceptible pause, she shook her head. The way she did it, her slight hesitation, produced a flicker in Talbot's brain, a fragment of cognizance he did not attend to as he would have only a few months earlier. He was on vacation, the war was over, and a beautiful woman had joined him for his meal.

For the next few afternoons, he took his naps in his room, the window opened, the gulls cawing, Marie-Claire interrupting his rest in ways he did not mind at all. She had a habit of coming in after her morning on the beach, removing her bathing suit as she entered his room and leaving it in a sodden heap. She did not want to track in sand, she explained. She made her way to the bathroom — paraded, really, her breasts and torso white and damp, her legs and arms oiled and bronzed — usually pulling Talbot to her as she went, drawing him into the tiny shower. As she dragged a fragrant bar of soap over his back, his chest, his thighs, she pressed him about when he would be leaving, why their unexpected acquaintance that seemed to satisfy a need in both of them, had to end. She proposed spending the night with him at least once before he departed. How glorious it would be, she said, to awaken in a man's arms again. Near the end of his stay, after a meal of the freshest fish and more glasses of a light

Clairette blanche than Talbot cared to count, they retired to his room to share what turned out to be a vigorous, if bittersweet, farewell.

When Talbot awoke, Marie-Claire was gone, as was all the cash in his wallet. He waited the better part of an hour, hoping that perhaps she'd gone to get them something for breakfast. When that did not seem to be the case, he made his way to the lobby and sought out the hotelier, asking if he'd seen the woman he'd been with the past week, Marie-Claire from the Loire. The innkeeper erupted in laughter, tried to recover himself, then laughed again, his hand held out in front of him like a stop sign, pleading with the monsieur to wait, please, so he could gather himself.

"I was not aware she had invented a story," the innkeeper finally said. "I thought you knew who she was and were a forgiving sort. She is not from the Loire. She is the daughter of the mayor here. Her father and husband—yes, she is a married woman, monsieur, with three children—are jailed, collaborators who profited from their service to the Germans. But now, of course, the well has dried up. So she, apparently, is developing new sources."

Four years in the clandestine services, Talbot thought, and I bought everything she said. Damn it all.

Talbot thanked the innkeeper with a tight smile, his well-cultivated control masking his shock and embarrassment. He asked that his final bill be readied and left the inn, walking several blocks up and down the sloped streets to the makeshift office where the U.S. military had set up shop. After several questions and a bit of discussion, Talbot secured a check that represented an advance on his pay that he could cash at the banking office down the hall. He headed back towards the inn, taking in for a final time, the charm of the narrow streets, the pungent smells near the pier, the relentlessness of the sun making its way across a pale blue sky. Talbot lamented that the peace and sense of restoration he found here had been spoiled by Marie-Claire's unnecessary lies. Retrieving his duffle, he paid his bill and decamped to the station to catch a train to take him east. He would begin his work with a team in Florence in a matter of days.

•   •   •

The route hugged the glimmering coast of the continent—the architecture and vegetation astonishingly different from the southern coastline where he'd spent his boyhood. As the train made its way from station to station, Talbot saw contingents of Allied troops, some arriving and others so buoyant and filthy it was clear they were headed home. Beyond the olive drab uniforms, the vista outside his window bore little evidence of the war so recently concluded. But Talbot imagined the accusations and recriminations that flooded these seaside communities, some shopkeepers and farmers having stayed true to France, others now shunned for having cooperated with the occupiers. As he rode, he ruminated. Marie-Claire. Had she asked him for money he would have given it to her. Her deception mattered less to him than the fact that he had not detected it. He had blunted his sensors, taken himself off-duty after the slog of daily mendacity that had characterized his life in Turkey. But in letting go of his created identity, he had relinquished an important set of skills, something he resolved not to do again. Europe was far from a safe place and to navigate it, he would have to reactivate his instincts, employ the skills his spymasters had taken pains to teach him.

The train traversed Monaco then crossed into Italy, stopping first in Pisa at a badly damaged rail station that had only recently returned to service. He exited the train to find something to eat, astonished by the rubble that filled the alleys and laneways. Fully ten hours after boarding the train in France, he arrived at the Santa Maria Novella station in Florence. He made his way to the Hotel Minerva, finding his new colleagues had taken over the hotel bar. After exchanging names and the barest details of what each had done in the war—polishing off a dozen bottles of wine in the process—the group broke up, dispersing to their rooms, with plans to reconvene to begin their work in the morning.

They spent the following day examining Florence by grid, noting the extent of the infrastructure damage and familiarizing themselves with the political leaders who seemed to be asserting influence. Their mission was to counter any communist pull that might impede Italy taking a democratic path. They could tap a healthy budget to fund the relocation of any especially problematic individuals. The task group solicited insight from nearly everyone they encountered: the American soldiers waiting for passage home, the men who'd run the last of the Germans out of town; factory owners whose businesses had been co-opted during the war; shopkeepers who had little to sell; women lined up at the fruit markets who spent their days scrounging for enough food to feed their families.

After his long train ride and a first day of back-to-back meetings, Talbot almost begged off that evening's private tour of the Uffizi Gallery, a get-to-know-you event for the task group. But reluctant to make waves, he skipped dinner for a shower he hoped would refresh him enough to enjoy the guided tour. Ancient and imposing, the Uffizi and the priceless array of Italian Renaissance artworks within it had somehow survived the war. Workers were in the process of moving items from the collection out of protected spaces underground to reinstall them in the upper floors of the gallery.

The docent, Talbot was surprised to learn, was an American—a young woman who had been stranded in Florence for the duration of the war. She spoke about various pieces as they circulated through the Uffizi's rooms, noting the particular care American bombers had taken in the massive raids of 1943, precision bombing that had spared not only art pieces at the Uffizi, but many of the city's historic structures. It was the Germans in retreat who had bombed the Ponte Vecchio bridge a few blocks away, she noted. Moreover, despite the Italians' best efforts, the Germans were believed to have made off with several works of art, including the small oil painting *Vase of Flowers* by the Dutch artist Jan van Huysum.

"The smaller casualties of war," the docent observed, "but to the art world, tragedies nonetheless."

Talbot thought he heard the barest trace of an accent as she spoke but nothing he could exactly place. He found her presentation outstanding and approached her afterwards to thank her and let her know how much he had learned. He was also curious how an American civilian had subsisted in wartime Italy.

"Talbot Bentley," he began. "Thank you for a fascinating tour."

"Eleanor Halsey," she responded. "So glad you enjoyed it."

"Tell me, has it just been harrowing for you?"

"I'm not sure I understand your question," she responded guardedly.

"I'm just surprised you weren't locked up at some point, is all. They let an American stroll through the streets when they were shooting at us just up the road?"

At this, Eleanor smiled wearily, remembering. "Ah. Yes. That. There was lots of hiding involved, subterfuge and deception," she said. "I stayed with friends from the university for months and when that got dicey, a professor from the university took me in. I ended up at the Convent of Santa Maria Novella. Me and quite a number of Jewish children."

Talbot took in her tall frame and her fair looks, the light blond hair pulled into low braid, the bright blue eyes.

"I would think you'd have a hard time passing for an Italian nun," he observed.

"You'd be surprised," responded Eleanor. "Men tend not to see women wearing a habit and wimple. Just doesn't seem to register. And as the city fell apart, no one had any interest in combing through monasteries and convents looking for subversives. Most Italians—the police, the soldiers, everyday people—were too busy trying not to get shot dead in streets themselves. Their instinct for self-preservation saved the lives of many, many Jewish children."

"It worked out pretty well for you too, except for the minor problem of being stuck here for five years unable to get home."

"Six, actually. I came here to study in 1938. I know, I know. What was I thinking?"

Members of Talbot's group began to speak a bit louder and to circulate in his peripheral vision. They were ready to return to their hotel.

"Listen, Eleanor," Talbot began." We're headed back to the Minerva. Any interest in joining us there for a drink?"

She looked over at Talbot's colleagues, seeming to genuinely consider his offer. "Perhaps, well… no, thank you. You are very kind but it was a lengthy tour and a long day. I hope you can understand. I do appreciate your offer. It would be lovely to spend some time with Americans for a change. But tonight, I'd have to say no."

So, thought Talbot, she is practically inviting me to ask her out for another time.

"Tomorrow night, then? Dinner? Or would lunch work better?" he asked.

Her face lit up, her shoulders relaxing in relief.

"Dinner tomorrow would be perfect. I know exactly where to take you."

•　　•　　•

The next night, they walked from the lobby of the Minerva to a dimly lit trattoria several blocks away. Eleanor had enjoyed a day off, as the gallery was still only open sporadically, and she'd used much of the afternoon to prepare for her date. She arrived at the Minerva early, wearing a bright blue cotton dress with a boat-neck and cap sleeves that revealed an expanse of smooth, pale skin from her neck to her shoulders to her arms. Surrounded by dark-haired, dark-eyed Italians, she stood out in a way that captured the eye of every man who saw her. Most especially Talbot.

Once they were seated and the wine poured, Eleanor wasted no time. "So, tell me — where did you spend the war? Not here, I suspect, since that was your first time at the gallery."

Talbot rolled out his well-practiced story. "I served on the command staff in North Africa. At the end of '43, I was deployed to England to prepare for the invasion of France."

"So, it was your idea to invade France! Well done, Talbot! Terrific planning!" Her eyes sparkled at her joke.

"Yes. Completely my idea. Ike followed my instructions to a tee." Talbot moved smoothly off his storyline. "And you? Where is home and why did you come to Europe when it was preparing to explode?"

"Junior year abroad. Or that's what it was supposed to be. I was attending Smith and earned a spot in an arts program that allowed me to come to the University of Florence to study sculpture. If I did well enough, I planned to stay and earn my degree here."

"And that didn't happen."

"It did not," said Eleanor, dropping her gaze. "Not at all. When I finally understood that Europe was falling in on itself, there was no safe way to get out. But I had some friends here by that point, good friends, who kept me out of harm's way."

"So, you can leave now. I'm sure you're eager to see your family."

"My father died of a heart attack when I was a fifteen. He was a professor of economics at Smith and they graciously allowed my mother and my brother and me to remain in faculty housing after we lost him. Mom worked as a secretary in the mathematics department. But last year, she passed away from cancer. My brother was killed in the Pacific. So, it's just me now. No rush to head anywhere. Lots to sort out."

Talbot was stunned by the magnitude of Eleanor's loss, how she had managed to hold herself together to shoulder it. "I'm so sorry, Eleanor, for all of it. I can't imagine how hard this has been on you."

"I'm not the only one. Not at all. I look around and loss is all I see. And—although it's probably terrible to say—it helps, I think, to know you're in good company. No point in feeling sorry for myself. Who would notice? So, you move on. Make a plan for what's next."

"And what is next for you, do you think?" Talbot asked.

A hint of a smile played at Eleanor's lips. "I'm not sure. Perhaps my situation will sort itself out before long."

•   •   •

Over the next few months, Eleanor shared with Talbot all she had come to love about Florence.

"The Renaissance began right here—in the Florentine Republic," she explained, as they walked along the portico bordering the Uffizi, where merchants called out from their stalls to market handcrafted leather, wood, and art pieces. "The Medicis—the bankers—fueled the art scene, supporting a stable of artists that included da Vinci, Donatello, Michelangelo."

"And they supported a few popes, I seem to recall," Talbot offered.

Eleanor laughed. "That's one way to put it. They made sure their choice rose to the top job, using bribery, corruption—you know, the usual. They had their hands in lots of things. And the cultural movement they funded went on to transform Europe."

She took Talbot to the Piazza del Duomo with the immense Cathedral of Saint Maria del Fiore, explaining the construction of the main building encompassed a 150-year project. She pointed out the green and pink marble on the exterior which came from nearby Impruneta, also the source of the terracotta tiles that covered virtually every rooftop across the city. She introduced him to the Baptistry of St. John, where Dante himself was baptized, with its many paneled doors that practically told the entire Christian story, and the gilded mosaic ceiling that did the same. They traversed the Piazza della Signoria, where she had spent so many evenings as a student, to see the copy of Michelangelo's David, along with works by Giambologna, Donatello, and others. They walked along the Arno, noting progress in the effort to restore the Ponte Vecchio and the shops embedded in the bridge's structure. Eleanor impressed Talbot with her detailed answers when he asked about the provenance of a particular piece of art—the context of its creation or the point it was trying to make. Ten years his junior, Eleanor's knowledge of Renaissance history and insight into the current day made Talbot aware of some distinct holes in his education.

Talbot loved listening to Eleanor follow ideas around corners, test them with contradictory perspectives, tie them to the history she deeply knew, and share theories she had read about or formulated herself about how Europe would progress and finally recover. Ever the artist, she continued to consume books and articles about sculpture and painting and spoke expansively about areas of study she still wished to pursue. But when the conversation grew personal, when Talbot gently probed for details about life during the war, a strand of melancholy emerged, Eleanor's brow creasing as she worked out answers to his questions. This inclined him not to ask, not wanting to increase the emotional distance between them. As it was, Eleanor was slow to respond to his obvious interest in her. Her attachment to Florence—and to Italy—however, was unambiguous, a connection so uncompromising Talbot was almost jealous of it.

"I became myself here," she explained one night as they sat at the Caffè Gilli on the Piazza della Repubblica. She took a sip of her espresso and nibbled a corner of a hazelnut nocciolino, the chocolate so rich Talbot could smell it across the table. "I was a teenager when I arrived and now I'm an adult who understands the vagaries of the world—that nothing is promised. When I lost my brother, then my mother, I was surprised to realize beauty still existed in the world. I'm literally surrounded by it." She told Talbot that through her hardest months, the very curves in the city's ancient architecture, the graceful columns and arches, the mathematical precision that joined them, soothed and reassured her in some primal way—evidence the world would survive the current terror and return to an understandable order, and that she, too, would recover from her grief.

When they walked through the city, Eleanor happily took his hand and leaned into him when he slipped his arm around her. She responded to his kisses at the end of the night, clasping her hands behind his neck to pull him closer. But she went no further, never inviting him to stay overnight at her little apartment or intimating that she wished to stay with him. There was a formality to her, a reserve, something Talbot attributed to the fact that she had no mother, no sister, no best friend to take stock and assure her Talbot was a safe bet. Talbot took his cues from her and didn't push, knowing she was young and, believing her inexperienced with men, trusting their intimacy would eventually come, that she would see they were an awfully good match.

CHAPTER
FIVE

1946

The European Continent

They spent their Florentine Year, as Eleanor came to call it, traveling across a reawakening Europe. They took the train to Rome, transfixed each time by the beauty of the countryside, the cypress trees seeming to stand at attention as the train moved through the swell of green hills. They passed through the medieval villages of San Giovanni Valdarno, Montepulciano, and Orvieto, with their red-tiled roofs and ancient cathedrals, most located on fortified hilltops that seemed to touch the azure Tuscan sky. They took long weekends in Paris, seeing for themselves the city's purposeful revival, its poets and musicians putting forward prodigious works meant to interpret for the rest of the world the depth of the city's suffering during Occupation.

Talbot put in for a week of R&R, suggesting to Eleanor they go to London, where he had plans to get together with Harold Warren. His former deputy and his wife, Molly, were coming from New York for a meeting at England's oldest bank, Hoare & Company. In little more than a year, Harold had established himself on Wall Street, much of his work now devoted to helping Europe's damaged cities find the capital they needed to rebuild and move forward, hence the meeting at Hoare.

Eleanor readily agreed to go to London, and as was her habit, confirmed he would book separate quarters for the trip. They had dated for a year now and despite often passionate farewells at her doorstep, despite her turning 26, she kept a firm boundary in place that baffled and frustrated Talbot.

They caught an early morning train out of Florence that carried them to the edge of the continent, where they crossed an unusually placid Strait of Dover by ferry. On the train ride to London, Talbot remarked that Eleanor had arrived, for the first time seven years, in an English-speaking country — English with a British accent, but still.

"I hope my ear is attuned to it," she smiled. "You're the only person I speak English with at this point. If I can't understand your friends, will you translate?"

And in fact, when they met the Warrens for drinks that night, Talbot saw Eleanor had a little trouble getting into the flow of the conversation, amid Harold's frequent interjections and Molly's happy, fast-paced chattering. Eleanor's eyes narrowed, her focus intense, absorbing the slang, the colloquialisms used by this quintessentially American couple, their references to popular culture in her own homeland that she acknowledged she would need to reacquaint herself with. She believed them to be old family friends, Talbot not making clear his and Harold's shared history in Turkey.

"So, when are you coming back to the States, Tal?" asked Harold, a question he had been posing in various ways since they'd ended their duty in Istanbul. "Any interest in banking? We can use a smart lawyer like you, although I'll have to fix it so you're not disqualified by your Georgia Bulldog education — or should I say lack thereof."

"Ha ha, Harold. Tell the snobs in New York that there are fully educated people out there who are proud and happy they didn't go Ivy League — men like me who would not have it any other way. While you were freezing your asses off in Connecticut, we were having luaus at the beach on Christmas break. That, by any measure, proves who's really smarter."

"Well, at least we know Eleanor got a decent education, even if she did have to deal with rotten Boston weather," Harold offered.

Molly jumped in. "Eleanor, tell us about Smith. I've only ever driven through there."

"It's lovely. A bit secluded, as you saw. Northampton is a small town. My father taught there so I suppose they had to take me." She smiled and gave a little shrug as the others objected to her self-deprecation.

"And Florence? How did you end up there?" Molly asked.

Eleanor recounted her decision to study sculpture in Italy, how she'd taken for granted that the university would be a shield from Europe's political turmoil. "By the time I understood what was really going on, I couldn't get out. The American consulate had closed. The university suspended classes. So, I moved in with friends, and later hid out at a convent, of all places."

"And a professor helped her, too," Talbot prompted, reaching for Eleanor's hand, "and kept you for months, didn't he?"

"I stayed with him and his wife and their children for a while, yes, living in their attic. But after a point, I didn't want to put them at risk. Any accusation that found its way to the authorities, the police, or the security apparatus could turn lethal. A classmate was hanged after his neighbor said he'd been seen with a communist. No proof. His neighbor just called up the police and that was it. Another—a beautiful artist named Patrizio whom I knew from university—was killed for the opposite reason. After the Allies landed and the Italians switched sides in the war, the new government went after fascist students first—as if they believed by killing off the evidence, they could pretend the terror hadn't really happened, that the Black Shirts and Mussolini hadn't created the god-awful mess they had."

"I would think you'd be eager to get out of there," offered Harold, "to get back to normal life."

"Normal life," Eleanor mused. "What would that be? My parents are gone. My brother was in the Navy and died in '43."

"Eleanor. I'm so sorry," Molly offered, turning to her husband with a wince.

"But I'm here. I can help, maybe," Talbot finally said. "I try to bring a little normal to the situation, maybe even a little fun. Like getting together with the two of you."

"He's wonderful medicine," Eleanor agreed. "As are you both. Tell us more about the glamorous goings-on in New York, now that the war has ended."

•   •   •

They dined with the Warrens three times in London, laughing with them through a production of *Annie Get Your Gun* in the West End. They were an easygoing couple and the visit was cordial, even if Talbot sensed Eleanor never fully relaxed. Throughout the excursion, a comment from a waiter, a question from a shopkeeper, seemed to throw her off for a second, inclining her to turn to Talbot, wide-eyed, for help. "The accents!" she cried, after a bus driver—a Scotsman—welcomed her to the trolley so incomprehensibly, she threw her hands in the air and fell helplessly into the first open seat. "All I hear are mumbles and consonants. It's harder than when I first learned Italian." Talbot laughed and promised to continue to serve as translator.

The next morning, he and Harold met for breakfast to reminisce privately about the war, their memories still vivid of close calls and near-misses they would never disclose to the women. There was a sacredness in the recounting; it made the safety they now enjoyed feel that much more astonishing.

Wonder of wonders, here they were, facing the rest of their lives without the high stakes.

Harold reached for the cream, noting to Tal that no amount of that and sugar could make this thing the English called coffee drinkable. "Forget all the bomb damage. Crappy coffee tells me it will be awhile before our former Allies are really back on their feet. But anyway — Eleanor. Wow. She's a peach. But what in hell was she thinking, staying in Italy like she did?"

"Naïveté, Hal. She was so consumed by her studies, she was oblivious to what was going on around her. She had a tight group of friends she says were smart and fascinating — and they all seemed to reinforce the idea to one another that they were immune from the threat around them — that things would return to normal. She's young, remember. We've got ten years on her."

"So maybe that's it… the age difference," began Harold.

"What do you mean?"

"Well, Tal, she doesn't seem comfortable with us. Maybe it's because we're older, or because we're kinda provincial compared to her. We don't speak Italian or French. Just good ole American."

"Yes. Wall Street bankers with backgrounds in signals intelligence are notoriously sheltered rubes. You don't have a clue about the world so I never should have subjected her to you two."

Harold smiled, shrugging his shoulders as if to say he had no other explanation to offer.

"Harold, to tell you the truth, I don't think it's her age or even how long she's been away from the U.S. I think it's that she's just been through hell. She left home and never saw her family again. She practically lived underground during the war. And she hasn't recovered from it. She's still in pieces. She's broken. She covers it up pretty well most of the time, with this great job she has at the preeminent museum in Florence. She's got a lot to be proud of, making her way as she has. But man, it's made her so cautious, so wary about everything. She doesn't entirely trust me yet. But I love her and hope she's almost on the other side of this. She's got a lot of healing to do."

"And you intend to be the agent of this healing?"

"I do. If she'll have me. I've never known anyone like her, Harold. There's just so much to her. She's brilliant. The stuff she knows about art and art history—it just pours out of her. And how easily she speaks Italian and French…"

"Her English seems a bit rusty," Harold observed.

Talbot laughed. "Yeah. She didn't use it for seven years."

"Unbelievable what she's been through," said Harold.

The men sat companionably for the next few minutes, the waitress bringing a fresh basket of pastries and offering more coffee, which they declined.

"So, the one thing," Talbot finally said, "is she's still keeping me at arm's length if you know what I mean. She has this real flirty side to her that comes out when she's had a few. But there's a line she doesn't cross. And you know, I'm trying to appreciate that."

"You always were one to take on ambitious projects and a traumatized, orphaned American seems right up your alley, Talbot. But let me suggest something. Take Eleanor back to States where she can sink some roots in familiar ground. She needs to remember who she is after all this time overseas, get away from the disruption here, the destroyed buildings, the displaced people, the food shortages. A dose of normal, boring life would do her good, I think."

"That's exactly the plan, Harold, absolutely. But she's so attached to Florence, it's like wrenching her from a lover. Still, I think I can do it. I'll remind her that the U.S. is not exactly a cultural wasteland."

•　　•　　•

"You were a champ, putting up with my friends for an entire week," Talbot said as they settled into the train that would take them to Dover, the first leg of their return trip to Florence. "I know it was a lot. Thanks for being willing to dive in."

"The Warrens are lovely," Eleanor responded. "I hope we see them again."

"Yeah. Me too. Maybe on their side of the pond next time."

"Now what is that supposed to mean?" she asked, wide-eyed, head cocked to one side.

"I have news," he said simply.

He explained that on his trip to Berlin, just before their holiday in London, he'd met with U.S. military intelligence, and learned they were about to boot him out; they were handing him over to the Central Intelligence Agency. CIA was taking over coordination of America's intelligence gathering. It was a step up, he said, the country needing its most experienced hands to join the fledgling operation aimed principally at getting eyes and ears on the ground in the Soviet Union now that they were no longer allies.

"I turned in the transfer paperwork and submitted my final reports before we left," he told her. "I have about six weeks before I have to be in DC."

"You're leaving then," she said, her face inscrutable.

"I have to go, yes, but my new orders clarified some things for me. Really, really important things. I should have done this months ago and I wish this were a more romantic setting—but Eleanor, I'm hoping you'll come with me. As my wife."

Rather than receive his proposal of marriage with ebullience or tears of joy, Eleanor became contemplative, crossing her arms, head still cocked, looking out the window of the train car to the horizon as if she were reasoning through a math equation. Finally, she turned back to him and reached both hands for his.

"Yes, I will," she finally said, her expression serious." But I have questions."

At this, Talbot let out a laugh and pulled her into his arms, deeply relieved that she agreed to be his. Hands on either side of her face, he kissed her and told her to ask away, whatever questions she had.

"Will we marry here? Or in the United States? I would prefer something small… so perhaps here, or maybe it should be in the States—to make sure there aren't legal questions. And do we have money for this? Can we afford to marry? Do we need papers?"

•   •   •

Two weeks later, much to the chagrin of Talbot's mother who had hoped to stage competitively extravagant nuptials inside St. Phillips Cathedral in Atlanta, they were married by a U.S. Army chaplain inside the vast Cathedral of Santa Maria del Fiore. Preparing for the ceremony had proven complicated and not because of the challenge of finding a suitable dress or a florist to create the bouquet. Eleanor's passport had gone missing years earlier, she said, a victim of her many moves during the war. She had only a tattered birth certificate, written in longhand and signed by the doctor who had delivered her at home. After some back and forth with Washington, given that her parents were no longer living and unavailable to help, the State Department issued Eleanor a U.S. diplomatic passport, with its attendant rights and privileges. The chaplain had helped greatly in securing the passport and the local paperwork for an Italian wedding: Tal was one of many American officers who'd found their brides while on assignment on foreign soil and the chaplain had learned his way around the landscape.

They did not advertise to the parish priest of the great Catholic cathedral that theirs was a Protestant ceremony; he stood across the transept, watching throughout, realizing as he heard the short, simple ceremony that lacked wine and wafer, that he had been wrong to allow these Americans and their unadorned Christianity into this sacred space. The only witnesses for the ceremony were eight members of Talbot's working group who were charmed by Eleanor and Talbot's happenstance romance and were looking very much forward to the celebration in the Hotel Minerva bar that would follow.

When the chaplain pronounced them wed, Talbot leaned in to kiss his bride, seeing tears gathered in her eyes. Eleanor was as raw and emotional as he had ever seen her. Finally, he believed, she would open herself fully, unreservedly, to him. As they made their way down the long aisle of the cathedral toward the massive wooden doors, her arm linked securely in his, he lifted his eyes toward heaven, grateful for this most holy moment. Above, in the balcony that ringed the sanctuary, a man skittered behind a pillar — Italian, well dressed. A church official perhaps? He turned to Eleanor and knew she spotted the uninvited guest, too. The welling tears spilled down her cheeks as she bit her lip, causing Talbot to resent that this outsider's intrusion had spoiled an otherwise perfect moment with his lovely, tender wife.

CHAPTER
SIX

1947

Washington, DC

As Talbot hoped, Eleanor's guardedness receded in their first years of their marriage. They returned to the States alongside thousands of veterans, all of them flush with relief at having survived the war, infused with optimism about what lay ahead. The Bentleys set up house in a sunny one-room apartment in Georgetown tucked into an historic building that faced the Potomac. The built-in bookshelves offered an ideal place to display the small collection of art pieces Eleanor had shepherded from Italy: a small oil of the Ponte Vecchio a classmate had painted, a clay sculpture of a starling that represented her best work, a blue and white painted tile Talbot had brought her from Lisbon set up on a small easel, and a small art deco box, cross-hatched in black and gold. Talbot had bought it from a merchant in the portico of the Uffizi, presenting it to Eleanor with her engagement ring inside. It was the perfect size to store the matchbooks she continued to collect from restaurants across the city. She hoped one day to add an example of abstract expressionism to the collection, even if it was just a framed print.

She and Tal scoured second hand shops for furniture, got to know the grocer on the corner, and professed their faith in front of congregants at St. John's Episcopal Church. While Talbot charted his course in the CIA, Eleanor learned her way around the city, map in hand. Her artistic appetite was satisfied by the collections within the Smithsonian's growing portfolio of museums.

Talbot made a point to get out of the office early every so often, so she could guide him through her newest discoveries in the city. He savored the tours she curated especially for him, much like she had done in Florence when they first met, walking him through galleries to explain the significance of a piece by Andrea del Verrocchio or Brunelleschi. He trailed her through the National Gallery and its rooms of Old Master portraiture, reaching for her hand as she interpreted an artist's brush technique, the use of light, why the Rembrandts, in particular, pulsated from the canvas as they did.

"Somerset Maugham identified it," Eleanor said as they stood before Rembrandt's portrait entitled *A Polish Nobleman*. "He writes about these aspiring painters in *Of Human Bondage*, toiling away in Paris, making little progress, and one concludes the greatest portrait painters paint both man and his soul—the man, the physical being, but his emotions and passion as well. That's the difference. Painting with the heart, as Maugham wrote."

Talbot found her depth, her intelligence, her beauty, distracting and stirring. He was proud of her and proud she was with him. On warm evenings, after their tours of the galleries, they often enjoyed a picnic dinner—simple sandwiches and a thermos of tea. They would linger on a bench near the Reflecting Pool, the Lincoln Memorial to one side and the Washington Monument to the other, the humming, growing city extending beyond.

"Reminds me of my bread and cheese dinners in Florence—before the war," she said the first time they picnicked there. "Sitting in the piazza, thinking our great thoughts. It was all theoretical—what Hitler and Mussolini were doing."

Talbot studied her, imagining the girl she had been in 1938, how easily she could have been lost to the violence that overtook Europe. "Did the university just wall you off from news from the outside world?"

"We weren't paying attention. We knew Jewish students left school because of the new laws. We just didn't know what to make of it. When the Black Shirts high-stepped across the plaza, we didn't take them seriously. Italy, with Mussolini, was theatre. Big gestures—literally!—and passion. The soldiers seemed like boys playacting. We thought sane voices would prevail before anything went sideways. We never imagined the school doors would close."

"Dictators are not easily deterred."

"Gosh, Tal, now that you mention it, Mussolini *was* kind of opinionated. And Hitler—not the best team player—always wanting to do it his way." Eleanor stood and paced in front of the bench, a hand stroking her chin. "I had not considered this, but you may be correct. The next time I'm in the middle of a worldwide conflict, I shall keep in mind that dictators tend to…dictate, not cooperate and I shall plan accordingly."

He loved this part of her, giving as good as she got, the playfulness that emerged more and more. She had finally grown to trust him, he believed, and it spilled over to their physical connection which had improved vastly since the early, fumbling days. She responded to his advances always and had begun to take the initiative herself. Some mornings she climbed into the shower with him, insisting it was only because she wanted to conserve water, before pulling his hips to hers. More than once after dinner, she appeared in front of him as he read the evening paper, silk robe open, nothing underneath, waiting until he noticed, then laughing at his shocked face. "I thought you were doing the dinner dishes," he managed to blurt on one occasion.

"It seems I'm finished. But if you're not interested I can keep myself busy."

As a younger man, Talbot had encountered women like this, frank in their sexual interest. He had never imagined he would find it in his wife. It felt like an undeserved gift.

Many Fridays, they met for cocktails and long discursive dinners with a growing circle of friends. They often walked Rock Creek Park on Saturday mornings, occasionally running into people Talbot knew from his office. Sundays, they slipped into the pew at St. John's right across the street from the White House, exchanging winks as they tallied the number of politicians, journalists, and other self-important types who tended to arrive just as the bells chimed eleven, ensuring their attendance would be duly noted by the greatest number of parishioners. In addition to DC celebrities, the sanctuary was filled with scores of young families — so many that the nursery committee was forever pleading for more volunteers to cope with the boom. Given his Episcopal upbringing, it was all quite familiar to Talbot, who volunteered to usher every quarter or so and always wanted to stay for the monthly coffee hour after the service. Eleanor, who had not been raised in a church, took a little time to warm up to the whole idea. She found the rector, Reverend Leslie Grant, who'd served as a chaplain in the war, approachable and warm, even if some of his assertions about righteous living tended toward the simplistic. But she found his sermons and her nascent exposure to a church community helped her better understand the prevailing post-war perspective — the twin ideas that the country was blessed by God and therefore knew what was best for the rest of the world.

Leaving the service each week, Talbot and Reverend Grant developed a little routine.

"How 'bout you join me for a round of golf at Congressional next Saturday, Reverend?" Talbot would ask as he reached for a handshake.

"How 'bout you agree to serve on the vestry, Talbot, so you can help me get a handle on the business side of things here? Then maybe I could afford to spend a Saturday golfing." Eventually, both men made good on their proposals, although

Talbot's travel made regular attendance at vestry meetings difficult.

Eleanor bristled at times with the chatty, cheerful congregants who buttonholed her with intrusive questions, asking her to contribute to the church cookbook they were putting together, to bring a casserole to the Wednesday pot-luck, or to volunteer in the nursery when she didn't yet have children. The women of St. John's found her difficult to slot into an understandable category, disinterested as she was in helming a committee or working her way into the church bridge club.

After a year in the apartment, they scraped a down payment together and bought the Arlington townhouse, Eleanor thrilled they finally had their own space, with walls they could paint any color they wished and a garage that meant no more battling for street parking. Soon after that, they met Caroline and Rémy Auclair at a homeowners meeting and a fast friendship began. Eleanor had the Auclairs to thank for her employment, Rémy, more precisely, who worked for the city of Arlington Planning Department and had put in a good word when the library had an opening. After a protracted interview process, she was hired on the circulation desk, later moving into positions of more responsibility.

The Bentleys made regular road trips to Atlanta to see his family, the pressures of work fading along with the thick city traffic as they ambled down Route 29 through Virginia. Eleanor found the view out the car window captivating, the Blue Ridge Mountains giving way to rolling hills and the Carolina cotton fields, the temperature warming the farther south they drove.

"It's almost like a different country," she said on their first trip south. "So rural and spare. More lovely and quiet than I expected."

"You've never been this way before? Never visited a Florida beach?"

"Of course not," she responded. "Why would I?"

It seemed reasonable to Talbot that a Smith professor might have had the means and inclination to take his family on a Florida vacation.

"So where did your family vacation?"

"Cape Cod," Eleanor responded. "Or Boston. But we rarely left Northampton because my father didn't like to be away. Perhaps that's why his heart gave out when it did."

At his parents' house in Atlanta, cocktail hour began promptly at five, after Tal's father came in from the Piedmont Driving Club. Eleanor held up well through arcane discussions that dissected everything from the Soviet threat to the coupling and uncoupling of people Talbot had grown up with. Often, this was followed by a little dinner party meant to help Eleanor get to know Tal's old friends and the important members of his mother's circle. The two women in his life enjoyed a polite if not warm relationship, his mother often asking, out of Eleanor's hearing, if there was a baby on the way, or at least plans at some point, for that to be the case.

"We'll see, Mother. It's not really anybody's business but our own."

"You're nearly forty-one, Talbot," she'd responded. "It's getting embarrassing."

•　　•　　•

His mother would remain embarrassed and disappointed. The children Talbot anticipated did not materialize and as they approached their third anniversary, their relationship seemed to stall. It had not matured into the comfortable interdependence Talbot had expected, something akin to the durable connection his parents enjoyed. Instead, Eleanor grew more aloof, dutifully tending to her library work, disinclined to share much about it with her husband. Despite his broad hints that he'd love to spend a day with her at one of the museums as they once did, she no longer offered him a curated tour. Their Saturdays walking Rock Creek Park—once sacrosanct when he was in town—grew rare, Eleanor preferring to sit with her coffee until noon, reading and re-reading sections of *The Washington Post*, before heading out to lunch with Caroline or a trip to Giant for groceries.

Tal blamed preoccupation with her job, and began making broad suggestions that they head to the Shenandoah Valley or Virginia Beach for a weekend, or plan a night out with friends from their Georgetown days. Instead, Eleanor planned a weekend away without him—a trip to New York to shop and meet old friends from Smith.

Her trip coincided with a ten-day assignment Talbot had in Europe, assessing the political winds as the Marshall Plan helped Europe begin its healing. The billions of dollars flooding into the Continent were doing magnificent work, he saw. Eleanor would be thrilled. He thought of her the entire time he was there, especially on his overnight in Italy, and again in Paris, where he picked out some French brassieres and panties for her—lacy, sexy little things he hoped she would see as an invitation.

When they reunited, she seemed especially happy to see him and eager to learn about his trip. Her time with her friends had been therapeutic, he thought, as she seemed to be making a renewed effort to connect with him in ways that might knit their relationship back together, restore the intimacy of their early marriage. She'd even bought him a gift: a beautiful Cheney briefcase in chestnut brown leather, nicer than anything he'd owned before. He would jettison his old Swaine attaché immediately, just to show her how much he appreciated her gift.

So. They'd been apart, but she was still thinking about him. A step in the right direction, he thought.

"Parliaments across Europe are leaning into democracy, Ellie, one by one," he said between bites of lasagna. He'd stopped by their little Italian place after he'd landed at Andrews Air Force Base that afternoon, the owner happy to pack entrees and bread into foil trays for him to take home. "It's a very, very hopeful sign. Greece has run the communist rebels out and

Turkey is stable. Italy is rebuilding—Florence looks like a jewel. We'll have to go back soon so you can see it. But Germany— wow. Berlin is a tense mess."

"All the former Allies fighting over it?"

"Sort of. There's still so much to put back together. Transportation doesn't work. Unreliable food supply. But the longer-term concern is that the Soviets might wall off their sector. They say they have to protect Germans in the east from the fascists in the west."

Eleanor scoffed. "Oh, I'm just sure Germany is crawling with fascists these days. All the people who slept through the Nuremberg trials and still think fascism is the ticket. But that's a little farfetched, isn't it? To think they could build a wall around a city, across neighborhoods, separating families. Wouldn't a wall have to be ridiculously high to keep people from crossing over? Sounds unworkable to me. Soviet hyperbole."

Talbot paused before he answered. "We think it's years off, but they're serious about it. We've heard them talking. So in the near term, they'll be busy placing assets—human and technical—in the western sectors."

Was the source credible? She wanted to know. "Maybe they just want to distract attention from other things."

"It's solid, Eleanor. The squishy intel never gets very far, certainly not to my team. And there's an operation we're getting going that will soon help us verify that and much more. But enough geopolitical intrigue. How was New York? All you'd hoped? How are your friends?"

"They're well. We did all the corny things: tea at the Plaza, buggy ride around Central Park. We plan to get tickets to *The King and I* when they go on sale and see it the next time we get together."

"Tourists," he chided.

"Make fun of me if you like. I enjoyed every minute."

"What else? I want to hear every detail." He reached for her hand, happy to be connecting with her, to see her relaxed and comfortable with him.

"It was fine." She rose to take her plate to the sink, her back to him as she rinsed it.

"Where'd you go?"

"What? I'm here. Just cleaning up."

"Ellie," he began, "it feels like you don't want to broach anything, I don't know…personal. Just politics and generalities."

She turned to look at him, baffled, and gave a little shrug. "No, Tal, I just answered your question and we'd sorta reached the end of that conversational string. Ok. What else?" She leaned against the kitchen counter and began counting on her fingers. "Let's see. One, I loved being in New York and we're all going to get together in a couple months and do it again, as I said. Two, work is work. Nothing really new going on. We're about to audit the catalog—usual stuff. Three, I had a wonderful dinner last night with the Auclairs at Rive Gauche in Georgetown. Rémy says the Coq au Vin is the best you'll get outside of Paris so we'll have to go. French chef and everything. Four, the Electrolux broke—just spewed dust everywhere as it gave up the ghost—so we need to get a new one. So that is the sum and substance of what you missed while you were gone. I'm glad you had a good trip."

"It was fine. Got done what I needed to."

"Excellent," she responded, patting him on the arm and leaving the room.

Had she heaved her plate of lasagna at the wall, he would have felt just as thrown off. Why did she hold him at arms' length? What point was she trying to make? Was it intrusive, his wanting to know how she spent her days, what she was feeling? Joy, boredom, insecurity, confidence, worry, hope—she seemed to want to manage it all smoothly and by herself, a stubborn vestige, he suspected, of her wartime trauma and accumulated losses that continued to contaminate their life together.

Her phlegmatic interiority had once fascinated Talbot. He'd seen it as a sign of her depth, her brilliance, that she was the kind of introvert who needed space to think, to process, and recharge. He realized now that it had become a tool for her, hardening in an instant into a wall he couldn't scale, a door he couldn't enter if she wished him not to. He wondered what wire he had just tripped to make her run away from an intimate conversation, a normal conversation between two married people. If he didn't know better, he might suspect she was involved with someone else. But there was no evidence of that. When he reached for her in the night, she still responded. With the lights out, her breath on his neck, her hands pulling him to her, he could believe their problems were minor and solvable.

A baby, he hoped, might draw them closer. Among their circle, having children was a given and, comments to his mother notwithstanding, Talbot expected to have a family like virtually everyone he knew. He'd overheard Caroline and Eleanor discuss the kind of mothers they hoped to be, test out names they might use, paint colors that would work in a nursery. It gave Tal confidence he would join the parent ranks in due time.

•　　•　　•

Nine months later, Talbot spent a soggy week in London, darting from hotel room to meeting room for conferences with the Royal Air Force about a planned joint endeavor. As his plane touched down at Andrews, he looked forward to seeing Eleanor, enjoying a glass of bourbon, eating a hearty something without cream sauce, and sleeping in his own bed. But the military staff car left him at the doorstep of a dark and empty house. Her car was in the garage so he assumed she was out with Caroline, somehow missing that he was due home this evening. He fixed his cocktail, swilling his bourbon and waiting for his wife.

As he debated whether he was more hungry than tired, whether to rustle up something to eat or head to bed, Eleanor arrived, stepping from a taxi looking pale and tired. Talbot greeted her at the door, taking her by surprise and causing her to drop her tote bag in the doorway. The afghan blanket she often pulled around herself on cold evenings spilled out. She tucked it back in the tote then stood to face him.

"Welcome back, Talbot. I missed you," she said quietly, reaching her arms around him and leaning hard into his chest.

"What is it, Eleanor? Are you not feeling well?" He extended his arms, leaning back so he could look into her eyes. They were dull, distant. She would not meet his gaze.

"I had a doctor's appointment," she said. "I didn't plan on hitting you with this the minute you arrived home. But…he had news for me."

Talbot cupped her face. "Tell me."

"It's not serious. But it's not good." She leaned back into his shoulder so he could not search her eyes as she spoke. "I had some tests run over the past few months, Talbot, and they seem to indicate I can't have children."

Talbot was stunned, realizing suddenly that this must be the source of her sadness, something she had worried about and carried alone without leaning on him, never giving him the chance to share the burden; suffering, while people they knew seemed to grow their families without effort. She continued.

"They said I can't hold a pregnancy—the way I'm built, the way my body responds. And they can't really treat it," she said, her demeanor composed, eyes moist, but not giving way to weeping as another woman might—as he might have expected. "It just happens with some women."

Talbot didn't entirely accept this. He had a million questions. There was always something that could be done, some intervention. Wasn't there? Didn't some women stay in bed for their pregnancies, then bear healthy children? What about surgery? Could that correct it? How could this door be slammed shut like this when he didn't even know they were trying to open it? Why had she borne this alone?

He stroked her hair, kissing the top of her head, thinking.

"Eleanor," he began slowly, "we still have each other. We have us." She looked up at him, as if to verify he truly meant what he said. "We're still a family—just us two—whatever happens. But, maybe there is something that can be done medically. And we haven't talked about adoption, but we could look into that at some point. Lots of couples do that."

"I don't want to," she said simply, her smile wan. "I think we need to accept this and not be eaten up by it. God knows I've spent enough time worrying about it."

"But what did the doctor say exactly? What did he recommend? Has he got experience with this? Because I think we at least need to get a second opinion."

Eleanor seemed unwilling to volunteer further details and given her obvious fatigue, he didn't push. She said she needed him to sit with her and accept it. She asked him not to take this on as a problem to tackle as he was accustomed to doing— strategically, from multiple directions, calling in the experts, applying pressure.

"Maybe we should talk with Reverend Grant. It might do us some good to sort out what's just happened." Eleanor shook her head and told him to stop, saying her sorrow and disappointment had consumed her for so long, that she had no more energy to discuss it. Only later did he realize he'd made a terrible error, not wading into their sadness and parsing fully what it meant for them, as painful as it was. Maybe if they had met together with her doctor, or consulted an adoption agency— even if it never resulted in adding a baby to their family—it would have drawn them closer, revived their marriage. A grief shared might have turned them toward one another instead of opening a fissure that only grew with time.

"Anyway, your job, Talbot—it consumes you. Maybe that was not going to be ideal for raising children. And I've been thinking that perhaps, I'm meant for other things. I have my job at the library and I've had the idea of volunteering at the National Gallery—now I won't have to give any of that up. And that's good and in a way, it's… I don't know, liberating."

He tried to agree with her, to affirm and soothe her. But learning they would never be parents turned out only to liberate her from him, to turn her attentions toward professional interests and away from the family she and Talbot comprised. Where he had received her news as a gut punch, an emotional loss he would need time to absorb, Eleanor behaved tactically, re-sorting her list of priorities as if not having children were merely an item to take off life's list, not a wrenching, irreplaceable loss. Although they never discussed it, Talbot believed she struggled with shame in not joining the province of motherhood, shame she covered by seeming not to care, her natural reserve amplified and impenetrable.

Their physical relationship persisted, soon characterized mostly by bedtime encounters after the lights went out—Eleanor no longer climbing into the shower with him or wafting past him in an open robe but receptive when he reached for her. The relationships he soon developed with other women, he told himself, were an inevitable consequence. It wasn't sex he was primarily after but confirmation that women still found him interesting, brilliant, in charge. A man in his line of work, with the stress and the secrecy, needed a counterweight, a mechanism to verify the fact of his charms, elicit admiration from those around him, most especially his romantic partner. Even with the playacting and temporariness that characterized his serial intimacies—he didn't love these women—it gave him great satisfaction to know he held them in his sway. The way they followed him down this road — from the initial earnest interest, that gave way to flirting, then word games and double entendre, that finally led them to his bed — told him, at mid-life, that he retained essential powers.

The general kindness and deference Eleanor showed Talbot kept him from provoking fights with her, from threatening divorce unless she opened up to him. There were, in truth, no divorced men at CIA because personal failure could too easily be conflated with professional incapability; how could an officer who couldn't move his marriage in a particular direction do the same in clandestine maneuvers? Instead, there were men whose wives lived apart from them because aging parents needed a hand or their teenagers needed to continue school in a particular neighborhood or they owned houses realtors just couldn't sell. Such arrangements satisfied the agency's code. Talbot rationalized that his extracurriculars were required to maintain the status quo in his marriage, and therefore, stability in his job.

He had found ample opportunities at work, young women assigned to his office or elsewhere in CIA, overt in their appreciation of his physical attributes and his verbal ripostes, women he nudged, inch by inch, into an intimacy that enthralled them both. The trick was to have his fun while making sure his playmates didn't expect things to progress to something deeper. When they did, when he sensed they were growing too attached, he could place a call and have his lover shuffled off into another department. When he encountered these women later, in the cafeteria or an elevator, after they were transferred out, he would offer a smile and a shrug, as if to say he had nothing to do with their changed circumstance. The slight crease that appeared between his eyes as he did this, the concern it communicated, reassured them it was not a matter of Talbot's waning interest. Several of them soon left CIA, abandoning dreamed-about careers in favor of safer, more traditional lives that didn't put their hearts at risk. Others remained in their jobs, tight-lipped and ashamed that they'd allowed their boundaries to be breached as they had. They could not expose Talbot, as that would involve exposing themselves.

CHAPTER
SEVEN

April, 1960
Washington, DC

Their affair had raged for nine months now but "affair" was not a term Helen liked to use. In her mind, she and Talbot were a couple. Partners. They practically camped out at his townhouse when Eleanor left on her New York weekends—four times so far. They would leave the office separately on Friday afternoon, calling out loud and conspicuous goodbyes to each other and wishes for a good weekend. Helen would drive home, feed her cat, and when possible, make small talk with the neighbor on the other side of her duplex. She'd often tell a little story about her weekend plans—she was headed out to dinner with a girlfriend and might spend the night, or she was heading to see her parents, or she was going with a hiking group to the Blue Ridge Parkway for the weekend—just to provide a little context for her absence. Then she'd drive in the direction of the bus stop, park her car in a lot nearby, and catch a bus to Arlington. Talbot would scoop her up when she arrived and their weekend would fully begin.

On this day, Helen stepped from the bus and hopped energetically into Talbot's car, slinging her canvas tote bag into the footwell, not even glancing around before kissing Talbot on the cheek. His retrieving her like this just felt more appropriate, more dignified to her, until he reminded her to slide down in her seat as they pulled onto his street, so she'd be out of view until the garage door was safely closed. Once it was, Helen grabbed her tote and leapt from the car, face flushed and eager. Every time Talbot brought her home, inviting her inside his life, moved her a step closer, she believed, to something permanent. It was proof their relationship was more substantial than whatever dalliances he'd involved himself in before. "What if I live here someday?" she mused to herself. "What if, before long, we're just Tal and Helen, coming home together?"

They made their way up the stairs to the main level, where the nubby creme furniture was enlivened by an array of art pieces Eleanor had brought with her from Europe after the war and collected since. There were a few framed photographs, mostly of Eleanor and Tal or of Tal's family, none featuring Eleanor's relatives. Helen found it all rather bland, too neat, more like Holiday Inn than a home where a two people shared a happy life.

"Hungry?" Tal asked, loosening his tie as he walked toward the kitchen. "I can make you a sandwich."

She came up behind him and slipped her hands around his waist. "I'm hungry," she purred, "but not for a sandwich."

"You're relentless," he laughed, turning to face her then lifting her to the counter. He walked between her knees, pressing them apart as she protested, his hand reaching.

"Not here," she breathed. "Let's get comfortable."

He lifted her in his arms and carried her down the hall to his and Eleanor's bedroom. As he lay her down, unbuttoning her skirt so she could shimmy out of it, the phone in his office rang. Helen groaned.

"Leave it, Tal," she pleaded, as she undid the garters on her stockings. "It's Friday. You're busy."

He winced. "Can't, honey. That's the work line. But stay just like that. Exactly like that. I'll be right back."

Talbot retreated down the hall to pick up the call.

Helen removed her skirt and blouse then considered whether to pose on the bed in her bra and garter belt, to put on the new silk nightie she'd brought, or to disrobe entirely. Ten minutes turned into twenty, then thirty. When Talbot made her wait like this, she made the best of it, doing a little poking around to ease her irritation.

On her first visit to the townhouse, she'd swiped a key ring she'd found as she'd looked through the bureau drawers, giving in to an impulse she could not articulate or explain even to herself. Of course she'd never told him. In the first drawer she'd opened, she'd found Talbot's T-shirts and boxers lined up with military precision. The next held little stacks of Eleanor's panties, bras, and slips—white and utilitarian. Helen had reached in to feel the fabric and knocked the little pile askew, uncovering several keys on a ring underneath. Underneath the keys, were a pair of brassieres, one black and one red—lacy, satin, low-cut and to Helen, alarming. She looked at the label. French. She had nothing like this in her wardrobe. Was this the kind of thing Tal liked? Maybe these were old things, placed at the bottom of the stack because Eleanor no longer used them. Helen had replaced the items and arranged them as she'd found them, deciding the key ring must be a duplicate, hidden here as a back-up and not something Eleanor would miss. So she dropped the key ring in her pocketbook and at night, when she was alone and missing him, she often pulled it out to look at, her talisman of how deeply Talbot had let her into his life. The ring held a house key, two car keys, a smaller key, perhaps to a safe or safe deposit box, and a large key she thought must unlock a door at the library.

Over time, she'd tried the keys here and there, surprised to discover the large key opened Tal's office door and the smallest key unlocked his file cabinet. How had Tal's key ring—now Helen's key ring—found its way into Eleanor's lingerie drawer? Helen supposed they'd been knocked in by accident and Eleanor hadn't bothered to notice, unhelpful wife that she was. Helen had used the keys just a few times when Tal was away from the office, opening his office door not to snoop so much as to stand in his space and study it without him in it. She found a copy of her personnel file in the cabinet—education, background, start date—and wondered if he spent time looking at it, thinking of her. There were dozens of work-related files too, notes on operations already executed and others in the planning phase. Grand Slam was his big project now—something to do with the Soviet Union and taking photos. Helen had developed a habit in the months since she'd obtained the keys, of peeking into her file, hoping to see his effusive praise for her work. But so far, nothing.

As Talbot's phone call dragged on down the hall, Helen turned her eye toward the Bentleys' bathroom. She wasn't entirely sure what she was looking for. She just liked touching things that were his. Nothing much of interest on the vanity— Tal's shaving cream and razor, his toothbrush. There was a dish with bobby pins, a can of Aqua-Net, but the rest of Eleanor's toiletries and make-up were obviously with her in New York. Helen opened the cabinet under the sink to find neatly stacked towels and sheets. She pulled each of the three drawers open, where she found cotton balls, band-aids, some cough syrup and, happily, no condoms. None. She supposed that was nothing Tal and Eleanor needed to have on hand anymore. The very idea cheered her.

With little left to explore, she made her way towards Tal's office to encourage him to wrap up his call. The daylight waned—he'd been talking nearly an hour. She opened the door gingerly, smiled, then showed a bare leg. Clearly preoccupied, Tal waved her in, holding up one finger to promise he would soon end the call. She planted herself in front of his desk and began to slowly remove her bra. Talbot rose to his feet and waved her off, turning his back to her and stumbling though remarks to end the phone call, claiming to the caller that there was someone at the door, that he'd review all they'd discussed, and would be back in touch. At last, he hung up.

"What are you trying to do to me, woman?" Talbot asked, coming around the desk and pulling her into him, hands on her backside. She looked around this office, thinking how it was so like him—black leather sofa, dark mahogany desk with his Cheney briefcase on top, the lid propped open. Prints of Amen Corner at Augusta National hung over the well-stocked bar cart—gin, vodka, and of course a full bottle of Jim Beam. She inhaled and pressed contentedly into the body of her lover. She liked being exactly here.

"Bedroom? Or here?" Talbot nodded toward the sofa.

She turned around to face him.

"Both," she laughed. "First here and then in bed, and then on the kitchen table and then the floor of the den…"

"As you wish," he responded.

•   •   •

After a squeaky, sticky interlude on the leather sofa, they soaped each other up in the shower then relaxed at the kitchen table over BLT's, both of them satiated for the moment, Helen especially content.

"So who called?" she asked. "I mean, if you can say."

"Knox. We're moving on that project."

"Must be important for you to talk that long on a Friday with me…waiting."

Tal smiled. "It is. He was sharing the latest and we had some timing issues to consider."

"The weather plane?" Helen winked.

"The weather plane." Talbot winked back.

•   •   •

The next morning, Helen awoke first, the crisp spring sunshine streaming in the window suffusing her with a sense of well-being. Talbot lay naked with his back to her, his breathing slow and rhythmic. She moved her hips into his and her hands to his torso, eliciting the response she was looking for.

"Morning," he mumbled, rolling over to pull her face to his.

"Pretty nice way to wake up, wouldn't you say?"

"Agreed," he said, beginning his usual machinations, reaching under her nightie, kicking clear of the bedsheets.

"So, Tal. Maybe it's time we take the next step together."

Talbot seemed not to hear her as he nuzzled her neck, kneed her legs wider.

"Right, Tal?" Helen tried again.

"This is right, Helen," he said as he entered her. "So, so right."

"It is right. Exactly right. So… baby," she whispered, breathing into his ear. "What do you think about what I said? If we made this permanent. If we lived here—or somewhere—together."

"Honey," he moaned, ignoring her question. It was a tactic he'd used many, many times—pretending to miss the ask and continuing on. But this time, Helen wasn't having it.

She pulled off and faced him, drawing her knees up as a barrier to further overtures, pulling the afghan from the foot of the bed over them. "Talbot. The least you can do is answer me."

"Answer what?" he asked, teeth clenched, jaw muscles working. "What do you want to discuss at this exact moment, Helen, when we were enjoying each other, enjoying the morning?"

"Enjoying the morning? Is that all this is to you? Just some morning fun?" She jumped to her feet, clutching the afghan in front of her. "Is that all this is, Tal?" she repeated, anger rising, "Am I just a transient thing for you? Are you kidding me? After the way I've been there for you? Supported you? Because you don't have a wife who's even interested in you?"

"Helen," he began, quietly, reasonably. "Who do you think you're involved with? I'm a CIA officer. A married intelligence officer. Divorce would end my career. End it. But we can still be together and even travel together, and have this, this incredible time together… this connection. But we can't be more than this right now, Helen. You understand that."

She could not process what he was saying. They were a pair. They were in love, weren't they? How could he stay married to someone else when he loved her? Or was that it? He didn't love her.

"But you…you always want to be with me. You want it as much as I do and I see it! You're sad when we can't be together. I love you, Tal. I thought you knew I did—and that you love me and wanted me for more than just the occasional weekend."

The look on his face told her everything she didn't want to know. He looked regretful, like he felt sorry for her, felt bad that she was disappointed. Not at all like a man in love, intent on soothing and keeping his worried lover. He reached for her hand.

"Helen. You're fantastic. You're fun. You're so, so smart." He locked his eyes on hers. "But did we ever talk about love? A future together? No. We didn't. Because right now, we can't have that."

"Tal, I just… I thought…" Her tears fell as she moved to him, straddling him and pulling his head to her chest. "How could you give this up—us together, the way we fit so perfectly, what we do for each other. Are you saying you could actually walk away from this—from us—when it feels this good to be together?"

Talbot smiled, reaching his arms around her and kissing her as tenderly as he could, brushing away her tears, urging her not to cry. He laid back on the bed, pulling her on top of him. He took his time with her, moving slowly, pausing to lock eyes with her, Helen interpreting his deliberate pace as some sort of commitment to her, that he couldn't, in fact, walk away from her. It struck her that he had used the words "right now"—they couldn't be openly together *right now*. He'd said it twice. That meant he was planning for down the road. That's how she interpreted what he truly meant to say.

Helen did not broach the subject of them moving toward something permanent again that weekend. Instead, she resolved to accelerate the timetable through her sexual pliancy, her attentiveness to his needs. They found some old movies on TV Saturday afternoon, which they watched entangled in one another's arms. By Sunday, after she'd helped tidy up to erase any evidence of her presence in the townhouse, she boarded the bus for the hour-long trip back to Bethesda. And despite what he had plainly said, his clear unwillingness to put his career at risk for her, Helen was convinced he was looking forward, as she was, to a future together.

CHAPTER
EIGHT

April, 1960

Washington, DC

Eleanor returned from her New York weekend more upbeat, with renewed interest in Talbot and his work, the progress of his golf game, what he'd like for dinner. His perpetual wish was that she would remain in this more open frame of mind, not drift back into herself. She was turning forty in just a few weeks and he'd reserved a room at the Italian restaurant off Dupont Circle for a surprise party. He phoned Caroline to ask for her help contacting friends from the library, several neighbors, and people they knew from the club so it would be a lively enough gathering.

"Do you think you could get any of her college friends to come for the party" he asked, "the ones you get together with in New York?"

"Come here?" she'd responded, "to DC?"

"Well, yes, Caroline, if we're going to have the party here, they would need to come here, yes."

"Sorry, no, I just meant that bringing people in from out of town involves arranging places for them to stay, transporting them from the airport or the train station. And we're three weeks out so it might be a lot to pull together."

"Aren't most of these friends in the Northeast? It's a three-hour train ride. Not so complicated, Caroline. And we have a guest room. It would make for a bigger surprise."

Caroline waited a beat before responding. "First of all, Talbot, unlike you, with all your hopping around on business trips, not everybody finds it so easy to just pick up and go. And to be honest, they just don't seem like those kinds of friends. I mean, they've known her a long time, and they like to go out together, but they just don't seem that close to her. And we did raise a glass to our girl at Tavern on the Green when we were up there last week. I think we just focus on the people here and we'll have a big enough surprise."

Talbot relented, accepting that his newest tactic to get a look at Eleanor's old friends would not be successful.

"Sure. You're right, of course. It will be good with just the people here. Can you help with flowers? I thought it would be nice if we brought some in."

•   •   •

Two days before the big event, Helen came upon him in his office, scanning the Yellow Pages for a bakery able to provide him a suitable birthday cake by Saturday night. He wanted something unusual, he said, more upscale, beyond frosted yellow cake.

"It's a little late for that," Helen said, sounding to Talbot more scoldy than supportive. They had not found a window to be together since their weekend at the townhouse at the beginning of the month and when they had spans like that, she tended to grow irritated and impatient with him. He camouflaged his annoyance by catering to her, praising how expertly she'd drafted a letter, how perfectly she prepped a file for a meeting.

"So I'm finding out. Not something I usually do, ordering cakes and so forth."

Helen paused a moment, crossed her arms, then said she knew the place to call. She could get it ordered and delivered to the restaurant Saturday evening.

"Excellent. Thank you." Tal leaned back in his chair, taking in the angry set of her mouth, her crossed arms. "Helen, you know Eleanor has no other family."

"I'm well aware."

"Do you want to come?" he asked suddenly. "You could bring a date and it might be kind of...I don't know... fun." He winked.

"Bring a date?" she asked incredulously, her voice low to make sure she wasn't overheard. "Uh... it's not like I have a lot of time for DATING." She gave a tight, angry smile.

"Oh right. Of course. You do work so hard, Miss Sizemore. Well, we'll miss you," he said loudly, before scribbling, "I'm so sorry, honey. THANK YOU!" on the legal pad before him.

She looked at the note then back at him. "I'll get right on that cake order, Mr. Bentley," she said, backing out of his office door while giving him a hard stare.

Despite her annoyance, Helen approached the task with her usual tenacity, reporting mission success to Talbot within minutes. Initially, the head baker protested it was too late for her rather involved request of a hummingbird cake.

"So I reminded him of all the business I steer his way—birthdays, baby showers, staff breakfasts, all those hush-hush celebrations we have around here that we don't even acknowledge. I asked him to 'kindly recommend another bakery.' I said, 'If they're good, who knows? I might call them the next time I need something. Whom do you recommend I call?' And he backed right down, said he'd put a rush on the fresh fruit he would need to create the cake, that he didn't in the least mind spending his Friday night at work. I ignored that little dig and said, 'That's why I always call your bakery. You always come through.'" She concluded her story and waited to hear Tal's praise.

"And so do you, Miss Sizemore. I appreciate your handling this." He offered a quick nod, the cue for her to exit so he could return his attention to his work.

"That's it then?" she asked with a scoff. "That all you need? Fine."

Before resuming his work, Tal ruminated on his growing Helen problem. Their last encounter at the townhouse hadn't moved her in the direction he'd hoped. He had several maneuvers in mind to address it and normally would not initiate anything so dramatic when he was covered up with work and this current, consequential assignment. But the way she had begun looking at him, the very posture of her body when they were in the office together, signaled to anyone paying attention that a boundary had been breached. She was too casual now, her tone too sharp with him when she was upset. She was acting entitled — that was the word — and it was only a matter of time before someone detected they were more than boss and subordinate. He had tried to get her to back off when they'd had that fight at the townhouse, but she had not relented. Time for the phone call that could take care of this for him, move the entire thing out of his hands and into the purview of government bureaucracy. He placed the call, feeling a fleeting pang of conscience, before turning to the files on his desk that needed his full attention.

Top of mind was the project he and Knox were wrestling with, one he hoped would bring him approbation from the higher-ups, maybe speed his rise within CIA. It was nearing zero-hour for the next stage of Operation Grand Slam, timed to give the president the upper hand when he sat down for talks with Khrushchev in Paris in just a few weeks. American negotiators would come armed with an accurate picture of

Soviet military strength thanks to photos U-2 spy planes had been snapping for years now. They wouldn't reveal these photos, of course, but the images had allowed the Americans to see past Soviet feints. Years earlier, Tal and his team had recruited two of the world's best scientific minds for the project. Aircraft designer Kelly Johnson had dreamed up the ultra-light, ultra high-flying, and very odd-looking U-2 while Polaroid Company co-founder Edwin Land, already a wealthy man from his raft of patented inventions, had built the high-resolution cameras for Kelly's plane.

Eisenhower had been wary of the whole thing, but they'd worn him down, convincing him to use all capabilities at hand so the Soviets couldn't continue to lie about how many ICBMs and long-range bombers they had. And when Ike had gotten a look at the first round of U-2 photographs, he was sold. The photos showed "every blade of grass," in Ike's words and zero evidence the Soviets were preparing for war. Recent missions had traversed the Semipalatinsk Test Site, the Dolon Air Base where strategic bombers were stationed, the missile test site near Saryshagan, and the Tyuratam missile range. No massive armament program was underway. There was no "missile gap," despite what *Washington Post* columnists continued to claim. Why had Eisenhower — the former Supreme Allied Commander, liberator of Fortress Europe — gone soft against the Soviets? the columnists yammered. The opposite was true, Talbot knew: the president wasn't worried because he'd seen for himself the limited cards the Soviets held. But the president, Director Dulles, and Talbot's team had to endure the wrong-headed criticism because publicly refuting the allegations would expose the U-2 surveillance program.

Talbot and Dulles had assured the president that even if the Soviets discovered the overflights, they couldn't stop them. Cruising at 70,000 feet, no MIG or Soviet missile could reach them. And if the unthinkable happened like a mechanical mishap, the pilot was equipped with fatal dose of cyanide and would pull the "destruct" lever in the plane. None of the carefully chosen flyers in the program wanted to end up in Soviet hands. Each was brave and brilliant and went into the operation knowing the risks.

The next flight was set for Sunday over several especially sensitive Soviet targets. Talbot blamed his preoccupation with mission details—the weather forecast had scrambled the schedule—as the reason he forgot to order a birthday cake. Two big projects coming together at once, he chuckled. The party Saturday night would be a perfect distraction—he could knock back a string of bourbons and everyone would assume he was just celebrating his wife. Sunday, he'd keep up with mission progress by phone and look forward to the congratulatory handshakes he'd receive Monday.

His series of afternoon meetings concluded, Talbot gathered his things and headed out to the reception area and Helen's desk. Two pieces of typing paper, a carbon in between, were rolled into the typewriter carriage. This afternoon? That was ambitious, Talbot thought, and impossible. He laid a piece of tissue flat in her trash can. Not tonight, Helen, he thought. Time for both of us to move on.

CHAPTER
NINE

Sunday, May 1, 1960
Arlington, VA

Talbot fell into bed after Eleanor's birthday party, enjoying a single hour of dreamless sleep before his wife jostled him. His three-thirty call.

"How 'bout some coffee, Tal?" she asked. "Tal? You awake?"

"Yes. I'm up. Coffee, yes," he said swinging his feet to the side of the bed, rubbing his hands across his face.

"It's on your desk in your office. All you have to do is walk down the hall. Your reward awaits once you actually get moving."

He laughed and thanked her, splashing some water on his face before heading to his office for what he hoped would be a perfunctory check-in on this phase of Operation Grand Slam.

Instead, he learned Grand Slam was shaping up to be a grand disaster. The U-2 had gone missing, the USAF communications specialist confirmed to Talbot. The pilot, a Captain Powers, had been expected to land in Norway hours ago, but there was no sign of him. Talbot knew the cleanest outcome, for the country anyway, would be that he'd crashed in the sea, hopefully not in Soviet waters, never to be heard from again. Chances were slim he'd been shot down over the Soviet Union, slim that the fragile plane—laden with technology—would be identifiable if it had crashed or the pilot triggered the destruct button. Talbot hung up and phoned his deputy Derek Knox.

"We've got time," said Knox. "It's early. He's only a few hours overdue. He'll turn up."

"Any chatter about a shoot down? Indications they tracked the plane or he ditched over Russia?" asked Talbot.

"None," said Knox. "If Powers got into trouble — depleted oxygen, engine failure — once he knew he was going down, he'd activate the destruct button and bail. He wouldn't leave anything for the Soviets to find. He's well-trained. He knew the drill."

"If they hit him, it means they saw him coming."

"Again, unlikely," said a confident Knox. "He's 70,000 feet in the air. Soviet radar is trained miles below that to track their air traffic. MIGs can't fly that high so they couldn't engage him. Wish we had a better idea of what's going on, but let's not overreact." They agreed to wait to bring in Director Dulles until they knew something concrete and to speak again in a few hours.

Talbot spent a few more restless hours in bed, reasoning through the facts he knew, coming to terms with the probable loss of the pilot. When he and Knox spoke again late morning, there was nothing new. Powers' overflight was to have lasted nine hours; he was now nine hours overdue, with no wreckage spotted in the Barents Sea, no chatter picked up from the Soviets. As Tal's anxiety swelled, Eleanor hovered, replenishing his coffee, offering bourbon which he declined, and retrieving the plate of toast he'd allowed to grow hard and cold. He gave her no details of the apparent crisis and she didn't pry.

That afternoon, Talbot gathered at the office with Director Dulles, his immediate boss Robert Bissell, and the rest of his team to review the cover story developed during mission planning: NASA — the new aeronautical agency that had replaced the National Advisory Committee for Aeronautics—had lost a weather plane.

"We've got a U-2 ready, painted up with a NASA emblem, that we'll show the press when it's time," explained Bissell between anxious drags on his filterless Camel cigarette. "Unarmed, civilian plane, aloft to take gust-meteorological measurements across the globe and conduct cloud atlas photography—just charting world weather patterns."

Talbot continued. "The U.S. military is not involved—this is a scientific endeavor the president knows nothing about—and he's looking forward to the upcoming meeting with the Soviet Premier in Paris."

"So, no sign of wreckage yet?" Bissell asked.

Knox shook his head. "Still time for something to surface. Let's have some patience."

When the president called in to the meeting moments later, it was clear he was well out of patience. Eisenhower was furious. He and Khrushchev were just coming to understand one another, he thundered, thanks to the Soviet Premier's carefully planned tour of the U.S. months earlier, which had yielded a reciprocal invitation for Eisenhower to visit Moscow after the Paris summit. The timing of this fiasco, he roared, could not be worse.

No one responded right away, Dulles sitting with his face in his hands, Bissell staring out the window, chain-smoking, and Knox, head bent, examining flight tables on the clipboard in his lap. Talbot finally waded in.

"Sir, I know the mutual regard you've developed with the Soviet Premier—the personal relationship—is critical to keeping us out of a hot war. We will do everything we can to protect that. But sir, thanks to the intelligence this project has collected, we can count the number of long-range bombers parked on the tarmac on an air base outside Leningrad." Dulles lifted his headed and nodded for Talbot to continue. "The reason we can sleep at night is because we know—we have photographic evidence—that the Soviets are not preparing a surprise attack, that we are not on the verge of nuclear war. So if we've lost a pilot—and we all feel awful about that—it was a risk we agreed to take because these surveillance flights have made the entire world safer."

After a long, loud sigh, the president said he hoped that was the case, ordered them to find out what the hell was going on, and hung up the phone.

•   •   •

Talbot arrived home that evening and picked at the soup and salad Eleanor prepared for dinner, more interested in his bourbon and Coke. After she cleared the plates, Eleanor returned to the table and sat quietly, waiting.

"We've lost an asset, Ellie, a big one," he finally said. "Along with a human being. Can't seem to find them anywhere."

"Soviets aware?" she asked.

"Potentially involved. It's possible they knew what we were doing. I mean, there were signs they were on to us a couple years ago, but they couldn't respond so we continued."

"Continued what, exactly?"

And since he expected all this would be splashed over the newspapers before long, he told her a sanitized version of what happened—that a surveillance plane might have strayed into Soviet airspace. That yes, sometimes the "straying" was intentional and this time, the aircraft might have been shot down.

Eleanor's eyes grew wide absorbing the implications of Talbot's words. She reached across the table for his hand.

"You don't know anything for sure yet, Talbot. Let's wait to see how this plays out. No need to worry until you know something. But I'm sorry you're in the middle of this, Tal. I know you're exhausted." She rose and carried the remains of his drink to the sink. "I don't think more drink will do you any good. But sleep might. Go on to bed. I'll clean this up and join you in a minute."

Talbot gave her a weary smile and did as she suggested.

CHAPTER
TEN

Sunday, May 1, 1960
McLean, VA

Late Sunday morning, Caroline phoned over to the Bentleys, partly to thank them for Eleanor's lovely birthday party, more so to give Talbot an opportunity to express his appreciation for her contributions towards its success. He answered the phone, his tone abrupt and hurried.

"Tal? Hello. Just calling to say I think we did well, pulled it off…"

"Yep."

Sometimes he could really be an ass, thought Caroline, who had not expected to have to fish for a thank-you for assembling the guest list, the menu, the flowers.

"Everything alright, Tal?"

"Need to keep the line free, Caroline. Work issue. I'm sorry. I've just got my hands full. I'll tell Eleanor you called and, you know, you loved the party, happy to help with it, happy to see her and so on. I'm headed out this afternoon so call then. Good for you?"

"Of course, of course. I'll catch up with her later. Unless — does she need me, do you think?"

"She's fine. You don't need to come. Call her later. That works. Gotta run."

Caroline stared at the handset, hearing it drone with the connection severed. *Some CIA somebody is in hot water,* she thought.

"That was quick," Rémy smiled as she entered the kitchen, a week-old copy of *Le Monde* spread on the table before him. It was his habit on Sundays to drive to Rosslyn to retrieve the paper along with breakfast pastries from the French bakery there that doubled as an international newsstand. Their eight-year old daughter sat at the table with him, a Nancy Drew mystery in her hands. "Let me guess. The Bentleys are still lazing in bed and can't even rally to offer a proper thank you for your help with the party." He extended his arms toward his wife, who folded herself into his lap.

"Not exactly. Talbot picked up. But he's in the middle of some sort of work problem and wanted to keep the line free."

They exchanged a long look before Rémy spoke.

"They have two phone lines, no? He's got that work line he's so proud of, so..." Caroline cut him off with a nearly imperceptible head shake, her eyes cutting toward their daughter. But the girl had caught the tone. She lifted her head from her book and looked at one parent then the other, her interest in another potential mystery peaked.

"Where are your brother and sister, Colette?" Caroline asked. "Round them up and we'll head to the park."

It would be easier for the adults to discuss adult things with their children distracted by the park's many charms.

•   •   •

Caroline met her future husband when she was an undergraduate at American University. Daughter of a Long Island construction manager, she had resisted her parents' plea that she enroll in Oneonta or the teacher's college in Buffalo and get a teaching degree — something safe. Like many Americans imbued with a post-war sense of possibility, she wanted to study government and public service and decided AU would be the best place, situated as it was in the Nation's Capital, the new center of the world. She first laid eyes on Rémy in a course called A Changing Europe, a survey class that she joked later, could be summed up in a single sentence: Fascism, Socialism, and Communism are bad and can't hold a candle to American democracy. She'd told her roommate she'd written exactly that on the final exam, "And Voila! Got the A!"

At thirty, Rémy enrolled in AU to collect the final few credits of a degree he'd abandoned early in the war. When the professor coaxed him to tell stories of his experience in the Resistance, his humility, along with his seductive accent, caused most of the women in the class to fall deeply in love — some of the men, too — imagining his brave exploits that involved sabotage and helping downed Allied flyers escape to safety. Caroline, with her simple background and unclouded love of country, stood out from the string of aggressive coeds who worked hard to get his attention. After two years of dating, his degree in his pocket, he asked for her hand and she said yes, their decision to marry also securing the paperwork he needed to remain in the United States.

When Rémy was hired into his position in the Arlington Planning Department, Caroline began work as a temp for the federal government, providing an extra set of hands at events when the State Department hosted foreign dignitaries. Soon after, the Auclairs bought their townhouse next door to the Bentleys. The youngest couples in the complex, they came to know each other at a homeowners meeting, watching the spectacle of angry, older residents appealing to the board to address what they believed were outrageous parking, trashcan, and mailbox violations that threatened the very post-war world order itself. Across the room at one meeting, Eleanor happened to catch Caroline's eye as a resident articulated the deep, deep damage caused when the trash collectors come later in the day, as opposed to the early morning. He bolstered his argument with points and sub-points, photo evidence and notarized testimony he'd collected from other residents. Both Eleanor and Caroline were doing their utmost to suppress laughter that threatened to erupt loudly, convulsively and their eye contact only made it worse. Each scooted into the hall to relieve the pressure, Rémy having fled moments earlier. The women found him bent at the waist, tears streaming, at the speaker's tragic tale.

"Had he spent a few days in Europe during the war, perhaps the trash man coming two hours late would not seem like the end of the world," he said, extending his hand to introduce himself to Eleanor.

She stopped, tilting her head to take in his accent, assess his background.

"I lived in Italy in the war," she said, squeezing his hand. "I could not agree with you more."

After the meeting, they brought Talbot into their new little circle, realizing only then they were neighbors on either side of a shared wall. Within a few weeks, the four met for cocktails after work and spent a Saturday morning at the Rosslyn bakery for coffee and croissants. Dinners together at Georgetown's trendier places followed, evenings when they lingered so long at the table that several times, the waitstaff turned off the lights before the diners got the hint. So began their four-way love affair, all of them grateful to abide in this warm company. The women connected immediately, Eleanor impressed with Caroline's resolve to earn a degree in something other than teaching, her independence in staying in DC to make her life. Caroline found Eleanor sophisticated and worldly in a manner unlike any American woman she knew. That she had followed her love of sculpture across the ocean, ignoring the peril, seemed a singular, astounding thing. Caroline savored the guided tours Eleanor laid out for them in the city's museums, and most especially the coffee breaks they shared as they went. Both were buoyed to have found a friend in Washington who valued them apart from their husbands' accomplishments.

Talbot recognized in Rémy a grateful Frenchman who was aware his survival was due in part to the work of Allied intelligence units that had provided money, radios, resources, and personnel to support the Resistance in the war. The men did not speak of this directly, or of Tal's role in it, but seemed to understand each other, the life-and-death situations each had confronted and survived. It made the humdrum of their post-war lives especially sweet. When either man had a leaky pipe, shelves to install, or shrubs to prune, they called each other for help. That soon expanded to taking in Senators' games at Griffith Stadium and later, golf and fishing weekends with a few guys from Rémy's office.

On warm weekend evenings, they enjoyed steaks or burgers that Tal prepared on his patio grill, Eleanor overseeing the salad and potatoes, the Auclairs contributing an apple tart, chocolate soufflé, or perhaps macarons, depending on what Remy deemed best from the bakery. After the plates were cleared, it was usually Eleanor and Rémy who sat outside in the fading light, their heads together, loose-limbed and slightly drunk, retelling anecdotes from the war years the other already knew well, raising a glass to missed chances, to lives lost. Rémy, Caroline knew, had relished living life on a taut string, each decision pivotal to his very survival. He'd felt fully alive and essential, he admitted, when life was dangerously unpredictable.

While their spouses commiserated, Tal and Caroline held their own colloquies, comparing how each continued to navigate marriage to a partner still coping with psychic wounds from the war.

"Will she ever get over this?" Talbot mused aloud one late spring night just a few years into their friendship, as he and Caroline stood over a sink of dirty dishes, watching through the window as Eleanor and Rémy smoked his Gauloises on the patio.

"This? Meaning losing those years, losing her family, her education? I don't believe you 'get over' it, Talbot. You incorporate it. Or maybe medicate it. Try to eradicate it."

Caroline smiled, looking up at Tal and taking a wet plate from his hand. "Irradiate it, maybe?"

He laughed. "Eradicate might be the best option. Just seems like she's missing something, like our life together isn't enough to keep her interested, let alone happy. I wish I could 'eradicate' whatever this unmet need is."

"I know what you mean. The pedestrian things Rémy spends his time on — should this little plot of land be zoned low-density? Medium? Sometimes he comes home practically enraged at the stupid things people get so worked up over. Outwardly, he seems so calm and settled. I think that's the French in him, wanting to appear relaxed and patient. But it's a ruse. He's still kind of restless, as if he wished he could use his talents on more significant things."

"You seem pretty significant to me," Tal said, drawing a surprised look from Caroline. He reached for her face, twisted a flyaway strand in his fingers. "He'd better watch it, Carrie, that someone else doesn't move in while he's distracted by his memories."

Caroline gave a nervous laugh and turned her attention to drying the flatware still on drainboard.

•   •   •

So began a brief, if intense interlude between them, Talbot reaching for her whenever they found themselves alone, planting a quick kiss on her cheek and later, her neck, his actions growing bolder, and eventually sexual, over the months. Given the bond between Eleanor and Rémy, it had not seemed wrong to Caroline at first — more like parity — that she and Talbot should have their own intimacies to balance the emotional attachment of their spouses. But over time, she found Talbot so adept, so smooth in the way he approached her, that Caroline realized this had nothing to do with balancing things out or

Talbot's attraction to her, specifically. He simply liked attention from women and had a sexual appetite to satisfy. That made what they were doing a different sort of thing, more tawdry and embarrassing, from the way it had first seemed to her. When she questioned him, he tried to say that Eleanor was vaguely aware of his needs and what he did to meet them—that she was a reasonable, modern woman who understood him. Caroline wasn't so sure. Was there a wife anywhere who didn't mind her husband straying?

So she did her own fact-finding, bringing it up, obliquely, when Eleanor remarked that Talbot was getting yet another new secretary—his third in five years. Caroline asked if the churn was typical at CIA. Eleanor had laughed.

"Caroline. Of course not." Eleanor fixed her bright blue eyes on Caroline's, head at a tilt, holding there until Caroline blinked.

"So what's going on?" Caroline asked.

"You've met him. He's a skirt-chaser. And he's caught a few, I think, and once he does, their days are numbered."

"And you're okay with this, Eleanor?"

Eleanor shrugged as if it was of no consequence, but her eyes betrayed her sadness. "I do wonder how he can sit there in church every Sunday and not have at least some pang of conscience. But I can't do a thing about it, Carrie. I don't know anything for sure and I sort of wall off my doubts, ignore clues. Look, when I lived in Italy, this was just a feature of the culture. Italian men say 'I do,' then choose a mistress and then another and it's simply a fact of life. And transient. Nothing to upend your marriage over. So I look at it that way. If he's doing something with these girls, they are no threat to me if they come and go. I'm still here."

Caroline didn't want to be shuffled off if this thing with Talbot ended badly, pushed out of the vibrant circle around which her life now revolved. His read of things wasn't accurate: Eleanor put up with his extracurriculars, but they hurt her. That was enough for Caroline to end it, to reconstruct a boundary with Tal. Without explicitly saying that she'd talked to Eleanor, she began to put herself out of his easy reach. She didn't venture into the house during their cookouts when Tal was inside milling around for the condiments or some other invented must-have. She no longer volunteered to help him shop for Eleanor's birthday, or drop his car at the mechanic's, or pick him up from the airport—things they'd done to help one another out over the course of their friendship, opportunities for them to be alone. And she consciously turned her attention back to Rémy, reminding herself how fortunate she was to be married to him and not some guy from back home. Soon after, on a little getaway to the mountains, they conceived Colette, with Oliver and Elise coming along soon after.

Unaccustomed to paramours spurning him, it took Tal a number of weeks, a handful of declined invitations, to realize what Caroline was doing, that their private chapter had ended. Once he did, he marked the occasion by sending her flowers, with a card that read, "That was fun." When Rémy asked her what "fun" might Talbot be referring to, she mentioned she'd lent him Bowle's *The Sheltering Sky* and he'd liked it immensely.

"Surprising," Rémy responded, "considering what a bleak story it tells. I mean, I appreciated it, but it's not exactly fun."

"I think he meant it was fun trading books we liked," Caroline said. "That's what it was."

"What book did he lend you?"

"*The Stranger*," Caroline said.

•   •   •

When their third baby—Elise—was on the way, Rémy announced that as much as he loved his neighbors, the townhouse just didn't work for them anymore. They moved a few miles deeper into Virginia, to McLean and a home big enough to accommodate them all. They kept the townhouse to rent out—there were plenty of young staffers on Capitol Hill in need of housing—and stashed the rental income into college accounts for the children. Once she settled in her new house in the tree-lined suburbs, it was to Caroline like the affair with Talbot had never happened. Preoccupied with her growing family, the pantry-groping and sweaty sessions in the back seat of her car in the National Airport parking lot seemed like bad dreams, things that had happened to an entirely different person.

Eight years on, their little foursome had survived, still close and intact. Talbot observed the resurrected boundary without complaint, deepening her fondness for him, as if he were a little boy who'd made a bad choice but was now fully reformed. She had grown closer to Eleanor, accelerated by her guilt, perhaps, the two taking girls' weekends in New York where they drank and talked and smoked and groused together. While Tal had the impression there was some kind of gang of girlfriends they got together with, Caroline had only met two of Eleanor's friends on these trips; sometimes only one came. She and Eleanor would typically meet these friends for brunch on Saturday morning, followed by a long afternoon of shopping at Macy's, then Bloomingdale's. Next came drinks, then a show if they'd managed to get tickets. And after the curtain fell, about the time Caroline thought she had just enough left in her to crawl back to the hotel and collapse, Eleanor inevitably insisted they take a cab to Little Italy in the Bronx for a late-night bite.

"I surrender!" Caroline had cried the first time Eleanor had pressed the idea. "I clearly don't have your stamina! You all go on. Have fun. I'm out." And so they did, Eleanor laughing the next morning that the outfit she'd worn—and by extension, everything in her suitcase—now smelled like a bulb of garlic.

While the women were away, Tal sometimes drove out to Rémy's, bottle of bourbon in tow, arriving after the kids were settled in bed. But sometimes, Caroline knew, Rémy called over to the Bentleys' on Friday to set up plans and didn't hear from Tal all weekend. Caroline wondered what, exactly, absorbed his time. She had some ideas.

•   •   •

The Auclair children raced down the pebbled paths of the park energized by the warming weather, winding their way among the cherry trees, darting to pick fallen blossoms or pluck from the bed of daffodils. Caroline slowed, turning to her husband and laying a hand on his arm, allowing the children run ahead, out of earshot. "I worry about them, Tal and Eleanor. He can be reckless sometimes."

Rémy turned to her, his face fixed and still. "Probably what makes him good at his job."

"Yeah, but you and I know he skates very close to the edge and I wonder, based on how rattled he seemed on the phone, if something's caught up with him."

"Something he mishandled? Or something he let slip to the wrong person? Or maybe…something he did with the wrong woman?" He held her gaze as he spoke. This was nothing they'd acknowledged before, Talbot's extramarital habits.

"I meant work. Operationally. Maybe a risk he took that caught up with him," Caroline stammered, resuming their walk, fearing her face would give her away.

"I always thought, and I think you know it too, my love, that it's his indiscretions—and they are legion—that could trip him up."

Caroline offered a silent nod.

CHAPTER
ELEVEN

Monday, May 2, 1960
Washington, DC

Helen arrived at her desk an hour early Monday, determined to force Talbot to deal with her, at the very least to find a private window for them to discuss their situation. She had stewed the entire weekend, thinking about Eleanor's party, mad at herself for supplying the spectacular cake that she was sure contributed to its success.

Her life, she realized, her every thought and action throughout every day, had become centered on making Talbot's life easier. She handled everything for him now — arranging their trysts, prepping his files before a meeting, booking time with the director at critical points in his projects before he even asked, calling down to his barber shop to find a window to ensure he could get right in and not have to wait, picking up a bottle of bourbon to take on his little golf trips. It just went on and on. With her sites set on taking over such duties permanently in his life, she felt she'd had to bail him out and order the birthday cake for his cold fish of a wife. But what had infuriated her — sent her spiraling into the weekend — was his failure to respond to her invitation Friday afternoon. She'd been in the ladies room, touching up her lipstick, neatening her hair, expecting he'd respond, that he would understand her need to see him. She returned to find the tissue in her trash can. Flattened out without a ripple. No note. No coded apology. No meeting, damn him. He had some nerve.

Rather than recognize his rebuff as a restatement of their difficult conversation in the townhouse weeks earlier, Helen — plucky, determined as ever — decided to redouble her efforts. She would be prepared for him when he arrived at the office, notify him she'd already blocked off time on his calendar this week for them to meet privately. It was past time they sorted through important issues.

She heard the door open and steeled herself to address him. But it was the personnel liaison, not Talbot, who arrived in front of her desk.

"Congratulations, Helen!" the woman chirped. "Deborah Mitchell, Personnel. I've got news about what's next for you."

"Next?" Helen repeated stupidly, unable to process why this woman was here now, with Talbot due any minute. "What do you mean 'next'?"

"You've been promoted. I've got your transfer papers right here," said Mitchell. "The chief sent me to let you know." She dropped her eyes and read from her clipboard. "You're being elevated from executive assistant to Supervisor, GS-6, commensurate with your excellent work record here at CIA, your language skills, and your background. So, again, congratulations." The liaison looked up and smiled.

Helen paused, mind racing. A foreign posting — it had to be. She'd skipped an entire pay grade and a GS-6 had to mean $4800 a year — maybe $5000. That meant the agent ranks, which she'd made clear to Personnel was her goal, her dream. If she were deployed overseas, she could rendezvous and travel with Talbot. He'd feel more like hers — a "geographic bachelor" as the term went in CIA. They could resolve the Eleanor issue later. Tal had a hand in this, she thought. He's moving the ball for me.

"I'm speechless," she said finally, feeling a need to stand to absorb the news of her apparent good fortune. "And I'm so happy because I've been waiting and hoping and I know openings are scarce right now. But I'm thrilled. Thrilled." she nodded, hands clasped at her waist, shoulders thrown back in a "reporting for duty" kind of way. "So! Tell me where I'm going."

The liaison pulled out a manilla folder from beneath the clipboard.

"Well, as I said, this is a supervisory position. You are moving to the third floor, to run the secretarial pool. The entire group."

Helen leaned into the desk to steady herself. She felt hot, suddenly, as she grasped what was really going on. This was no opportunity. This was sidelining. Talbot was clearing the decks, cleaning things up. Had he even considered how this could sabotage her career — her future — to take this detour into purely clerical work? Clerical work! As she opened her mouth to protest, she saw a warning in Mitchell's eyes: should Helen react to this promotion in the wrong way — emotionally, uncooperatively, or fling an accusation — she could very well be escorted not to the third floor but out of the building by a security guard. Who knew what Talbot had inserted into the file folder Deborah Mitchell clasped in her hands? Helen knew she must keep her own counsel for now.

"Oh my. Well. Wow. I'm so surprised. The whole pool? Gee. When?" Helen saw relief in the liaison's eyes.

"Right away. They're waiting for you. This officer is getting a new girl so I'm here to move you to your new spot."

"Now? Well. So efficient. And exciting! Okay, then. I guess I need a few boxes to move my things."

"Left them right outside the door," said Mitchell. "I'll get them." She retrieved the boxes and re-entered the office just as Helen plucked a tissue from the box with particular vigor, gave her forehead a stab, then savagely balled the thing up and dropped it in the trash can.

"Ink," said Helen. "There was a blob of ink on that one so I threw it out."

"Ah," said Mitchell, "then I'd be careful wiping your face with it."

Helen gave a nervous laugh and they began placing her things into the boxes. She palavered as she packed—making little comments about the items she was boxing up, asking about the vending machine options on the third floor, the number of secretaries she'd be overseeing, saying again and again how lucky she felt to be making this move. Mitchell observed Helen's skittish chatter with a wrinkled brow, placing a hand on Helen's arm to reassure her this was a good move for her, a step forward in her career. Helen sighed deeply, allowing her shoulders to sag for a quick minute, absorbing her circumstance but not admitting to what she was feeling.

"Well," said Helen as she placed her coffee mug into the box. "That's about it. I'm just going to leave a note for my boss—you know, tell him where I'll be if he needs me—to make the transition smooth for the new girl… for my replacement."

"Certainly. I'll take this box and meet you on the third floor."

"Perfect. Thank you. I'm just so thrilled about all this!"

"Well, good," said Mitchell, eyebrows raised, a hint of caution in her voice. "No reason not to be."

Once Mitchell exited, Helen collapsed into what was once her desk chair. Her chair. Her desk. Her office. Her Talbot. What had he done? He'd betrayed her, that's what. He'd thrown her aside, or at least, hadn't fought to keep her. He was behind this and didn't even have the balls to face her.

Well. He owed her. He would be very, very sorry he'd done this.

She rose and used her stolen key to open Talbot's office door. She walked behind his desk and dropped into his chair, willing herself to think, to pull herself together. She reached into her pocketbook for a Salem and her lighter. Her hand found Talbot's

Minox and she briefly considered returning it to his drawer. But no. She would not give it back. He didn't deserve to have it, however precious it had been to him in the war. And if he discovered it missing, he couldn't even ask her for it because he wasn't supposed to have it.

She riffled through the files on his desk and finding nothing interesting, moved to his file cabinet. Using her key, she pulled out a drawer and quickly scanned the documents in the front folder, the one that held urgent business. There she saw foreign maps, timetables, talking points for the upcoming Paris summit, correspondence with the British Royal Air Force, and an undated press release from the National Advisory Committee for Aeronautics about the loss of a weather plane. She snapped photos until the little camera stopped clicking. Then she wrote a note on the legal pad on Talbot's desk, mindful to write something that couldn't boomerang back on her:

I got promoted! But I'll see you around, you can be sure of that.

She rose and took a last look at his office.

"Goodbye, Talbot," she said aloud. "You've done a stupid, stupid thing."

•   •   •

Arriving at her new station, she was welcomed with applause from a handful of her new charges—the few who'd arrived early—all of them young and eager, much like she imagined she had come across only a year earlier. As Helen fumbled through some introductory remarks, Mitchell reappeared, pulling a fresh-faced blonde carrying a box of office supplies out the door by her elbow. *She's Talbot's new girl,* Helen thought frantically. *This cannot stand.*

Eyes misting, as if she were grateful to be among them, she thanked the secretaries around her.

"I look forward to getting to know all of you better as we support our officers here and agents in the field," she said. "First, which desk is mine?"

The women laughed, one of the veterans stepping forward and offering to help her settle in. She escorted Helen into her new office which featured a door and a measure of privacy Helen had never before enjoyed in her work life. Her misery lifted a bit as she considered this perfect spot from which she could place phone calls that would not be overheard.

"Okay, then," she said, placing her box on the desk and returning to the doorway. "I have some matters I must attend to right now, but I'll be right back out in just a few minutes."

Her new team looked at her with uncertainty, unsure of what to do until the new boss was available.

"Coffee. Everybody get coffee or tea or whatever you'd like and just...do what you know to do, or visit with each other or just...anyway, we'll circle up at nine."

The awkward spell broken, members of Helen's new team grabbed their pocketbooks, some giving her a little wave as they exited the office to enjoy this little bonus time. She stood in the sudden quiet, worried, thinking, planning.

CHAPTER
TWELVE

Monday, May 2, 1960
Arlington, VA

Talbot managed a few hours of sleep before his alarm sounded, his mind kicking fully into gear as soon he was conscious, resuming the tumbling and twirling that had occupied it the day before. He hauled himself out of bed to prepare for what he expected would be a brutal day. He was due to meet first with the Inspector General, to review how the mission team had come together and, he worried, to suss out if safeguards had been breached. He steeled himself with several cups of coffee, watching the sun rise over the back patio as he scanned *The Washington Post* to see if any of their reporters had sniffed anything out. Not yet.

He lingered in the shower, hoping to calm his roiling stomach, and nicked himself shaving, trying to hurry through it with an unsteady hand. "Get a grip, man," he told himself. "You've been through worse." But the truth was, he hadn't. Even in his undercover work in the war, he'd had a measure of control, an understanding of the risks. In this case, something had gone completely haywire and he didn't have a clue what had happened. And the risk inherent in clandestine overflights that he'd so blithely dismissed with Dulles and the president now felt outsized and ominous.

Talbot returned to the bedroom to whisper to a sleeping Eleanor that he was heading to the office. She had escaped the cocoon of bedclothes, one leg snaked on top of the coverlet, hands folded under her cheek, her breaths deep and even. Talbot stroked her arm, the skin so smooth and lovely, still so familiar. He was grateful to her for handling all this with steady calm, bringing fresh coffee throughout the day Sunday, encouraging him to eat, reassuring him that things would work out.

She stirred, turning to see her alarm clock then dropping back on her pillow, drawing the coverlet to her chest.

"Going now? Running late?"

"Just a bit. Gotta meet with Bissell and the guys from the IG's office at 8:30," he said, hating the unease his voice betrayed. "They're coming to my office."

"Your office? That's good. You don't have to sit half the day in some strange conference room somewhere."

"Maybe. But it also gives them lots of time to eyeball everything—my shelves, my desk, the secretary's area."

"Well, I'm sure Helen will make sure everything is set up per regulation."

Talbot tamped down the urge to tell Eleanor he didn't expect Helen to be there. He breathed a shaky sigh and wondered what would happen if he confessed, if he told Eleanor what he'd done—with Helen, with the others before her? Would telling the truth, admitting he'd been weak and stupid, draw them closer—give them a chance to start over, be honest with each other? Would it wipe the slate clean and enable Talbot to be the upright man he presented himself to be on the Sundays he ushered at church, escorting little old ladies to their preferred pew? Or would it fray the remaining tethers that held them together? I'm being irrational, he thought. Telling her the truth right now won't fix what I've got to deal with at the office.

Seeing the tension in his jaw, the worry in his eyes, Eleanor sat up and reached for his hand.

"Talbot. It's nothing you did, right? They could bug the place and they wouldn't have anything on you. I know this wasn't your mistake. Probably something mechanical—the plane failed. It's awful you lost someone—I know that really troubles you—but you're not responsible for that, right? I mean, you can't think the Soviets were tipped off to what you were doing and just lying in wait."

"I can't see how."

"Okay, then. Even if you had a sloppy guy on your team who said more than he should to somebody, nobody did anything intentional. Maybe the Soviets did get lucky. They're watching the skies all the time and they saw a trespasser. But even that— and I can't imagine that happened—is not your mistake. You'll be fine. I'm not worried."

Eleanor's confidence in him heartened him. Her kindness, her belief, made him ache to be the person she believed him to be.

"I've seen these things go off the rails—an officer losing his job, his pension, his reputation—based on a set of facts put together by creative minds who need a scapegoat."

"Not this time, Talbot," Eleanor said. "Just tell them the truth and show them you have nothing to hide."

"Right. Nothing to hide." Talbot gave Eleanor a quick kiss on the cheek and headed out to his car.

•   •   •

The querulous Helen was not waiting when Talbot arrived at his office. He heaved a deep sigh, the unoccupied desk a symbol of at least one problem solved. The desktop held only a monthly calendar, his appointments penciled in, no coded messages that he could see that might point to past or upcoming assignations. A crushed tissue sat in the trash can; if this was some kind of message from her, he would ignore it. Helen would have no access privileges beyond the third floor, so chances of an unexpected encounter were low. He'd requested that her replacement be "mature and experienced"—code within the ranks for someone asexual and unattractive. A man, even. He needed a respite in this moment, to un-complicate his life.

At that moment, Mitchell from personnel—the woman he usually called when he found a transfer of his secretary was in order—stepped into the office. A younger woman followed shyly, carrying an apparently heavy box Talbot rushed to help her set down.

"Ladies," he said. "What have we here?"

"As you know, Mr. Bentley," Mitchell began, her tone stern, eyebrows raised for emphasis, "Helen Sizemore has been promoted. Miss Key is her replacement—not exactly the experience-level we would like you to have—but it's the best we can offer on short notice. I trust you can get her settled in and handle things from here?"

"Yes, ma'am. Thank you, I appreciate it."

"I'm sure you do," said the liaison, offering Talbot a curt nod as she exited.

He turned to the young woman. "Talbot Bentley. Welcome. Glad you're here."

"Frances Key. Bridgie."

"Bridgie?" Talbot echoed. "You're called Bridgie?"

"Got the nickname from my friends. I grew up here. You know, Frances Scott Key Bridge—Key Bridge, so Bridgie."

"I know it well and take it often. Okay, Bridgie, let's get you settled in. You say you're from Washington, huh?"

"Arlington. I went to Wakefield High School. Tops in my typing class and started here two years ago, after I graduated. Very excited to get promoted into your office. I thought I'd be in the pool forever."

Holy shit. She's twenty, thought Talbot, who vowed in that moment to keep his distance. He had to, he told himself, despite her pretty face framed by silky blonde hair, the fluid way she moved her trim, young body. She reminded him of Eleanor when they'd first met.

"Well, set up your desk however you'd like and let me know if you have questions. I have meetings this morning in my office so just take lunch when you need to, head home when you need to—don't worry about me."

"What do you need me to do? Do I have assignments?"

"Uh, for now I'd say just answer the phone and let callers know I'm tied up. Take names and numbers and I'll return calls when I'm free. My calendar is there on the desk so you can see when I have open time if someone needs to schedule a meeting. Other than that, there will be couriers bringing documents, briefs, that sort of thing, so collect the relevant information on those, hang on to them, and I'll get to them as soon as I can."

"Yes, sir. Thank you, sir. Can't wait to get started." Frances gave a clap and turned toward her desk, essentially dismissing Talbot to go about his business.

CHAPTER
THIRTEEN

Monday, May 2, 1960
Arlington, VA

Brought fully awake by her conversation with Talbot, Eleanor took several deep breaths to settle her own anxiety. She'd never seen him so worried, not fully in control as he worked so hard to be, confident he could see around corners to anticipate what lay ahead. So there was something to this, some kind of threat he perceived but felt he could not confide in her about.

She rose to shower and dress, another week at the library ahead of her. She was glad to have a place to go, colleagues who whispered cheerful greetings when she arrived, facile tasks to distract her from what was happening with Tal. It was not work she particularly enjoyed; she'd only become a librarian because no one would hire her at any of the city's museums. She lacked a key qualification to be a Smithsonian docent or curator: she was female and in DC, where the cultivation of the arts mixed in an odd, regulated way with bland government bureaucracy, museums were the provenance of men. For all its trying, Washington retained a provincial character in which men were thinkers and doers and women, dutiful helpers who got the work done behind the scenes while camouflaging their own ambition and agency. Had she stayed in Europe, her training would have secured her work more vivifying.

Eleanor's job as Head Research Librarian was not a sinecure exactly, although the staff members who worked for her handled the bulk of patron requests. Usually it was high school students and their teachers who approached the Research Desk in need of a fact or two: serious scholars crossed the Potomac to the Library of Congress. This left Eleanor wide swaths of free time to read (under the guise of patron research) and spend her lunch hour in various museums along the National Mall. When she walked the rooms of the National Gallery, she was reminded of the thrum of her early life—the energy, the rich history and artistry that had surrounded her in Italy. She still missed Florence despite her harrowing experience there. She hoped one day she would have the chance to return to the place where the first outlines of her future began to take shape.

Eleanor's weekends in New York—social and artistic diversions, she explained to her husband—ensured her ennui did not deepen into depression. For years now, she had been taking the train from Union Station to Manhattan to meet up with old friends for a couple of days of restorative conversation, inside jokes and shared stories, protracted gabfests that would be constrained if husbands came along.

"Besides," she explained when Talbot expressed interest in joining her, "we go to shows, stay out late, and behave completely irresponsibly. You don't want to do that."

Early on, Talbot had protested that he did.

"I would love it," he said. "I want to meet your friends and hear what you were like all those years ago, hear about your family before—well, before things came apart. We could go up to Boston and visit Smith and see if any of your dad's professor friends are still around."

Eleanor insisted that keeping him and the life they shared now separate from her growing-up years helped her manage her sense of loss.

"I can't just open up everything like that and let you wander in," she said.

"But you can't just park your past somewhere—everything you've been through—and ignore it, can you? I'm interested in it, Ellie, because I want us to be close, to understand not just what happened to you in the war but how you got to be you."

"You don't talk much about what you saw and did in the years before we met," she chided. "You keep all that in a rather neat box, don't you?"

"Because it was clandestine activity, Eleanor. Not the real me. We're talking about completely different things here."

Eleanor would promise, at intervals, that he'd be invited along soon. But it was Caroline she eventually asked to accompany her, much to Talbot's surprise. His invitation never came and after a year or so, he stopped pushing. So, Eleanor saw her friends, wallowed in the memories of the family she had lost, then got back on the train and returned home to pick up the thread of her life with Talbot. And indeed, when he met her at the station, he often commented that her time away was obviously good for her because she seemed especially happy to see him upon her return.

Since the moment she married, Eleanor had let go, piece by piece, of the moments and milestones around which she thought her life would unspool. Like many people reared in happy families, she had expected to recreate a home much like her parents': noisy, curious children complicating and enlivening every moment, a kitchen rife with the aroma of favorite, familiar foods, holidays celebrated practically the same way every year, treasured friends and neighbors who helped shoulder burdens both anticipated and unforeseen. And somehow, she had planned to wedge a career in the arts into the tableau, to put her costly training in Italy to good use.

Instead, she was a librarian living a childless life on the rim of the world's most political city, where private people tasked with consequential jobs tended to keep their own counsel. The couples they'd first met in Georgetown were less available now, having become serious people, raising two, three, four children, living an entire world of experiences Eleanor and Talbot would never know anything about. Their busy families limited their capacity to delve into art and culture, as Eleanor wished to do. The only exceptions were the Auclairs, with whom she and Talbot had grown intensely close, people with whom they could debate politics and recent works of fiction, who were usually up for a last-minute cookout and ice-cold gin and tonics. But even they had children, now, that constrained their schedules and created other priorities.

So Eleanor quietly ended her quest to surround herself with like-minded souls as she had enjoyed all those years ago on the piazza in Florence—people who could name the best contemporary painters and had a thoughtful understanding of what the European Continent looked like before the war. She settled for what she had, grateful for the friendship with Caroline and Rémy, and skated on the surface of life, not expecting much. In this way, her deep, deep disappointment in her childlessness, in failing to find work she loved, could not wreck her further.

Talbot no longer looked so forlorn when she left for her New York weekends and she had a few theories as to why that was so. They'd settled into a comfortable, stable understanding. They visited his aging parents regularly, spent analeptic summer weeks in Virginia Beach at a little cottage she'd found. They had season tickets to the National Symphony and involved themselves (at Eleanor's urging) in fundraisers for a new Washington ballet troupe that was to perform Tchaikovsky's *Nutcracker* at Constitution Hall next year. While they seldom spoke authentically about what mattered most to them, their sexual connection thrived, evidence of that on Saturday night when he'd slid a hand up her skirt as they left her birthday party.

So she had a life, she told herself, an active life that she didn't spend time and energy and regret comparing to the life she had hoped to live.

As Head Research Librarian at the Arlington Public Library, Eleanor helped formulate a proper budget and hire new staff. And when that paperwork needed to be delivered to city hall, Eleanor was happy to do so, letting Rémy know ahead of time so they could enjoy a neighborly visit. It was their habit to take their paper bag lunches to a bench outside and discuss privately all the things they missed about Europe. Eleanor wished they still lived next door but knew their split-level in McLean better accommodated the five Auclairs.

She had no visits to city hall on the day's agenda, just a couple of meetings scheduled with patrons who needed very specific research questions answered. It wasn't the complexity of the questions they had but the demeanor of the patrons that determined whether Eleanor got involved. The difficult ones — often retirees who no longer had secretaries to summon — objected to anyone but the Head Research Librarian handling their requests. These, Eleanor invited into her office, closing the door to accomplish what they most needed — for her to listen and take them seriously. "Yes," she nodded solemnly, as they explained why they needed a bit of information. "Very important. I understand," she assured men who needed factual support for the fiery letter they were sending to *The Washington Post*, or to set straight a golf buddy who had his facts wrong. She had learned a lot from these patrons, often retired government employees who hadn't quite let go of their former jobs and still had a driving need to exercise influence. Her gift was turning them from angry skeptics to happy patrons who might even entertain the notion of supporting their local library with an annual donation.

Arriving well ahead of the library's nine a.m. opening, she greeted the girl at the Circulation Desk and climbed the stairs to her office.

"Morning, Mrs. Bentley," one of her juniors called out. "Phone message for you. It was ringing when I walked in. She said she tried to reach you at home."

The woman handed Eleanor the note. A call from Helen, requesting she return the call to an unfamiliar phone extension. Probably calling to commiserate, thought Eleanor, because she just loved being in the middle of things, being the one who knew the most about Tal's comings and going. Unless. Unless something's happened to Tal.

Eleanor entered her office and closed the door. She picked up the phone, paused, then returned it to the cradle, deciding she didn't wish to speak to Helen, that it was probably improper for Plucky Helen to call her. Eleanor wanted to wait until she heard from her husband.

CHAPTER FOURTEEN

Monday, May 2, 1960
Washington, DC

Bridgie's fresh face, her very presence, tamped down Talbot's anxiety — but just for a moment. He walked through the door to his office and adjacent conference room and began scanning for anything out of place, signs that anyone had been in to slip cameras in the overhead lights or listening devices on his phone. His eyes ran across his bookshelf once, then twice, before settling on Trotsky's biography of Lenin. And there he saw the slightest gleam from the spine of the book, a lens, smaller than a baby tooth embedded in the "o" of Trotsky. The counter-intelligence team covering all the bases. He wondered how long it had been there. It drew his eye when he moved around the room, the lens catching and reflecting the merest ray of light, depending on where he stood. Amateurs, he thought as he moved smoothly around to his desk chair, the bookcases at his back, to begin his morning routine, wondering if they knew, that he knew, that he was being surveilled.

His already-acidic stomach heaved when he saw Helen's farewell message. How had she gotten inside his office? Her clearance didn't permit her anywhere near his files without him present, yet she'd obviously been at his desk. He turned toward the bookcase, a confused, concerned look on his face to communicate to those monitoring the little camera that he found all this highly improper. If they questioned him about it, he could honestly say he had no idea how she got in. They might even have pictures of her doing it. "*See you around. You can be sure of that,*" she wrote, the line producing in him a flash of anxiety he hadn't truly experienced since his OSS days in Turkey.

His mind worked to solve this puzzle as his face remained placid, neutral, businesslike. He reflected on the intense months of planning for Grand Slam and wondered if he'd overlooked something. Had Helen, or any member of his team, dug a little deeper for information than job duties required or asked questions that went beyond the scope of the project? Had he said too much to Helen who, it now seemed, had access to his office and could match up a stray comment with facts in his file cabinet? She would not do that, he told himself. She was not a particularly complex person and her mission, recently, had become gluing herself to him, making him happy. She could not think that interfering with his work would bring her closer to her goal. He'd have to get a message to her, feel her out and continue this thing a little longer until he was sure she'd had no role in the mission mishap.

Talbot considered the other members of his team. Intelligence work attracted a different breed, men and women who enjoyed the risk, the exhilaration that comes with pulling off a complex operation. But within the walls of CIA, where supervisors took their measure and Congress exercised oversight, intelligence officers colored within the lines. Talbot had followed each strict requirement in putting the planning team together and formulating the action steps. He'd set approvals in sequence and neither Bissell nor his peer assessors had objected to these latest overflights. Had one of them let something slip? Spoken too freely, in an elevator or a taxi or a restaurant and someone clever had pieced things together? And had those conclusions been furnished to the Soviets as highly placed intelligence?

Talbot felt he'd already endured a long workday when the Inspector General arrived at precisely eight-thirty. Larry Horne seemed an unimposing man, a quiet accountant who used his training to ensure CIA budgets were not exceeded and procedures properly followed. His demeanor belied a history few at CIA knew: he'd been a member of 99th Pursuit Squadron—a Tuskegee airman—who'd escorted bombers over Europe in the war. Shot down over Ploesti, Romania, he evaded capture and made his way to the coast, where the Soviet Army plucked him up and returned him to Ramitelli Airfield in Italy. His war exploits had pried open the door for him at CIA—he was among three Black officers—but rather than tap that resourcefulness, the leadership had consigned him a fairly circumscribed job at headquarters. Talbot was among those who privately dismissed Horne's inquiries as generally superficial, non-complex. But Talbot and the others were unaware of Horne's knack for pursuit.

"Morning, Mr. Bentley," he began, hand extended. "Is that the same secretary?"

"Helen was so good at her job, she's been promoted," Talbot responded, palms up, nothing to hide. "Frances arrived this morning."

"Yes, sir. I see. Mr. Bissell isn't joining—no need, really at this point. But may we sit in your conference room to review what we know?" Talbot led the way.

The door closed, the men settled into their chairs, Horne pulling a legal pad and the CIA manual of regulations from his briefcase. Talbot asked if any new information had surfaced.

"Nothing. Not a sign of anything to answer our questions. What do you think happened, Officer Bentley? Was there anything that worried you going into it?"

"Just the weather and nobody had control over that. We pushed back a few days because of storms over the targets. The 'go' window shifted around until right before take-off. But no, I didn't have a bad feeling in the least. Previous flights were uneventful. In and out. Got great photographs. Done and done."

Horne nodded. "Communication protocols. Did your team observe those, far as you know, sir? Is it possible someone on your team was careless—that details of this mission slipped out due to some chitchat in public?"

"Slim to none. They know better."

"Sir, do you have any suspicion that anyone on your team, or serving in a support role to your team, took any steps to intentionally sabotage this mission?"

"Absolutely not. Everybody's a pro, Larry. Trustworthy and reliable."

"Ok, then. To this point, the Soviets haven't said 'boo.' So our best guess is that the pilot Powers had engine trouble or his oxygen supply failed. He went off course and ditched in the ocean. Never to be seen again, unfortunately. We're holding off notifying next of kin just in case something surfaces. Per Director Dulles, we'll give it a few more days, then NASA will announce they lost a weather plane and ask the world to look around for it."

"What kind of read are you getting from the director? He and I haven't spoken today."

"He regrets upsetting the president to this degree, but they all supported the surveillance program so we live with the results. Director Dulles will give a full brief to the National Security Council this week—the president, the VP, Secretaries of Defense and State, Chairman of the Joint Chiefs. You know, we've got the big national civil defense drill, and as a part of that, the Council will convene at High Point. Director Dulles will share the latest with the team there."

"Ironic that the drill is this week. Millions of Americans practicing taking cover in case the Soviets send over their ICBMs — from all those sites we've got pictures of."

"Well, maybe the summit with Premier Khrushchev will produce some kind of agreement. Maybe before long, we can end these drills and people won't have to buy cans of green beans to stock the fall-out shelters they've built in their basements. That's the hope, anyway."

"Let's hope. Disposition of the files?" Talbot asked.

"Please keep them here, your file cabinet locked, and I'll have them picked up next week for archiving. Thank you, Officer Bentley. I appreciate your time."

•   •   •

Talbot felt immeasurably better — regretful of the loss of life, certainly — but Horne's perfunctory interview seemed to indicate this thing was manageable. No mention of Helen getting into his office, no scapegoats identified, the weather plane cover story ready to roll out. Horne had his answers and he could fill out his little report and move on.

Talbot emerged from his office to find his new secretary sitting at Helen's old desk, sorting through the stack of newspapers and documents that had arrived while he was meeting with the IG.

"Bridgie, how's it going?" he asked.

She turned and gave him a wide smile. "Well, other than not having a clue what I'm doing, good I guess! How 'bout you?"

She was bright and enthusiastic, more confident than Helen, younger and prettier, appealing in a schoolgirl kind of way. He considered for a moment if he should ask her to bring up lunch from the cafeteria so they could eat together in the conference room. He could continue her orientation to her new job as they ate, get to know her a little better. But he suddenly pictured

Eleanor as he left their bedroom earlier—the unwavering belief she seemed to have in his integrity, her certainty he had not mishandled this mission. And at that moment, the connection to his wife seemed the more important thing.

"Finished my meeting and I've got some more calls to make. For now, just continue to play traffic cop for me. If I'm on the phone, take a message and keep a list. I'll be in and out of my office this afternoon."

"Yes, Mr. Bentley. Will do."

"Take lunch when you like. And tomorrow: I'll be out most of the day—so maybe bring a magazine to keep you busy."

At this, she laughed. "You trying to get me in trouble? You're not going to find me doing that. Ever. I don't bring personal stuff into the office."

"Smart girl," said Talbot, wishing he himself had adhered to such a practice.

CHAPTER
FIFTEEN

Tuesday, May 3, 1960
High Point Command Post, VA

Early Tuesday morning, Talbot climbed into a CIA staff car that took him directly to Andrews to catch a helicopter with Bissell and Dulles for a trip to High Point in the Virginia hills. Eisenhower, his staff secretary Andrew Goodpaster, and other top cabinet officials were scheduled to arrive later in the morning. No reports had surfaced overnight to contradict Washington's story of the missing weather plane so Talbot's worry had begun to abate, his trademark confidence reasserting itself.

The leaders were convening as part of the country's tenth civil defense drill—Operation Alert—a rehearsal to ensure if the Soviets launched a surprise nuclear attack, the American government could carry on. That afternoon, in cities across the country, emergency messages would blanket television and radio stations. Sirens would signal citizens to rush below ground into subway stations and bomb shelters, and children would duck under their school desks. Timekeepers would confirm whether Americans were getting better at this—if they beat last year's times. Millions would likely die if the Soviets struck, but it was believed that rehearsals could improve the numbers.

High Point was a facility built for COG—Continuity of Government—located west of Washington. If DC blew up, the president had access to everything he would need to run the country—sleeping quarters, meal service, and a staff of physicians, firefighters, engineers, and secretaries. The bunker could be sealed from blast radiation, allowing those inside to survive in the filtered air long enough for radiation in the atmosphere to dissipate. The usefulness of the elaborate facility was dependent, of course, on successfully getting the president there should the unthinkable happen.

Dulles said little to Talbot on the flight, asking only for quick review of where things stood, a confirmation that nothing, to Talbot's mind, had surfaced that might explain what had gone wrong and where the hell Powers was. Bissell jumped in to say that Powers had clearly done his duty—destroying the aircraft and losing his life in the process.

"He was a patriot, I can tell you that," Bissell declared. "Wife was a little looney, but he was solid."

Talbot agreed, saying he had reviewed countless times how the mission had come together and could discern nothing contrived or unusual among this team.

Dulles nodded. "Let's hope you're right."

The three men stepped from the helicopter into the clear sunshine, each looking the part with felt hats on their heads and briefcases in their grips. They were ushered into the bunker and through the maze of hallways to the war room, outfitted with the latest communications and computer gear.

Once Eisenhower and his entourage arrived, Dulles suggested that with the heads of all relevant agencies in the room, they review the U-2 issue first. The president agreed. But as Dulles launched into the known facts and the successful release of the weather plane cover story, the teletype machines began to clatter, the bell on the United Press International machine signaling an urgent message. Within minutes, a young navy ensign brought a tear sheet and waved it before Goodpaster who read it then moved closer to the president to whisper a few words. Eisenhower stared straight ahead. The teletype machines rattled and rang as the men grew quiet.

"Mr. President? What is it, Andrew?" Dulles asked.

Goodpaster turned to the group and read from the tear sheet: "Dateline: Moscow. Soviet Premier Khrushchev, speaking before the Politburo this afternoon, announces his military has shot down an American plane that violated sovereign Soviet airspace."

Talbot felt heat rise in his face, the muscles in his neck draw taut. This was his project. He'd been the one to assure the president that this exact scenario could not happen because there existed no Soviet weapon that could shoot high enough. If there had been a mechanical issue in the plane, the pilot surely hit the destruct button. That's what had to have happened — not a shoot down. Unless Talbot and his team had missed something.

Dulles raised a hand, to silence the murmurs. "Our story still holds, people. Pilot lost oxygen supply, fell unconscious, and strayed off course. Nothing here contradicts that. We shrug and tell the world the Soviets overreacted to a weather plane."

Talbot cleared his throat and asked to speak.

"I agree with the Director. There can't be much left of the aircraft, Mr. President, plunging from the presumed altitude. Any debris — the guidance system, the cameras — is probably splintered metal now, which NASA can continue to say were systems related to the collection of weather data. Period."

"Disagree." This from the Chairman of the Joint Chiefs. "If there's anything left of that plane that reveals what it was doing, the Soviets will say we've committed an act of war. We need to get out in front of this, prepare to provide a rationale for what we were doing if the truth comes out."

"Perhaps we should go ahead and admit we crossed a line," said a defense liaison from the State Department, "but we frame it in terms of fairness. The president's been advocating for the Open Skies Treaty, but Khrushchev won't bite. We remind the world the Soviets can see just about everything we're doing because we're an open society. So maybe we admit we took a peek into what they're doing to keep the world safer. Fair is fair."

"No, I think Bentley's got it right," said Dulles. "We don't want to get into a back-and-forth. We want this whole story to just fade away. Evaporate. Deprive it of oxygen." He turned to Eisenhower. "Mr. President, I recommend we stick with the NASA explanation and wait to see if Khrushchev makes any more noise. Mistakes happen. The plane flew off course. That's that."

The ensign returned and leaned in to whisper in Goodpaster's ear. The staff secretary blanched then stood to speak.

"Mr. President, Mr. Dulles. With respect. It's not fading yet. Khrushchev is saying the plane went down below Sverdlovsk—right in the middle of the damn country—nowhere near Pakistan or Turkey or Afghanistan. So if it 'strayed,' it strayed a thousand miles from the border—which makes our position less plausible. Reporters are going mad at the White House demanding that we clarify this."

The president cringed, a few breathy swear words escaping as he rubbed his forehead. He announced he would like to run through the rest of the morning's agenda—the review of the national civil defense drill preparations—as quickly as they could. But he and Goodpaster would not stay through the two p.m. sirens: they would get back to the White House to sort out how to respond to Khrushchev's latest assertions with the press team.

Within the hour, a cursory review of the systems at High Point was completed, staffers touring the visiting group through the bunker, reassuring them that systems and processes were tested regularly. If the seat of government needed to be moved in the event of a disaster, the High Point facility and the hundreds who worked there were fully prepared. Talbot was not the only member of the group who found that scenario far less remote than it had seemed only a week earlier.

The room was tense as the meeting adjourned, Dulles holding a whispered conversation with Goodpaster, followed by one with the Chairman of the Joint Chiefs. Talbot and Bissell stood off to the side, clearly not invited into the conversation, Talbot thinking about how wrong he'd been when he'd anticipated a week full of approbation and acclaim for his magnificent work on Grand Slam. His conversation concluded, Dulles waved them over and the three men headed to the helipad.

In succession, the phalanx of helicopters took off to ferry Washington's brain trust back to the city. Talbot stared out the window, taking in the varied greens of the Blue Ridge Mountains, already so vibrant for May. His mind puzzled through his next steps—bracing for how he would defend himself and his team for their obvious miscalculation about the Soviet ability to shoot down a U-2. As his chopper touched down gently on the tarmac at Andrews, he thanked God for two things: that his had been a safe landing—and that the U-2 pilot's had not.

CHAPTER
SIXTEEN

Thursday, May 5, 1960
Washington, DC

Talbot trudged through the next few days, sensing a sort of inertia within CIA, he and his colleagues waiting to see if the Soviets would have more to say or if this thing was losing steam. NASA continued to dutifully assert that a weather plane had gone missing north of Turkey while the autopilot was engaged. They trotted out the repainted U-2 for the press to see, full of weather gauges and equipment they insisted were just like those on the lost plane. Deprived of oxygen, they said, the pilot likely passed out, the plane ran out of fuel, and went down. Members of Congress made themselves less available, those who'd been briefed on the U-2 program wanting to avoid any direct questions. Reporters continued to pester the White House press team for information on the weather plane's original flight path, apparently the only cohort in Washington eager to keep the story in the headlines.

Settling into her new role, Bridgie proved cooperative and eager to please, Talbot refraining from seizing on perfectly good double entendres given the current crisis. The lack of sexual undercurrent made him feel even worse, producing an office atmosphere he found listless, stale. For once, he came to work only to work, something he hadn't done in years. He encountered no fallout from Helen's transfer. She hadn't tried to contact him and he stopped worrying about how she'd gotten into his office because no one up the chain had made an issue of it.

On Thursday morning, just as Talbot stepped into his office, he was summoned to Director Dulles' office.

"New reports are coming down the wire," Dulles said. "Another speech by Khrushchev to the Supreme Soviet. Get up here."

When he arrived, the director's office was a tomb. Dulles' secretary sat with an elbow on her desk, gnawing her nails. When Talbot announced himself, she simply pointed toward her boss's office.

Dulles stood at his desk, a teletype sheet in his hands and others scattered over his desk. "Talbot. Here's what we know. Khrushchev just said he needed to amend his statement from two days earlier. Made a real show of it, apologizing for not providing more details of what happened on Sunday."

"Details? Shit. What details?"

"Well, the plane's intact. And apparently in pretty good shape. And so is the pilot. Frank Powers is in Soviet custody—the exact scenario you and I claimed could never, ever happen."

Talbot shook his head. "No. Oh no. That goddam pilot was not supposed to survive if something… He knew the deal. What in hell? Do we know if he's conscious? If he's said anything?"

"Oh, he's conscious. Conscious and talking, interpreting the flight logs they found in the plane, confirming he was using a high-powered camera to take photos of Soviet military installations. Khrushchev described the survival kit to a T: the Russian phrase book, 1500 rubles, the message written in multiple languages promising a reward for help, the pen loaded with poison—no question he's got his hands on it. 'Why, would a weather plane be equipped with such things?' he asked his comrades during his speech—and they just laughed and laughed. The whole room of 'em. He claims Soviet radar tracked the plane all the way across the Russian steppe. They saw it coming and shot it down."

"Saw it coming? They don't have that capability."

"Apparently they do, Talbot. How did you not know their radar has improved to that extent—and the range of their missiles? We've been taking all these pictures for years—apparently of the wrong things."

The search for a scapegoat was on, Talbot realized. Well, there was nothing they could pin on him.

"On top of that, you initiated this mission on May Day. MAY DAY, Talbot, their big military holiday when there's not much flying over the Soviet Union, making the U-2 that much easier to see."

"The timetable slipped because of weather but given the altitude…" Talbot began. Dulles waved him off.

"I offered my resignation, but the president wouldn't take it. But he wants answers. This is about to get real ugly, given a few other things that have popped up. Return to your office and get yourself squared away. I'm sending Chamberlain to speak to you."

"Chamberlain? Counterintelligence? Why on earth?"

"Why? Because, as you're well aware, your secretary got into your office. Sat at your desk. The IG has moved this into Chamberlain's court."

It struck Talbot that Horne's interview with him might not have been so cursory after all.

•   •   •

Herbert Chamberlain was a retired army lieutenant colonel and lawyer who had honorably served throughout the European theatre. He'd opted to retire in 1949 when it became clear that despite the valor he'd displayed from Normandy to the Rhine, he'd never make full colonel. His and Talbot's paths had crossed when both were stationed in Italy after the war, Talbot impressed by his ability to suss out the facts of a situation quickly and mine nuance to arrive at the truth, or something close to it. Chamberlain was the top deputy to James Angleton, the head of Counterintelligence who operated under the belief that the CIA was rife with Soviet moles. Chamberlain served as something of a check on Angleton's zealousness, applying sound investigative tactics to assuage Angleton's endless suspicions.

Chamberlain and his team arrived within the hour at Talbot's office, equipped with a thermos of coffee, cigarettes, and a tape recorder. Chamberlain directed Bridgie to manage Talbot's calls for the rest of the day, saying that if they went past six, she was free to leave.

Seven hours? Talbot thought. This interview could run seven hours? He ushered Chamberlain, two assistants, and a secretary into his conference room. Chamberlain gestured for Tal to sit at the head of the table then pointed to one of his assistants.

"Jerry? Go ahead and set up."

Jerry Engwall heaved a tape recorder from a leather suitcase, placed it at the center of the table, and began running wires to place microphones on the table.

"We don't want to miss anything," Chamberlain explained. "But I'll remind you that you're here voluntarily, consenting to this interview pertaining to the loss of an aircraft dispatched through your task group. Not that you or your group did anything wrong or illegal. But we need to understand how the Soviets intercepted this aircraft so it doesn't happen again. Fair enough?"

If only it were that benign, thought Talbot. There would be tremendous political pressure to find the culprit, identify an error — accidental or otherwise.

"Sure. Of course. I want to understand what happened as much as anybody."

"I'm sure you do. We rolling?" Engwall nodded. "Ok, we're here with Officer Talbot Bentley, lead on Operation Grand Slam. First, Mr. Bentley, tell me about your team. Let's start with your deputy."

"Derek Knox—I've known him for ten years. Met him right after the war. He was an early recruit like I was. Excellent case officer. His analysis is always thorough. He was on the team for the Guatemalan thing—missed a few details and that got a little messy."

"What do you mean? Which details?"

"Well, if you remember, the idea was to slip in and dislodge a president who'd gotten too friendly with the Communists. And now we're paying millions to keep a different clueless idiot in place who threw out his country's Constitution and became a dictator. So, our intel on the guys on our side lacked some depth—Derek made some wrong assumptions because there was a lot we didn't know given the limited operations we'd run in Latin America. We'd kinda assumed they'd be as reliable as the Brits and Aussies were in the war. Our mistake."

"Did Derek Knox ever mislead you?"

"No, no. Never misdirected me or gave me false information. The analysis has been wrong at some points, but that's part of the game."

"The game. Right. How did you settle on the date for the mission? This will probably scuttle the Paris meeting. So, anybody especially keen on this day, so close to the summit?"

"We were just watching the weather. We wanted good pictures and the forecast was for clear skies so it could have been twenty-four, thirty-six hours later or earlier. The Pakistanis agreed to let us use their base to launch and we didn't want them to change their minds. So this was the moment. Three previous flights this year were flawless. Milk runs, except at the end of the last one, when a few MIGs chased us near the border. We thought they'd just gotten lucky— stumbled on us—because we had no signs, no chatter, no photos that indicated improved Soviet capabilities. Based on that, the president told us to carry on, so we did. We thought we could continue to get in and out."

"Except you didn't."

"No. Obviously. Do you know how the pilot is doing?"

"Powers? Eyes on the ground say he's banged up and in a Soviet hole for who knows how long. Said way more to them than he was supposed to, based on what they're saying to us. So we're investigating more of his background, why he's being so cooperative."

Over the next few hours, Chamberlain asked Talbot about each member of the six-person team, what Talbot knew of their backgrounds, their work experience, why they'd been assigned to this project. He asked about their private lives—anything Talbot knew about troubled marriages, financial issues, unmet career aspirations that might have proven frustrating. Talbot had little to offer.

"We just didn't discuss all of that, Herbert. If Knox, or Scholls, or Mendicino had some kind of agenda, if they were steering this across a timeline one of them wanted, it's news to me. The goal was surveillance to collect intel on ICBMs so Khrushchev couldn't lie to Ike. We knew we would raise Soviet eyebrows at the summit, when the president trotted out the numbers and the data. But hell, by that point, it wouldn't matter because we'd force the Soviets to negotiate from a more honest position. If anybody on the planning team was pissed and felt passed over or under-appreciated—well, that got past me completely. You'll have to ask them."

"Oh, we are, Officer Bentley. My juniors are in with all of them, separately, right now, asking them the same things I'm asking you. There is one more employee, however, I need to ask you about. Helen Sizemore."

Shit, Talbot thought. Shit. Shit. Shit. He withdrew a cigarette from his case to buy some time, mind racing to defend what Chamberlain might ask.

"Helen?" he said lightly. "She's been my secretary for about a year. Until this week. She's been promoted to the third floor to manage the secretarial pool. Did her job well."

"She did lots of things well, wouldn't you say?"

"Yes, she was competent, punctual, good with dictation."

"And good in the sack?" Chamberlain sat back in his chair and waited.

"Herbert, can you excuse the team for a moment? I'd like to have a private word."

"Hell, Bentley. They know. Lots of people know. We've watched it all for a few years now and when it doesn't compromise the work, Counterintelligence just keeps an eye on it, on Helen and all those young ladies who came before her. You're an effing rabbit, Bentley, sorta like Dulles, now that I think about it."

Talbot worked to appear unbothered, keep his face neutral, maintain his relaxed posture as he drew on his cigarette. "She knows nothing about this operation. She was just…well…we became close, and then it was…convenient."

"Not sure she'd appreciate hearing how you put that, Officer Bentley. Ok. We'll come back to that." Chamberlain flipped to a page in his notebook. "Tell me about your wife."

"My wife?"

"Yes. Your wife, uh, Mrs. Eleanor Halsey Bentley. What does she know about this episode?"

"She knows we lost an asset and that I met with the IG earlier this week."

"What did she know before the mission? That's what I'm asking."

Talbot thought what he might have said to Eleanor. Had he disclosed something? "I don't routinely discuss my work with her."

"Of course you don't. I'm not saying you would. I'm wondering if something could have slipped out. Inadvertent.

You working late at home and her overhearing something. Accidentally."

"I don't think so," said Talbot. "She respects what I do, doesn't pry. She's got her work and I've got mine. But I'll give it some thought."

"You 'spose she respects what you do with Miss Sizemore?" Chamberlain asked. Talbot tamped out his cigarette, stabbing with vigor into his Churchill ashtray.

"If you're asking whether she's aware of Helen, no. She doesn't know," he said finally. "She wouldn't stay with me if she did."

"Ok. I'll accept that for now. Does the wife have any contact with your secretary?"

Talbot found the question odd, disconcerting.

"What do you mean 'contact'? She's been by my office. They've met. They're not pals, if that's what you mean."

"Any reason Miss Sizemore would call your wife on the phone earlier this week?"

"What?" Tal asked. "Helen called her? Shit."

"She called us too."

"Why? Because she's pissed about the transfer? Pissed at me? Look, Mr. Chamberlain—Herbert—I was breaking it off with her. Called Deborah Mitchell to find her a new job because Helen didn't realize what this was—just a little fun, a little distraction. Somewhere along the line, she decided I was her great love and she wanted me to leave Eleanor and be with her. Which I was never, ever going to do. So if she called you and called Ellie to rat me out, fine. I cheated on Eleanor with my secretary. My mistake. That has nothing to do with mission failure and how we figure out if the Soviets knew we were coming."

"We're in the process of seeing what has to do with what. Right now, it's too early to say."

A knock sounded at the door. Bridgie stepped through the doorway and gave a little shrug, a fixed smile on her face. Before Talbot could object to the interruption, a man stepped around her and handed Chamberlain a file. The deputy head of Counterintelligence opened it and flipped slowly through its contents. The man who'd brought the documents stood against the door, hands clasped behind, suit coat straining over the weapon at his waist.

Chamberlain withdrew a stack of photos from the file and slid them, one at a time, across the table. "Recently, we came into possession of some film and the lab has just finished developing it. And we now have photographs that appear to be pictures of documents in your possession. See the numbers at the top? Those are copies assigned to you."

Talbot had trouble catching his breath. He could not believe what he was seeing. "Those are mine, yes. But how? Who photographed them? They haven't been out of this office, or out of my conference room. I don't even take them home."

"Maybe you can tell us, Officer Bentley, why your old Minox was used to photograph them."

"It couldn't be my camera. Mine's still in my desk. I'll show you." He rose and went into his office. Chamberlain followed, photographs in hand. Tal pulled out his center desk drawer growing agitated when he couldn't find the camera. "It was here," he insisted. "Right here."

"You know, you were supposed to enter that Minox into inventory," observed Chamberlain. "Once you started work here, it reverted to property of the U.S. of A."

"It was a souvenir," Talbot protested, knowing how feeble he sounded, that he had no defense for failing to return the spy gear. A nervous chuckle escaped him, exposing just how rattled he was. "I used it all over Europe and, hell, I just got attached to the thing. And I just, you know, wanted to keep it with me. Not to use it. Not at all. Just to remember how well it had served me in some pretty tight jams in the war."

"So let me ask," he said as he handed the stack of photos to Talbot, "is there a reason you gave that camera to Helen Sizemore so she could photograph these documents?"

"What? I did nothing of the sort."

"Well, she did this for some reason. We've got her on film doing it."

As Talbot leaned on his desk, flipping slowly through the photos, Chamberlain looked up at the man who'd delivered them and gave a small nod. The man approached Talbot and asked him to extend his arms behind his back.

"Sorry to have to say, Officer Bentley, but we've gotta take you into custody. You're under arrest for violating your security clearance. We'll be taking you to the DC jail while we sort this out."

"Oh, come on, Herbert! You know me. Have you talked to the director? To Bissell? They know I did nothing to undermine this mission. Can I at least make a call?"

"You can at the jail. And Dulles knows. Bissell too. They can't help you. Boys, let's take the service elevator and stay out of sight as best we can. We'll say you've taken a leave, Bentley — the stress of the mission and all that. But with the press crazy to name the villain in this U-2 thing, I can't promise they won't land on you before we get through this mess."

And for the first time in his memory, Talbot found himself unable to mitigate the emotions that overtook him, unable to calibrate all the tiny muscles of his face, unable to move in that casual, confident, relaxed way of his, to present the self-assured Talbot he wished the world to see. His shoulders shook. He heaved a sob and his face crumpled.

Bridgie's eyes were wide as they walked her new boss out the office door.

CHAPTER SEVENTEEN

Thursday, May 5, 1960
Washington, DC

Late Thursday, two men slipped into the Arlington Public Library, bypassing the Circulation Desk and making their way, quietly, to Eleanor's office. They found her standing at her desk, gathering her things to head home. She started at the sight of them, at the stealth they had employed to enter her office and close the door without a sound. They spoke in low tones, informing her they had been sent from CIA to say her husband was booked on charges related to his work and would remain in jail overnight. Eleanor melted into her desk chair, her breathing accelerating but her demeanor composed.

"What is he accused of doing?" she asked. "Or do you routinely jail case officers when missions go awry, just to have someone to blame?"

Eleanor recognized the men who stood before her, although she did not know them well. She had seen Ted Dixon and Ronald Duckett, separately, at arts and social events in the city, Talbot introducing her to one of them walking with his wife in Rock Creek Park, never exactly saying how he knew them. The men exchanged a look, uncomfortable with her question. It was a moment before Dixon spoke.

"Mrs. Bentley, we don't know the details of this case. We're here to advise you of the whereabouts of your husband, that you can go see if him if you wish to, and that he will need an attorney. We also ask that you keep this quiet, for now, as the investigation continues. That's it. We aren't here to litigate this with you. Just to inform you. Do you have any more questions?"

Eleanor shook her head then asked if they knew how Talbot was doing, if anyone else had been arrested, if they had spoken with his secretary, Helen. The men declined to offer any further details.

"It's still very early in the investigation and we have no information on the direction it's going, who they've talked to," Dixon said. "We do need to advise you that someone from CIA will be in touch with you and will have some questions. Probably in the next 24 hours."

"I'll expect that, then. Thank you."

"And again, the less you say the better. We're not releasing anything to press at this point."

"And why is that?"

The agents exchanged a look. "We don't want to tip off anyone else who might be involved with this case."

Eleanor swallowed then nodded. The men left her office one at a time to make an unobtrusive retreat from the library. She picked up her phone, thoughts racing — what to do first? Contact a lawyer? Speak with Talbot? Call Helen and see what she knew?

After seven rings, she hung up the phone and rose from her chair, leaning on the desk to steady herself. Clutching her pocketbook, she turned off the lights and walked through the library doors, choosing not to acknowledge looks from colleagues, curious about the men who'd come to her office so late in the afternoon without taking even a glance at the library shelves.

• • •

It took Eleanor a series of additional phone calls to retain a lawyer willing to take Talbot's case, which in turn, delayed her own interview with CIA investigators, as she wanted that attorney at her side before she sat for questions. She'd called three lawyers from their old Georgetown circle, several who had worked their way up in the city's top firms, but each offered excuses—"full plate," "conflict of interest," "above my pay grade"—as to why they best not represent Tal. One finally steered her to his former intern, George Jeffrey, a George Washington Law School grad who'd turned down offers from several prestigious firms to open his own practice. He agreed to represent Talbot and to sit through Eleanor's initial interview. But she would need to obtain separate counsel, he cautioned, if the case against Talbot grew more complicated.

Chamberlain and his assistant Engwall arrived on her doorstep as she returned from work Friday, Jeffrey a step behind them. A team would be coming to do a search as well, they explained, if she would consent. Or they could get a warrant, they said, but if they took that step, the press would likely discover the story. Eleanor said a search would be fine—she had nothing to hide—Chamberlain promising they wouldn't make a mess. But first, they had questions. Eleanor offered to make coffee or tea but found no takers. After a nod from Chamberlain, Engwall set up his tape recorder in the living room and they began.

Chamberlain asked first about Eleanor's background, dates and times she easily confirmed, questions Jeffrey raised no objection to. She detailed her growing up years, her study abroad in Italy, when she had met Talbot after the war. When they began to press her about her husband's habits—did he take calls at odd hours? Did he leave suddenly to do errands on weekends or at night, or take last-minute out-of-town trips? Jeffrey locked eyes with Eleanor and shook his head. He did not want her to answer. She did anyway.

"Of course he does," she said with exasperation. "He works for CIA!"

"Can I speak with Mrs. Bentley a moment, gentleman?" asked Jeffrey, rising swiftly, slipping a hand underneath Eleanor's elbow to pull her out of the room and down the hall.

"Mrs. Bentley," he whispered, "they are fishing with those broad questions. Please don't answer when I tell you not to. What you just said can be construed any number of ways and it won't help your husband."

"Oh, please, George! I told them nothing they don't already know. It's what intelligence officers do—taking calls at all hours and running off for meetings in the middle of the night. I didn't say 'Why yes! He's at the Soviet Embassy! He's meeting with foreign nationals!'"

"True, but if they can construct a timeline, where Mr. Bentley claimed to be in a work meeting, and they can show he wasn't with, or speaking to, CIA personnel, it looks nefarious. So keep it neutral. Tell them he did his job, nothing beyond that."

Eleanor said she would. But she needed a minute, she said, to pull herself together to continue the interview.

"Of course, Mrs. Bentley," said George kindly. "Do what you need to do. I'll tell them you'll return shortly. But don't be too long."

"Just need to compose myself," Eleanor assured him, heading towards her bedroom. She stopped first at Talbot's office and stood for a moment in the doorway, breathing in the familiar smell of her husband—the leather, the liquor. Atop his desk was his Cheney briefcase—an impractical gift, she'd concluded, that he had mostly used when he traveled to carry non-classified files, his toiletries, and magazines. If they take this in their search, Eleanor worried, she'd never see it again—this peace offering she'd brought back from her very first girls' trip to New York. So she carried it into her room and slid it into her deepest bureau drawer, covering it with her lingerie, placing her laciest bras and panties on top. Then she powdered her nose and ran a comb through her hair before returning to her guests.

"I apologize—truly," she said as she entered, a tissue clutched in her hand. "This is just so completely unexpected and, well, enormously upsetting." She gave a wan smile.

"Of course, understandable," said Chamberlain. He asked if there was anything she wished to re-state or clarify.

"Only that Talbot is dutiful in his work and that he responds to phone calls and requests for meetings with his CIA colleagues at all hours. Nothing he did raised my suspicion—no strange people turning up here or awkward run-ins in public—ever." She turned to George as she concluded, who offered a tiny nod.

"What about Miss Sizemore? Does he ever meet her outside of work?"

"Who?" asked Eleanor. George stood to interrupt, intent on shutting down this line of inquiry.

"Mrs. Bentley is not well-acquainted with Miss Sizemore," he offered, "and she has nothing to say on this."

"Who is Miss Sizemore?" Eleanor asked again.

"Helen Sizemore," clarified Chamberlain.

"Oh. His secretary? Helen? She's rather new, I think. I've only seen her a handful of times."

Chamberlain eyed her, chin in his hand, a lazy plume of smoke from his cigarette curling above his head. "Right, then. I think that's all we need to cover." He stubbed out his cigarette and stood, handing his legal pad to Engwall who secured it in a briefcase. "But—forgive me—you say your father taught at Smith? The years, exactly?"

Eleanor stilled, eyes fixed on Chamberlain, thinking.

"Well, I was fifteen when he died. 1935. I left to study in Florence in '38. But give me a minute to think, and I can be more precise."

A sharp knock sounded at the front door.

"That's fine, Mrs. Bentley. That gives me enough of an idea. Just looking for general dates. The guys are here, I believe, so we'll just let them look around now."

Chamberlain was good as his word, directing the team to poke gently through closets, to replace sofa cushions they dislodged, close the drawers they opened. Eleanor and George waited at the kitchen table.

"You were in Italy? In 1938?" George asked, eyes narrowed, appraising. "Your husband told me you met after the war. I didn't realize you'd been stuck over there. You must have had quite the adventure."

"You could call it that. Had my father lived, he probably would have forbidden it, but it was just my mother, my brother, and me. I was enthralled with the idea of studying in the sculpture program at the university in Florence. Tunnel vision. The continent erupts and I was pinned down until 1945. Then, I met Talbot, who rescued me and brought me back home."

"I can't imagine what that must have been like. And how fortunate you met your husband when you did."

"Fortunate?" Eleanor cast her arms out, acknowledging the ongoing search, the situation in which she was now embroiled. "I guess we'll see if that's the case, won't we, George?"

He nodded, then pivoted to Talbot's situation. They would meet at the jail the next day. Eleanor was to come mid-morning, after Tal's bond hearing and expected release.

A half-hour later, the search was complete, the officers toting away some documents they'd discovered in Tal's desk drawer, his overcoat, his passport, and little else. Before they left, they placed taps on the Bentleys' phones, testing to see if this went beyond Talbot and the plucky secretary.

•   •   •

George Jeffrey figured his representation of Talbot Bentley would either make his career or end it. George found Tal a blend of straight-arrow patriotism and bravery—his service in the war had been exemplary—mixed with a roaring hubris that blinded him to the threat posed by serial extramarital liaisons. It appeared the most recent one could cost him everything he'd worked his entire life to achieve.

"So, Mr. Bentley, tell me about this woman... Helen Sizemore," he'd begun, when they met at the jail, the afternoon of Talbot's arrest. "Your secretary."

"Former secretary. She got promoted. And it's Talbot. Tal is fine."

George found him smooth and relaxed, despite the alarming setting: they were meeting inside the jail's cinder block conference room. Talbot reclined slightly, appearing as comfortable in the metal folding chair as he might in a leather armchair. He drew deeply on the cigarette George had offered, looking more like a man considering what cocktail to order than a CIA officer facing multiple felonies.

"Ok, Talbot. And please, call me George. Former secretary, then. How long did she work for you?"

"About a year. She came in June last year."

"And she's already moved on? Is that common, to move secretaries after eleven months? I would think she's just beginning to get her bearings."

Talbot smiled. "I guess for me, yeah, it's common. I tend to... well, it's almost not fair, these young girls coming into my office, helpful and solicitous. Usually attractive. And, I sorta..."

"You became intimate with Helen Sizemore?" George asked, his tone clinical, not judgmental.

Talbot studied his cigarette before finally answering. "Yeah, we developed this...thing. Good at first. And I told her, yes, we were having a great time together. But I couldn't leave my wife."

"And how did she respond?"

"Not well. Sullen. And she'd gotten a bit too familiar with me in front of other people and that began to worry me. So she had to go. HR moved her out Monday and sometime after that, she turned in the camera to the IG who passed it along to Counterintelligence, alleging I was running some sort of espionage operation."

"Have there been other women?"

Talbot winced.

"Talbot. I need to know what we're up against. Never good to surprise your lawyer."

"I've had five secretaries." He appeared to be counting. "I've slept with four."

George kept his eyes glued on his legal pad.

"Anybody else?"

"Not at work."

"Has there been anybody else, Talbot?"

"One."

George lifted his head and sighed. "It would help me if I didn't have to pull this out of you. I'm not your adversary. I'm here to support you and frame this case in the best possible light for you. The affairs really aren't the point and we will certainly argue that Miss Sizemore is simply being vengeful and angry and therefore her allegations are not credible. But that grows more complicated if stories about women you've slept with dribble out and dribble out. You lose credibility. Better to acknowledge it all up front."

"My neighbor. My wife's friend, Caroline."

"Last name?"

"Auclair. She's married to a French guy. You'll like this—he's a former resistance fighter. They live in McLean. It was just a brief little thing years ago—nothing serious. We're still friends with them. No one ever found out. I think her friendship with my wife got to her and she ended it. Ancient history."

"That's it?"

"All I can think of," said Talbot with a rueful smile.

"So. Helen Sizemore. You say she's lying. Is this out of character for her? Are you surprised she's taking this tack?"

Talbot said he was, given how cooperative and compliant Helen had always been. He explained, somewhat matter-of-factly, how easy it was to conduct this and his previous affairs because of the ample privacy intelligence officers were afforded. When an office door was locked, no one asked questions. And with Helen, there had been the serendipity of the business trips they'd been dispatched on together.

"She's a good worker," Tal said, "Smart and organized. Conscientious. Doesn't make many mistakes. Owns it when she forgets something. Never had any complaints about her job performance. She's determined, ambitious. Then she started talking about us living together. So I put in for her transfer and they needed someone on the third floor, so it came right through — the morning after the U-2 thing which is how all this got bungled up together. I still don't know how she did it — how she got in my office and into my file cabinet. They're always locked when I'm not at my desk."

"So she needed keys?"

"She did. I never gave her any."

"Do you leave yours lying around? Could she have duplicated them?"

Talbot thought. "I don't see how. I keep them in my pocket. But..."

George waited. "Talbot, I need to know everything."

"She's been in my house."

"So you have extra keys there that Miss Sizemore might have run across?"

"I keep a spare set at home in my office. It's not locked, but I don't think she's been in there alone...unless she went looking around while I was in the shower or something."

"So — and this is just an initial theory — she could have found the keys on a visit to your home, used them to access your office, then taken photos on the camera she delivered to the IG's office. That would make this intentional, Talbot, that she planned, far ahead of the failed mission, to set you up. Does that sound like something she would do? Something she's capable of?"

"Why would she possibly do that? She didn't know I was ending it."

"Maybe it wasn't a spur-of-the-moment decision based on her transfer. A possible defense here is that she had an agenda — not sure to who's benefit but most definitely to harm you — and you were blinded to it because A) you assumed her security clearances had not placed a dangerous person in your office. And B) you were in love with her."

"I never loved her."

"Oh, I know, but we may have to argue it that way. Love is blind and all."

Talbot swore.

"But before we get into that, I need to know about the other women, especially Caroline Auclair, just to make sure they don't pile on. And then, I'll schedule a chat with Miss Sizemore."

CHAPTER EIGHTEEN

Saturday, May 7, 1960
Washington, DC

Talbot spent two nights in jail before he was freed to home confinement, the judge's order specifying he could only leave the townhouse for meetings with his attorney. The preliminary hearing was held in a closed courtroom, two members of the DC police standing guard at the judge's order, waving off questions from members of the press, insisting there was nothing newsworthy going on behind the closed doors.

Saturday morning, Talbot and George walked out of the jail, heads together, chatting, Tal's expression relaxed. They approached Eleanor's car, George saying the hearing had been routine—a good sign that nothing significant had popped up in the past two days in the investigation to incline the government to keep Talbot behind bars. The men shook hands and set a time to talk the next day. George walked off towards his car, Tal giving a hearty wave before he climbed into the car next to Eleanor. Once the door was safely closed, he slumped in the seat and stared out the window at security officers as they paced— sidearms at their hips—and the vista of barbed wire that encircled the jail compound.

"This is shit, Ellie," he said, his voice low, angry. "I did nothing. NOTHING. I'm being set up. Set up because—well, for something stupid that has nothing whatsoever to do with this mission going south." He raked his hands through his dark hair, his eyes weary, depleted. "I am a loyal American. What the hell else do I have to do to prove that? They know that. I've done what this country has asked of me my whole adult life. You know that, right? Please."

Eleanor pulled the car through the gate and onto Washington's crowded streets, thinking how days earlier, she'd ferried a self-satisfied Talbot home after her surprise birthday party, drunk, cocksure, full of swagger. Now she'd sat through an interview with CIA Counterintelligence—an interrogation, actually—her house searched, and she was ferrying Talbot home from jail. The DC Jail, in fact, known for having electrocuted spies during the war. Six of them. Germans. Was that what awaited Talbot?

"And what was this something stupid that tripped you up, Tal? A paperwork error? Saying too much in the cafeteria?" Eleanor shot him a glance as she spoke, surprised to see pain in his eyes and color rising in his face. She didn't relent. "Why don't you tell me who set you up and turned our lives upside down—the thing that landed you in jail for being a suspected spy?"

"Helen. I got involved with Helen."

Eleanor stared straight ahead.

"I broke it off. And that made her angry so she made up a story, apparently, that I was working against the mission, betraying my county."

They rode in silence as Eleanor absorbed his admission, pieces clicking into place now. She made the final turn onto their street, pulled into the garage and shut off the engine. She turned to him, her face tense, steeled for what he would say.

"How long?" she asked. It was the least important thing in all this, with both their marriage and his freedom at stake. But she wanted him to say it.

"Started last year. Not even a year ago. It was nothing, Eleanor. Nothing to me. That's why I ended it. Had her transferred out. And it set her off."

"Nearly a year? And you say it was nothing. Although, now that I think about it, I recall the two of you took several trips together." Talbot dropped his head, hand massaging his temples. "How nice for you. You and your lover. How convenient."

"Eleanor, you know things have been tough between us — you can be so damn remote and distant — and I thought…"

"Talbot, do not even try to pin your screwing around on something I did. You think you deserve whatever you want. You always have. That you can just grab whatever thing you like, anything that crosses your mind because it pleases you. Me. Helen. Whomever. I'm sure there have been others, Talbot. And it's a shame you didn't see how all this is connected. That when you're off having sex with anybody who's willing to have you, you make yourself more distant — to use your word — from me. So this is on you. You and the dick you couldn't keep in your pants. But please, do tell me the story. How did she set you up? What could a secretary possibly do to make the CIA believe her over you?"

"She got into my filing cabinet and took photographs of documents — maps, coordinates — things she doesn't have clearance to see. That cabinet is locked and my office stays locked when I'm not there. I don't know how she got in. She used my little Minox — the one from the war — to take the photos. Then she handed the camera over to the IG and said, 'Gee, I found this in my boss's office. Is it important?' And the IG referred it to the Counterintelligence Unit."

"Plucky Helen," she murmured, like a reflex. "Getting them to investigate you for being a spy."

"I'm charged with violating my security clearance — for allegedly giving her access to these documents. They can hold me on that while they continue to investigate if I had anything to do with the U-2 mess."

"And did you?"

"Shit no, Eleanor. Why the hell would you even ask me that?"

"Well, Talbot, it seems I may not know you as well as I thought I did."

They made their way into their townhouse, Talbot saying he really needed a shower. Eleanor was grateful for a few minutes alone, for time to process Tal's admission and how it tied in with what Chamberlain had asked her. The phone rang, Caroline's anxious voice coming through the line, eager to hear how things had gone with the bond hearing and whether there was anything she could do to help.

"It's because he had an affair, Caroline," Eleanor said. "This happened because he made the wrong woman mad."

Caroline said nothing.

"Hello?"

"Sorry," Caroline breathed. "I'm just a little stunned."

"Yeah, well, me too, Caroline. What else has he been lying about? Where his allegiance lies, maybe."

"Eleanor. A man doesn't live like he has, following the rules, serving his country for decades, then decide to serve the Communists. He's just…" and here Caroline hesitated, "he's a playboy, Eleanor. I'm sorry. But he is and, well, we've talked all around it for years, but we both know it's the case. But being a shit husband doesn't mean he's a traitor."

"I suppose," said Eleanor. "But I have a feeling there's a lot more I don't know."

For a second time, Caroline said nothing.

•   •   •

Over the next few weeks, the more perceptive among the Bentleys' neighbors, friends, and Eleanor's colleagues pieced together that Talbot's sudden retreat from view, the absence of his Corvette from the flow of commuters exiting and returning to the neighborhood each day, might be linked to the U-2 story topping the headlines. With the spy scandal driving both gossip and newspaper sales across Washington, enterprising reporters began to dig for more angles to the story to keep it going. One, who used his connections to camp out at the bar at Congressional Country Club, was sitting near the Bentleys' ostensible friends as they rather loudly listed all the places that in recent days, the Bentleys had failed to appear, including the golf course and St. John's Church. Had Talbot, big CIA man that he was purported to be, simply blundered, or done something illegal and anti-American? They mused over their martinis, one of the women saying she'd always thought he was a skirt-chaser, which in her view made him roundly less trustworthy. Within days, the reporter unearthed the pertinent court records and made the connection. CIA intelligence officer Talbot Bentley had indeed been arrested then released weeks earlier, just after the U-2 was shot down.

When the curious deigned to ask her about it, as they encountered her at the mailbox or in the case of her workmates, at her office, Eleanor assumed a forbidding reserve that even the nosiest were reluctant to pierce. Eleanor went about her days at the library, her errands around Arlington, as if nothing were amiss. Talbot developed a habit of trailing her through the house when she returned home at night, overly solicitous and annoying, so she began driving out to the Auclairs' several evenings a week to find comfort and to decompress, to get away from Tal's anxious, hovering presence. She knew he needed her, that this could be an opening to repair things and be honest, finally, with one another. But she was unsure if she could take that step.

"He's mad with worry," she told Caroline as they sat on the Auclair patio one night, sipping gin and tonics in sweating glasses, watching the sun slip below the horizon after an oppressive June day. Rémy was inside, dumping Chef Boyardee Spaghetti-O's into a saucepan, the children anticipating this delicacy with delight.

"What's the attorney saying?" Caroline wanted to know. "Has he been able to convince the government that it's not sabotage or espionage or whatever they want to call it but just a pissed off woman who should have known better, who's probably set him up?"

Eleanor smiled at her loyal friend. "It's Tal who should have known better, Caroline. Truly. Helen is a child. Only a few years out of college. She wasn't mature enough to understand what was happening and to keep out of Tal's clutches. You know how he operates." She fixed her eyes on her friend as she took a long draft of her drink. "Did I mention? She called me the day she was transferred out of his office. Early, before I got in. I never called her back."

"To say what, do you think?"

"To tell me about them, I'm sure. Maybe if she'd been able to rat him out, devastate me, and blow up our marriage it would have been enough for her. But I didn't return the call—and here we are."

"This wasn't triggered by anything you did or didn't do, Eleanor."

"Oh, I'm not so sure about that. Did you know there were others, before Helen? He's admitted it, all of them young and eager and probably just positive they'd end up married to him. Too inexperienced to realize what clichés they are, sleeping with somebody else's husband."

In the growing twilight, Eleanor couldn't see Caroline flinch, an involuntary shiver that prompted her to wrap her arms around herself, despite the warm night. Once the sun was fully set, Eleanor rose and patted her friend's cheek before making her way into the house. There she found Rémy, who pulled her into an embrace and whispered intensely in her ear. Eleanor nodded, responding with a passionate, almost bitter whisper of her own.

CHAPTER NINETEEN

Wednesday, June 1, 1960
Bethesda, MD

The satisfying jolt Helen felt in asserting herself, in introducing chaos into Talbot's tidy life, was short-lived. Her single-minded quest to ensure he knew he wronged her prevented her from anticipating how the chaos would envelop her.

The way he'd dismissed her after she came through for him in getting the cake, his gall in getting her transferred, opened her eyes, finally, to who Talbot was. A user. Using her to make himself look good to his wife and friends, never considering how he was hurting her. Helen had felt enraged, an emotion new to her ordered, educated, calibrated life—a life he'd upended by seducing her then failing to recognize that what they'd found together he needed to protect. When she snapped those photographs, she'd been oblivious to the story developing a world away, that the operation Talbot had been directing all these months had failed. She had just wanted to muddy the waters a bit, make him sweat. Had Eleanor picked up the phone that morning and given Helen the chance to express her outrage, the Minox and its exposed roll of film might still be rattling around in her pocketbook.

But now, he'd spent a few nights in jail and faced serious charges. She'd been suspended from work for three weeks—just temporary, she was told, until certain questions were resolved, specifically the provenance of the photos on the Minox and what she might know about the loss of the U-2. She had been interviewed at work first by the IG. Then the Counterintelligence people came to her duplex multiple times, pressing her in ways that surprised and worried her. She was on their side, after all, standing up for truth and integrity. They seemed skeptical of her version of what had happened that Monday morning, no matter how many times she repeated it: she'd found Talbot's door unlocked and had simply entered his office to hand him a sheaf of documents and tell him she'd been promoted. But here was Jerry Engwall, back for a second time in three days, reviewing answers she'd repeatedly provided.

"If Officer Bentley was not yet in the office on Monday, May second, Miss Sizemore, why did you try the door? Why expect it to be unlocked?" he asked. He was seated in her small sitting room, ignoring the coffee she'd prepared, his ubiquitous tape recorder on her small coffee table, whirring away. "You'd just learned you were promoted and Miss Mitchell was there to help you move your things to your new location. So help us understand why you tried a door you expected would be locked and continued to handle documents on Officer Bentley's behalf, when you were, effectively, no longer assigned to his office."

In their initial conversations, she'd explained that she was so surprised by her promotion that she'd unthinkingly barged into Talbot's office expecting him to be sitting at his desk. But Engwall continued to press why she hadn't left the office when she found it vacant. So Helen began to improvise.

"Well, as I said, I was very surprised Mr. Bentley wasn't there. But I like to finish what I start. I'm extremely thorough," she said brightly. "When I realized he wasn't in, I just thought, 'He must have unlocked his office and gone down the hall—the men's room, probably. I'll leave him this paperwork, and a note to explain I've been promoted—'see you later' and all that. And

I saw the camera just sitting there and thought it seemed out of place, that it might be important."

"Was it his habit to come to work before seven, go in his office, and shut the door?"

"Oh, yes. Sometimes. He worked a lot. I just thought I'd try the door and see."

"Miss Sizemore, let me try it this way: was Officer Bentley known to come to work, unlock his door, then exit his office? Did he give you or anybody else routine access to his office when he wasn't there, in violation of security protocols?"

Helen jiggled a leg, casting about for an answer that would not make matters worse, implicate herself. Even if the door was unlocked, she knew full well she wasn't allowed to go in when Tal wasn't there.

"It was stupid. I just wanted to finish up, leave Officer Bentley those papers. I wasn't thinking. And Miss Mitchell can tell you, I was just rushing around, getting ready to leave. But when I saw the camera…I don't know. I thought, as I said, it looked out of place. It was not a device I recognized. That's it. I thought I should turn it in to the IG."

"Your fingerprints are on it," Engwall said.

"Of course they are. I found it."

"No, ma'am. On the shutter. Did you take photos of anything in Office Bentley's office?"

A rush of heat spread from Helen's neck into her cheeks. This was new. They were accusing her? She fell silent trying to work her way to a reasonable answer.

Engwall continued. "Yours were the freshest prints and they're all over the device. We believe you're the only one who has handled this camera for quite some time."

"Well, I picked it up. I must have grabbed it and touched the shutter. Maybe that erased other fingerprints…earlier fingerprints."

Engwall looked up from his legal pad. "You deny you took any photos?"

"Well, yes. No." How had this fallen apart so fast? This was supposed to implicate Talbot, not her. Ah. There it was. "I mean…I had to. Talbot—Officer Bentley—made me take them," she said finally, eyes shining, relieved to have arrived at this solution. "He was my boss so I did as I was told."

"So you took the photos, then you had second thoughts?"

"Exactly. Yes. He asked me to take pictures of some files, which I did, but as I was packing up for my transfer, I thought better of it and I took the camera to turn it in."

"And he asked you to take these photos when?"

"Sometime…um…in April, I believe."

Engwall looked at her with a sad reluctance, knowing the surveillance images captured May second showed her removing the Minox from her purse, pawing through documents on Bentley's desk, then unlocking the file cabinet and removing and photographing the U-2 file. He had hoped she would come clean, explain how she came to possess the camera and the office keys so he'd better understand who was behind all this. He replaced the cap on his pen, stowed his notebook, clicked off the tape recorder, and asked if could use her phone. After a hushed conversation, he returned to Helen's sitting room and picked up the coffee cup she'd prepared for him, the contents now cold and muddy. He asked, casually, how long she'd lived in the duplex, if she had nice neighbors, how long her commute to the office was.

Happy to be answering a series of benign questions, Helen believed the danger had passed. She relaxed into the tattered armchair she'd had since college, reaching for her coffee cup and holding it in her lap, eager to outline her daily commute. Her relief was short-lived. A loud rap sounded at her door, causing her to jump, the coffee sloshing first into the saucer, then across her white linen pants. She opened her door to find two federal agents waiting to take her into custody.

"But! But!" she sputtered. "I've explained! I took the pictures, but he made me do it!"

"That doesn't quite align with what we already know," said Engwall.

"Of course. You believe Talbot over me."

"We don't have to believe either one of you, Miss Sizemore. We have your prints on the camera. We have surveillance images of you using a key to enter a secure area you are not permitted to be in alone, then sitting at your supervisor's desk and withdrawing the Minox from your purse."

Surveillance images? Helen's thoughts careened wildly. Did they have photos of her and Talbot in the office, Helen splayed out on the desk or pressed against the wall? She closed her eyes and began to cry.

"We know you were in possession of keys you used to open the office and unlock the file cabinet. You pulled out files and snapped the photographs."

With that, Helen collapsed, prompting Engwall to gently lift her by the elbow to guide her to the door. She wailed that this would harm her career—she had an outstanding personnel record! They were making a terrible mistake because everything she did, she did at Talbot's behest. While she waited in the government car, two agents, equipped with a warrant, searched her apartment. The key ring in the drawer of her bedside table was among the first items they bagged and labeled. Next to the key ring was a memo pad from the inn in Warrenton, receipts from hotels in Las Vegas and London, and a tie clasp that signified honorable discharge from the army—an odd little assortment of keepsakes, it seemed, bound to complicate her contention that she was forced to do what she did because of Talbot's sexual coercion.

CHAPTER TWENTY

Monday, June 13, 1960
Washington, DC

Since Helen had no long record of service, coming to work out of college with no previous employment, the government placed her in detention and delayed her bond hearing to more deeply investigate her background. They learned she was fluent in several languages and had inquired about enrolling in a course in Russian at the Defense Language Institute. Believing her a spy, they ordered her isolated from other detainees and her meals served in her cell, hoping to keep her situation out of the press as long as possible. Jerry Engwall was assigned to speak with people in the office who knew her and to canvas her neighborhood.

Her next door neighbor — an avid gardener who spent a lot of time in his front yard — told Engwall that more than once, he'd chatted with Helen on a Friday afternoon when she'd outlined plans to drive to the mountains to hike, only to have his wife return from work and mention she'd just passed the bus stop and seen Helen waiting not three blocks away. The teenage son of the family who lived on the other side of Helen's duplex smirked when Engwall arrived to ask questions.

"Miss S? Oh yeah. I've seen her. I play basketball in the rec league at Cabin John Park," he said. "She goes there — always with the same guy."

Engwall took down the boy's description of the man—it was Bentley—then asked what the boy had observed them doing. Were they talking? Meeting anyone else? Looking at folders or documents?

"Uh…" he looked at his parents and gave a little shrug. "They were going at it. Outside. Going at it standing up…leaning on a tree."

The boy's mother retreated into the kitchen, hand over her mouth. Engwall didn't flinch.

"When did you first see them?" he asked.

"Almost… a year ago? Yeah, I think that's right."

"How many times?"

The boy thought. "Maybe…four?"

Engwall nodded. "What else did you observe?"

"Observe?" the boy repeated. "Well, they seemed to like doing it."

"I meant how long are they there? They're obviously out in the open—visible to others—so I'm just trying to get a sense of these little encounters."

"The first time, the guys and I weren't exactly sure what they were doing. We're playing ball and I see this girl walking across the meadow at the back gate, off the path and into the woods where it gets pretty full, pretty dense with bushes and scrub and trees and stuff. And I notice because she's wearing a dress—not what people usually wear to the park. Then this guy in a suit shows up, carrying a basket or something and he's obviously headed the same way. There aren't many people their age at Cabin John who aren't with kids or a scout troop or something. So a couple of us creep closer to get a better look. And holy crap, I say to my buddy. That's my neighbor! At first, we think maybe they're wrestling or having a fight. And then it hits us, what they're doing. We couldn't believe it. But it was kinda embarrassing, grownups doing it in the woods. I mean it's funny. But it's not like I want to see it, you know?"

"I'm sure you don't. Did you ever observe them meeting other people, or pulling files from briefcases—that kind of thing?"

The boy's eyes grew wide and he shook his head. "Never saw anyone else come with them, or approach them. It was just the two of them."

Engwall handed him a card. "If you think of anything else, give me a call."

The investigator headed back to the office armed with a much fuller picture of the risks Helen Sizemore seemed willing to take to Talbot's benefit.

•   •   •

The second morning she awoke at the DC jail, Helen was advised an attorney was waiting to meet with her. Finally. Her parents had promised to bring in her cousin the lawyer, whom they were confident could quickly resolve this misunderstanding. Todd Sizemore handled many of her family's legal issues—wills, real estate—nothing remotely like this. But when she was escorted to the conference room, it wasn't her cousin there to console her, but George Jeffrey wanting to ask her a few questions.

He rose as she entered, extending a hand.

"Miss Sizemore? I'm George Jeffrey, representing Mr. Bentley. I wondered if we could speak."

"Talbot?" she said. "Did he send you here?"

"He knows I'm here, yes."

"Is he alright?" she persisted. "What is he saying about this— about me? I need to talk to him."

"He's okay, Miss Sizemore, but I'm not sure you'll have the opportunity to speak. But I'm here to ask you a question. Won't take long, I promise. Why did you do it? Why did you fabricate a story that could land you both in prison for years?"

Helen blanched. "I've fabricated nothing. Talbot made me do what I did," she said. "Now he's ruined my life, with his promises and lies."

"Promises? What did he promise you? What did he lie about?"

She sputtered, recognizing she was veering into territory that could undermine her contention that she'd been manipulated. "Well…he promised that taking those photos was part of my job. He lied to me. I was not authorized to do that and it's landed me here."

"But what were you promised for doing it? Money—some kind of payment?"

Helen looked puzzled. "Payment?"

"Yes—payment for taking the pictures, perhaps getting them into the hands of someone else?"

"Someone else? I have no idea what you're talking about," she said. "I'm saying I was only doing my job at CIA, Mr. Jeffrey. Or at least what I understood to be my job, as requested by my superior."

"And was sleeping with him just doing your job? Or was that something different?"

Helen blinked, her throat so dry she knew she couldn't speak.

"Because what we have to tease out here, Miss Sizemore, is what you chose to do versus what someone asked you to do. But thank you for speaking with me today. I've got what I need. And—if you'll permit me—it's time you hire a lawyer. This thing isn't going away."

•   •   •

Alone in her cell, Helen could feel her heart thudding in her chest as she realized what her impulsivity, her resentment, her jealousy could cost her. She wanted to take it all back—to ask for another interview with Chamberlain and Engwall to confess the affair, say that she and Talbot had fallen in love and the transfer had upset her so, that she had behaved recklessly—but not because she was involved in anything criminal. Only because she was hurt and felt she was losing Talbot. Her parents would be shocked when they learned the real story, but she knew it was time for her to change course to save her own skin.

Cousin Todd arrived to meet her the next day and within a few minutes learned this was not at all the case he'd anticipated.

"So he didn't pressure you into taking the photographs? You did it because…"

"Because he hurt me. I was angry. I wasn't thinking."

Todd nodded, made a few notes on his legal pad, and told her he was working on getting her bail. He would try to secure a plea deal for her, one that could still involve jail time and require her to testify against Talbot.

"I'm not ready to drop the idea that he made sexual advances that you felt pressured to respond to. He was your boss. It was wrong."

"I loved him, Todd. I thought we had something."

"I don't want to hear it. Whatever you felt has nothing to do with the case we need to make to get you out of this. He crossed a line. That's a fact. So. I'll keep working. In the meantime, keep your mouth shut, okay? No more talking to other people's lawyers or anybody at the CIA for that matter."

Helen nodded mutely.

CHAPTER
TWENTY-ONE

Monday, June 20, 1960
Arlington, VA

Talbot became a caged tiger, drinking too much and eating too little, pacing the townhouse, hungry for information about his own situation and what Powers might be saying to his Soviet interlocutors. Khrushchev had bailed on the Paris Summit after Eisenhower refused to apologize for the overflights. The papers declared the president's stock had fallen, that Nixon's election was no longer a sure thing. Talbot's misery, he imagined, was broadly shared across CIA and official Washington, what with the Soviets, in gleeful daily briefings, dribbling out details of all they were learning about the spy plane they'd captured. And because of Helen and her schemes, Talbot was the one blamed for it—for poor mission analysis at a minimum and covert espionage at the worst, one *Washington Post* columnist noting

Bentley is a former OSS agent whose loyalty had been questioned during his service in Turkey during the war. Sources say his apparent anti-American activities related to the shoot-down of the U-2 over the Soviet Union resulted in his suspension from duty and the criminal charges he now faces. Further, sources allege a co-conspirator — a female and some say, a paramour.

Anti-American? The hell.

Daily, he took calls from his mother, who relied on her Southern reserve to manage her emotions when they spoke. While her unrelenting belief in him was reassuring, he learned later she usually wept after their calls. His father made plans to drive up, but he was older, more frail now and Talbot worried about him managing steps in the townhouse and the added stress that being in Washington would cause. Talbot convinced him there was no need to come now, but gratefully accepted his offer of additional resources should the case drag on and additional payments to lawyers required.

•　　•　　•

In a meeting with government investigators, George Jeffrey learned of Helen's star turn on film, the images they had of her pulling the Minox from her purse and taking the photos.

"So that's one thing to cross off the list," George told Talbot. "Surveillance footage confirms you didn't take the photos—you didn't even have possession of the camera. Now we just have to convince 'em that she did it on her own, not because you asked her to."

"She took those photos when the U-2 was already missing. If I was making her do it to sabotage the flight, I was a couple days late."

George nodded his head and sighed. "Well, you weren't supposed to keep that camera. The government's floating the idea that you must have had a purpose in keeping and concealing it—and they're going to try to attach that to the espionage statute—and probably go beyond that and try to suggest you might have used it over the past number of months and years to take photos of maps and documents that made their way to our enemies."

"We've been flying over the USSR for years now, successfully, uneventfully. So if I've been supplying them with maps and timetables all this time, why didn't they use them before?"

"Maybe over time, the data helped improve their capability to take out the U-2. So—and I'm speaking theoretically, Talbot, I'm on your side—the government's theory of the case might be that maps and schedules you provided helped them figure out where the U-2 would be most vulnerable during the flight. It might have helped them tailor their missile development so they could shoot this plane down."

"Fiction," Talbot said. "I had no part in helping advance their capability."

"We gotta explain why you kept the camera, Talbot. They'll push on that."

"It was a souvenir to me—a relic of the war. Helen stole it and kept it. I haven't had it in my hand in months. She took the photos to get back at me. That's it. That's all. There's nothing to it beyond that."

"Miss Sizemore is sticking with the story that you coerced her. She thought her job was at stake so she did whatever you asked her to do—including taking photos of documents in your file cabinet. Her lawyer has hinted that if we push back too hard on her version of things, she'll say you sexually assaulted her. That you raped her repeatedly—on business trips, in a park near her house. So we need to step carefully and not push her into making those allegations out loud."

What was the word Eleanor always used to refer to Helen? Plucky? Well, she was far more than that. He and Eleanor had vastly underestimated her.

•   •   •

In truth, Chamberlain and Engwall had concluded Helen had been all in with Talbot. She had been the one booking reservations at the inn in Warrenton and saving little mementos from their time together, the one hopping city buses to reach rendezvous sites, participating with enthusiasm amid the flora of Cabin John Park. But their boss, counterintelligence chief Angleton, was always eager to expose a turncoat and made it clear that those facts were less important than the imperative that they identify the saboteur at whose feet they could lay this failed mission.

Rather than apologize for spying on the Soviets, the narrative had now been reshaped by Angleton and fed to press secretaries across official Washington, that the overflights were a brilliant, necessary tool that not only kept tabs on Soviet missile development, but had helped draw out and expose spies at home—perhaps even a spy cell within CIA, eager to trade on information. Instead of outrage at Eisenhower or Dulles for conducting illegal spy missions, public sentiment began to shift to how the secret overflights had done immeasurable good in revealing there was no missile gap with the Soviets, and in cleaning out rats within the intelligence agency.

•   •   •

Six weeks after Bentley's arrest, Chamberlain and Engwall sat in a CIA conference room, sorting through their notes and the clutch of documents around which the government would build its case. The search for others associated with the apparent espionage had come up empty, no sense of alarm detected in the wiretapped calls of the *rezidentura* inside the Soviet embassy, no coded calls placed to the Bentleys' home or shadowy strangers turning up on their doorstep. Talbot and Helen seemed to be the only players.

"How are we handling Sizemore's access to Bentley's office?" Engwall asked. "Did she poach the keys somehow? Did he make her a set?"

"We can say he gave her the keys."

"Weird to give a secretary full access to his office. Wouldn't there be things in there he would not want her to know about? Things involving his wife maybe, or other women? I just can't see a guy with lots of secrets allowing unfettered access like that."

"Good point. Maybe she copied the keys without him knowing. Ask some of his former secretaries if they recognize the key ring. Maybe see what his wife says about how careful he was with his keys."

"The wife. What do you make of her?" Engwall asked. "Did she just look the other way? Are we going to take the position she was aware of Bentley's extracurriculars?"

"Yeah, she's a bit of an odd one. I don't know. I'm inclined to leave her on the periphery—the unknowing, trusting wife who didn't have a clue."

Engwall pulled out a notebook and flipped it open. "We're having trouble finding more about her background. She says she was in Italy during the war—trapped there as a college student—which I guess we can chalk up to extreme ignorance, going to Italy while the war drums are beating. But when we backtrack to Massachusetts, where she was raised, we can't find much."

"Her dad taught at Smith, right? What do they say?"

Engwall shook his head. "Nobody remembers him specifically. I mean it's been almost thirty years now, so the faculty has come and gone a few times over. We did talk to a retired assistant to a former dean who remembers a Dr. Halsey, but she thought he was a bachelor. Didn't recall the family. We'll keep looking. May not even be important."

"The family continued to live on campus after he died, according to Mrs. Bentley. There's got to be something. Keep digging," said Chamberlain.

"We are." Engwall crossed his arms and thought a minute, "What if Sizemore did this just to hurt him—because he tried to get out from under her—excuse the expression. That could exculpate him. Woman scorned and all that. The plane going down, the photos—just terrible timing for him."

"Jerry, the government's gonna focus more on the fact that it was his camera, his documents and maps that were photographed, his team that led the U-2 mission that resulted in a massive black eye for the United States. Whatever Sizemore might have done in retribution, Bentley created the conditions where top secret information was shared and we think, possibly, made its way around the world so the Soviets were ready when that plane crossed into their airspace."

"We have no evidence of intent on Bentley's part—that he was purposely careless, or that he enlisted his secretary to do this. Just her contention."

Chamberlain shrugged. "His office. His camera. His secretary. His files. Is it espionage? Is he a traitor? Can we tie it to the shoot-down? I don't know. But we need to keep looking because that's what Angleton and Dulles and the president need us to do so they're not the ones losing credibility with the American people in the middle of the Cold War."

CHAPTER
TWENTY-TWO

Wednesday, June 22, 1960
Arlington, VA

Eleanor had begun to keep a bit of distance from Talbot, steering clear while he paced, refraining from asking for updates on his case because it could launch him into a rant he could only soothe with Jim Beam. She reminded him daily that she believed him, that she would stand by him, despite his betrayal, despite the vicious way he was depicted in the newspapers that subjected her to wide-eyed stares at work. She didn't take her colleagues into her confidence, still greeting any attempt to draw her out with a chilly smile. She did take a call from Reverend Grant, the rector of St. John's, who offered her whatever she needed — a visit, conversation, prayer, or simply an ear so she could express how she was feeling in a private, confidential way. This surprised her, his direct acknowledgement of the Bentleys' crisis, and his promise that she would be safe expressing herself to him. She thanked the reverend, sincerely, who promised he would call again in a few days to check on her.

Mostly, she turned to Caroline for support and Rémy, when he was around. Having her husband's loyalty questioned, the breadth of his indiscretions so publicly exposed, left her feeling vulnerable and exhausted in a way that surprised her. So, as she had done throughout her marriage, Eleanor decided she needed a few days away — to take a weekend in New York. She told Tal she needed some uninterrupted, private time to think about her current situation and what she needed to do about it. She called George and asked if he could be on call in case Talbot needed anything. After making a few other arrangements, she booked her train passage—not inviting Caroline to come along—and informed her husband she was heading out of town. Her plan struck Talbot as utterly unreasonable.

"You just went up there in April," he protested, "and you're taking another vacation?"

"Not a vacation, Talbot. I need a break. I know you're dealing with a lot, but so am I. And I need a few days to myself to sort things out, without your pacing the halls. Without this simmering anger."

He looked at her in a way he never had before, unsure of himself, vulnerable.

"Sort things out? Are you coming back?"

"For heaven's sake, Talbot, I'm not leaving you. I'm taking a breather. I'm used to you traveling and going to work every day. We've been in this townhouse together every day for a month. It's hard to think about what I need, what I ought to expect, when you're there right in front of me all the time and I'm so damn worried about you."

He nodded, his eyes clouded.

"George is around—so are the Auclairs—and they've both said they can bring over dinner or just stop in if you need them too. I'll be home Sunday night. There's nothing happening with your case this weekend so it seems like a good time for me to see my friends and let down."

He nodded again and said he understood.

•　　•　　•

Friday, June 24, 1960
New York, NY
Eleanor took a bigger suitcase than usual, blaming it on an uncertain weather forecast that suggested she might need sweaters and rain gear. From her bureau drawer, she withdrew

the Cheney briefcase, which had safely weathered the search of her home. She reached under her lingerie for the key ring she stowed there, but couldn't find it. Patting the lace, slowly at first then a bit frantically, she felt under the piles but found nothing. Had the keys somehow tumbled down behind the drawer? She would have to worry about that later. She lifted the briefcase and placed it inside her Samsonite, covering it with her clothes and snapping the locks shut before Tal saw what she was doing.

When the taxi arrived to take her to her train, she felt a pinch of conscience, seeing Tal standing in the doorway, beleaguered, alone. "Call Caroline and Rémy," she said as she kissed him goodbye. "They'll be good company."

Three hours later, she stepped from the train at Penn Station, disappearing into the crowd of afternoon commuters weaving toward the subway. She caught the train to Brooklyn, riding as far as Borough Hall. She climbed the stairs to the street, circled the block, then returned to the station, descending to the subway platform a second time, joining the handful of people leaning against the columns and station walls. Together, they boarded the next train, one going the same direction as the one she'd just stepped off minutes earlier.

At Grand Army Plaza, she left the train, took the stairs up to the street, and walked toward the plaza. She took a seat on the bench at the Soldiers and Sailors Arch, sitting quietly, feeling the sun on her face as she gazed at the memorial to the defenders of the Union, scanning the crowd on the street. Eventually, she removed her boiled wool jacket, folding it into her tote and replacing it with her cardigan. A few minutes later, she unpinned her pillbox hat and swapped it for a faded scarf, into which she tucked her blonde hair before knotting it under her chin. Prepared now, she stood and made her way back to the station where she caught another train, this one heading north — the direction from which she'd come. This she would ride all the way to the Bronx.

She left the train at Arthur Avenue, relaxing a bit as the smell of fresh bread, the familiar hints of rosemary, wafted from the doorways of the line of restaurants in Little Italy. She walked a few blocks before arriving at Mario's, where she spotted her dinner companion, already seated. She waved off the maitre d' and approached the table.

"My lovely," he said, rising to place a soft kiss on her cheek, help her fit the suitcase under the table. "How was your trip, Mishie?"

She winced and took a quick look around. "Don't call me that here, Gilberto, please."

PART TWO

~~TOP SECRET~~

EO 12958 3.4(b)(1)>25Yrs
(S)

SC-02040/59
Copy ___I___

31 March 1959

THE CRITICAL NEED FOR   COLLECTION

The threat to the security of the United States and the West stemming from our ignorance of Soviet guided missile production and deployment is judged to be a more serious risk than that attendant on overflight operations to obtain the information we sorely need. This is the view of the United States and British intelligence communities as well as of outside consultants, the Hyland Committee.

The Soviets claim that the power balance vis-a-vis the United States is changing. We believe that if this is true the missile factor is the key.

CHAPTER TWENTY-THREE

Eleanor

Many who heard the story of a teenaged Eleanor Halsey, traveling from her home in Massachusetts to virulently fascist Italy in 1938 to study art, questioned how in the world her mother could have been so ill-informed to allow it. Talbot's onetime colleague in Turkey, Harold Warren was one. When he met Eleanor in London before the Bentleys married, his instincts told him there was another layer to this woman, that her unpracticed English pointed to a riddle he couldn't quite unravel. The military chaplain who married them had raised a baffled eyebrow, pressing Eleanor why she hadn't evacuated the minute Britain declared war in 1939. Americans were repeatedly, forcefully advised to leave, the chaplain insisted, and the chartered planes and ships marshaled for the evacuation were packed with sudden refugees leaving behind businesses, homes, entire lives. In comparison, Eleanor had had little to leave behind. Then there was Talbot's mother, who always wondered about Eleanor, most especially because she never spoke of any relatives or shared much about her parents, beyond her stories of the unusual perch she'd enjoyed when artists came for a semester-in-residence at Smith. Wouldn't an orphaned girl have an aunt or cousin somewhere inquiring as to her wellbeing? But as his mother found fault with every woman

Talbot brought around, he paid little attention to the questions she raised.

She had indeed left her home to study in Italy. That was true. She adored her life in Florence—the art history classes that reached back into the centuries to help her organize the random and disparate things she knew into discernible artistic movements and eras; the hours in the studio in the company of vibrant young friends more worldly than she, who encouraged her and bolstered her confidence. But more consequential than this, were the hours spent with her advisor. After their first wine-soaked dinner, when he'd offered to tutor her personally so she could stay in the program and in Florence, her schedule began to revolve around him. Her professor, she found, had far more than sculpting technique to teach her.

Professor Cossutta—Gilberto, as he invited her to call him—was a favorite of his students, the females especially, sunglasses atop his head, pulling his wavy black hair from his face. When he was pleased with a particularly well-wrought sculpture, a clever question from a student, or a well-timed bawdy joke, his smile extended to his eyes, his pleasure and approval so total that his students were compelled to work as hard and as long as necessary to replicate it. Not quite forty, he was younger than most on faculty, often arriving to class with his tie slung around his neck, suit jacket draped over his tanned arm, white shirt unbuttoned to his breastbone. Why he always ran late was a topic of constant conjecture among both faculty and students.

Early in the semester, Cossutta began to reserve vast swaths of time for Eleanor, bristling when students more capable pleaded for time on his schedule. She impressed him, he told her, with her determination, her courage in coming all this way to Florence, despite her limited background and the layered challenge of having to conduct herself in Italian. Their sessions in the studio typically began with Cossutta coaching, cajoling, pleading that she work more delicately, that she pay closer attention, that she not rush. He offered detailed explications of how she could correct her approach, his hands placed over hers as she worked the wax or clay.

After concluding the technical work, they often remained in the studio late into the night, lingering over cups of cooling tea and the occasional bottle of wine. He asked about her upbringing, her parents, her town, saying he wanted to know her better, what drove her, and what was important to her. He often digressed into lengthy analyses of the current moment, insisting the world was at a turning point that would change the map forever. She listened patiently, absorbing his perspective, believing him wise.

"Why do you rip through this, my lovely?" he asked urgently one night, as she struggled to mold a piece of clay into something recognizable. A bird, she hoped, a starling—but it was not coming. "There is no parade at the finish line. There's no value in going quickly and recklessly as you do. This is crude. You rob the piece… the entire moment of creation … of its elegance. In your desperation, you forfeit the creative joy you seek."

It was not the first time he had sounded this theme, but this night, it was tinged with disapproval that felt personal to her. It was past midnight and she was bone tired, her long days filled with demands she could not seem to meet. She dropped her arms at her sides, her modeling knife clattering to the floor, tears gathering in her eyes.

"My lovely," Cossutta said gently, bending to pick up the knife. "Stop. Do not pound the clay to make it submit. Seduce it." He stood behind her, placing his hand on her hip, so close she felt his whispered breath on her neck. "We learn what it wants to be, my dear. We wait for it to speak. Then we coax it into form."

And at this, she gave in, to her art, to the professor's long seduction, leaning back, feeling him press into her as he encircled her with his arms.

•   •   •

Evenings in the studio soon gave way to assignations at an inn with a lovely view of the Arno, not that they spent much time gazing at the river. It was always the same room, a standing arrangement with the innkeeper, she later realized. Gilberto was married with two small children, but he reassured his young lover that his family was no impediment. When his wife turned up at the studio one night to find her husband uncorking a bottle of wine and his student wearing only her sculpting smock, she apologized for disturbing them and backed out the door, telling her husband she would take the soup she'd brought him back home and leave it on the stove.

"Don't look so shocked, my lovely," Cossutta said after she left. "My wife prefers this — my involvements with students — to a permanent mistress, someone long-term as most men choose. Mistresses, after a few years, forget their place, develop a sense of entitlement — showing up at family parties or at Mass on holidays, demanding attention. But my wife knows there is no danger of that, as my students are here for just a season, enriching my life as you are doing now."

She nodded but stayed mute, confused and hurt by his casual appraisal of this intense thing between them. Gilberto was relentlessly possessive with her, always wanting to shape her plans for the day, to know who she'd eaten lunch with, hear what her classmates were saying about the bellicose Hitler, glean news from the letters her mother sent. She had learned when she wasn't properly forthcoming with him, when she was vague or slow in answering what she believed to be mundane questions, simply because she was tired or her mind was elsewhere, she paid a price. He withdrew, criticizing her harshly in class and keeping his distance, skipping their private sessions in the studio. So she grew acutely attentive to him, developing antennae that read the signal embedded in a raised eyebrow or a narrowed eye, acquiescing to the rhythm he set in their relationship.

When they were alone, he kept his hand on her, stroking her arm, gripping behind her neck, praising her looks that he found so startling, so unusual — the light blue eyes, the flaxen hair, the pale skin so unlike, he said, the Mediterranean women he was accustomed to. He developed an extended ritual of freeing her long hair from the bun she usually wore for school, of running his fingers through it to loosen the pins, gripping her skull with his long fingers, pressing. Then he would undress her, assessing aloud the vigor and quality of her response to him, evaluating her always. She, in turn, became more expressive, more demonstrative and daring because pleasing him — eliciting that look of complete pleasure and approval on his face — had become the most important thing to her. This would prove to him, she believed, that theirs was more than a casual affair that would run its course over a school term.

Only much later did she recognize that Cossutta's intensity stemmed only partly from his attraction to her, far more from his commitment to shape her, to ensure she absorbed his outlook on the world. Over their many hours together, he taught her the particulars of various political systems — democracy and capitalism, communism, socialism, the dictatorships that dotted Africa and of course, fascism — answering her questions and slowly coaxing her views into alignment with his. Familiar only with the system she'd been raised in, she was astounded at all she learned, savoring their back and forth that made her feel intellectually mature and worldly.

"Could Patrizio be right, do you think?" she asked as they lazed on the bed at the inn. They had skipped class in favor of a long afternoon together. Having emptied two bottles of Amarone, they would not be heading back to the studio.

"Right in what way?" asked Gilberto.

"That done right, the Fascist system ensures the correct leaders hold power, leaders who make decisions that protect the people from corrupting influences."

Cossutta laughed. "You were raised to know better," he chided. "Surely you know how Marx and Lenin destroy Patrizio's argument."

"Still," she smiled. "I love hearing you lay it out. When you answer my questions, it dispels my doubts."

Six months later, as Hitler's tanks rolled into Poland and Mussolini crowed in celebration from his balcony in Rome, she found Gilberto in his office, where they whispered in growing alarm behind his closed door. He cautioned her to watch herself, to avoid the authorities whose intolerance of any perceived opposition would only grow. Afraid and deeply in his thrall, she looked to him for direction, willing to do anything he asked. And what he asked, finally, after months of indoctrination, was for her to relinquish everything she knew, to take on what he called a life of higher purpose and honor, to help rid the world of the dangerous, oppressive ideologies he had outlined for her, the wrong thinking that had closed the university and threatened their safety. It was, after all, what had brought her to Florence in the first place.

"The world needs you now, my lovely," he told her. "With your clever brain and your creativity and the glorious way you look, doors will swing wide for you."

She could be anything, he said, French, Swiss, even American. So, with the help of a folder of information produced by Gilberto's network and an extended tutelage in American history, Marisha Yahontov, child of Vyatka, Russia—now called Kirov, Soviet Union—became Boston-born Eleanor Halsey.

•   •   •

When Marisha's fevered interest to study painting first asserted itself, her mother, Svetlana, considered how it might be leveraged to the party's benefit and by extension, her own. A true believer, Svetlana had cheered the Bolshevik takeover in 1917, earning a post on the local soviet where she'd served twenty years and giving her access to better housing, better food, and a better education for her children—a living example that some comrades are indeed more equal than others. Svetlana survived the party purge by the People's Commissariat for Internal Affairs—the NKVD—that began in 1936, perhaps because she was female but probably because Stalin had fewer eyes on Kirov, his focus more on rivals in the Supreme Soviet and the Red Army. Although hundreds of thousands of committed communists were eliminated—scores of people Svetlana had known and worked with were executed or sent to the Gulags—Svetlana clung to her belief in the rightness of the Soviet system. When Marisha asked to go to Italy to study art, Svetlana immediately consulted the local committee, believing the request would be seen as evidence of Svetlana's own loyalty and commitment: she was willing to send her young daughter into Fascist Italy to be used however the state wished. It was up to the committee to approve and endorse such a plan and secure the papers the girl would need to travel. After discussions within that soviet, and endorsement by higher-ranking committees, it was determined that another pair of eyes in Florence could be useful, aiding in intelligence gathering as Mussolini grew more erratic and hostile. Marisha would study sculpture while monitoring student attitudes toward Mussolini and, tangentially, Hitler.

Marisha had responded tearfully, protesting she wanted to study oil painting in Rome, not sculpture in Florence. She was dreadful with clay, she cried. Her mother had responded with an angry retort and a sharp slap to her cheek.

"You are being given a gift, Mishie. Do you know how unusual it is for a girl like you to be given permission to leave the country to attend university? A handful of people are allowed to do this, only the most talented and committed, who will bring honor to the homeland. You are not needed in Rome. You will go to Florence or you won't go anywhere. Besides, you are no better with oils than with clay."

Absent an alternative, Marisha soon came around to her mother's point of view, noting Florence was not far from Switzerland, that she might be able to take a trip there, or France, perhaps, to see the treasures in the Louvre. As she neared her departure, her mother informed her that there was another condition she needed to agree to before she would be permitted to go.

"When Soviet students are given the opportunity to study overseas," her mother began, "there are certain obligations involved, reports you will need to send back home."

"Reports? Grade reports, you mean? My school progress?"

"Don't be dense, Mishie. As you go about your business, you must observe your surroundings. Listen to your classmates, your professors, people on the street. Learn how they feel about their leader, their attitudes toward the German beast. Find people who share your views. It will take patience. Then you will write me or your Papa, and describe what you see, note what people are saying. Detailed, thorough reports will reflect well on you and protect our family."

This idea of monitoring others was familiar to her. Her mother and father regularly discussed neighbors and friends, constantly evaluating whether a person's loyalty was drifting or remained pure to the state, information that her mother documented with the local soviet. Marisha agreed, without telling her mother that all this listening and observing would not be her first priority.

When she arrived in Florence she at first encountered only the most ardent Fascists, devotees of Mussolini who believed his years in power had finally set things right. Her letters home described the enchantment of the starlit piazza while dutifully recounting conversations with classmates. As time went on, the communists in the group revealed themselves to her, inviting her to join them in the Comintern to help bring communism to all parts of the world and pointing to Professor Cossutta as the leader of their hidden band. When she wrote her mother to say she had gotten to know her program advisor particularly well and that they shared much in common, Svetlana presented the letter to her committee and they applauded; the professor had deemed Marisha acceptable and would use her in the cause.

•   •   •

"This is what love of country requires," Cossutta reminded her in a tense whisper in his office a year later, "putting the good of the Motherland ahead of yourself."

He was gathering files to burn, identifying anything incriminating—positive appraisals of the work of Jewish students, applications he'd sent to groups and associations for grants and financial support for the art department, appeals Mussolini might overlook but the Nazis would object to. With the university shuttering its doors, no grants would be of use, anyway.

"I don't understand this. We just signed the pact with the Germans. I thought that would keep the peace—make us safe."

"It is a temporary strategy, my lovely, until the Soviets and the Germans can split Europe up between them. But once the Germans move into Florence, they will rout out any communist, pact or no pact, and they'll kill any Jew they find. So we must lie low for now and begin to prepare you for what's ahead."

"This can't be real. To be honest…I had thought I would return home if war broke out." She paused, considering the prospect of never seeing her family again, her five brothers and sisters, her taciturn father who spent his days unloading cargo at the Kirov wharf, her calculating mother, who had set all this in motion. "But if you think this best…"

"It is, my lovely, the best course. And we have a little time to ensure you are ready."

•   •   •

As Italy careened into war, Gilberto safeguarded her in his home. She was given the codename Starling, the NKVD sending tutors to drill her in English, American geography, and history and introduce her to her purported Massachusetts roots. Small details of American life gleaned from Cossutta's colleagues who'd taught in the U.S. became filler to strengthen her background story because it was the details, Cossutta warned, that could give her away. She sat through hours of American movies to study how Americans walked and moved and ate their meals and listened to recordings of radio shows to tune her ear to English conversation. She read English-language classics — books forbidden in Kirov — that included *Little Women*, *The Scarlet Letter*, *Main Street*, *Of Human Bondage* and multiple works by Edith Wharton, F. Scott Fitzgerald, and Mark Twain. Each night, after hours of work and study, she and Cossutta climbed into bed together, his wife relegated to a pallet in their children's room, the children not seeming to notice.

She did not hide out with her former classmates during the war, as she would later claim, for two reasons. First, they knew her as Marisha, the identity she was working to erase, and second, because few of her friends remained in the city. Some took up arms on either side of the war, while others risked their lives in the Resistance. A few fled to Spain while others simply disappeared into the ether. Weeks after the university closed, Marisha went to the studio hoping to find an unlocked door and perhaps retrieve a few pieces of her work. As she stepped off the bus, there was the beautiful Patrizio, swaying from the grand cypress tree at the university entrance, his brown curls lifting in the wind then settling on his broken neck. She rushed back to Cossutta in tears to tell him what she'd seen. He patted her head and gave an impatient cluck.

"Child. He was the last of your class who knew you and could expose you. It was a necessary step and this way, he avoids the suffering that will come with the defeat of his beloved fascists. Don't waste your tears."

That those who knew her true background could be eliminated like this, their silence guaranteed through death, horrified her. But as she looked into Cossutta's eyes, they offered no sympathy. Instead, they held a clear warning that her emotion had no place here. He seemed almost repulsed by her grief. She swallowed her tears and steadied herself, wishing desperately to return to safer territory with him. "But there's Remigius," she said finally. "He knows me, too. He's still around."

"Rémy? He's with us. You needn't worry about him."

When the tide of the war began turning toward the Allies, Gilberto secured a place for her in the Convent of Santa Maria Novella, presenting her as a stranded American who'd been hiding with the help of her university advisor—the first test of her new identity. Equipped with a forged Massachusetts birth certificate, the nuns accepted Eleanor Halsey completely who, to their ears, sounded like every other American with her flat intonation and occasional twang. Given the melange of languages native to the people they'd hidden and sheltered during the war, each camouflaging true identities, backgrounds, and religions, there was little chance anyone would note the odd Slavic vowel that asserted itself now and then, a fault Eleanor worked tirelessly to overcome.

By the time Talbot Bentley arrived in Florence, the transformation was nearly complete, Eleanor living in her own little apartment and working at the gallery, having absorbed her new identity to the point her dreams came to her in English. After they arranged their first dinner together, she rushed to Cossutta to tell him she had found her mark.

"You know where this leads, don't you, lovely? It leads you away from Florence and me. I had thought you would infiltrate an American embassy somewhere in Europe, a clerk gathering tidbits of information here and there, but this could take you to the United States itself."

Eleanor shivered. "Can you find out about him? Find out what he's doing here. That can help us decide if he's the right one to pursue."

While Eleanor and Talbot spent the subsequent months taking romantic walks along the Arno, Cossutta's intelligence network got to work, tracing Talbot's travel across Europe and concluding that his story about serving in North Africa during the war was invented—likely cover for some kind of covert work. Reversing his route from the French coast to Florence, they discovered some details of his sojourn, hearing the story from a loquacious innkeeper about the French widow who'd stolen his money. He could be distracted this way, then, Cossutta observed. His boundaries might not be difficult to breach.

Eleanor did as she was told, drawing close to Talbot but struggling as she did so. She managed well with the handholding, even the kisses at the end of their dates. He was an attractive man and treated her with a deference and respect she was drawn to. But she could not bring herself to go from Gilberto's bed to Talbot's, even though this is what her lover wished her to do. They fought over it, Eleanor insisting she just needed time to adjust to the idea because he, Gilberto, was the one who held her heart. Her confession did not move him.

"Fine, then. He will assume you are inexperienced, waiting for a proposal of marriage. He will desire you even more because he can't have you. It's how men are. And with Eleanor's story — no parents, dead brother, the lost American who couldn't get home — he will assume lingering trauma. He won't pressure you, his chaste little flower."

Then came the day Talbot asked her for her hand, as they traveled back from their harrowing visit to London, during which Eleanor was convinced she'd be exposed as a fraud with her inability to decipher most of what the British had to say and her realization of all she didn't know about her purported country of origin.

Talbot wanted to marry her. He believed her to be who she said she was. He would soon start work for a new agency — an intelligence agency — and she could be there alongside him, as it all played out. It was a gift, enabling her to accomplish what she and Gilberto and the people behind their work needed her to do. But the other, awful side of that was relinquishing Gilberto, the man who had shaped her into the woman she was, to whom she still looked for affirmation and assurance. She told him she wasn't quite sure how she'd manage without his guidance, his constant supervision and correction.

"Starling will have new handlers, who will do as I have, monitor Eleanor's assignments to support the work."

Hearing him use her code name — and her new name — speaking so matter-of-factly about what lay ahead, brought a rush of tears, so little did he understand what he was to her. He was her wise teacher — the brilliant sculptor Cossutta — who had nurtured her talent in her first year in Florence. He was her first lover, who had instructed her how a woman should properly respond to a man. He was her interpreter of the world, who had draped a filter over her eyes so she saw the world as he did. She would make him proud of her, she decided, cement a place in his life more permanent than the girls who had preceded her. But her resolve did not lessen her heartbreak and on the day of her wedding—when she saw Gilberto in the cathedral balcony, smiling in the way she knew so well, as if this were a happy wedding like any other—her tears threatened to overwhelm her.

Soon after Talbot and Eleanor left Florence, Gilberto made his way south to Brindisi, where he caught a ferry to Albania. An exfiltration team awaited him there, spiriting him across eastern Europe and into the Soviet Union. He was received as a hero in Moscow by members of the Ministry of State Security. Within weeks, his wife and children were similarly transported out of Italy, men in dark suits arriving on their doorstep commanding them to leave everything they owned behind if they wished to see their husband and father again. The family arrived at Tushino Airfield, a military installation outside Moscow, weary and bewildered.

"What have you done, Gilberto?" his wife spat when he approached her, arms spread to embrace her. "What in God's name have you done to us?"

"You'll get used to it, my lovely," Gilberto said. "There are benefits here I'm sure you'll enjoy."

After a trip down the motorway, they arrived in Moscow, Gilberto pointing out the many churches designed by Italians centuries before. His wife did not utter a word. The driver stopped in front of a tall, concrete apartment building and Gilberto announced they were home. His children, young teenagers now, gathered the odd assortment of welcome gifts they'd been given, while his wife took in the drab street, the grim-faced Muscovites, heads down, hurrying about their business. She saw no markets filled with flowers and fruit, or friends cozied up to tables at a sidewalk trattoria, sharing a caffè or glass of vino. It was so unlike the lyrical pulse of Florence, that once she exited the car, she collapsed in a loud, dramatic sob like the Italian mother she was, wailing for her citta natale, bella Firenze, Firenze pefetta. People rushed past, knowing it unwise to pay attention to the emotional displays of strangers, unwise to pay too much attention to anything on the streets of Stalin's Moscow. Cossutta gave a cluck and instructed the driver to help him hoist her to her feet and get her inside their new home.

CHAPTER
TWENTY-FOUR

Friday, June 24, 1960
Arlington, VA

Soon after Eleanor departed for New York, Caroline phoned Talbot to say she would be there late afternoon, just as soon as the babysitter arrived. She'd bring provisions: three porterhouse steaks and baking potatoes, salad-makings, and a bottle of bourbon to replenish supplies. Rémy would be along after work with a dessert of some kind from his little French bakery. Learning the rest of his day had been planned for him, Talbot offered little resistance, saying he would love their company, that Caroline needed to pick up some charcoal, too, because he couldn't remember the last time he'd grilled out. He thanked her for opting not to join Eleanor on her trip. Caroline said Eleanor had asked her, specifically, not to come, so she could be available to Talbot.

Caroline's breath caught when he opened the front door. The last month had taken its toll. This was a man diminished. He looked thinner, less substantial. His broad shoulders slumped as if surrendering to what lay ahead of him, dark eyes tired and clouded, stubble across his cheeks and chin. He ushered her in quickly and she dropped her grocery bags the moment the door was safely shut, reaching out to embrace him.

"Talbot," she said again and again as he leaned heavily into her. "Talk. How are you? Really? Tell me."

He shrugged as he searched for words, finally leaning down to retrieve the groceries. Caroline followed him into the kitchen, lifting the potatoes out of the bag to wash them while he made room for the steaks in the refrigerator.

"It still doesn't feel real, Caroline. Even if it were only losing my job, I'd feel at sea. But losing my job because I'm accused of betraying my country? Sometimes I rant, as Eleanor could tell you, over this idiotic investigation, and at myself, too, for the stupid mistakes I made. Other times, I just want to crawl into a hole and be left alone. The idea of ending up in prison—I can't even take it in. And after my service, Caroline. Faithful service I rendered to this country that apparently counts for nothing."

"You're a patriot, Talbot, I know that. I know what you've done. Rémy knows. We'll be character witnesses when the time comes."

"You'd testify to my character? You sure about that?"

It took her a moment to realize what he meant. Whatever Talbot was working through, their affair was not something she was willing to rehash with him—even if Talbot felt the need to clear his conscience.

"We don't need to go over that, Talbot. Ancient history. It's been years. So just strike that from the list of things to worry about. It never happened."

"But it did, which makes you the wrong person to put in a witness box to testify that I'm a stand-up guy."

"Talbot. Nobody knows."

"All the more reason you need to steer clear of this so it doesn't blow up your life. And I know it's a little late to say this, but I'm sorry. I'm sorry I crossed the line and dragged you over it with me."

Caroline smiled, impatient to move off this topic, fluttering across the kitchen to fold the grocery bags, stow the bourbon in the bar cart. Rémy would arrive soon and she didn't want a whiff of this conversation in the air. "No need, really Tal. We're adults.

We both participated. We had our little thing and it was foolish so let's not give it any more oxygen."

"I appreciate that, Caroline, I really do. I appreciate you. I don't deserve how big-hearted you've been—I mean, we're still friends, for God's sakes, all these years later. And Eleanor. Wow. She knows everything now and she's still here, still standing by me."

Caroline blanched. "Everything? She knows about us, too?"

"Oh, no, no. Sorry. Not that. The others. I've told her everything about the women…the incidents…the activity at work. Had to. My lawyer insisted. But I didn't mention you. She needs you too much, Caroline. Loves you. I couldn't take that from her. Not now."

Caroline let out long exhale. "Scared me there for a moment, Tal. Listen. Why don't you get ready for dinner? Maybe a shower and a shave will help."

"Am I that rank? I hadn't noticed."

"I didn't mean that. I just thought dressing for dinner might make you feel more like yourself—distract you, maybe, for an hour or two."

Talbot nodded and climbed the stairs to his bedroom.

With the potatoes in the oven, Caroline turned her attention to the kitchen and beyond, where newspapers were strewn amidst empty coffee cups and abandoned highball glasses. So unlike Eleanor to leave the house like this, Caroline thought, evidence of her friend's ongoing distress. Caroline collected the glassware and stacked the papers then ran a cloth over the credenza to catch the dust, pausing to look at a photo of the Bentleys taken on their wedding day. Of the two, Talbot was the radiant one, handsome in his uniform, the glint in his eye full of pleasure, longing, joyful anticipation. Eleanor looked unsure and hesitant. While Talbot had his arm around her shoulder, his hand clearly pulling her to him, Eleanor's arms hung stiffly at her sides, as if she were not fully on board with the proceedings.

Thinking about the wedding night, Caroline surmised, wondering what she had gotten herself into.

A knock at the door signaled Rémy's arrival. He bore a full grocery bag and a box of profiteroles, so fresh and fragrant that he said he'd almost consumed them on the drive over. He handed the sweets over to Caroline as Talbot reappeared, clean-shaven and smelling of Old Spice, dressed in crisp khakis and a sports shirt. The men exchanged a fierce embrace.

"You okay?" Rémy asked, his hand clutching Talbot's shoulder, eyes intense and searching.

"I'm okay today. Okay because you two are here."

"Well, then. I will man the grill tonight," he announced, withdrawing the pepper, cognac and cream he planned to use to prepare steak au poivre. Caroline cheered in anticipation and he laughed, reaching to pat her cheek.

"I know, my sweet, you can already taste it, eh?"

After setting the steaks in the marinade, Rémy said he was going to scoot next door for a moment to check on the townhouse they still owned. The tenants—a revolving cast of single college students and interns—had reported a trail of water on the ground floor that needed investigation. He didn't think it would take long—not as long as the steaks would need to marinate.

"Prepare my drink, Talbot. I'll be right back." He headed back out the door.

En route to the bar cart, Talbot detoured by the Hi-Fi cabinet and put on a Perry Como record. The needle dropped and after the merest scratch, music filled the house, restoring a bit of normalcy to the proceedings. Talbot stood listening, snapping along to the opening bars of "Route 66."

"Wish I could head out on Route 66 right about now," he called to Caroline.

She gave a sympathetic nod as she assembled the salad. "I bet you do."

He embarked, then, on his bartending duties, preparing a bourbon and Coke for Rémy and delivering a gin and tonic to Caroline, leaning against the counter to watch her tear the lettuce and chop the carrots. When the record transitioned into "Mood Indigo," he pulled her into his arms and swept her slowly across the kitchen floor. She acquiesced to the moment, heartened to see this Talbot, her old friend, moving in his smooth, self-assured way. She relaxed into his arms, her cheek on his. When she pulled back at the song's final notes, Talbot's eyes were closed, fat tears threading down his face.

"Takes me back to the war," he said, shrugging. "Simpler times. We knew exactly who the enemy was." He released her and said he would set the table.

•   •   •

Rémy's visit next door took longer than he'd forecast, his brow creased when he returned.

"Might be a bigger problem than I thought," he said.

"An expensive problem?" Caroline asked.

"Hope not. We'll see. I'll need to spend a little time over there in the next few days."

"Rémy, my friend," Talbot began, "wish I could help, but the only place I'm allowed to go is to my lawyer's office."

"Not your problem, old man, and nothing we need to worry about tonight. Let's just enjoy one another and our little feast. Bring my drink to the patio and I'll get started."

Within the hour, they were seated and inhaling their dinners, the steaks so tender, Talbot said, he hardly had to chew. They pushed their chairs back from the patio table as dusk descended, the air still and warm, at the cusp of summer.

"Grilled to perfection, Rémy. Thank you," said Talbot. "Feels like I've eaten at a five-star restaurant." Caroline nodded in agreement, rising to refill their glasses and retrieve the dessert.

Rémy placed a hand on his chest and gave a small, appreciative nod. "Avec plaisir," he said. When Caroline returned with the profiteroles, he reached out and pulled her into his lap, wrapping an arm around her. "I wish Eleanor could have been here — like the old days — before kids, before..."

"Before complications," Talbot offered.

"Indeed. Yes. Before complications." Rémy lifted his glass. "Here's to our friendship," he began, taking a long pause before he continued. "And here's to things becoming uncomplicated in the months ahead — to the facts emerging and getting past all of this."

"Yes," agreed Talbot. "Here's to the truth in all things."

CHAPTER
TWENTY-FIVE

Friday, June 24, 1960
Arlington, VA

None of his tenants had been home when Rémy went to inspect his townhouse. There was no leak, but there was unquestionably something that needed immediate attention. Unlocking the townhouse door, he moved down the hall to the bedroom that shared the longest wall with the Bentleys' home. Making his way to the closet, he pushed aside the blouses and skirts that belonged to the inhabitant of the room, exposing a cabinet door embedded in the wall. His tenants understood this was a fire safe that held documents the Auclairs once kept in a safe deposit box but could now keep here, to save from having to pay the bank month after month. Given the tenant turnover, he doubted any of the current residents even knew it was here.

But it was a recording device, not a safe, tucked inside that cabinet. With the briefcase now miles away, the machine no longer served a purpose. There was no transmitter to trigger a recording and given the intensity of the investigation of Talbot, Rémy had been ordered to remove and destroy the tape. Dismantling the taping system would require a more complicated intervention he would undertake in the coming days.

After nearly fifteen years in the United States, marriage to the quintessentially American Caroline, three happy children, a job

that enabled him to own a home and a rental property—
something that never would have been possible in Europe—
Rémy remained a communist of unwavering belief. Did he have
an interest in living under that system? Did he believe Stalin's
assertion that gaiety was the most outstanding feature of the
Soviet Union? Not in the least. But with de Gaulle stumbling
around France, insisting French communists present a danger
because they take their orders from Moscow, Rémy believed it
would be some time yet before his own country would be
hospitable to his viewpoint. So here he remained.

Even so, he held a simmering contempt for Americans that
had built steadily since the closing days of the war. The simmer
grew to a rolling boil when Joe McCarthy's half-truths rallied the
anti-communists and sabotaged the careers of countless
entrepreneurs, artists, and scholars. Americans had cheered
him—Eisenhower hardly had a negative thing to say—until
McCarthy started offending the wrong people.

Rémy found the average U.S. citizen ignorant of the toll the
war had taken on the world, and once the Traités de Paris were
signed, these self-interested Americans gave little thought to
restoring a world blighted by war. The vitriol against Stalin had
been immediate and unwarranted, as American military
advisors and troops wormed their way across Germany and into
Berlin, blanketing Europe with personnel to implement the
Marshall Plan. Talbot himself had been a part of that—his
assertive, get-out-of-my-way-because-I'm-right attitude so
typical of the Americans stationed across the continent in the
post-war years. The Red Army had sacrificed profoundly, but
Americans talked like the entire war was fought in Normandy,
the Ardennes, and the Pacific. What of Stalingrad, Leningrad,
the Ukraine, his blighted France? While the rest of the world
staggered toward recovery, American industry hummed on the
strength of the expanded economy the war had created,
advertisements convincing citizens they needed console

televisions, clothes dryers, air conditioning, electric garage doors, of all things. Even Caroline had made a point just a few weeks earlier of showing him a magazine ad for the 1960 Ford Galaxie Sunliner that came with a removable roof.

"A convertible car, Caroline?" he'd asked. "Who needs such a thing?"

"Nobody needs it, Rémy, but wouldn't it be fun? Taking the roof off and driving into the Blue Ridge mountains? The kids would love it. They'd probably want to take their friends."

He had simply smiled, hoping she'd been seized by a fleeting notion she would just as quickly forget. While American automobile engineers spent their time dreaming up new, obscene and unneeded luxuries, engineers elsewhere still struggled with the logistics of getting food to starving people in Eastern Europe, Russia, Asia, and Africa.

Rémy knew what it was like to be hungry, his years with the Maquisard having taught him that he could subsist on very little. The stories of those days that had so captivated his college classmates were mostly true and led people to wrongly conclude certain things about him, as Talbot had. Camouflaging his politics, he had secured a visa to the United States then admission into American University, situated a little over a mile from the Soviet Embassy in DC. He studied urban planning, more useful than the Renaissance sculpture he'd studied in Florence. Twelve years after their first meeting, Rémy laid eyes on a woman who bore little resemblance to the small-town Russian girl who'd sat next to him in their introductory sculpting class in Florence. Marisha's transformation—the assertive way she dressed and carried herself, the very western way she conversed over dinner, the blood red fingernails curved around her cigarette—was utterly convincing. In fact, Rémy thought, the two of them were so embedded in these post-war identities they'd created, he sometimes forgot who they really were, the mission that had brought them here in the first place.

Their activities grew out of orders Rémy received and later, instructions given to Eleanor on her trips to New York. Caroline was invited on Eleanor's "girls weekends" as an antidote to Talbot's persistent requests to join his wife in New York, and with that, the enterprise grew more elaborate, as operatives were brought in to act as friends Eleanor knew at Smith, Caroline's unwitting presence providing additional cover. While he had married her to gain a foothold in the United States, over time he had grown to love and appreciate her, so reliable and open-faced in a way French women were not. He saw their marriage as something genuine, completely separate from the work he was sent to the United States to do. The only time he'd wavered was when Talbot had drawn Caroline into his bed, the taping system picking up their sometimes raw conversations in Talbot's home office, while he and Eleanor conversed on the patio. Rémy had seethed, quietly furious, contemplating whether he should confront her, sweep up the children she so adored and return to France, leave her and the whole mess behind. His handler had chided him for his immaturity—for talking about it with Eleanor—and demanded he keep his mouth shut and be grateful Caroline had unwittingly provided such useful blackmail material should they need it. The handler worked out of the Soviet Embassy, a purported defense attaché whom Rémy believed ran a number of agents in Washington. When Rémy needed to get a message to him, or had tapes or documents that needed to be processed before Eleanor's next trip to New York, he used dead drops in Rock Creek Park, near the Lincoln Memorial, or sometimes in Arlington National Cemetery, where a cutout would collect them and courier them across the city.

As a young man, his continent under siege, Rémy came to believe the Soviet system was the fairest path. In the years since, he had dedicated his creativity, his intelligence, and his skills to ensure that system would spread. But he hadn't truly understood how complicated living out this mission with a partially invented identity would become. His children were no longer vague, ill-formed ideas; they were flesh and blood Americans he helped with homework and tucked into bed at night. But with Eleanor positioned to gather information from the highest realms of American intelligence, Rémy could not see abandoning this work even if he'd been permitted to. He was confident he would do it well enough so that his wife and children would never discover where his loyalty truly lay. Talbot's arrest had made things more interesting, more urgent, perhaps. And if they had to end their friendship—if Tal went to prison and Eleanor relocated to get away from the heat—it was a small price to pay for important work. Caroline would adjust, he believed. She loved her friend. But that hadn't stopped her from climbing into her friend's husband's bed. Perhaps she'd feel relieved if the Bentleys were forced to move out of the Auclairs' circle. It would tidy up a few things for all of them.

CHAPTER
TWENTY-SIX

Friday, June 24, 1960
The Bronx, NY

"Tone, Eleanor," Cossutta said, his flashing eyes a warning. "Do not direct your irritation at me."

"Who else, then?" Eleanor sat, giving the dining room a once-over. Those seated around her were familiar to her, most of them Italians whose identities were known to Cossutta and Mario, the owner. On their meeting nights, these were the only people who could secure reservations.

"I'm being scrutinized," she hissed. "I've been interviewed—twice. My house has been searched and if Talbot goes to jail, I may be out on the street. Pardon me if I seem irritated."

Cossutta lifted the bottle of Chianti from the table and languidly poured her a glass, a gesture he had relied on for as long as she had known him, his antidote to difficult questions.

"All is well, my little Starling," his use of her code name the subtlest reminder that she reported to him. He was in charge. "So stop it. We are in this position because of your excellent work over many, many years. Release this—whatever it is—that is making you so disagreeable and be proud of what you've accomplished, even landing your erstwhile husband in jail."

"I can hardly take credit for a coincidence, Gilberto."

He shrugged. "I disagree. The goal was to derail the summit, diminish Eisenhower in the eyes of the world, and it's done. The stain extends to the vice president who now has no chance of becoming president. Given his contempt of the schemer Nixon, the Premier is extremely pleased. And you played an essential part in our getting to this point. You mined information and sent it where it needed to go, helping our friends improve their capabilities. They were prepared when that odd bird flew by."

"How did they down it? Do you know?"

"I have been told little. Your information aided improvements in the missile battery near Sverdlovsk and gave them an idea of the flight path. Perhaps a surface missile took it out. Or a MIG—which can't fly as high as the U-2—got under it and shot upwards. Or maybe the MIG was hit by the missile, came apart, and debris flew into the American plane. That might explain why it was missing a wing and floated to earth mostly intact. But your fingerprints are not on this anywhere, my child, so you needn't behave so peevishly. And we have the happy accident of Talbot himself in the crosshairs, due entirely to his own appetites. So," he lifted his glass and smiled, "saluti."

From the time they met, Cossutta had impressed on Eleanor the value of certain attributes, chief among them discipline to manage herself, to modulate her emotions. The only place he welcomed her expressiveness was in bed. Outside of that, he was quick to compare her to a child if she questioned a decision, betrayed anger or disappointment. But his nonchalance—his dismissiveness—fed a growing ire inside her. She swirled the Chianti in her glass, searching for a way to make herself understood. She lit a cigarette and leaned in.

"I'm in the crosshairs, too, Gilberto," she said quietly, reasonably. "We're lucky they didn't find the briefcase and begin to figure out who the hell I am."

He leaned back in his chair—physically discounting her viewpoint—and sighed, looking impatient and somewhat baffled at her refusal to drop this line of conversation. He took a labored breath, as if to communicate how taxing he found her, having to make a further attempt to correct her thinking.

"I'm sorry you're feeling set upon, Mishie, but can you step outside your current discomfort to see the bigger picture? We'll be rid of Talbot! Might that restore the spring in your step? It does mine. And should it appear the government is closing in, we'll pull you out. Send you home. Return you to your family as you've often wished, while we circulate the story that Mrs. Bentley, cheated on so publicly, so brutally, by her husband, has fled to Europe where she lived during the war, in search of peace and privacy and equilibrium. Once we get you into Eastern Europe, you'll disappear. I could even join you if that suits. Or we could stay here, together—I do love New York—renewing an old friendship that began during the war."

She stared hard at her old professor, the ease with which he proposed options for her future. She considered for a moment the wife he'd parked in Moscow then abandoned for a more vibrant life in New York—for freedom, essentially, to teach his art, enjoy the rich culture of the city—and have contact when he wished with Eleanor and other women, certainly. Did his wife share his dedication to his mission or, like Eleanor, had she been dedicated mostly to pleasing him? His black hair was shot through with gray now and the brown eyes that had once been so vibrant were rimmed in red. With the stoop of his shoulders and his softer middle, it was harder to conjure the man who had once proved so alluring, who had so easily convinced her to turn her life over to him and join the Soviet cause. Eleanor doubted the female undergraduates he now taught at Fordham were lining up for private interludes in the studio with him. But years ago, he had been a force, casting a spell on her, stoking her need for his approval, withholding it when he wanted her to do something especially difficult. First in small things, like who she socialized with at university and later, in directing her to marry Talbot. She had agreed because seeing Gilberto happy, receiving his praise, had been paramount to her—her anchor—offering her a sense of hope, of security, when the world was reeling and her parents were thousands of miles away. To keep him happy, she agreed to leave him, to live her life as the American Eleanor—hoping that one day it would pay off for her, that somehow they would reunite.

And so they had, in 1950. As Talbot readied for a trip to Europe, part of a team assessing the effectiveness of the Marshall Plan its third year, her old professor arrived in the United States to reassert himself in her life. Newly hired into the Fordham Fine Arts Department, his curriculum vitae indicated he had spent the years after Florence in Greece, sculpting and teaching workshops to tourists. Soon after he got to New York, he sent a message through Rémy that Eleanor should report to him immediately. As Talbot had packed to fly to Europe, Eleanor mentioned, as casually as she could, that she planned to make a shopping excursion to New York while he was gone.

Talbot had paused, his brow furrowed. "Alone?" he had asked. "That's not something you ought to do alone, Eleanor."

"Talbot. Don't be old-fashioned. It's a good way for me to pass the time without you," she'd insisted. "There are a couple of girls from Smith in the city so I won't really be alone. We talked yesterday and they have a line on tickets to *Carousel*—the new musical that just opened."

"But we would have a ball there together, Ellie. I'd like to see *Carousel*. It's supposed to be superb. And we could look up the Warrens—Hal and Molly—see how the banking business has been treating him."

"I'd love it, Tal. But…another time. Plus, my love, I can't get an early start on Christmas shopping if you're with me. I'll just do a quick up and back while you're out of town and we'll plan another trip together."

Tal declared himself disappointed, saying at the very least, he would see if Rémy were available to see her safely onto the train. The next morning, minutes after he headed to Andrews for his flight, Rémy arrived and handed her a small valise.

"This is for me?" Eleanor asked, unaccustomed to lugging things of that size, so unlike notes easily hidden or destroyed. "What's in it?"

"Schematics of buildings where Tal and his colleagues have set up offices so the Centre can rent adjacent space, tunnel inside walls, that sort of thing. The *rezidentura* has been working on these for months—some are hand drawn and updated just days ago. They offer an idea of how quickly the American intelligence operation is growing. So. Take these to Cossutta who will get them where they need to go."

Later that morning, Eleanor arrived at Penn Station where she stowed her luggage and the valise in a locker, then walked the two miles to Bloomingdale's. She bought socks and ties and aftershave for her husband, circling the sales floor multiple times to ensure no one was following her. She went next to the matinee performance of *Carousel*, surprised to discover that it was a reworking of a Hungarian play she had studied as a girl—just as tragic and unsettling as she remembered it. After taxiing back to the train station to retrieve her luggage, she arrived at her hotel just after six in the evening, to wait for the man who, for good or for bad, had made her who she was.

CHAPTER TWENTY-SEVEN

1947

Washington, DC

When newlywed Eleanor arrived in Washington, DC, she found it not exactly as described. Cossutta had prepared her for a chorus of politicians, bureaucrats, reporters, columnists, neighbors, shopkeepers, bus drivers absolutely aligned, sounding the refrain that her homeland must be subjugated and destroyed.

But Washington, she found, was focused more on catching up from the frenzy of the war years, less about the Soviet threat. The city itself felt new, improvised—wholly different from the centuries-old seats of power she knew in Europe and Russia. This was an earnest, clumsy, work-in-progress, as war-focused enterprises returned to non-military use and soldiers swapped uniforms for civilian suits. Rows of neat little split-levels were going up outside the Potomac River in Maryland and Virginia, burgeoning suburbs swallowing up farmland, creating new communities where veterans, full of hope and optimism, could start their families and begin to heal. Talbot's work involved countering the Soviets, but to Eleanor's surprise, it also included vast efforts to rebuild Europe, to provide for the millions of refugees searching for home and safety.

The young couples they befriended in their first years in Georgetown had stunned her with their diverse views of

Truman, taxes, the nuclear threat, the missile gap with the Soviets. The group often lingered long after the dinner check had been settled — coffees, brandies, other aperitifs spread across the table — debating issues and testing ideas. It was an echo of the evenings she had loved on the piazza, absent the anxiety and tension: unlike pre-war Florence, no one in post-war Washington worried their opinions could be twisted into something the government would one day use against them. These conclaves were chatty and good-natured, full of sarcasm, jokes, contemporary references, and slang that Eleanor absorbed and folded into her expanding American vocabulary.

"Korea will be Harry Truman's undoing," a friend announced one evening, a section head at the Department of Agriculture who lived with his wife in their building. Eleanor flinched hearing a government employee assert such a thing out loud against a country's leader. Any frustrations her mother had with her soviet had been shared with her husband in whispers — quickly recanted if Eleanor inquired about it. In Florence, Patrizio and the others had loudly trumpeted Mussolini's brilliance; digs were murmured with hand over mouth, communicated with gestures, raised eyebrows, scoffs.

But in Washington, Eleanor found no single party line promoted by the State to ensure people moved in a unified direction with a shared perspective and viewpoint. Unity of belief and message, her mother had taught her, enabled leaders to create a cohesive culture and protect the people from injurious, corrupting influences. But this Washington? It was a political and cultural stew. Everybody had opinions about everything — lawmakers, of course, but also her neighbors, the mechanic who fixed Tal's car, the proprietor of her favorite dress shop. A local TV show called *Meet the Press* featured influential people with wildly different viewpoints, arguing and debating. The questions the newsmen threw at the officials would have cost them their jobs and shut down their newspapers back home.

American artists, too, expressed themselves in a way entirely new to her, celebrating a world at peace by trying daring things, causing a sensation among their patrons and drawing headlines in the Arts section of the *Post*. Caroline took Eleanor to a modern dance concert at American University, where they watched, rapt, as young, sinewy bodies draped across one another, grasping and twisting in a raw display of sensual freedom. It was a long way from the Kirov Ballet. Caroline had been the one to comment on how arousing the whole thing was, saying maybe if she'd been with Eleanor in Florence among Michelangelo's naked statues for years, she'd be more used to it.

"But in Florence," Eleanor protested, "the statues stand still. These bodies—" she searched for words—"writhed. I've never seen a body do that. Except maybe Tal's—but certainly not in public!" Caroline laughed and winked, suggesting they stop by the box office and inquire about getting season tickets.

Freedom of expression, Eleanor began to understand, was a thread that wound through all of American culture, the subject of books and newspaper columns and lectures—even dance recitals. Americans were preoccupied with *this,* she saw, not destroying the Soviet Union. This was their organizing principle.

When she and Tal began attending services at St. John's— Eleanor faking her way through the *Book of Common Prayer* because her re-education in this area, too, had been lacking—she had expected something akin to a low-key rally, a celebration of all that was good about America wrapped up in hymns and recitations. When, in his homily, the rector began to extoll the high virtue of Capitalism over Communism, she felt a rush of satisfaction. Exactly as described, she thought, the greed the Americans are known for—thinking only of themselves.

The rector continued.

"Under Capitalism," he declared from the gilded, elevated pulpit, "you can make a lot of money. Making a lot of money enlarges the tithe you can give to the poor to relieve their suffering. As Saint Luke's gospel reminds us, 'For unto whomsoever much is given, of him shall be much required: and to whom men have committed much, of him they will ask the more.' And God has bestowed on this country, and on you, my dear people, more than our ancestors could ever have imagined. So here is your charge: make your money, fairly, ethically. Then give it away to the good of others. I trust I'll see you all at the mission fair next week where you can explore ways to do so."

And so it went, each time they attended. No condemnation for godless Russia, just prayers for its people, that a religious sensitivity would arise to proffer hope. Rector Grant didn't pound the pulpit as he made his case: he laid out his argument gently, in a way that inclined Eleanor to listen. And as she listened, not wholly believing, a door nudged open, behind which she parked the inconsistencies—ideas and concepts that didn't quite fit with what Cossutta had taught her. The economics of it all, for one thing. Her government collected and redistributed resources according to need. It was the fairest way. But Americans were buying their own homes and cars, working two jobs if they wanted, happy in their autonomy, in their striving. Was that better, all that hustling to find opportunity? These were the questions she would sort through at some point, when she knew more and was better equipped to find the holes in the rector's logic, spot the fallacies in the stories the news anchors shilled. Her lack of contact with Gilberto made possible her extended musings about the world she now inhabited, absent his particular filter.

One afternoon, she took her musings to the Freer Gallery, attracted more by the familiarity of the Italian Renaissance-style building than the Oriental and Egyptian art in its galleries. As she studied an ancient tapestry, she felt a jostle, later finding a folded note in her jacket pocket. The first message from her handler—a reminder of what she had been sent here to do. The message specified a drop site outside the National Gallery where she would receive instructions and return information. The requests were fairly simply at first—Talbot's itinerary for an overseas trip, names of people he traveled with, met with, or mentioned; new words or phrases she overheard when he spoke on the phone. She was asked to host dinner parties for Talbot's colleagues, neighbors, friends who held government jobs, and take photos with her new Polaroid camera—her guests fascinated by the astonishing technology and envious that she'd been able to find one to buy. Each time Eleanor deposited the envelope of muddy images at the drop site, she was quite sure they would be of little use.

Two years after she arrived, she retrieved the message that Rémy and his new wife would be moving in next door. They were not to acknowledge their shared past in Florence but instead, act out the little charade at the homeowners' meeting. When she spotted him there, she wished she could rush over and throw her arms around him—the face so familiar, an emblem of her formative experiences in Florence. Once their contact was established—Rémy securing her the job at the library, the friendship extending to include Talbot and Caroline—Eleanor no longer needed the drop sites. She handed her notes directly to Rémy. He provided her a film camera, which she used to take photos of items in Tal's desk drawer, briefcase, coat pockets, and wallet. Within a few days of turning in the completed roll, she would find a camera with fresh film behind a volume of *The Collected Plays of Lillian Hellman* in the Fiction section of the library.

Cossutta sent a letter every so often, routed through Florence and mailed to her office. These always took her by surprise, a jolt to her life and routine. The letters—ostensibly just her old professor saying hello, hoping she was finding time to pursue her art—were reminders that he was watching, that he knew what she was doing and expected her to continue in the cause. At first, she scoured the pages for signs that he missed her, that he wished to have her back, near him. But eventually, she no longer looked for hidden meanings, reading each letter once then dropping it in pieces in a city trash can.

As tension with the Soviets grew and CIA operations broadened, monitoring Talbot grew more sophisticated. While Tal was away on business, Eleanor and Rémy set up a wiretap on his work line and embedded two tiny cameras into the wood paneling in his office. Rémy told his wife he had been at the Bentleys helping Eleanor put a new rug in Talbot's office. It had taken some time, he said, to position it just right.

Despite all she was doing to undermine Talbot, Eleanor began to settle into her American life, growing comfortable as his wife, living into the fiction she had created. When she considered things through the eyes of Eleanor rather than the Soviet operative she was, she found a lot to like. She convinced herself that all she was doing was what her parents had done in Kirov: monitoring those around them, keeping an ear tuned to anything the Soviet government should know about. That's all it was. But she was very glad she worked here, in the United States, where her time was mostly her own. She could visit and revisit museums as often as she wished. She could read what she wanted, see movies and shows that intrigued her, absent any concern a neighbor would see and take exception, or worse, that Tal would chastise or correct her as Cossutta had so often done. She lived in a home more expansive than she could have imagined for herself, finding deep pleasure in choosing drapes and furnishings, and curating her humble collection of art. Talbot accompanied her to estate sales and antique stores as she searched for new treasures, praising her discernment when she found something she simply had to have.

Daily, when he was in town, Eleanor consulted the *Better Homes and Gardens Cookbook* Talbot's mother had sent her on their first wedding anniversary to produce American dishes completely foreign to her — meatloaf with ketchup glaze, chicken fried in Crisco, gelatin salads topped with whipped cream and walnuts. The bounty she found in the grocery store was unlike anything she'd seen, even in the best years in Italy. She liked her library job, buoyed by colleagues who invited her to baby showers and graduations and brought cakes on birthdays. When she and Talbot visited his parents, she reveled in the very idea they could just drive there—no nosy passersby asking about their itinerary as they loaded up the car, no checkpoints along the way to verify that itinerary. They drove unmonitored through miles of gorgeous countryside, the Blue Ridge mountains framing the highway when they headed south, stopping for gas or food that was always available to them.

So it was to be expected, perhaps, that three years in, her double life had created an accumulating pressure inside her, the dissonance harder to manage. In growing so comfortable with her husband, her peaceful life, she feared she might forget she was playing a part, might make an observation or blurt out something that exposed her. She couldn't very well rejoice in the abundance at the market or marvel at their freedom of movement. But she thought about it all the time. She certainly couldn't comment how nice it was that their neighbors never informed on them to authorities. But it astonished her. Her solution was to circumscribe her conversations with Tal, be quieter, more withdrawn, disengaged. He repeatedly asked what was troubling her, where she had gone. She claimed not to understand what he was asking but believed the distance she created was vital to protecting her cover and continuing her work.

But did she have to continue that work? Her contributions to Soviet intelligence seemed minor from her standpoint, inconsequential even. Talbot was a mid-level officer, pushing papers, overseeing budgets—not the key intelligence operative Cossutta hoped he would become. Perhaps Rémy could take over monitoring Talbot—there was so little going on. She would never disclose anything, of course. But what if she became the woman she pretended to be and could live a regular life, here, as an American, perhaps with children one day? Given what she'd sacrificed already, that seemed to her like a fair exchange.

When Cossutta summoned her to New York that first time, she believed the timing was perfect, her opportunity to negotiate easing out of her commitment. Eleanor prepared for their reunion in hopeful anticipation, wholly unprepared for what her onetime lover would demand.

CHAPTER
TWENTY-EIGHT

1950

New York, NY

Eleanor checked her make-up, reapplying a layer of lipstick as she waited, wondering what Cossutta would think of her now, nearly four years after they'd last met. She wished to appear competent, mature in his eyes, to show his confidence in her had been properly placed, that he could trust her judgement now, in wishing to step away.

When she heard his tap on the door, she gave a little start, taking one last glance in the mirror, exhaling to settle herself. She opened the door and there he stood, hand on his hip, a half-smile on his face. He stepped through, eyeing her as he closed the door behind him, placing a package he carried on the credenza. He reached to cup her face in his hands, to take her in, surprising her with a fierce kiss on her mouth.

"My lovely little Starling," he breathed, clasping her hands and drawing back to see all of her. "Here we are." He reached to run a thumb over her lips, rubbing off the cherry red lipstick she had just applied.

"We are, Gilberto, finally," she managed, gesturing to the little table and chairs in the room, feeling a familiar vulnerability that had been a signature of her days in Florence.

He continued to stand before her, hands encircling her wrists. "Look at you. So American now, Mishie, with your painted face and your silk stockings." He swept a hand at her and chuckled. Was it disapproval she heard in his voice? Contempt? "What happened to the long hair I loved? What a shame, Mishie. Must you now go to the salon every week for the working ladies to cut and curl it?" He raked his fingers through the hair at her temples then withdrew to examine his fingertips. "Ack. Lacquer. I can only imagine what your mother would think."

His criticism stung and confused her.

"I'm doing exactly as I promised, Gilberto, exactly what you prepared me to do." She worked to hide the edge in her voice, forcing a smile. "I'm not the teenager I was when we met."

"You've done the job so well I hardly recognize you. But there is a remedy. Underneath those clothes—so *haute couture*, Mishie—I'm sure I'll find the girl I remember."

"Gilberto," she stalled, taking a seat at the table. "You've only just arrived. Please, let's sit a moment and catch up. We haven't been together since…well, I haven't seen you since my wedding day. I want to know how the years have been for you—really— the direction of your sculpting and what you're assigned to do here. I have some things to say too. Shall we order up some drinks? "

His eyes narrowed. Then he chuckled.

"Listen to you, Mishie, speaking as if we are peers now, as if we're meeting to pass to the time of day. Surely you know we are not here, together, in New York City of all places to discuss sculpture. We're here to discuss business and to renew our…friendship." He approached, bringing his face close to hers, one hand leaning on the table, the other reaching up her skirt for her garter, unclipping it so her stocking began a slide down her leg.

"We can chitchat after, Mishie. Right now, it is time we reacquaint ourselves after our long separation, understand?" He straightened and began unbuttoning his shirt. "So. Go wash that face and hurry back to me. Now, my lovely."

And because she had never set a limit with him, had always done as he asked, she acceded, absent any consideration of how she wanted this reunion to proceed. Silently, she retreated to the bathroom, the naughty girl who'd blundered into her mother's make-up. She felt nineteen again, when she'd first grown aware of the high cost of disappointing him. As she ran the washcloth over her face, she wondered if she could fit through the small window above the bathtub. She examined her scrubbed face, eyes full of alarm, fearing there was no clean exit from this path, both her work for the Soviets and pleasing Gilberto. She removed her clothes and slipped on her robe, obedient, always, to her older, wiser professor.

Gilberto perched on the side of the bed, eager, his clothes puddled on the floor. Nearing fifty now, she still found him beautiful, his compact body and trim stomach, the arms and shoulders muscled. But the look on his face, the set of his jaw, was not the same as she'd known in Florence. Silently, he pulled her to his lap—none of the seductive preliminaries, the modulated choreography that first drew her in. He took her in an ardent, urgent coupling, still seated upright, his forehead pressed against her chest, his hands gripping her hips. It was brief. He didn't whisper her name, draw his tongue across her neck, caress the skin of her thighs and breast. Instead of the smooth elegance he'd used to court her, he was brusque and businesslike. When he was finished, he lay back on the bed, forcing her to rise off him and pull away. Eyes fixed on the ceiling, he waved a hand, kissed his fingertips, as if to say that was just the thing he'd wanted. Then he pronounced himself exhausted, moved beneath the covers, and closed his eyes.

She felt a rush of heat at his selfishness, his disregard of her, but she could not summon the words to object. It had always been this way between them. He set the terms, first in how she was to approach her art, then in the rhythm and interplay of their liaisons, and now, in the ways she was obligated to serve the Soviet state and the wider world. Her questions, her opinions, her preference, her needs—he had never asked her what she thought and over time, she had learned not to speak up. But in their years apart, she'd grown accustomed to being attended to, listened to, consulted. Not once had Talbot satisfied himself then pushed her off to retreat under the bedcovers. Talbot. Would he sense what she had done?

While Gilberto slept, she showered and dressed then called room service to request cocktails and dinner. He awoke refreshed and pleased to see sustenance before him, but asked that she call room service one more time to see if there were any Italian wines available. He was annoyed there were none, saying in the future, she might need to bring something with her, or they might book a different hotel.

"And when do you suppose that might be?" she asked.

"Every few months, we will meet to review operations and reacquaint ourselves," he winked.

Midway through their meal, Cossutta rose to retrieve the package he'd left on the credenza. "This is for you to give Talbot. A briefcase, made by Cheney. Very exclusive. And we've customized it, shall we say. Inside is a very sensitive recorder, triggered by sound. It will transmit his conversations to Rémy's tape machine next door."

It was a step beyond what Eleanor wanted to do. "He rarely carries a briefcase," she said, waving a hand. "There are very few documents Tal can take out of the office."

"So then, he will leave it in his office at home and it will pick up chats he has with colleagues who come to your house—to supplement what we get through the wiretap. You can bring them to me when you come."

"Gilberto, I can only take so many shopping trips to New York before it draws attention."

"You'll arrange weekends with these college girlfriends we've invented and insist on museum trips as the artist you once aspired to be. Talbot won't begrudge you that. We can also line your travel up with his so he'll have no idea how often you're away. We have detected no surveillance on you or on Rémy because the Americans—unlike the Soviets—are lazy and stupid." He laughed. "So very stupid. I'm sure you have seen this for yourself. Their devotion to money and comfort makes them too undisciplined to ensure their citizens are behaving properly. But that is all to the good for us, no? A government so loosely constructed—so careless—cannot possibly survive. All your work contributes to the undoing."

"I'm just saying it would be disruptive for me—for my life—to come to New York that often. I have a job now and taking time off work, putting off plans with our friends—someone might notice."

"Disruptive for your life you say?" he said sharply. "I'll remind you that your life is what we direct you to do. Has anyone ever commented about your movements? Your travel? Approached you?"

"Approached? No. Of course not." She took a long pull of her water glass, not wanting to meet his eyes. "You're right, Gilberto, they don't pay attention to ordinary people here. What am I thinking? When I've been walking along the mall, where the museums are, or sitting in Rock Creek Park, DC police have zipped past on their bicycles without a look—more times than I can count. Same in Arlington when Rémy and I have our lunches. And there was the one time," she paused, giving a little laugh, "and you may know about this, when I'd taken photos of a group Tal had over for drinks. I was instructed to take the film to the Soviet Embassy inside a copy of *Anna Karenina*. I told the library I was looking for verification that it was a signed first edition. Of course it wasn't. But no one—not Talbot, none of my colleagues at the library—questioned it. This freedom of movement—just going about unchecked—is a stunning thing. A different world, to be sure."

Her attempt to appease him, to assure him her perspective aligned with his, had failed. Cossutta's eyes clouded. He placed an elbow on the table, chin in hand, a plume from his cigarette circling above him. "Those we work for would not appreciate hearing your praise for this 'freedom of movement,' Mishie."

Eleanor swallowed hard then started to speak. He waved her off, the small shake of his head silencing her.

"Indeed, it is a different world. But remember: it is not better. It will not last. In the Soviet Union, there is proper vigilance, scrutiny, most certainly of foreigners and their families. We know who they meet with, how they spend their time. Here, chaos rules, with all these freedoms, all these opinions, and that will rot this country from the inside out. You understand that, no?"

"I do," she lied.

"Ah. Good. See that you remember that, remember who you are, and what you're here to do. Because if you don't, we will pull you out. Send you home. That's it. Your erstwhile husband could meet an unhappy end, too. Depends."

She gave an uncertain nod and resumed eating her dinner.

Cossutta reached for the wine bottle then pointed at her with his free hand.

"Why do you insist on doing that?" he asked.

"What? Eating? Drinking? I'm enjoying my meal. With you. What am I doing?"

"Holding your fork in your right hand like an American. So…pretentious."

"Gilberto," she sputtered, "it's…it's…how I eat now. This is not to show off or make a point. I can't very well switch back and forth. For God's sakes, it's part of my cover."

"No need to overreact. It's just off-putting, is all. Like you've forgotten who you are."

"My life depends on my forgetting," she said. "We did a lot of hard work so I could present myself as an educated American woman. So that's all I'm doing. That's it."

"As you say. So. We have one more matter of business today. An issue that has concerned me that is, thankfully, easily resolved."

Now is the time, Eleanor thought, to see if she could open the door, at least plant a seed. "Can we discuss the future of my work?"

He shook his head. "Not that. Your fertility. You no longer need it. In fact, it presents problems."

Eleanor's heartbeat accelerated. "What do you mean? That you don't want me having children? We never discussed this…"

"Two issues, Mishie. One, you cannot afford to get pregnant and deliver a black haired baby built like me — not with your tall, athletic American husband. But more than that, there is too much at stake to risk your becoming pregnant at all. Next time you're here, we will take care of it."

"I've been reading. They are working on pills."

"Not pills, my dear. A hysterectomy. No point in taking any chances."

•   •   •

He insisted on a second interlude with her and she cooperated, knowing there was no distracting him when he wanted her, no pleading fatigue. After, he pulled her into the shower with him, dragging a washcloth between her legs as if to make up for his lack of consideration earlier. Rather than arouse her, it merely irritated the soft skin of her thighs. They returned to the bed, where he announced that a back rub would help him relax and within a few minutes, he fell into a deep sleep. His snores helped muffle her sobs. Eleanor lay still, facing away from him, sheet pressed to her face to catch her tears, a fist at her mouth. She had always imagined herself a mother, but here was yet another thing she would be made to relinquish. Would her own mother have agreed to this? She wished she could speak to her — that she had a single person in her life she could trust who could advise her what to do. Given Cossutta's threat to send her away or even harm Talbot, she believed she had no choice but to cooperate.

Sunday night, Eleanor returned to Washington with the beautiful new briefcase. When she presented it to Talbot, the pleased look on his face, his effusive gratitude, nearly broke her. She knew now that she was a danger to him, and resolved to do whatever she had to, to protect them both.

CHAPTER
TWENTY-NINE

1951

New York, NY/Arlington, VA

Nine months later, while Talbot was on an extended trip to London, Eleanor boarded the train for New York a second time, heading to a hotel in the Bronx to meet Cossutta, close to Little Italy where Italian wines were plentiful and cheap. After a restless night, Eleanor awoke to find a chipper Cossutta, urging her into the shower, reminding her not to wear a speck of make-up, forbidding her even coffee before her appointment. In the cab ride to the surgical center, he reminded her not to open her mouth in front of the medical staff.

As she sat in the exam room, a thin sheet clutched awkwardly around her naked body, he explained that this was his niece, mildly retarded but sexually active. He had promised her mother, now deceased, that he would take care of her, make sure the boys she allowed to take advantage of her didn't impregnate her. The staff agreed this was the right thing to do; in fact, it was something they were asked to do all the time.

When Eleanor swam up from the anesthesia, pain sliced across her middle. As she remembered where she was, a deeper, unrelenting pain swelled within her soul. A day later, Cossutta came to retrieve her, ignoring the protests of nurses who insisted the patient needed at least a week's convalescence in the facility. He said he had to take her home because her younger siblings needed him, too. He couldn't manage their needs with her across town in the hospital. Reluctantly, they let her leave, the uncle listening earnestly to every scrap of post-op instructions they offered, promising he would do his utmost to ensure she recovered fully.

Laid out on the bed in the hotel, she endured a difficult week, Cossutta having to get a hold of more penicillin once her incision turned red and angry and began to ooze. She vomited repeatedly, eventually realizing it was a reaction to the painkillers she'd been prescribed. Cossutta made another call and got her some promethazine, which stopped her vomiting but sent her into an immediate dreamless sleep. Each time she awoke, her torso still felt like it was on fire, as she only had aspirin, now, to address the deep gash in muscle and tissue. But uneasy with the blocks of time she lost on the promethazine, she began to drop the pills Cossutta gave her into tissues, which she then gathered and stuffed into her pocketbook. Holding onto multiple doses of the sedative gave her some kind of insurance, she thought, if things truly became intolerable.

• • •

His trip overseas concluded, Talbot was surprised to arrive home to an empty house, the change in time zones and the several glasses of bourbon on his empty stomach making him especially irritable. When he saw Eleanor step from the taxi, pale and unsteady, it alarmed him: had she contracted the flu or worse during his week away? She had been unprepared to see him when he opened the front door, dropping her tote as she reached for him, the afghan she had clutched around her for the past five days spilling out into the foyer. He pressed her to explain what was wrong, where she had been, when she had fallen ill. Why hadn't she asked the office to locate him? He would have rushed home, he said. She responded in an unfamiliar, hollow voice, recounting the terrible conclusion she'd just learned from the doctor that she was sterile. She said she had just come from his office and only just found out. So what he was seeing wasn't physical illness, she insisted, but emotional pain.

As he grew more animated, eager to solve this for her, for them, to find another way, she nearly wept. His kindness. His heartbreak. His belief in her. His wish to find an answer that would restore her hope. But she knew she now must make herself immune to his reassurance, immune to Talbot himself, with his easy charm, his persistent interest in her. She didn't want a second opinion, she said, and she didn't want to adopt. And inside her head, spun a whirl of realizations, about how she'd have to maneuver around the scar now — make love to him in darkness, change clothes when she was sure he wouldn't walk in on her. She and Talbot would never be the same; rather, the Eleanor she had created and Talbot — would never be the same. She had a dance to do, keeping her distance, but still keeping him on a string. She needed him to do her job, to fulfill the obligation to Cossutta, to keep herself in place and Talbot safe. To stay in the home she'd grown to love, keep her job at the library, preserve friendships she'd made — even if they were mostly false and based on lies — to hang on to this stilted independence she had found.

Sunday morning, Talbot said he felt like church might do him some good under the circumstances. Eleanor was still in bed, the Sunday paper in her lap, feeling incrementally better but not completely herself.

"I understand if you're not up to going," he said, moving towards the bathroom to shower. "It's been a tough few days."

"If I stay home, every woman in the Ladies' Auxiliary will call this afternoon and poke around to find out why."

"This is true. It could work out for us, though, Ellie. If I say you're under the weather, we'll have a half-dozen casseroles here by dinnertime. Maybe cookies too."

She laughed, eyes rolling heavenward as if she were weighing the enticement of homemade cookies against spending the afternoon answering the phone.

"I'll come," she said, casting the covers aside.

"Do you want to shower first? Or," he snapped his towel in her direction, "we could save water and do it together."

She claimed to need more coffee, urging him to go ahead.

When she announced herself ready to go, Talbot commented on the raw silk sheath that hung loosely over her slim body — so different from the skirts and tops and belted dresses she usually wore.

•　　•　　•

After the usual preliminaries — the hymns, the announcements, the anthem — Reverend Grant climbed into the pulpit to read the Gospel.

"From Matthew," he began. "'Ye have heard that it hath been said, Thou shalt love thy neighbor, and hate thine enemy. But I say unto you, Love your enemies, bless them that curse you, do good to them that hate you, and pray for them which despitefully use you, and persecute you.'

"Now, were I to ask who our enemy is, our collective enemy, I imagine most of you — most of official Washington for that matter — would say the Soviets. This verse tells us that the only way out of the anxiety we're all living under isn't building more missiles or more nuclear weapons or radiation shelters. It's love. Prayer. 'Doing good to them that hate you.' As we sit here under the nuclear shadow — our new bomb shelter is even now under construction in the basement — I wonder: how might our world transform if we loved our enemy?"

Eleanor wrestled with his argument in her mind, realizing that despite her upbringing, despite Cossutta's indoctrination, she no longer had a clear picture of who her enemy was, who it was who deserved her prayers and love and consideration.

CHAPTER
THIRTY

Friday, June 24, 1960
The Bronx, NY

"So, Mishie, despite your grousing, you are not in peril. There are any number of directions we can take you should you need to disappear." Cossutta reached for another piece of garlic bread. "Kirov, perhaps? It is pleasant enough. The weather may not be as comfortable as Washington, but it's come a long way in the twenty years since you were home."

"There is no home to return to now, Gilberto. You know that. My father has been dead ten years, and I assume mother is still in the home for the aged in Gorky—unless you have new information. My brothers and sisters are scattered. But sure. We can keep Kirov on the list."

She picked at her veal parmigiana, nodding and smiling at Cossutta's small talk, her mind working. What sort of person might she have become had she stayed in Kirov or returned there once the war began? With her mother's influence, her worldview might have turned out much the same. But she would not have had this man regulating her every thought and action.

For twenty years, she had taken his opinions as her own, at first to please him and earn his favor and later, to keep danger at bay. In so doing, she had failed to give expression to her own life except in the smallest ways—the art pieces she brought into her home, the books she consumed by authors banned in the Soviet Union—*Dr. Zhivago, We, Cursed Days*. She wished now she had accepted Cossutta's assignment—she could have done nothing else, as in love with him as she'd been—then come to, woken up and realized what it would cost her. What if she'd had the courage to turn herself over to the Allies once they arrived in Florence? Her knowledge of Russian, Italian, and English might have been an asset they'd been keen to use. But as dependent as she'd been on Cossutta in those days, she had never even considered it.

And here he sat across the table from her, a blot of red sauce on his collar and a wineglass in his hand, the man who had so utterly constrained and directed her life. Who was he to speak so dismissively to her, as if she were still a young girl? To chastise her for legitimate worry?

"If you're finished, my lovely, you're welcome to go on. I'll walk you out."

Eleanor nodded and gathered her things.

•   •   •

As Eleanor exited the taxi at the Concourse Plaza Hotel, she heard a distant swell of cheers and applause; the Yankees were playing at home tonight. They were good this year, she'd heard Talbot say—with Maris and Mantle and Berra. She pictured the stadium packed with fans hoisting beers and boxes of popcorn and for the first time, she envied them. Cossutta found this obsession with sports infantile, evidence of misplaced values, Americans paying more attention to scores and standings than the state of the world. They were cowards, he said, pouring their aggression into battles on the baseball diamond and the football field because they didn't have the courage to wage an actual war. But it struck Eleanor that if all that aggression and hostility were confined to playing fields, there might be less available for battlefields. She wished she were sitting amid a crowd that believed winning a baseball game was the day's most pressing concern. Tal had invited her many times to see the Senators play at Griffith Stadium. She regretted she'd been only once; it was unlikely he'd be free to ask her again.

Eleanor settled into her room, sweeping for surveillance devices in the light fixtures and elsewhere as was her custom, then uncorking two bottles of Amarone. Mario routinely sent over a box of cannolis from his restaurant when she was in New York for these meetings with her "uncle." She poured herself a glass and picked a cannoli from the box.

Within the hour, she heard his familiar knock—a knock she had dutifully answered, year upon year, in hotels on two continents. She opened the door and he strode through, giving a little shake of his head and gesturing at the traveling clothes she still wore. Wordlessly, he turned and reached for the top button of her blouse. She pulled back from him, moving to the club chair by the window, holding up a hand to preserve a boundary around her.

"I'm tired, Gilberto. Can we please just…not."

He threw up his hands and swore.

"Then why are you here, Mishie? We could have communicated any number of ways, but I assume when you agree to see me, it's to do more than discuss operations. Your petulance has grown so very tiresome. And unattractive."

"I came because we need to discuss what's happened in person."

"There's nothing more to discuss. I've had a long day and I'm not interested in games. Work out whatever it is you are feeling—quickly, please—so we can relax and salvage what's left of this evening."

When she failed to respond, he stood to face her, hands on hips.

"Do you take pleasure in disappointing me this way? When we have much to celebrate, getting to this point after these many years?"

She stayed at the table, head bowed, working the hem of her skirt between her fingers. "Maybe I do."

He looked confused. "Do what?"

"Maybe I do want to disappoint you, Gilberto. Maybe I'm tired of pleasing you at my own expense. Maybe I would like to have a part in making decisions for a change."

"Decisions? That is not your role, Mishie."

"Role? Have I no say in what happens to my life and my future? Have you ever thought of what this has cost me?" Blood pulsed at her temple. She worked her hands under her thighs so he would not see them tremble, would not see the pills she had extracted from the hem of her skirt.

Cossutta looked at her for a long minute then moved to the closet. He slid one foot then the other out of his soft leather loafers and reached for a wooden hanger for his jacket. Staring at her all the while, he slowly stepped out of his pants, draping them over another hanger, then unbuttoned his shirt. He returned to the bed and sat, emitting a long sigh, the burdened professor preparing to explain a simple concept to his recalcitrant pupil one more time.

"I will remind you that you've had a glorious life full of purpose and significance because people far more experienced in these things, far more perceptive, make the decisions. Not just me. Others above me." He removed his shirt then pulled off his briefs. "You've lived in the West, worn beautiful clothes, driven a car, owned a home—even had a job with a measure of responsibility—not because there is anything remotely special about you but because of the things set in motion *for* you. I helped give these things to you, Mishie, you understand? The People's Committee for State Security helped give you these things. What you did was for the greater good, but you — YOU — have benefited immensely, tremendously. And it is unseemly — and impermissible, frankly — for you to whine about it now and think you have some say over your circumstances."

He sat naked in front of her, unapologetic, expecting her to acquiesce as she always did.

"Things you set in motion for me," she repeated. "Like the hysterectomy, so I would never become a mother. You certainly set that in motion, wanting to make sure children didn't complicate things. You find it 'impermissible' for me to regret that now?" Tears welled in her eyes.

"Oh, per l'amor del cielo! You had a job to do, Mishie. An important job. One you agreed to, not when you met me but when you left Kirov for Florence. A child would have been dangerous — it could have distracted you. Consider it a kindness that you never had to grapple with that."

"Rémy and Caroline had kids. Rémy grappled just fine. You grappled just fine with your own family. You robbed me of that, Gilberto. All of you did."

His jaw tensed. He rose suddenly, yanking the covers back to get into bed, his back to her, muttering to himself about her ungratefulness. As he did, she moved her hand over the top of his wineglass, dropping three promethazine pills into the Amarone.

He turned toward Eleanor, his breath rapid, skin flushed from his cheeks to his chest. He placed his hands on the arms of her chair, leaning into her face, eyes fixed. "I would suggest we end this conversation before you say something that might haunt you later. These emotions, Mishie, how many times do I have to say it? They do not become you. They're so..." he cast about for a word, "weak. American. Short-sighted. In fact, I believe we have indeed reached the end of your usefulness in this country. It is time for you to leave. Excellent timing, now that I think about it. That will solve things entirely." He moved a hand to her upper arm and squeezed hard, drawing her towards him, forcing her to stand.

"Now I suggest you join me in bed. Wash up and calm yourself. Do not make me ask again."

She nodded, recognizing she had not timed this well, that she had crossed into treacherous territory and said far more than was safe. She had always been hyper-vigilant to his moods, calibrating her behavior and viewpoint to mirror his. She had never challenged him like this and having done so this one time, his immediate reflex was rid himself of her, remove her from his world. She had always complied with him because on some level, she had always known this is how he would respond. She prayed he would stop short of hurting her.

She heaved a sigh and leaned forward, resting her head on his shoulder. He reached an arm around her, moving his hips into hers. She didn't resist, nuzzling his neck, the scent of garlic on his breath, sweat on his bare skin, familiar and repellent.

"Okay," she said. "Okay." She reached for a tissue to dab her eyes then reached for his hand.

"I'm so sorry. Gilberto. I'm sorry. This has just been a lot to bear and I have no one to talk to about it—no one to voice my thoughts to but you. I've been upset—and it's made me mean and foolish. I see that now. And Gilberto, you're right as you always are. If I'm honest with myself, I know a child would have limited me. I couldn't have contributed as deeply as I wanted to do. That's the most important thing. So forgive me for getting emotional. Women can be a ball of sensitivities sometimes, can't we? You know that as well as I do."

"A perpetual problem, my little Starling, and one you must master. I have begged you to work on this." His hard eyes did not match his sympathetic words.

She gave him an apologetic little smile. "I won't do it again. I assure you." She handed him his wineglass and began unbuttoning her blouse. "I'm sure my face is a mess with all these tears. Give me a minute—let me get cleaned up."

He reached for her face, gave her cheek a sharp pat, then turned to the Amarone.

Eleanor closed the bathroom door and locked it, standing a few minutes with her face in her hands—her world, once again, reduced to a hotel bathroom, a tiny realm of privacy where she could think. She didn't undress but turned on the shower and smoked successive cigarettes, cracking the window to let the smoke escape, giving the promethazine time to work. She had finally arrived at the crossroads that had loomed for so many years. It involved more than political systems and power, whether the world and the people in it were better off as communists or socialists or free-wheeling capitalists. It had to do with the life she wanted to live and never had. She knew she could not for one minute longer subjugate herself to this system or this man.

After fifteen minutes, she cracked the bathroom door and listened. He was snoring. She'd had no idea how potent nine year-old promethazine pills might be. Potent enough, apparently. Soundlessly, she removed Talbot's briefcase from her suitcase and placed it in the closet; Gilberto would have to figure out how to dispose of it. She placed their wineglasses on the bedside tables, rinsing his, but leaving a residue of wine in hers. She emptied the bottles of Amarone into the bathroom sink, dribbling a bit on his pillow and placing the bottles on the bed. He would think they had gotten very, very drunk. She withdrew a few things from her suitcase — a canvas tote, then a nightgown and panties which she dropped beside the bed. She stuffed her make-up and hairbrush into the tote, and grabbed her cardigan. Then she slipped on her shoes and stepped into the hall, easing the door closed behind her. She avoided the elevator to run down the staircase so she would have more places to hide if he awoke quickly and found her gone. She was grateful there was no one at the front desk when she whirled through the revolving door and out into the street.

CHAPTER
THIRTY-ONE

Friday and Saturday, June 24-25, 1960
Washington, DC

Cossutta was mostly correct that the U.S. government had not kept an eye on private citizen Eleanor Bentley these many years, had not followed her comings and goings. Her fake birth certificate, her origin story in Massachusetts, had gone unquestioned, as the Cold War accelerated and there were more urgent issues to track. But her sudden trip to New York caught the attention of both George Jeffrey and the Counterintelligence team. With Talbot marooned in their townhouse, it struck both as an odd time for a shopping trip to Manhattan. And indeed, the merest investigation revealed it wasn't a shopping trip at all. The Americans, it turned out, were not quite as stupid or lazy as Cossutta believed.

As Eleanor had failed to retain a lawyer to represent her interests, George continued working at the margins, managing the back and forth with the government for both Bentleys, knowing there might be a point where the interests of his two newest clients diverged. With Eleanor claiming she had no living family, George decided to poke around at Smith, hoping to find a former colleague or friend of her family who might direct him toward a distant relative, or a benefactor, perhaps, who would remember Eleanor and her father's service to the college.

Instead, he learned that the one "Dr. Halsey" who'd been on faculty at the school was still living outside Northampton, a spritely 80-year-old who had taught geography, not economics, and had never married. He was also hard of hearing which made their long-distance phone conversation a challenge.

"The Dr. Halsey I'm looking for died in 1935. He would have been 52, 53. An economics professor. His family remained in faculty housing after his death, the wife doing clerical work for an office on campus. Is it possible your paths simply didn't cross?"

"How old do you say he was when he passed away?" asked the retired Dr. Halsey.

"Fifty-ish."

"Impossible. We'd be nearly the same age. Had he been here, we would have bumped up on one another all over campus. It's not a large community. We met regularly as a full faculty, socialized frequently. You've got your facts wrong, sir. My hearing may be poor, but my memory is not. As for a family living in faculty housing: I can think of no professor I've known over these many years who ever did such a thing. That housing was reserved for single people, newly marrieds sometimes, for a semester or two as people transitioned in and out. But there was no school housing that could have handled a family of four, year upon year."

Intrigued by George's questions, Dr. Halsey said he would ask around among his friends and former colleagues one more time. But he was quite sure George had the wrong place entirely. Had he tried Vassar?

•   •   •

Believing he had a fairly full picture of one Helen Sizemore, Jerry Engwall turned his attention to Talbot's wife, Eleanor. Much like Talbot's attorney, he had failed to unearth much about her that confirmed her life story. There was no birth certificate on file in Northampton, no record of her matriculation at the university in Florence, no manifest with her name on it that confirmed she'd sailed to Europe in 1938. But an absence of proof meant nothing: Eleanor could have been born outside Northampton, and records could be misfiled, lost over time. What he needed was something affirmative, something that contradicted what she claimed. So far, he'd found none of that.

Engwall learned in a scheduling call with Jeffrey that Mrs. Bentley was headed to New York and would be unavailable for further questions or interviews until the following week. She was taking the train. So Engwall called a buddy at the FBI office in Manhattan and asked that a subject arriving at Penn Station from DC, midday Friday, be tailed. Late Friday night, the buddy phoned.

"Hey Jerry, it's Clark. You got it right. Something's going on with this girl," he chuckled.

Engwall's stomach flipped. "What can you tell me?"

"Well, she got to Manhattan then rode the subway up and down the tracks, changing trains, changing directions—classic anti-surveillance activity—before she ended up at Mario's in Little Italy in the Bronx. Met a man there."

"An affair, you think?"

"Maybe. Brian came with me tonight and we both think it's something beyond that. All the train-changing, plus she changed her hat, her jacket like a pro. The guy she met—kinda old and foreign. Had an accent of some kind—thought it was Spanish, but it's Italian. We waited across the street while they had dinner and watched through the window—their posture, their gestures—seemed kinda tense between them. She seemed mad."

"Lovers' spat maybe?"

"Maybe. So after they finish, she got in a cab, and he went to the subway. We followed her to the Concourse Plaza Hotel a few blocks away. About an hour later, he shows up. So we did our usual thing. Brian puts on the old uniform smock from the laundry and took some men's shirts to the front desk. Said he needed to deliver them but forgot the customer's name. Brian describes him and the guy at the desk gives a little smirk and says, 'Yeah, that guy isn't here, you know what I mean?' So Brian says, 'A regular, huh?' And the desk guy just laughs harder. Says he's a prof over at Fordham. Teaches art. He's come to the hotel with a bunch of different women. Brian keeps him laughing and then palms himself on the forehead and says he just realized he's at the wrong hotel. Says there must be another old foreign guy somewhere doing some extra-curricular canoodling and waiting for his laundered shirts. 'Great story, though' he tells the desk guy as he leaves. So at the very least, your girl is stepping out. You want me to stay here? See if he stays with her all night?"

"Could you? Hope you didn't have big Friday night plans. This investigation is kind of important."

"Yeah. We can manage. And I've got more. Brian popped over to Fordham — it's only a few blocks away. Looked him up in the faculty directory. The guy's name is Gilberto Cossutta. Italian. He teaches sculpture and Renaissance art history."

"No kidding. Wonder if she met him during the war."

"Guess that's for you to find out, Jerry. Thanks for the fun and games. I'll be in touch."

•   •   •

As a near-comatose Cossutta snored at the hotel, Eleanor took a direct route to Penn Station, making it easy to track her. When she arrived at Union Station in DC in the early hours of Saturday morning, a member of Engwall's team watched her sit quietly, pensively on the station's torn vinyl seats until well after the sun rose. Around eight, she left her seat and entered the phone booth outside the station. She placed two calls, weeping violently through the first one, stabbing at the air with her free hand. She was more composed during the second call, but tears still slipped down her face. Then she stepped outside the phone booth to light a cigarette and hail a cab.

CHAPTER
THIRTY-TWO

Saturday, June 25, 1960
New York, NY/Washington, DC/Arlington, VA

While Eleanor was en route from New York to Union Station, Jerry Engwall heard back from the sources he'd tapped to glean something about this Italian professor who'd suddenly appeared in Eleanor's life. Engwall was unsurprised to learn he'd taught at the school Eleanor Bentley said she had attended in Florence. So theirs was a long-standing relationship, perhaps one of the few anchors in her life, he thought. Given that they seemed to be romantically involved, Eleanor could not very easily introduce the professor into her life with Talbot.

The team on the Europe Desk at CIA had been up all night running down the professor's background. They had encountered gaps—years where he didn't seem to be employed and years where they couldn't find him at all. Cossutta stopped teaching in 1939, as the war in Poland forced the university in Florence to close. They'd spoken with the current dean of the art department at the University of Florence, who had subsisted during the war years by doing commissioned portraits and small art projects—even consenting to painting a ghastly mural of Hitler and Mussolini inside a Florence restaurant. He recalled being puzzled in those days at Cossutta's lack of employment when he had a young family to feed. Cossutta had been frequently seen in the company of a female student in those years, but that was not unusual; these types of relationships were common among university professors. Post-war, when the university began hiring again, the dean held a couple conversations with Cossutta who seemed eager to return to teaching. But soon after, he said, Cossutta and his family left Florence. The dean never saw the young student again either.

"So here's our analysis—very raw," said the lead officer on the Europe Desk. "He went off somewhere in Eastern Europe to teach, a place where we really don't have good eyes, and three years later—1950—came over to Fordham, somewhere along the line shedding the wife and kids. He's been there about ten years now. Lives pretty quiet, hasn't really made any waves. Busy dating life, apparently, according to the reception desk at the Concorde."

"Divorced?"

"Not that we can find."

"Okay. Keep looking, will ya? I'm curious about that three-year gap."

"We're on it, Jerry."

The second he hung up, Engwall's phone rang. It was the Bentleys' attorney.

•   •   •

Eleanor rested her head on the back of the seat as the cab made the short trip across a city just waking up. The route took them down Louisiana Avenue, across to Constitution and past her favorite places—the National Gallery of Art, The Smithsonian Castle, the Museum of Natural History—the Capitol Building and the Washington Monument standing watch on either side. Tourists were already filtering into the city, armed with pamphlets and guidebooks, cueing up at museum doors, their children hopping around in anticipation. She recalled winding through these galleries with Tal and Caroline, the delightful surprise of encountering a piece just added to the collection, the borrowed pride she felt for a city striving to establish an artistic core. She doubted she'd have the chance to do so again, given what she was about to do.

The cab pulled up to Lafayette Square where George Jeffrey waited at the curb. The cabbie hopped out to open Eleanor's door, eager perhaps to place the woman with the tear-ravaged face into someone else's custody. George paid him then reached for her tote. He'd spoken with the rector, he said. He was waiting in his study.

They entered the empty vestibule that served as the reception area for St. John's Church. George paused, placing a hand on her arm.

"Mrs. Bentley, I was happy to make myself available for this meeting. But if you need to make a confession or pray or get some counsel, I'm not sure I need to be here."

At that moment, Reverend Grant emerged from his study to wave them in. His kind face brought a fresh rush of tears from Eleanor. She shook her head at George, unable to speak. As she entered the study, the Rector pulled her into an embrace then gestured for them both to sit. She sank into the sofa with George next to her, the rector in his rocking chair in front of them.

"So," said Grant reaching out to clasp one of Eleanor's hands within his two. "Here we are, Mrs. Bentley. Time to end this then? Time for a new chapter."

"It is, Reverend," she responded.

"What the hell is happening?" George demanded.

And for the first time in twenty years, Marisha Yahontov spoke the truth of her life aloud, her story building, cascading, tumbling out. There was her childhood in the Soviet Union, daughter of a party official eager to win favor with her comrades against the backdrop of Stalin's purges. The teenager who traveled to Florence, having made a deal with her mother to serve the State while she studied art. Then the development of the relationship with Cossutta that began with her admiration of his artistry and progressed into a devotion so complete that she relinquished her identity to serve his purposes. And finally, Talbot, the unwitting target who gave her the ticket she needed to come to this country, to spy on him, on America, to undermine efforts to hold back the Soviets.

As her story unspooled, Grant sat quietly, holding her hand and nodding when her emotions overwhelmed her, passing her tissues, telling her she could slow down — he had plenty of time. George, meanwhile had stood from her opening words and now paced, hand rubbing his jaw, his head, the back of his neck. He struggled not to interrupt, asking questions then withdrawing them, muttering "holy shit" again and again then apologizing, given the location of the meeting.

Eleanor sketched out her activities over the years, the photos she'd passed on, the names of people in his office, schematics of his building. And finally, the conversations picked up by the device in the briefcase that helped the Soviets improve their defense systems and had apparently played a part in Powers' U-2 falling out of the sky. At this, George stilled, one hand over his mouth, the other limp at his side.

And then she fell silent, eyes red-rimmed and puffy, and asked if anyone could spare a cigarette. George pulled out one for her and as he lit it, they locked eyes.

"What are you expecting me to do with this, Mrs. Bentley? If I should even call you that. You've got clergy here, so are you thinking we're your shield? Because I'm struggling here. I still represent your husband. This is espionage — and I cannot ignore it as Tal's lawyer — as the person hired to defend him. I'm sorry."

Eleanor shook her head. "I didn't bring you here for a religious confession, so I can waltz out of here, conscience clear. But saying all this — the truth I have wanted to acknowledge for so long — well, there's something to be said for that. But no, George, I'm not trying to shield myself. I'm trying to help Talbot recover his life. None of this is his fault. It's mine. I'll pay the consequences."

"And by that you mean?"

"You need to contact Chamberlain to get Tal out from under this." She turned to Grant. "I'm sorry I've lied all these years, in this, of all places. I called you because…if anyone could still summon some kindness for me, as I try to set things right, I thought it might be you."

"Mrs. Bentley, none of us is exactly the person we present to the world, or the person we believe ourselves to be. Although," and here he gave a little wince, "I'd agree, you have gone a bit farther than most."

"Well, thank you Reverend, for picking up the phone, for listening to me. I won't burden you further. But I suppose all of this is about to be splashed all over the papers—so you'll be able to keep up with what happens to us."

"Not a burden, Mrs. Bentley. You're a member of my flock. It's my duty to walk alongside even those lambs that stray far out of the pasture."

•   •   •

At noon, the phone rang at the townhouse. Talbot ignored it for ten long rings. It stopped then resumed a beat later. He lifted the receiver to find Jerry Engwall on the line, saying he and Chamberlain were headed over, along with Talbot's attorney. And Eleanor. She would be coming there too.

"Fraid she's out of town, said Talbot. "Shopping in New York."

"Actually, Mr. Bentley, she's back in DC. And we've got a lot to discuss."

CHAPTER
THIRTY-THREE

Saturday, June 25, 1960
The Bronx, NY/Arlington, VA

It was two in the afternoon when Cossutta finally roused himself, much of the prior evening a complete blank. He called out for Eleanor, the wine bottles on the bed clanking as he moved to sit up. When she didn't answer, he rose and looked around the room. Her suitcase was still here but her purse was not. The discarded nightgown and panties, the drained wine bottles, meant things must have gone reasonably well. But then he remembered their fight, her insolence, her unreasonableness, his threat to send her away followed by her rapid acquiescence and apology. So she was off pouting somewhere, he thought. She'd probably left him to get something to eat, then decided to shop, perhaps to gather things she would want to take back with her to Kirov, or wherever she ended up. She'd left no note, and failed to phone the hotel or get a message to him the entire afternoon. Her exposure to the Americans had ruined her, he decided, with her overwrought emotions and anxiety over her physical safety. When she returned, he would tell her, forcefully, that she'd been insubordinate, that she didn't enjoy the latitude she seemed to think she had. She had once been so useful, so compliant, he thought, so willing to do what was necessary. This country had been the worst kind of influence on her.

It was for this very reason that he hadn't brought his wife to New York when the job had been arranged for him at Fordham. He had worried she would be hard to control. She hated her life in Moscow and complained bitterly about it. Had he let her come to the United States, she might have exposed him out of spite. So when the Centre told him she could move to New York with him—the children dispatched to various boarding schools—he declined the offer. His wife had become quite attached to Moscow in the four years they'd lived there, he explained. How could he ask her to move away from a city she loved? He did arrange to fly her out of Moscow once a year—to the Greek Islands, Turkey, the Black Sea—some oceanside spot where he could fawn over her, assuage her anger, and remind her of the importance of his work. Had she been more trustworthy, she could have lived in New York with him, shopping at the Italian delis, strolling the Boardwalk on Coney Island, and eating Mario's fine pasta. But she'd never really gotten over leaving Florence. She was a woman who held grudges.

At dinnertime, Cossutta waved to the desk clerk, bypassing the subway to take a head-clearing walk to Mario's, Talbot's briefcase in hand. He turned down the alley next to the restaurant, cut across the back, and deposited the briefcase in the vast dumpster used by the fishmonger. A shame, he thought. It was a beautifully-crafted attaché.

Mishie must still be sulking in a Macy's dressing room or bistro somewhere, he decided, having spoiled his weekend entirely. He was ready for a bottle of wine—or two—to take his mind off all this. But whether it was his growing fury or a lingering fog from the sedative in his wine, he had failed to spot unassailable evidence Eleanor was not coming back: her make-up and the cardigan she carried everywhere were gone. Moreover, he failed to take countermeasures as he walked, no doubling back or quick turns to shake anyone who might be tailing him. It made Clark's surveillance of him almost too easy, the retrieval of the Cheney briefcase taking mere minutes.

•   •   •

Talbot expected to see Chamberlain and Engwall when he opened his front door, but there stood the rector, a tight-lipped smile on his face.

"Reverend, hello. I'm so sorry, but it's not a good time," said Talbot. "I've got a meeting."

"I'm aware, Talbot. Is there coffee? We may need some." He brushed past his perplexed host, casting about in the kitchen for supplies to make the coffee. "Any snacks around, Talbot?"

"A few profiteroles, I think," Talbot responded, surprised that the normally intuitive rector wasn't taking the hint. While Grant searched for a plate to lay out the leftover pastries, more people clattered through the front door and into the kitchen.

Eleanor stood before him, disheveled, her face a map of pain and sorrow. George stood next to her, head bowed. Chamberlain and Engwall, along with two men Talbot didn't recognize, approached and announced they had a bit of looking around to do.

"What's this?" asked Talbot. "What's happened, Eleanor? Are you okay?" He reached for her hand, to pull her into an embrace. She leaned hard against him, but said nothing. "Chamberlain? Who are those guys?"

"They're on our team," Chamberlain said. "Checking the usual—light fixtures, lamps, and the record player so we can't be overheard."

"Office is clean—now," one of them announced, displaying two tiny cameras in his palm.

"Guess the other guys missed those," said Chamberlain. "Always helps to know where to look." He turned to Talbot, whose face registered utter confusion, and placed a hand on his arm. "Ok, Officer Bentley — Talbot — as you see, we've got some things to discuss. Let's go into the living room, if you don't mind. Reverend, can you fetch me a cup of coffee?"

As Grant puttered in the kitchen, the assemblage took seats in the living room. Engwall withdrew the ubiquitous tape recorder from the case and one of the newly arrived counterintelligence agents pulled out a notebook and pen. Talbot sat next to Eleanor on the sofa, a protective arm curled around her shoulder.

"Talbot, some new information has surfaced about the U-2 deal and how it affects the charges against you, so we're here to discuss that."

"What is it? Helen admitted she's been lying?"

There was a beat of silence before Engwall waded in. "It's not Miss Sizemore we're here to discuss. It's what your wife has told us. What's she's admitted to."

George renewed his objection to their discussing the situation with all parties present, pleading for a word alone with Talbot.

"You're my attorney too," Eleanor reminded him, "and I am ready to proceed with this meeting." Talbot stared at her, unable to work out what was going on.

George threw up his hands, saying the only good thing about continuing the meeting was the grounds for appeal it would offer down the road.

"What the hell are you talking about?" Talbot demanded. "Can someone clue me in here?"

Eleanor reached into her pocketbook for a cigarette, Talbot leaning over to light it. She gave her husband a tired smile, and then, for the second time that day, began unburdening herself of the lies around which she'd wrapped their life. She spoke slowly, deliberately, about Kirov and Florence, how the professor who'd housed her during the war had in fact, been her lover. Talbot grew progressively more pale, removing his arm from her shoulder, raking a hand through his hair, his breaths coming short and quick, alarm and pain in his eyes.

"I don't believe this. How? How did you hide this from me? All this time? Why are you telling me this now? With all these people here?" he asked.

She gave a small shrug. "Because it's not over, Talbot."

Her husband's face contorting in pain, Eleanor explained how she had continued to work for the Soviets after they came to Washington, how Cossutta had re-entered her life some years earlier, operating out of New York to supervise her.

Talbot rose and walked down the hall to the bathroom, his loud retching that of a man bereaved, heartsick, in shock. Eleanor wept at hearing Talbot so physically ill, so disconsolate. The rector excused himself and went to Talbot, his voice low and steady as Talbot sobbed. When the two men returned to the living room, Talbot took a seat across from his wife, his head bowed, not looking at her.

"Tell me something. When did Cossutta come here? To the U.S."

"Ten years ago. 1950."

"About the time you started meeting your friends in New York."

"Yes. I went there to meet him. He summoned me. I had no choice."

"Was this pure business, Eleanor, all these times you were up there?"

Eleanor studied her cigarette. "He expected me to sleep with him. It was always a part of things." Engwall and Chamberlain exchanged a look. The other two men shifted uncomfortably. George continued to pace.

"So that explains, finally, why I couldn't come to New York with you."

Eleanor nodded.

"So Caroline? She's in on this?"

"No, no. We did go up to shop, and there were women we socialized with. But they weren't my college classmates, obviously. And when Caroline would wear out and go to our hotel—late Friday or late Saturday—I went to my meetings."

"Meetings," Talbot sneered. "Your trysts, you mean."

"He controlled me, Talbot, in every way. Please understand that."

"What did this involve, Eleanor, the things you were doing to undermine me?"

George interjected. "I'd like to wait until we've got the paperwork signed before we discuss all of this. I mean, we've agreed in principle to some things, but I have nothing in hand."

Eleanor waved him off and kept talking.

"At first, it was small things, Talbot. Minor things. Your itinerary. Names of people you met with or who called you at home. It was information so easy to collect, it didn't seem all that ...terrible."

"And you passed this along how?"

"Dead drops. I had three sites in the city where I left notes and retrieved instructions."

Talbot looked like he'd taken a blow to the stomach. "How could I not know this?" he asked no one in particular, "you running all over the city, doing dead drops, for god's sakes."

"I didn't run around, really. One was outside the National Gallery—lots of tourists there to hide what I was doing. Another was in Rock Creek Park. The third was inside my library. One particular shelf." She stubbed out her cigarette and lit another. "It was so easy—and infrequent—that I believed it wasn't important. And after a couple years, after we'd settled here, and this place began to feel familiar to me, I wanted out. Partly because I wasn't unearthing anything of value and partly because I wanted to make my pretend life real. But Gilberto arrived and made it clear to me there was no getting out."

Talbot went quiet, thinking. "I seem to remember, Eleanor, that once you began running up to New York every few months, things went to shit for us. Before that, I thought we had something pretty good. And then, out of the blue" — he snapped his fingers — "now I know why."

"Perhaps we can leave that aspect of things alone for…" began Chamberlain but Eleanor interrupted, speaking as if she and her husband were the only two in the room.

"I couldn't get out of it, Talbot. I wanted to. I did. I was 19 when this started — 19! What did I know about what I was getting in to? That first trip, I rehearsed how I would tell him I didn't want to do it anymore. But he threatened me — I was afraid he would hurt you, Talbot. Or worse. I created that distance so I wouldn't know as much about what you were doing — so there would be less to pass along."

"So you were protecting me! Aren't you thoughtful!" Talbot thundered.

"I did protect you, yes," Eleanor said, "the only way I knew how."

Talbot turned to Chamberlain.

"So what damage has she done? To me, to the country. Are you going to incarcerate her? Deport her?"

"She's admitted to multiple acts of espionage, Talbot, that involve surveilling you and passing what she found on to the Soviets. At first, she mostly monitored you — observable things anyone could find out. But then, they got her a camera, installed a recording device in your office, wiretapped your phone. We found a couple of small cameras in your office, but they don't appear connected to anything. We think over many, many months, she passed along bits of information on the flight plans on the U-2 mission. Nothing like the documents Sizemore showed us. But we think things you said on the phone here — sites you were targeting over there, your concerns about the weather, wanting to pull this together before the Paris Summit —

we think the Soviets cobbled all that together and it gave them a timeline and a flight path to intercept Powers and shoot him down. There's still a lot to be sorted out."

"I was surveilled here in this house."

"You were. Phone taps, a recording device in your briefcase. The FBI got their hands on that in New York just a couple hours ago. So—for now, we're gonna leave the tap on your phone lines while we continue the investigation."

Bewildered, hurt, humiliated, Talbot put his face in his hands. "And I'm the goddam intelligence officer who let her in, allowed this to happen."

Engwall spoke up. "And that's something we still need to resolve, Officer Bentley. How you were fooled. Whether you were fooled. You understand."

"I fooled him. I fooled everyone," Eleanor insisted. "He didn't know. You can see he didn't know."

"So you lived this lie with everyone at your office, with all our friends, with Caroline and Rémy…"

"Not Rémy, no," she said quietly,

"What the hell does that mean?"

Chamberlain spoke up. "It means, Talbot, that she had a partner. Rémy Auclair was working with her. And she's agreed now to bring him to us, and take down Cossutta and perhaps others in his cell. So we're not at the end of this yet, Talbot. Not by a long shot."

"Rémy too," breathed Talbot. "Jesus."

After a long silence, Chamberlain rose to conclude the meeting and forecast what lay ahead.

"Here's where we are. As Jerry said, there's work to do, unraveling the U-2 shoot down. We'll stay on that. For now, both of you are going to remain here in the house and out of sight. Mrs. Bentley, you'll call the library and explain with your husband's troubles, you've decided you need the next few weeks off. Because you left New York like you did, we expect

Cossutta's people will be watching your movements and we don't want to make it easy in case they want to talk to you—or take you. We have people in the neighborhood looking for vehicles or people who seem out of place. Cossutta is still up in that hotel room—we've got a team watching him—waiting for you to return, so you haven't set off any alarm bells with him yet. So for now, act as normal as you can, especially with the Auclairs. Let Rémy know about your quick departure from Cossutta; say you had a lover's spat, you're really, really sorry and need him to let Cossutta know. Hopefully, he buys it and we wait for Rémy to bring your next set of instructions—probably instructions on your exfiltration from Washington. Then we'll go from there."

"Do I follow instructions when I get them?" Eleanor asked.

"You do. If you're required to travel, we'll be with you. If you're asked to visit a drop site, we'll have people there. And if Cossutta or Rémy press you for information, you say you're trying, but you ain't got squat because CIA cut Talbot off from everything. The tap stays on your home phone line on for now—our side will be listening too—but we're gonna muddy up the tap on your office line so we'll be able to use it without them hearing."

Eleanor nodded hesitantly.

"Listen, Mrs. Bentley. You need to stay in the game and be cooperative. They're making their plans to get their hands on you, which will take a few days. Don't give them reason to think you're not on their team or they'll swoop in and take you before we're ready."

Eleanor nodded. "I'll do whatever you ask."

"Duly noted."

As the group dispersed, George spoke quietly with Talbot, saying the case would now pivot around Eleanor's cooperation, Talbot's future tied to how the next few weeks played out. He clapped Talbot on the shoulder, told him to keep the faith, saying they'd speak later.

Before he departed, Rector Grant promised to bring dinner one night next week, advising Talbot and Eleanor to get enough sleep and nourishment so they could manage themselves through this. Then he let Talbot know that, since he'd be missing the next vestry meeting, he'd mail the meeting minutes for Talbot to review. Talbot shook his head as he departed, noting the absurd kernel of normalcy embedded in the rector's remarks.

CHAPTER
THIRTY-FOUR

Saturday, June 25, 1960
Washington, DC

Approaching a month in pre-trial detention, Helen was losing both weight and hope. The feds had marked her the highest security risk so she couldn't get bail. Her attorney-cousin had shared no timetable for when her case might get a hearing. She remained isolated from the rest of the prison population so no one could pump her for information, but already, the press was breathlessly piecing together her role in the U-2 scandal. When a *Washington Post* reporter called cousin Todd and asked if his cousin, Beatrice, was the one who worked for Talbot Bentley in the FBI, he'd helpfully clarified that it was Helen who worked for Bentley at CIA.

"All I need," chirped the reporter and only then did Todd—unfamiliar with the tactics of determined journalists—realize he'd been bested. And when the neighbor on the other side of Helen's duplex confirmed to a second reporter that he'd seen government agents cart Helen Sizemore away, the alleged paramour had been identified.

During her long, unchanging days, Helen lay on her cot, recalling how it had felt each day to arrive at work, to sweep down the hushed, carpeted hallways toward the elevator, to fix a coffee, then review the calendar at her very own desk as she prepared for the day. She'd stand to receive important files from the courier who came to Talbot's office each morning, signing her name to his paperwork in an increasingly illegible script, the way Talbot and other senior employees did. At lunch, she'd sip iced tea and laugh with other secretaries in the cafeteria, all of them dreaming and plotting their next steps, whether it was attracting the attention of a certain person, or moving up in the ranks. She wondered how her little home was, who was feeding her cat, whether the neighbor on the other side of the duplex was cutting her side of the yard. Her houseplants were likely all dead now, she realized, the food in her fridge spoiled and stinking. And at this, she cried, angry at her own stupidity in falling for a married man in the first place, thinking she could outplay him. She no longer cared about having a career in intelligence: she just hoped to regain her freedom.

Late one afternoon, told her lawyer had arrived for a meeting, she was almost too despondent to rise from her cot to see him. She wasn't in the mood to hear him explain yet again he'd made no progress. But, she decided, at least she'd get to walk down the corridor, see a slightly different shade of urine yellow on the walls of the meeting room. An hour outside her cell would help pass the time. She arrived to find cousin Todd with a wide smile on his face.

"Get ready to go," he said.

"Go where?"

"Outta here. Just got a call. They're sending over a plea deal. Time served. Probation. No trial."

Helen asked him to repeat himself, sinking into the metal chair as he did.

"What's the catch? Do I have to testify against Talbot? Is that it? I'm not sure I can."

"Nope. No testimony. We don't want to go there and we don't have to. This is it. They're charging you under U.S. Code 18 section 1924. Unlawful retention of documents—that you retained them improperly in photographic form. But then you gave them back. They've dropped the security violations related to your entering Bentley's office and possessing the keys. That's gone. So you'll need to pay a fine—five-hundred bucks—but they've reduced it to a single misdemeanor. You could even continue to work for the government at some point if you wanted—just not at CIA."

"How did this happen, Todd?" she asked. "What made them offer this?"

"No idea, Helen. They came to me with this deal, tied up in a bow."

Todd explained government lawyers would be coming later so she could sign the deal. It would take a day or two to be approved by the court. After that, she'd be released and could return to her home, with the provision of monthly check-ins with a probation officer for the next twelve months.

"One more thing, Helen, and this is critical. We'll talk more about this when we meet with the government. The story about you that will come out in the papers is gonna be a little different from what's actually happening. You aren't to let on that you won't be testifying. When reporters call—and they will—you say you stand ready to provide your truthful testimony in the case against Talbot Bentley."

"What's the point of that? Talbot didn't do anything—well, not that I know of. Do they have something else on him?"

"I think it may be more complicated than that—like there may be some other people they want to confuse or draw out and you saying you'll testify helps do that."

Helen processed this new twist, then erupted in a convulsive cackle—her first laugh in many weeks, since before Eleanor's birthday, before she'd last been with Tal at the townhouse. But she suddenly found her situation very, very funny. They were asking her to do something clandestine. She recognized misdirection when she saw it. At last, she thought, the CIA is using me on a case. The very thing she'd wanted since she first joined the intelligence service.

•   •   •

Curled on her cot that afternoon, knowing she had only hours left in confinement, Helen wept over the wild turn her life had taken, how radically her perspective had shifted in just a few weeks. Had someone told her a year earlier—when she first arrived in Talbot's office—that her brief CIA sojourn would culminate this way, she would not have believed it. She had trusted her upbringing, her education, to create a smooth career trajectory, free of stumbles and mistakes, immune to sexual traps and temptations. Other girls, she once thought, stupid girls were the ones who made ill-advised choices and got caught up in terrible situations. Not her. Not Helen.

Her former self could never have imagined embarking on the affair or cultivating the spite and anger that ultimately led to her arrest. Love, she now knew, made you do strange things. Crossing one line made it easier to cross another. She resolved to be a little kinder to all those girls she once considered stupid now that she was one of them. It was a fitting end to her time at CIA, getting to play the role in public of the aggrieved secretary intent on telling the truth about her untrustworthy boss. She would enjoy that, maybe get a new dress in case the TV cameras came around. Helen Sizemore, ladies and gentlemen, portraying the scorned woman in a CIA production. But after this, she never, ever wanted to be in any type of situation—personally or in her career—that required her to lie and be convincing at it. When all this was behind her, after she'd fulfilled the terms of her probation, she thought she might move to Williamsburg—or maybe Virginia Beach, but away from Washington anyway—to start over. She intended to take the very hard lessons she'd learned from entering into a disastrous, disingenuous love affair and embark on a different kind of life.

CHAPTER
THIRTY-FIVE

Saturday and Sunday, June 25-26, 1960
Arlington, VA

Alone, finally, Eleanor and Talbot had so much to say but no words to say it. Once George and the others left, Eleanor sat mute at the kitchen table, steeled for Tal's assault. He milled about for a few minutes, dumping the coffee the rector had prepared into the sink and reaching for the Jim Beam. Without a word, he took his glass into his office, closing the door and lying down on his leather couch, an arm draped over his eyes.

After weeks of insomnia, pacing the halls to wrestle with how he'd become the fall guy for the U-2 mess, he had answers. He had indeed screwed up the mission but not through inattention to detail. He'd done it when he invited this woman into his life. His sense of failure gutted him—his willful blindness both as an intelligence officer and a husband. He'd ignored all the small things with her that didn't add up, acquiesced to the boundaries she erected between them without demanding she let him in. And why?

If he was honest with himself, it was because her remoteness justified his pursuit of women—made him believe he was entitled to find succor elsewhere to salve his wounds. But the bargain they'd struck turned out to be a far more complex and uglier deal than he could have imagined. He picked up the phone and called George.

"Where does this leave me?" Talbot asked. "Suspended animation until they decide what to do with the nest of Soviet spies I seem to have attracted?"

"We're in a hold, Talbot. The Feds want to get the Italian guy, isolate Auclair, and suss out how deep and wide this thing is. They can't do anything abrupt that could signal Eleanor has changed sides. And as all this plays out, you cooperate, and they won't find any evidence you were a part of this at all — correct?"

"Right. Not a shred."

"Okay, so once they get to that point, you get your freedom back. So just hold tight for now and play along."

"That's not as easy as it sounds, with us both here in the same house. What about Eleanor? Once all that shakes out, what happens to her?"

"She doing okay?"

"We haven't spoken. I'm keeping my distance."

"Understood. Helluva lot to take in. So, Eleanor." George sighed. "You know, the letter of the law calls for spies to be executed. Or spend the rest of their lives in prison. But in agreeing to cooperate in the investigation, helping bust up this little ring, she's protected herself. Switch sides, and you may get immunity. Or deportation."

Talbot was quiet for a moment. "How did I not see it?" he asked.

"What? That she wasn't who she said she was? For one thing because she's beautiful and, I don't know, intriguing. So you fell in love with her and decided you wanted her and of course, you thought she was safe. You believed her and you stopped evaluating. Turned off the antennae. We all do that. And we all wear masks, Talbot, to make sure people see only what we want them to see about us. Her mask fooled you and — I gotta be honest, so don't get mad — she didn't particularly want to see behind your mask either, considering all the women you've chased around in the past ten years."

"So she knew," Talbot said, "but couldn't let on because she had to keep it going. Makes it kinda funny how she reacted when I told her about Helen and the others when I got out of jail. She actually cried. She pretended she was so upset..."

"Talbot," George interrupted, "when we were at the rector's office this morning, and she was going through this wild story of hers, the only time she cried — the only time — was when she talked about you. Hurting you, the damage she's done to you. Now, I'm hoping she has genuinely turned — come in from the cold, shall we say — to save herself. To get out from under this jackass Cossutta who ran her and has had her under his thumb for twenty years. But I also believe she just couldn't do it to you anymore. Cossutta was thrilled, she said — thrilled you're in the crosshairs. But she was distraught about her life here coming apart and that made him furious. It got so heated that she said he told her he's pulling her out. And she knew if she's exiled somewhere behind the Iron Curtain, you'd most certainly go to prison. Sizemore too. So when she realized his plans, she played nice, did what he asked, then got the hell out of there once he fell asleep."

"Huh," was all Talbot could muster.

"So, when you get around to talking to her, bear that in mind. She's done a lot of terrible stuff. A lot. Made huge mistakes. But she cares about your welfare. Despite all she did, despite Cossutta's influence, somewhere along the line she grew to care about you. If she hadn't, we wouldn't know a thing about any of this. We'd still be in the dark and you'd be headed to prison."

They ended their call, agreeing to reconnect on Monday. Talbot lay back on his dark leather couch, uncomfortably warm under the sunshine streaming through in his west-facing window this late June Saturday. On a typical day, he might be coming in from the golf course, showering to head to a bar-b-cue, a cocktail party — maybe a show at Constitution Hall or a fundraiser — the political conventions were only a few weeks away. That used to be my life, he thought, wishing he could trade the bourbon he drank alone for a gin and tonic on Rémy's patio. Rémy. God, Rémy. Another searing loss among so many.

Feeling ill-equipped to cope with all of it, Talbot drew the curtains. It was barely six in the evening but given the toll of the past few weeks—his arrest, his exile from work, the shock of learning who his wife really was—he found himself unable to remain upright. He retrieved a blanket from the hall closet, removed his clothes, and returned to the couch to sleep.

•   •   •

The next morning, Talbot found Eleanor in the kitchen, sitting exactly where she'd been when he last saw her, a box of tissues on the table.

"You stay there all night?" he asked.

She gave a sad little grin. "No. I slept in our room. Got up a couple hours ago. There's coffee."

He poured himself a cup and sat across from her, seeing her, in a way, for the first time. The hair—still light, light blond. The crystal blue eyes, red and swollen. The slim, straight nose and high cheekbones. Russian, he thought. Of course she is. He sipped his coffee and shook his head. When finally he spoke, his voice was quiet, drenched in grief.

"Well, this is embarrassing. I'm a goddam intelligence officer. A pretty bad one, I've come to realize. They drill it into you—and I guess at this point, hell, I can tell you this—don't be fooled by the distraction, preoccupied by a small move that makes you miss the big one. So while I've been preoccupied with you, your sadness, this gulf in our marriage, I missed the big move: you were just creating space to operate. It wasn't about you and me at all."

"Talbot," she began, "the gulf, as you call it, was also to protect you. Partly to limit what I could pass along about your work. But also, so you could develop a life apart from me—find other people you could lean on."

"So you were being generous, Eleanor, or Marisha or whoever you are, wanting me to have a healthy social circle so I wouldn't catch on to how you were ripping my life and career away. You're quite the actress, Marisha. Had me fooled completely. I actually believed you loved me—that we could get back to who we'd been together. Couldn't see all the other shit— all the things you hid from me—because I loved you. Love is, indeed, blind."

"I did love you. I do love you," she began before he cut in.

"Don't even start. Enough with the manipulation—there's no point. It won't improve your case with the Feds—this last-minute change of heart, changing sides now that you got caught."

"I didn't get caught, Tal. I gave myself up because I couldn't do it anymore. I called George and he called Chamberlain. I told you: I wanted out ten years ago—once I grew up, once I realized what was at stake. But I was afraid. Afraid for myself and for you. Once Gilberto came here…"

"Your boyfriend. Yes. Tell me more about him."

"He's not my boyfriend. Not now. He was my sculpture professor in Florence—my advisor. It was pre-arranged, something my mother had a hand in. I got to the university and he took an interest in me. He was extremely well-thought of, admired for his talent—and I was flattered. Thrilled, actually. We spent hours alone in the studio and over time, he drew me in. Made my decisions for me. And once we began the affair, I was incapable…I couldn't break away."

"And at what point did you trade your training in art for training in espionage?"

"When the war began."

Talbot narrowed his eyes. "So 1939...until we met in '45? A six-year apprenticeship in becoming American. So when I met you..."

"I had just emerged in Florence with my new name, the background we had invented."

Talbot stared off in the distance. "Hal—remember him? The banker? Way better intelligence officer than I am. He knew there was something off about you." Talbot continued despite the tears gathering in her eyes. "When we met him and Molly in London, he made a comment to me that your English was 'rusty.' I just didn't want to see it. I'd been in Europe so long, everybody's accent sounded funny to me."

Eleanor nodded, head bowed. "My first test, that week in London. I was terrified."

He rose and put some bread in the toaster.

"And all those stories you told. So elaborate—about life at Smith and the artists you met there, the receptions and parties. Hell. Where did that spring from?"

"It was a version of how things go at many universities when visiting artists come for a term. I just imagined myself in the middle of it."

"What an idiot I was, thinking you'd stumbled into Europe because your mother didn't read the papers—that you needed me because you'd lost your entire family."

"I did come to need you," she said. "But I believed I had to follow the path Gilberto laid out."

Talbot rolled his eyes. "But at some point, early on, you wanted to quit. What changed?"

She gave a small, wincing shrug. "Because after we got here, I actually felt happy. Happy to be married to you, to have freedom and privacy. Our little place in Georgetown, interesting friends who said whatever they wanted—I saw the world, finally, not Gilberto's interpretation of it. America seemed pretty good. Not perfect. But better than what I'd grown up in. So when

Gilberto came, I planned to tell him I wanted to ease out—that Rémy could just handle things. But he was furious, enraged at how I had adapted to things here. He could see I liked it. He made it clear I'd be removed and they'd hurt you if I didn't follow my orders."

"Nice little story, there. You should have come clean then, Eleanor. You should have told me and we would have dealt with it."

"McCarthy was raging right down the road, Talbot. Have you forgotten? Imagine how we would have been treated—both of us. We'd both be in jail. Or dead, depending on who got to us first. I was trying to avoid that."

He scoffed. "Right. Yes. Thank you for protecting my career by maintaining your surveillance of me. Very noble." He retrieved his toast without offering her a slice. "So, whatever mixed feelings you had about the work, you must have enjoyed reunions with your lover."

"I did not." By now, her tears flowed freely, her tissue a torn scrap in her lap.

"It fits the timeline, Eleanor, of when you pulled away from me."

"The hysterectomy. I had a hysterectomy."

Talbot froze, the toast in midair, mouth attempting to form a syllable.

"He was afraid I'd get pregnant and it would interfere with my work. Or a baby would arrive that looked like him."

"You agreed to this?" he roared, dropping his toast, splattering coffee across the table.

"I never agreed," she said. "I complied. Because I was afraid. I was young. I didn't want them to hurt you."

He began to pace, throwing long looks at her as he sorted out the details, the timeline of what she had told him.

"So that's why…" she began.

"That's why you kept yourself away from me. Locking the door when you bathed."

"And why I looked the other way when you took other women. Helen. The others before her. And Caroline."

His head whipped around when she said it, frantically thinking for a brief moment that this secret between them mattered, that there remained a small portion of himself he couldn't reveal to her. But no, he realized. His reflexive response to keep this secret could be discarded now. There was no risk in her knowing this because there was no marriage to protect. He could drop the mask. He went to the sink and splashed some water on his face, grabbing the kitchen towel to dry himself, working it in his hands, gripping and twisting. He paced a few more steps around the kitchen, then sat back down at the table to face her.

"When did you find that out?" he asked. "Caroline, I mean."

"I knew then. I knew your schedule and when there were holes in it. And when I pressed him, Rémy verified it. He had recordings."

"It was stupid. Brief. We just fell into it, both of us feeling like we didn't understand the two of you, all you'd been through in the war."

"I know, Talbot. I saw it. And it was then—when you became involved with Caroline—that I knew I loved you, because of how betrayed I felt by the both of you. Isn't that stupid? Me, doing what I was doing, feeling that? I wanted a real life, for you to come back and want me, so I tried to quit the work. But Cossutta wouldn't let me."

"So he used you. Is that your defense?"

"He used me, yes. They all used me. But I know what I did."

"You traipsed around after me. Lied to me. Made me a laughingstock. Then you busted up the Paris Summit, Eleanor—a meeting that could have made the world safer. For Americans, for all your Russian friends in Kirov. That's what you did, ultimately."

She nodded, her sobs overtaking her, her voice breaking. "I'm cooperating now, Talbot. I'm working for the U.S. now. And I'm sorry. I'm sorry."

He looked at her, wanting to believe her, knowing he could reach his arms around her, let her collapse into him as she seemed so desperate to do. That in doing so, he would telegraph a way forward, that he still cared about her welfare, believed that she was sorry and believed that in some aberrant, outlandish way, she loved him.

He rose, used the dish towel to mop up the spilled coffee on the table, and headed to the shower.

CHAPTER
THIRTY-SIX

Monday, June 27, 1960
Arlington, VA

Just before noon Monday, Eleanor dragged the rotary phone off her bedside table and into the bathroom, uncoiling the phone cord and finding it reached just far enough. She sat on the side of the tub and placed a call to the Arlington Planning Department. A chipper voice happily transferred the call to Mr. Auclair. Eleanor turned on the shower and let it run.

Rémy picked up and greeted her in his loud, professional voice and inquired how things were going at the library. He was busy, he said, so he would look into the issue she described and call her back later. She told him to hurry. Ten minutes later, her phone rang.

"You've resurfaced. I was concerned."

"We had a horrible fight, Rémy. I came back early, but I haven't had any privacy to call."

"Where's Talbot now?"

"In his office, I think. I'm in the bathroom. Told him I needed a shower so I don't have much time. What about you? Are you alone?"

"More or less. I'm at the deli around the corner from the office."

"Where? Is that a good idea?"

Rémy heaved an impatient sigh. "Santucci's, Eleanor. You know it. It's loud and busy. Our old art teacher would be at home here. No one's anywhere near me. And we're the side that taps your phone, remember?"

Eleanor laughed, relaxing. "Of course. Right. Then, I just need you to get a message to him. Tell him I'm fine and I'm terribly sorry. I made an awful mistake. I know that. Whatever he wants me to do, I'm ready."

Rémy was quiet for a beat. "He's furious at you, Eleanor. Very. The plan to move you has been set in motion. You understand that. It only makes sense. You're disgusted with your husband and decided to leave the country."

"Right. Okay. Do you know how? When?"

"Just stay ready. When he's got it worked out, he'll send an escort who will come to the library, make an inquiry, and get you out."

"I won't be at the library for a bit. I'm taking a few days off."

"Hmm. Then we'll have to make an adjustment. Is Talbot making you stay home? Is he trying to keep you within reach for some reason?"

"No. I'm just tired of the looks and the whispers, Rémy. If we're at the end of this, I'd just as soon not play-act at the library."

"Toughen up, Eleanor. You need to be sturdier than this. It's fine for Tal to believe you're upset. Cry on his shoulder all you want. But when I heard what happened Saturday, I thought maybe you'd had some sort of breakdown—lost your nerve. And that doesn't play well with our friends up the line, you know? Since Caroline and I had just been with Tal for dinner Friday night, I couldn't very well call looking for you because as far as I knew, you were out of town. I did see people coming out of your place late Saturday, after I'd learned you were…missing, shall we say. I was sent there to take a look."

Eleanor shuddered. "Yeah, I arrived just as that party was getting started. Investigators asking more questions. A team of them—plus Tal's lawyer, of course, and the rector from St. John's."

"The rector?" Rémy asked. "What was he doing there?"

"Tal called him. Everything is pressing down on him now so he's looking for some help with his mental state, I guess."

"Poor ole Tal. He was pretty melancholy Friday night. Barely on this side of despair. Still can't believe how all this came together. What were they asking him on Saturday?"

"Nothing new, really."

"You were the properly distraught wife?"

"Yeah, my fight with Gilberto left me a little raw and that worked to my advantage."

Rémy gave little chuckle. "It'll be a tough thing to explain to Caroline, though, when you're pulled out and you don't stay in touch with her. Which you can't do, you understand."

"I do. Of course. But who knows, Rémy? Maybe we'll be able to collaborate down the road—in Eastern Europe, perhaps. I imagine we'll see each other again."

"May it be so, ma petite amie. I'll let Caroline know you're having a terrible time of it so when they take you, she'll just think you were overcome, you couldn't bear to stay in touch. Stay ready. I'll send a message when I have something."

Eleanor thanked him and said she'd be ready to move.

She pressed the button to disconnect the call.

•   •   •

Rémy hung up and exited the phone booth, giving a quick look around to ensure no one was paying him undue attention. He made his way to the counter and ordered his lunch, wishing for the millionth time that he could get a salami and bologna sandwich on a proper baguette, instead of an over-salted Italian loaf. Just one of the many sacrifices he continued to make—and was willing to make—to continue this work.

He thought about Eleanor, how she'd cooperated with assignments but had always been somewhat diffident; she could have gleaned much more if she'd been willing to dig a little with Talbot, ingratiated herself with his colleagues. It had been a bit of an issue, her lack of strategic creativity, but Cossutta had insisted she stay in the role—for his own reasons obviously—but also because she was so well-positioned. And he'd been proven right, Talbot moving up in the ranks to his career capstone, overseeing the U-2 project.

They had a lot to be proud of, accomplishing what they had and now, it was the right moment for their little partnership to dissolve. It had been messier than he would have liked, Caroline developing a deep but inconvenient friendship with Eleanor that led to the four of them socializing. He'd never liked his wife accompanying Eleanor to New York—always worried something random would cause a slip up and expose him—but it never had. The affair, too, had been useful, providing a point of leverage that could be exercised if needed. Rémy harnessed his fury at their infidelity, their scheming, into greater motivation to undermine Talbot and destroy his career. Things had worked out well.

He glanced at his watch. The man behind the counter was moving more slowly than usual, stopping to take a phone call midway through preparing a sandwich. No matter. Rémy was not in a huge hurry and he enjoyed standing amid the energy and aroma of the deli, sipping his Coke. He considered how Eleanor would handle leaving all this behind. In East Germany or the Soviet Union, she would not enjoy the autonomy and the abundance she'd grown used to. He did not envy her that. If he were pulled out, he could return to France and never even break his cover.

At last, the man at the counter called his number. Rémy collected his sandwich and his Lay's chips, left a generous tip in the jar, and walked out the door into the still June day. As he did, two men who had surveilled him for the past week came up from behind, each clasping an elbow, smoothly steering him into a waiting car.

CHAPTER
THIRTY-SEVEN

Monday, June 27, 1960
Arlington, VA

The running shower masked the hurried activity in the Bentleys' home. Talbot spent the first few minutes of the call to Rémy seated on the side of the bathtub next to his wife, leaning into the phone receiver she held between them, holding his breath and listening. Once he'd heard enough, he crept away to his office to phone Engwall on his work line. Intercepting Rémy unobtrusively, outside the deli, without making a scene at the Arlington Planning Department, would afford Rémy a longer window to entertain options for his future.

Talbot returned to the bedroom to find Eleanor placing the phone back on her bedside table, tucking away the now-stretched out phone cord.

"Brava," he said. "Completely believable." He sat down on the bed, eyes weary, shoulders rolled forward. "Engwall says what Rémy said in that call will be quite useful. They've probably already got him in custody. My old fishing buddy. My golfing buddy. Not exactly the grateful French ally I thought. Wonder what he'll have to say for himself—how he'll explain this to his wife."

•   •   •

That evening, they turned on the local news in time to see film of Helen's departure from the DC jail earlier that day. Cousin Todd clutched her elbow, steering her through the pod of reporters and photographers. Her make-up was understated, her hair tied back, and she wore a sleeveless orange sheath, a dress Talbot didn't recognize. She looked every bit the inexperienced recent college grad who might have been led astray by her boss. The anchorman explained in his This-Just-In voice that her lawyer had reached a plea deal with the government. He cut to an interview with Helen.

"Will you testify against your old boss?" shouted a reporter. Helen turned to the camera and placed a hand over her heart.

"I will do whatever my government asks me to do so we can learn exactly what happened in this case, who did what, and what it has to do with that plane going down over the Soviet Union." She looked pleased with herself as her lawyer pulled her away to a waiting car.

Talbot found Eleanor staring at him as the report ended, mouth slightly open, eyes holding a question.

"I have no idea, Eleanor. It just happened, okay?"

She nodded. She hadn't said a word.

"But she did her job right there. Your people will think the case against me is heading to trial."

"Not my people, Talbot. Not anymore."

Fifteen minutes later, the doorbell rang, the rector arriving with a chicken casserole. His wife, Ruth, had also sent a jello salad and lemon bars, having prepared it all herself, he explained, rather than alert the Episcopal ladies' meal calvary to assist.

"People are hungry for gossip," he said. "Ruth was not interested in feeding any of that so she did all this herself. So, how are you? Ridiculous question. Let me try this: anything I can do?"

"This is plenty, Reverend, truly," Eleanor responded. "Neither of us has had much of an appetite, but this smells enticing. Thank you."

"Okay, then. I want to let you both know that your man Chamberlain has contacted me and we met this morning. I asked to share that conversation with you and he said that was fine."

Eleanor swallowed. "I'm sorry you're entangled in this too, Reverend."

"No, no," he said. "That's not why I'm bringing it up. I wanted you to know I told him I knew nothing of this situation until Saturday, when Eleanor turned up in my study. I told him you're on the vestry, Talbot, and that the two of you have long participated in worship at St. John's. He asked me if I thought you were sincere, Eleanor, in your…what do we call it? Your change of heart? I told him that's impossible to determine, but actions give insight and time will let us know what's true."

Eleanor's eyes filled with tears. The rector placed both hands on her shoulders and leaned in, speaking quietly, only to her.

"Whatever your true beliefs, whomever you consider yourself to be, you're a human being, Eleanor. Flawed as we all are but valuable and worthy, too. This invented existence — the rootlessness that has characterized your last twenty years — has been costly. To Talbot, to the United States, and to you. To your personhood. Your soul. Much more so than you could ever foresee, I'm sure."

Eleanor nodded, overcome and overwhelmed, standing eye to eye with one of the few men she had ever known who had spoken with concern to her and for her, who wasn't pushing his agenda on her, determined to direct her a particular way.

"Thank you," she whispered, bowing her head as he promised to continue to hold her in his prayers.

Talbot walked the rector to the door, wanting a private word with him.

"Wish I could be as generous as you are, Reverend. I don't think I can get there."

"Take your time, Talbot. You're in an excruciating situation."

Talbot continued. "To put myself in her shoes—I can't do that. She's lied to me for so long. I can't just overlook her deception because she's sorry now."

"Of course not. It was a profound betrayal. Profound. But repentance is possible, Talbot. And remorse. And after that, after a time, perhaps forgiveness. But far be it from me to dictate any of that, to expect that will happen. I'm just here to remind her she must recognize the damage she's done to you and to herself, acknowledge it, before she can climb out this. And perhaps forgiveness will follow. Perhaps."

CHAPTER
THIRTY-EIGHT

Tuesday, July 5, 1960
The Bronx, New York

Cossutta sorted through some paperwork on his desk, information on the students who would be matriculating in his department in the fall. No one particularly special. Too many boys. The pool had improved now that Rothko was no longer across town teaching at Brooklyn College. The very idea of a college dropout working as a professor, he thought. This country. Cossutta shook his head.

But this was hardly the most pressing problem occupying his mind at the moment.

He'd received no message from Rémy. It had been a week. They'd spoken the day Eleanor had abandoned him at the Concourse, after it had finally dawned on the professor that she wasn't coming back. He'd had to get rid of the things she'd left himself, he complained, further evidence of her thoughtlessness. He laid out for Rémy the logistics of collecting her at the library and transferring her to the Soviet Embassy for exfiltration. Rémy was to make contact to ensure she had returned to Washington and verify her schedule for the week. But he'd failed to respond to escalating pings from Cossutta, the most recent being a long, yellow chalk mark on the sidewalk outside the Arlington Planning Department. Translation: call immediately. There had been nothing. The likely explanation was that he was with her, or with Talbot, or with Caroline, and unable to safely respond. It was possible Eleanor was angling for more time and Rémy was indulging her—the unfortunate byproduct of the friendship they'd developed. And the holiday. Americans closed everything down around the 4th of July. That had to be part of it. There was another explanation, however, that Cossutta did not care to entertain. He would wait to send up a distress signal. After all, any failure here would reflect on him, too. No need to overreact. Yet.

•　　•　　•

Washington, DC

Rémy would soon be in a position to communicate with his old art teacher, but the message would not be his own, shaped and massaged instead by U.S. counterintelligence agents. The U.S. marshals who picked him up outside Santucci's were joined by Chamberlain and Engwall and the agents assigned to the Bentley case, all of them gathering in the basement of a weathered building close to Talbot's office. The drive-under garage made it ideal for these kinds of interrogations, the marshals easily hustling the subject into the stairwell and into the makeshift conference room without drawing notice. Two members of the DC police force stood guard outside the room.

Rémy had sputtered in protest when he was seized—he was an urban planner for Arlington, for god's sakes. They were making an obvious mistake. By the time he took a seat at the dented and dusty military-issue table, the others circled around him, he changed his tack, relaxing and offering a little shrug. He leaned back in his metal chair, ostensibly studying the cigarette he smoked that Engwall had offered.

"You have an opportunity here, Mr. Auclair," Chamberlain began. "We know what you've been doing and who you work for—and it ain't the city of Arlington and it ain't the French. So you tell us the folks who are helping you and things will go better for you."

Rémy smiled. "Americans do this? Take people off the streets for absolutely no reason and make unfounded charges? Are you the Gestapo now?"

"Now, now, Mr. Auclair. That's sounds a little ungrateful. We're the sum bitches who beat those sum bitches. You know that about as well as anyone, I'd say. But let me ask: apart from objecting to how you were invited to this little party today, you like living here, right? Enjoyed the perks of your education, the freedom to pretty much conduct yourself as you like?"

"Of course," he said. "I'm grateful to live here and I love this country. My wife is American. My children are Americans."

"And did you just forget all that when you were running Soviet agents, leaving instructions in a tree stump in Rock Creek Park, so you could pass U.S. government secrets to the Centre?"

Rémy pulled on his cigarette, relaxing his face into an indulgent smile. "I've done nothing of the sort. It's a fiction."

At that moment, one of officers outside the door gave a little knock and peeked inside. Chamberlain gave him a nod. The door creaked open and Eleanor stepped through. Talbot followed.

Rémy rose, his smile pinched.

"You know these folks, Mr. Auclair?" Chamberlain asked.

"Of course…my friends…whom I trust are here to take me home." He stubbed out his cigarette and moved toward the door.

"Friends? Really?" Talbot asked. Eleanor stood next to him, head bowed, her hands braced on the back of a chair. "Am I your friend, Rémy?"

"Talbot," Rémy began, extending a hand. "They've confused me with someone else, obviously."

Eleanor lifted her head, eyes clouded and sad. "I told them," she said. "I told them all of it. About you, Gilberto, what we've been doing."

"Say whatever you wish. It has nothing to do with me."

"Oh, but it does, Mr. Auclair. Jerry? Go ahead." Chamberlain gestured at Engwall who withdrew his tape recorder and placed it on the desk. He pressed Play. The color drained from Rémy's face as he heard himself say:

"He's furious at you, Eleanor. Very. The plan to move you has been set in motion. You understand that. It only makes sense. You're disgusted with your husband and decided to leave the country."

Engwall snapped the button to stop the tape, a sharp click echoing through the room.

Rémy looked at those around him and gave a little shrug. "Well. I suppose I need a lawyer to straighten this out."

"Sure thing," said Chamberlain. "We'll get you one. And listen: tell him you got two choices: prison here, or deportation—probably to your employer, the Soviet Union. And you might want to know that we're headed to pick up your wife next. Family Services will take your kids for now. Well. I guess we're done here. Short and sweet. Thank you, Mrs. Bentley, Talbot." Chamberlain rose and began gathering his things.

"Wait, wait, wait." Rémy said. "Surely there are other options, yes?"

•   •   •

For all his European sophistication and bravado, his oft-repeated disdain for Americans uninformed about the world, Rémy discovered quite suddenly that he wanted desperately to continue to live in and among these coarse brethren. Within hours, he'd agreed to hand over the names of the agents he worked with, as well as diplomats within the Soviet Embassy who were actually intelligence officers, and leads to cut-outs he used. The city was crawling with Soviet spies, he said, but busting up his cell would make a big dent. In return, he wanted a deal that would keep him in the United States, even if it meant a prison term and confessing to Caroline. Chamberlain said he would work on it—no promises.

For the next week, Chamberlain and Engwall worked around the clock to pull together resources for next steps. Surveillance teams tracked the agents Rémy identified, tapping their telephones, trailing them as they did business in the city. Protection teams infiltrated the Arlington Library, St. John's Church, and the Bentleys' neighborhood—all of this scaffolded quickly because Cossutta would be impatient for Rémy's signal that Eleanor was ready to be pulled out. Somewhat surprisingly, Chamberlain invited Talbot into many of these conversations, tapping his expertise on aspects of the sweeping operation. He consulted Eleanor, too, to learn more about Cossutta's proclivities and what they could expect as they moved ahead. The planning conversations took place in a variety of locales depending on the participants: George's office—where Talbot was expressly allowed to go—the rector's study at St. John's, where Eleanor was thought to be bringing her husband's notes on the most recent vestry report, and even the top-floor conference room at the Arlington Planning Department, quietly commandeered by federal marshals.

Rémy's cooperation had bought him time. He was still heading off to work each morning, Caroline still insulated from the truth of who he was. On the day of his initial interrogation, he'd called his office to say he'd taken ill—just a stomach thing, probably bad salami. They'd allowed him to return home in time for dinner with his family and to play catch with his son. The following day, he was seldom found at his desk, his boss explaining to fellow planners that Auclair was working on a long-term density analysis with the Feds in the conference room upstairs.

From a phone in that room, he dialed Cossutta.

"Hello, professor," he said.

"Well, hello," Cossutta responded. "You've been busy, yes? Too busy to come to the gallery opening. A pity."

"Unexpectedly so. My friend took the week off from work, so that affected my own plans somewhat. Plans I'd had for us to do some sightseeing together must move now to next week when my friend is again available. So I'll have to pass on the gallery opening for now."

"I see. Well, these things happen."

"Did I mention? We're going to see the new display at The Museum of Natural History—the Fenykovi Elephant went in last year, but I've yet to see it. Have you been?"

"I have. It's stunning. Not to be missed. Mondays are less crowded and perhaps you can enjoy a bite of lunch first if your schedule allows."

"It does. My friend will be delighted."

"Might I recommend the split pea soup at the museum cafe? Filling and quite tasty. Unless you need a salad or sandwich in addition?"

"With a thick soup, we'll need nothing else, I'm sure. Thank you for the recommendation, professor. Always nice to be prepared. But tell me: how are preparations for classes going? Do you like what you're seeing?"

"Eh, the usual. New students with varied degrees of talent. Nothing earth shattering, but they will all progress. I appreciate your interest. Well, then. Enjoy your visit with the elephant. I look forward to hearing all about it."

"Of course, professor."

Rémy replaced the phone in the cradle and turned to Chamberlain and Engwall.

"So. Monday means Friday. Lunch means later in the day—say, three to five p.m. I told him she'll come willingly so there's no need for a second man—just the soup, not the salad."

Chamberlain nodded. "Then we'll put things in place."

"He also said this delay has raised no concern above him, at the Centre. They aren't on to me or her. Or you, for that matter."

Chamberlain nodded a second time.

CHAPTER
THIRTY-NINE

Friday, July 15, 1960
Arlington, VA

Eleanor was up early on Friday, not that she had truly slept. Talbot had taken to sleeping in the spare room, the two of them moving through the house like matching magnetic poles in constant repulsion. They were polite, the first one up making the coffee, Eleanor making dinner and leaving a plate for Talbot. She let him know when she left for the library and he always went to the top floor window before she did, scanning for anything out of place. Chamberlain had men positioned in the neighborhood and at various points along her route to ensure she arrived safely.

This morning was a little different, however, as this was the day of her kidnapping. The team had briefed her on how things would proceed, all of them confident they could keep her safe as long as she followed the script. Talbot paced in the foyer as she gathered her things, mouth opening and closing as he tried to find the right words to see her off.

"I hope it goes well, Eleanor," he began. "I hope you're safe today."

She turned to him, her face steely and remote in the way sadly familiar to him. She had recovered herself. Here was Eleanor the operative, emotionless and distant, armor back in place, no sign of the copious tears that had wracked her for two weeks. If Cossutta's men were following her, this is what they would see.

"You surprise me, Talbot. I would think you wouldn't much care, beyond wanting this ring of spies taken into custody."

He closed his eyes and gave his head a small shake. "Then you don't know me at all. I feel lost, knowing what you've done—what it's done to the life I thought I had. But I don't want you hurt. I'm worried about this whole operation. I wish I could be there to make sure nothing happens to you. Please be careful."

Her face softened, surprised. "Thank you, Talbot. Thank you. I'll do my best."

He watched her car from the upper floor window until it escaped his view.

•   •   •

Rémy kissed his wife goodbye and trundled into his car, anxious over what the day would bring. He pictured a placid Eleanor approached at the library by the man sent to retrieve her. If things went as planned, the man would be intercepted then secured in a vast sweep that would extend from DC to New York. After that, once things were sorted and settled, Rémy hoped his own future might snap into focus, his cooperation taken into account. His rapid conversion had surprised even him, the political philosophy that had driven him in the war years and after suddenly feeling dated now, impractical in the mid-twentieth century. But could he live safely, happily, in a country he'd denigrated for fifteen years, among people he'd dismissed for their artlessness, their solipsism? If it meant he could preserve his freedom and his marriage, Rémy concluded he could overlook most everything. The coq au vin at the Rive Gauche in Georgetown, profiteroles from his little French bakery in Rosslyn far surpassed anything available at the best restaurants in Moscow.

•　　•　　•

After her week's absence, Eleanor's return to work had been smooth, her colleagues sympathetic with her explanation that she had just needed to collect herself, have time to assess her situation. Each day, her work had grown more routine and ordinary. She entered the library on Friday morning appearing relaxed, waving to her assistant before she headed into a departmental meeting. At that meeting, she announced she had discovered some new, perhaps unwelcome patrons in the stacks—federal agents assigned to monitor her as the case against her husband grew more complicated. She offered an apology.

"Do they think you're involved, Eleanor?" asked the archivist, his blunt question making the others squirm.

"They probably think you're involved, Stan," she said, prompting trills of inauthentic laughter. "They're scouring everywhere to make their case. They've interviewed my neighbors. But be assured, this will end soon."

Eleanor was genuinely busy the rest of the day, speeding toward the confrontation she had waited so long to have. At two, she picked up the phone and called Talbot.

"What?" he said. "What's happened?"

"Nothing yet. But it will soon, I expect. I just wanted to say hello. And goodbye, if…well…I just wanted to hear your voice."

Talbot was silent. "I'm with you in spirit, Eleanor. Hoping for the best."

At three-forty, a man who had busied himself much of the afternoon among the periodicals, made his way up the steps to Eleanor's office. He entered and closed the door.

Eleanor turned. "May I help you?"

"I have a research question," the man said.

"Ah, yes. Shall we proceed to the research volumes? They're on the main floor."

She reached for her cardigan. "Sometimes it gets chilly there." She smiled. Her visitor nodded.

They walked down the steps side by side, Eleanor pausing to put on the sweater then stopping to fix her shoe, the thin, sling-back strap having slipped off her heel. Their slow descent gave Chamberlain's team time to slide into position.

Eleanor and her escort exited the library, the man placing a hand on Eleanor's back to direct her towards a black sedan idling at the curb a half-block down the street. A young man who appeared to be about college-age followed just behind them, nose buried in a comic book. A second, older man followed him, newspaper tucked under his arm.

Eleanor suddenly stopped, whispering something to her escort and shaking her head in apology. Her shoe again. She stepped over to the bus stop, placing a hand on the bench there to steady herself, so she could address the wayward strap. She reached down to her heel, pulling the leather this way and that, then straightened, drawing her arm up and slamming a fist under the man's chin. He staggered, briefly. The doors of the sedan flew open and two men walked determinedly in Eleanor's direction. A beat too late, they realized as the gentleman seated on the bench was not, in fact, waiting for the bus. Chamberlain stood and leveled his Colt M1911 at them both while the college kid and the man with the newspaper wrestled Eleanor's original escort into a delivery van parked in front of the library.

•   •   •

Two-hundred and fifty miles away, Cossutta was at work in the Fordham Fine Arts Sculpture Studio with a young woman he had encouraged to enroll in his summer tutorial, whom, he believed, could benefit from his particular touch. He'd called her in to work one-on-one this afternoon, to help distract him from the operation he believed was underway in DC to get Eleanor out of the country.

After a few words of inspiration, that she needed to listen to the clay, coax it into what it wanted to be — the same, tired words he used with all the young women he invited into his studio — Cossutta laid his hands on hers as she massaged the soft green clay on the table. He interlaced his fingers with hers, leaning into her hair, inhaling. The student seemed oblivious to his attentions. After a time, he tired of the clay work and invited her to sit with him at the small cafe table in the studio to discuss the flaws in her technique, an open bottle of Chianti there to lubricate the conversation. Before he could proceed, the Dean opened the door, his alarm at seeing a professor drinking wine in the middle of the day with a student apparent.

"Dr. Cossutta — a word?" he asked timorously, beckoning him to the studio door.

Cossutta complied, picking up his wine glass — then thinking better of it and setting it back on the table. Once he crossed the threshold into the dim hall, two U.S. marshals appeared.

"Afternoon, professor," said one as the Dean stood shaking his head, speechless. "You'll be coming with us."

"What? For what? For a midday respite with a student?"

"Well, no, but I'm pretty sure you shouldn't be doing that either."

"What, then? I demand to know what is happening. Norman," he pled to the Dean, "make them stop this nonsense."

The second marshal pulled out a set of handcuffs and snapped them on Cossutta's wrists. "Not really nonsense, professor. Not from what the warrant says."

The marshals muscled him down the hall and out the door, the Dean watching and still mute. The young student had seen it all from the classroom and made her way to the hall to have a word with the Dean.

"That guy?" she said. "After the stories I've heard, I'm not a bit surprised."

•   •   •

And so it went throughout the day—police officers, marshals, FBI agents, executing sealed warrants then launching themselves on targets up and down the Atlantic Coast. "The best kind of Blitzkrieg," Chamberlain joked, and one that produced a larger haul than he could have imagined, law enforcement finding two, three, four suspects at various locations where they'd expected to nab just one. Eighteen people were taken into custody without a shot fired, each confined separately at the DC jail. It would be up to the courts to sort out who was whom and given the assortment of Slavic accents among the detainees, it was bound to get interesting.

CHAPTER
FORTY

Friday, July 15, 1960
Arlington, VA

Talbot paced the townhouse, wearing a path from the front hall through the living room to the dining room, desperate for news, leaving the bourbon alone for now, wanting to keep his head clear. At eight, Chamberlain called and described a mission that had gone like clockwork, yielding documents and technology in addition to the perps in custody.

"Eleanor can tell you more. And I'll come by in a day or two to discuss where we are," he said, his voice exultant but weary. "We've given Dulles briefings every step of the way, Talbot, and I think we're getting close to clearing your charges. Eleanor's situation is still under discussion, Auclair's too. Give us a few days."

"Understood,"

"Just make sure you continue to abide by terms of your release, in case there's anyone else out there we missed and don't know about yet, who might be paying attention to what's happening at your house. We've still got surveillance on you and Eleanor, but please, watch your step, okay?"

Eleanor arrived home an hour later, accompanied by Engwall and a stack of takeout boxes from the Italian place on Dupont Circle. They entered through the garage and trudged up the steps where an anxious Talbot waited. Forgetting for a moment how his world had changed over the past two weeks, he reached for her when he saw her, easing her head to his shoulder, feeling her relax into him, a posture once so familiar that now felt startling. He whispered thanks to God that she was safe.

"Come. Sit. Both of you," he said, releasing his wife and reaching to unburden her and Engwall of their takeout boxes. Eleanor moved warily, appraising Talbot's show of concern after days of studied indifference. She went to the cabinet to retrieve some plates.

"I'm not staying," said Engwall. "I just wanted to make sure she got here safely and that you two got a bite to eat tonight. Helluva day. She can fill you in."

Talbot extended his hand. "Thanks," he said. "Truly. Glad things went as they did. Be careful getting home."

"Officer Bentley, the streets of Washington may be safer tonight than they've been in a while. I'll let myself out."

Talbot sank heavily into the kitchen chair across from Eleanor, accepting the lasagna she'd transferred to a plate. Before he could ask a single question, she began speaking.

"It was so smooth, Talbot. Everyone in place, moving exactly as we rehearsed it."

"Clockwork, Chamberlain said."

"It was, at least where I was. The targets? They were stunned, really, like they'd never even considered there could be snags, that I might not be on board."

"Swept up a lot of people, I heard."

"Yes. They've been putting photos in front of me for the past five hours. Most were people I didn't recognize, but others—I've seen them at the library, at Giant Food, outside the National Gallery. One guy—I swear I've seen at St. John's." She gave a shiver.

"So your side was there, making sure you were doing your job."

She looked up from her meal and locked eyes with him. "It's no longer my side, Talbot. It's not. Please hear me. I'm on your side. I know it's the right side. It just took me a while to get here."

Talbot's lips drew into a tight line. He rose, opened a bottle of wine, and pulled two glasses from the shelf. "Feels like we should celebrate a little." Eleanor nodded.

He drank nearly half his glass before he spoke again. "It's just hard, Eleanor. Hard to know where your heart is, what you truly believe — given the alternatives you were facing. Siberia or East Germany or something."

"I can't make you believe me," she said quietly, gazing past him, her shoulders giving a slight shrug. "But I know what I know. I know what's true. They can put me in jail here, but as long as they don't make me go back, trade me for a Western spy or something, I'll be satisfied."

"Happy to spend the rest of your life in prison?"

"Yes," she said. "Yes. Because for the first time since I was nineteen — no before that — since I was a girl too young to understand, I will be free. I can be myself. I've made some progress in that direction since you brought me here — whether you believe that or not. And if I have to continue that progress from jail, at least I'll be able to think for myself. Read what I want. Judge things for myself. I can't expect you to understand what that means to me. You've been free your whole life."

They sat at the table as the food grew cold, Talbot replenishing their wine glasses, both lost in their own thoughts, considering the depth of the love and lies between them. Finally Talbot asked about their earliest days, whether she had actually been interested in him or just found him a proper target for her work.

"I had never even spoken with an American man, Talbot. You were a new species to me." Her tongue loosened by the wine, she gave him a smile he had not seen in months. "I absolutely wanted to get to know you better. Here you were, so so confident and self-possessed—and still, you asked my opinion of things, paid attention when I showed you around Florence."

He allowed himself a chuckle. "I was a rube. I knew nothing about art and I needed to catch up."

"I remember small things, books you shared that you thought I'd like, you asking me to pick the wine, or to order for you at a restaurant because I knew the menu better. And my ring—the engagement ring that you gave me in that little art deco box we still have…"

"You'd spotted it in the artists' stalls outside the Uffizi. One thing I got right."

"You got a lot right. That box holds a place of honor in our bookcase all these years later. But…" and here she paused, eyes welling, "at the same time, it was excruciating, Talbot, with Gilberto telling me to climb into bed with you when he was still…"

"…climbing into bed with you."

"I was a girl. From Kirov, of all places. Idealistic, knowing nothing about the world. No experience with men. Here was my security, the man who defined things for me, saying 'Just give yourself away. It's not important.' What he did was cruel." She withdrew a cigarette which Talbot reached over to light. "It wasn't until we got here, away from him and whatever magic he conjured, that I realized I did like you. I liked us, this place, this way of life. And that grew into a love I had to keep at bay…because Gilberto wouldn't leave me alone."

Talbot sat quietly, appraising her.

"Can I ask you a question now?"

He nodded.

"The women. Were you looking for someone to replace me? A woman who could give you children, maybe?"

He considered her question.

"Be honest," she pleaded.

"It's not so easy," he replied. "I've told myself so many stories about why I did what I did, why I was justified, using them, lying to you. I'm not sure how to be honest."

"I know what you mean."

"I needed to feel important, Eleanor. They were young. They were impressed with me, my responsibilities, my shadowy service in the war." He gave a wistful smile. "Four of them in all. And Caroline, as you know."

"You have Caroline to thank for why those cameras they found in your office didn't work." Talbot looked at her, questioningly. "After they filmed some of your... exploits...during our little dinner parties, I disconnected them. Explained to Gilberto we'd had some electrical work done and the cameras were accidentally damaged."

Talbot shook his head then reached for his drink.

"Was there anyone you wanted to keep?" she said lightly, the tone contradicting the intense set of her face.

He closed his eyes before he answered. "Not one. Not a one. When they got too invested, I had them promoted. Transferred. Something that seemed to happen outside of my control so they could just move on and out of my life and not turn it back on me. Except Helen. She didn't want to move."

"Plucky Helen."

Talbot smiled.

"But why Caroline?" she asked. "She was the hardest for me to understand."

"Because she knew you best, Eleanor. She's smart and insightful and was the closest thing I could find to you. And maybe I wanted you to notice, so we could have a big, awful fight and say what needed to be said, and maybe I'd finally understand why you'd lost interest in me, in our marriage. Maybe it would be a way to find my way back to you."

•   •   •

In the hours before dawn, as she lay in her bed, Eleanor became aware of another presence in the room, of an arm draped heavily over her middle, of Talbot's rhythmic breathing at her neck. She leaned into him, clasping her hand over his, unconcerned that his hand might stray over her raised scar, no longer needing to hide it from him, wondering if they would have the chance to heal the invisible scars that saddled them both. She wondered: was this Talbot finding his way back to her, or preparing for their inevitable goodbye?

CHAPTER
FORTY-ONE

Monday, July 18, 1960
Washington, DC

Cossutta was ferried to Washington the day after the raids, complaining persistently that he was a simple artist—AN ARTIST!—wrongly denied his rights. He lobbied every member of law enforcement he encountered to send him back to Italy and avoid the costly unpleasantness involved in bringing charges against him. He railed against his solitary confinement through the weekend, calling it inhumane and beneath him. For perhaps the first time in his life, no one listened to the imperious Italian so accustomed to getting his way.

Cossutta was among a group called to a closed courtroom for a first appearance the Monday after his arrest, where he heard the breadth of the charges against him. He was alarmed at how many on his team had been seized but concerned more about one he did not see. It was Rémy, then, who was responsible for this disaster, whose mistakes had disrupted their work and Cossutta's comfortable life. It could not be Mishie, he told himself, for she had done her job quietly, ploddingly, obediently, year after year, as he had trained her to do.

Her early work had been so peripheral that soon after Cossutta arrived in New York, the Centre wanted her cut loose and returned to Moscow. He had objected, arguing he saw potential, that having her suddenly demand a divorce from her

CIA husband and decamp to Europe would invite unwanted scrutiny. But the real reason he fought to keep her was because of her use to him personally, physically, the weekends he enjoyed with her that steadied him, that he believed made him more effective, even if the intelligence she provided was spotty. He had tamed her, he liked to think, from the feral creature she'd been when she arrived in Florence into the cooperative agent she now was. His patience, the path he'd insisted they take with her, had paid off with the jackpot of intelligence she'd unearthed in the past year, earning praise from the Centre and the Soviet Premier. He had been pleased at this validation, as she had been his little project for so long. And despite her recent emotional outburst and the American airs she put on that he found so tasteless, he felt certain she would never betray him.

Rémy, in contrast, functioned closer to the center of the operation and more than once, Cossutta had found him somewhat careless — his phone call the previous week the latest example. With countless, safer ways to pass messages, he'd opted to pick up the phone, their most exposed option. Cossutta knew his line was clean, as were the lines in the Arlington Planning Department. But still. Rémy got sloppy when he was in a hurry and that sloppiness had probably led to something overheard, a slip that resulted in this round-up of Cossutta's network. The French, he thought. This is why Hitler had such an easy time of it until the Americans barged in.

As Cossutta left the courtroom, he signaled to the custodial officer that he was ready to make his phone call, that he needed to secure counsel before his arraignment. The officer told him he'd have to return to his cell first but would be retrieved within the hour so he could make his call.

•   •   •

Chamberlain and Engwall arrived at the Bentleys' townhouse late Monday afternoon — no tape recorder in tow this time, just a pile of paperwork for Talbot to sign. The charges against him had been dropped, but he would not be returning to CIA. His signature on the documents Engwall pulled out of his briefcase would trigger a healthy severance, ensure Talbot wouldn't sue the government, and guarantee his permanent silence on all projects he'd worked on in the course of his intelligence career. It was Eleanor, now, who was placed on home detention, while Director Dulles and his deputies, in consultation with the president, decided her future.

"And Rémy?" Talbot asked. "What happens to him?"

Chamberlain sighed. "His case is a bit more complicated, to be honest. We doubt he would have come forward if you hadn't forced the issue. There may be more to wring out of him. He'll keep his cover for a few more days and we'll watch. Either the bad guys try to establish a new link with him now that Cossutta's out—which could bring us a few more scalps—or they figure out you and Auclair are no longer playing for their team." Chamberlain gave a little grimace. "At that point, we'll take you both into custody."

"I'll be arrested?"

"That's what they'll think, Mrs. Bentley. You and Auclair would go into protective custody while government lawyers figure out what the hell to do with you."

"What about Caroline?" Eleanor asked.

"Still in the dark. No sense upsetting her applecart until we have to. Her husband is going into the office, working some long days, but for the most part, keeping his regular schedule. For now. Until we tie up some of these loose ends."

•   •   •

Tuesday, July 19, 1960
Arlington, VA
With the raids and arrests rolling out as well as they had, due in part to the intelligence Rémy provided, he had hope now that he could wrangle a deal without sacrificing the life he knew, the life he was very late in realizing he didn't want to give up. All

Caroline knew was that for past two weeks, he'd been working extra-long days, unusual in July when the city usually emptied out, its residents fleeing to Ocean City and Rehoboth Beach.

Early Tuesday morning, he brought her coffee in bed and said he'd been thinking: what if they moved to upstate New York?

"Where is this coming from?" she asked with a laugh. "You love it here."

"Two things have changed," he explained. "Our children are growing up without grandparents and we fix that if we lived closer to your parents."

"And the second?"

Rémy hesitated. "The Bentleys. Talbot. The Halcyon days with them are past now, no? They were our family here. And now, however his case ends up, it won't be the same." He watched her eyes, wondering if she was ready to put distance between herself and Talbot, eager to erase her private memories of him.

"We need to talk more," she said, "but yes. Let's think about it. My parents would be thrilled. It'd be a lot slower life. A lot. Upstate New York is pretty quiet."

"More like what I grew up with. And maybe it's time to slow down, Caroline. This town has sort of worn me out."

"You just want to escape the humidity."

"And the radiation cloud that's sure to cover Washington long before anything happens to the upstate." Caroline laughed and he kissed her, hope and guilt colliding, nearly overwhelming him. He had married well, far better than he deserved. If he got clear of all this, he would make it up to her. He would learn to be an honest man.

•   •   •

Rémy enjoyed a light day at work, now that the Feds were no longer camped out in the conference room. He actually handled real planning issues, invigorated by questions and problems that weeks earlier had annoyed him with their triviality.

At four-thirty, he placed a few files in his briefcase and explained to his colleagues that his long days of the previous week had caught up with him. He was cutting out a few minutes early. As he rode the elevator to the parking garage, he decided to run by Giant to get ingredients for Chicken Jardinière for dinner—he had been promising Caroline he would cook one night. The Giant supermarket could not be more different from the small family markets he knew in France, where inventory varied on every visit, but the produce was always ripe and bursting, the chickens freshly plucked. Maybe he should move his family to France. He would, he decided, if he got the chance.

As he pulled out into traffic he imagined life without the lies, the cover, the subterfuge. He would leave behind the way he'd lived since he was an eighteen-year-old fighter in the forests of France—a life fueled by deep belief and surges of adrenaline. It had been an addiction, really, something that he had hung on to after the war because it made him feel essential, important. Someone else could pick up the baton now. He was through.

At that moment, he heard the car window shatter in his left ear. His foot fell heavily on the accelerator and the car lurched into the side of the building across from the garage, the hood folding like an accordion. The Arlington police would later conclude the driver had a heart attack, or perhaps was seized by a stroke. There was so much blood, they missed, at first appraisal, the bullet hole just above his ear.

CHAPTER FORTY-TWO

Tuesday, July 19, 1960

Arlington, VA

Chamberlain was not entirely surprised when he got the call. He figured there were more operatives out there but had hoped to sniff them out before somebody got hurt. Members of the counterintelligence surveillance team had been slow to track Rémy when he left his desk early, all of them weary after a non-stop few days, mistakenly believing the operation was essentially over. They'd been on the other side of the building when they heard the crash and had raced to find the car wrecked and a man fleeing. Two agents pursued him on foot, wrestling him into handcuffs and throwing him in the back of their sedan. Chamberlain and Engwall arrived to persuade the Arlington police to ignore the prisoner writhing in the car and write up the incident as a single-car traffic accident with fatality.

"No can do," said the dutiful young police officer in charge of the scene. "Window on the driver's side is shattered—looks like a bullet. There's more to this."

"No, my friend," said Chamberlain, as he took the officer by the elbow and walked him away from the other cops, Engwall trailing behind. "There is not. Single car accident. That's it. Nothing more for you to do. Got it?" Chamberlain pulled out his ID and placed it before the officer, suggesting he take a second look. The officer studied it for a long moment, eyes darting between the two men before him, then gave a quick nod. Chamberlain went on to say he was taking custody of the body because of the deceased's ties to a federal case. After he directed the ambulance driver where to take the victim, he left the scene to travel the few miles to the Bentleys' knowing he needed to deliver this news in person.

· · ·

Talbot's reaction to Rémy's murder proved complicated, disorienting, yet another unimaginable event in a sudden string of them. He was relieved—and for this he felt a fissure of shame—realizing he would never have to face Rémy about his involvement with Caroline, never have to own up to it or explain it. There was the familiar sense, too, that he'd felt in his intelligence work when an enemy was taken off the field—a move in the right direction, a point for the good guys. But beneath all that was profound grief for the friend that he had once had, the man he'd lost when he learned of his treachery in the days before the assassin's bullet found its mark. The false friendship had nevertheless been an anchor these past ten years and there would be no way, now, to redeem it. No way to find out if there had been any authentic aspect to it at all.

Talbot's thoughts ran next to Caroline and the children, the promise he and Eleanor had made as godparents at their christenings years before. They had taken those vows in an entirely different, parallel life, but the children didn't know that. Talbot hoped they would never learn the truth about their father and decided he would push for whatever truth-bending was required to protect them.

"Are we next?" he asked Chamberlain. "Do you think we're targets?"

"Shooter's in custody. We think Cossutta sicced him on Auclair—based on the timing of a call Cossutta made from the jail. Seems Cossutta thinks Auclair triggered all this, not Eleanor." Chamberlain had sent his team to the jail to squeeze the detainees and threaten their immediate return to Moscow if they didn't give up more names. Each, independently, had named or described the man arrested at the scene.

"He'd been working as the defense attaché at the Soviet Embassy. We're filing to strip his diplomatic immunity because he ain't no diplomat. He's at the Arlington Jail, gun charges pending, but he'll be indicted for murder and espionage — spend the rest of his life in federal prison." Chamberlain paused and ran a hand across his jaw. "But hell, I'm damn sorry this happened. We've still got guys outside your house and we'll leave them in place. Right now, we can get you out to McLean to see Mrs. Auclair if that's what you need to do."

•   •   •

As Caroline drove her kids home from the neighborhood pool, she heard the traffic reporter on the radio describe a snarl in Arlington. She hoped her husband wasn't caught up in the closed intersection. After she arrived home, she rooted around the refrigerator to pull together something for dinner, finding a leftover cassoulet she could reheat and serve with salad.

When the clock approached seven, as she debated whether to delay dinner for him, Arlington police officers arrived at her door. They explained as gently, as apologetically as they could, that her husband would not be coming home. Shattered, in shock, she tried to shoo them out the door, saying she wasn't having it — they needed to leave and take their story with them. Talbot and Eleanor arrived just then, Talbot ushering Caroline to the sofa, handing her tissues, holding her as she keened. Eleanor rounded up the children and sat with them on the patio, the youngest, Elise, huddled on her lap, Oliver and Colette wedged together in a patio chair, until their mother appeared some hours later to tell them what had happened to their father. The story she offered that day would become the family truth; daddy had suffered a medical emergency and died when he crashed his car.

•   •   •

The brief obituary in *The Washington Post* mentioned Rémy Auclair's courageous service with the French Resistance, describing a peaceful if unremarkable life he had found working for the city of Arlington, one cut tragically short by a car wreck. Talbot argued there was no purpose served by exposing Rémy now and Chamberlain agreed: Caroline would never know the layers of falsehoods and betrayals that comprised her husband's life. It left her to believe her affair with Talbot was the ugliest secret between them.

Rémy's death severed Eleanor's last tie to Cossutta and the freedom she felt, especially in the first few days, of being out from under their malign control left her in tears every time she tried to articulate it. She felt exhausted, hollowed out, and strangely bereft—no one sending messages and instructions, let alone whispering in her ear to direct and appraise. Caroline read her tears as grief for Rémy, understandable and apt. The Bentleys stood near her at the receiving line after the funeral, minding the children for her and bringing things she might need—a sip of water, more tissues. Caroline drew them over repeatedly to introduce them to neighbors and colleagues, saying again and again that here were the friends Rémy loved most, that she didn't know where she would be without Talbot and Eleanor.

The emotional fog of those early, grief-filled days made it easier to convince Caroline of other things that were not strictly true. She was occupied with making arrangements for her husband's service when reports first surfaced about the busting up of the Soviet spy ring, so the entire episode mostly escaped her notice. She was overjoyed to learn the charges against Talbot had been dropped — not espionage, just a woman scorned — and she supported his decision to leave CIA because how, really, could you work for an organization that didn't trust and believe you? But with the affair with Helen a matter of public record now, she also knew his opportunities at CIA would be constrained. Talbot's decision to return to private legal practice, joining George's law firm as a partner, seemed a logical step, especially when Talbot said he was tired of getting by on a government salary.

"All of Washington thinks George is a magician, given what happened with my case," he explained to her one Saturday when she and the children came by for hamburgers and hotdogs on the grill. "George has got more white collar-criminal defense cases than he knows what to do with — least I can do is help."

"But you did love your work, Talbot, and it's a crime things had to end because of their ridiculous jumping to conclusions."

"A crime," Talbot snorted.

Caroline stared into the deep red of the wine in her glass, lost inside it for a moment. She lifted her head and gave a small, sad smile, looking first at Talbot, then Eleanor. "Everything's changed for all of us since we lost Rémy. If only we could rewind the clock."

Caroline went on to explain that her event work with the State Department had suddenly dried up, something she blamed on the extended leave she requested after the funeral. She would never know Talbot and Chamberlain had arranged it to insulate her from State Department visitors with diplomatic cover and malintent who might have known her husband.

"But with life insurance, his government benefits — we'll be okay. I don't have to find work right away. The kids need me around. Worst case is I move up to New York. My parents are begging me to do that. And what about you, Ellie? What are you going to do next?"

Of Eleanor's departure from the library, Caroline knew there'd been an incident—a library patron who got fresh when Eleanor walked him to the door, several other patrons—one an armed officer stepping up valiantly to defend her. Caroline never heard about the right hook Eleanor delivered to the man who came to her office that day, although it became the stuff of legend among the librarians, some forgetting they had not witnessed the moment, telling the tale as if they'd been standing on the sidewalk when it happened.

"Mmm. Not sure," Eleanor responded. "I never wanted to be a librarian, you know. I wanted to work in the arts. After everything that's happened…it just seemed like it was time for something new."

•   •   •

But the truth was, her future was not in her hands. Eleanor was waiting for the Feds to decide whether to indict her, and if they did, Caroline would learn the truth despite all that had been done to obscure it. By October, the lawyers still debating, Eleanor was released from home confinement but directed to stay within fifty miles of Arlington. By December, Tal's mother's was pushing for her son to come to Atlanta for Christmas, an invitation he declined, citing the mountain of legal matters he needed to wrap up before the end of the year. The Bentleys' phone remained tapped and Eleanor's contacts monitored— intrusions she welcomed if it helped her prove herself to them. A pattern developed, where things would go quiet for a couple months, giving Eleanor and Talbot a window of normalcy, then up would pop another lawyer with a question or a demand that Eleanor take yet another polygraph. Early in the new year, the CIA, oddly, consulted her when they needed help with a translation or nuance only a native Russian-speaker could provide. She suspected it was only to see if she was translating honestly. She would dutifully head down the George Washington Parkway to the newly opened CIA headquarters at Langley—a building Talbot would never enter—and review what they placed before her. Her first visit there, she remarked to Chamberlain how relieved she was that she would never, ever have to take photos of the state-of-the-art facility for a Soviet handler.

"Glad to hear you're not spying," Chamberlain said, shaking his head, his voice a monotone. "I'll be sure to let the director know."

·   ·   ·

There was a new director now, Dulles having resigned after the Bay of Pigs debacle and John McCone stepping in. He had held repeated meetings with Chamberlain in hopes of closing out the Eleanor Bentley/Marisha Yahontov file because with Cuba, Central America, and Southeast Asia simmering, McCone didn't need another thing on his plate. Angleton, still running Counterintelligence, continued to push—for expulsion, a prison sentence, something—still nursing his disappointment that his team hadn't come up with anything concrete on Talbot. So McCone turned to Chamberlain for his read of things.

"I don't think she's a threat—not at all," Chamberlain said at their meeting, a year and a half after the U-2 shoot down had so dominated the headlines. "This whole thing's gotten old and tired. I think we move on."

"Angleton could not disagree more," responded McCone. "He insists that a head should roll—somebody's—after all that's happened. He believes she could be a conduit for Soviet operatives still in the country."

"If that's the case, she's doing a terrible job. We just had her here, looking at some cable intercepts between the Soviet Union and Cuba. Her translation matches what the guys on the Russia desk gave us. Exactly. So if she's involved in any subterfuge at all, it's not to fool us."

McCone thanked him for his input, but said he owed it to his Counterintelligence chief to listen to his analysis.

George, meanwhile, was relentless in making the case to the U.S. attorney that Eleanor deserved her freedom, that she was a de facto juvenile offender, young and unknowing when she'd been recruited. Moreover, she had repented, turned, and delivered Cossutta's operatives. Talbot too, advocated for her freedom, insisting that as a former intelligence officer, he'd make the same argument even if she were not his wife; sending her back to the Soviets would be a terrible waste of intelligence. Their position gained purchase when the search of Cossutta's office at Fordham turned up a photo of Mishie at fifteen. On the back, written in Cyrillic and English in her mother's hand, was the name "Eleanor." The plan to enlist her in this shadow war had been set in motion fully four years before she'd left for Florence, perhaps before.

Throughout the months they were marooned in the townhouse, before and after Rémy's murder, while they waited for word on Eleanor's fate, Talbot's sense of betrayal ceased to be the only emotion through which he channeled all others. The analyst within him wanted to understand her better, understand the predicament in which she had lived her entire adult life. Through conversations that ran late into the night, they imagined different scenarios they might have lived had they never met, or if she had found herself earlier, broken away in Florence, or when they'd first come to Washington. They dreamed of paths they might follow now so each could reclaim a life of purpose when whatever this was, was over. They never really decided to stay together, never turned to one another to announce the answer to the unresolved question between them. If she were returned to the Soviet Union, that would be that. Until that was decided, it seemed pointless to separate, to devise a plan to live apart, craft a plausible explanation that would make sense to Caroline and her children, because they'd have to recant all of it and admit what really happened if Eleanor were indicted or expelled.

Over these endless hours together, Talbot began to believe that this woman he called Eleanor was rooting for him, that she earnestly sought to regain his trust, and might even love him. The pulsating outrage over what she had done took on a new texture as he learned more about her, his anger turning from his own losses and towards the mother who had failed her, had allowed her daughter's identity to be erased and served her up to the wolf Cossutta, who used her. He blamed himself that he had not loved her well enough to cause her to abandon what Cossutta asked her to do — that the force of his love should have somehow been enough to compel her to truth. She said he had it backwards: she had loved him through every bit of it — his affairs and her own lies — because she naively believed the only way to protect him, keep him safe and alive, was to cooperate with Cossutta.

A second, central thing that drew them together was their concern for Caroline and her children. They bore a guilt they could never acknowledge or confess, knowing Rémy's decision to cooperate with Eleanor's change of heart had cost him his life. So to feel useful, to find redemption, to pay penance, they became errand-runners and carpoolers, cheerleaders in the front row of piano recitals and baseball games. They babysat, delivered meals, took the kids shopping for Christmas presents for their mother.

And amid all their playacting, the stability and surety and love they worked to convey to the children, they began to show it to one another, to see a glimmer of a remade future with one another, one crosshatched with scars but that might still be worth having — if they were granted the opportunity.

EPILOGUE

February 10, 1962
Glienicke Bridge

It had taken nearly two years and interminable hours of negotiations. The exchange would take place across a bridge that spanned the Havel River at the border between West Berlin and East Germany. No matter that one prisoner on the West Berlin side of the water did not want this to happen, had no interest in living in a place that would never feel like home. This was the deal the Americans had struck; the prisoner's wishes did not matter.

Three detainees in all would take the walk to the East German side, in essence, trading one prison for another. The first offered three meals a day, a warm bed, access to books, ideas, conversation. The second meant a life constrained in a different way: perpetual surveillance, decisions about work and housing made by others, limited fruit and too much cabbage — whether they were welcomed as heroes or exiled to a labor camp. Had things been different, Rémy would be with them, the prisoner thought, his Gallic sensibilities surely struggling by this point to camouflage his disdain for the charade that theirs was a journey to freedom.

They waited in the van, the U.S. Army driver periodically cranking the engine to get a little heat going, while negotiators for both sides stood at the center of the bridge, toeing the white line that divided East from West, smoothing out the logistics. As a dense gray dawn overspread the landscape, the door of the van slid open.

The prisoner wanted to weep, to rail, to resist, to refuse to go, to make the case again that it was not fair to be consigned to a life in what was now, after all these years, an unfamiliar land. But histrionics would do no good. Their arms gripped by American soldiers, the three prisoners were guided through the snow to the deck of the bridge then suddenly released to make their way toward the Soviet military vehicle that waited on the opposite shore. Another man headed toward them, erupting with joy the moment his Soviet minder released him, running into the arms of the two Americans soldiers who awaited him. Overcome as he was by his sudden freedom, Captain Francis Gary Powers might have missed a cold look cast in his direction by the American army colonel overseeing the exchange.

"Dobro pozhalovat' domoy!" shouted the Soviet officer on the other shore, welcoming his three newly returned comrades.

"This is not my home," the prisoner spat. "I know nothing of life here."

"Your Russian is rusty, my friend," said the officer. "But you'll have ample time to improve. And let me remind you: you're not in America anymore. When you say things like that here, there are consequences."

Over the officer's shoulder, the prisoner spotted a broad familiar figure, her smile wide, palms clapped to the sides of her face, standing next to the truck that would take them away to a life reimagined. As the prisoner neared, the woman opened her arms, repeating the name of the returned prodigal like a chant. She leaned in for a kiss, to whisper regret over their long separation, her relief over this long-delayed return.

"Now you'll know how I feel waking up every day in a place I hate, Gilberto. Idiota. Stupido uomo egoista. Te lo meriti." You deserve this, Cossutta's wife hissed, but I do not. She pulled back to look him in the eye then laughed before trudging back to the truck, boots crunching in the snow, arms gesturing wildly that the soldiers were free to do what they wanted with her husband: he was their problem now.

•   •   •

A world away, Eleanor watched the report on the prisoner exchange on the evening news, imagining the life Cossutta would live now. The news anchor focused mostly on Powers' joyful return, with only a sentence about those handed into Soviet custody. There were no pictures, just a description of three returnees—a professor of Renaissance sculpture and two of his associates, described as having worked to undermine the U.S. government. There were still questions, the newsman said, about how the returning American pilot survived the crash of his plane, which handed prodigious technology over to the enemy. "Congressional investigators insist the question of how the Soviets intercepted the U-2 aircraft has still not been satisfactorily answered," he said, before turning to a preview of the televised White House tour the First Lady would soon be conducting.

Talbot scoffed. "Oh, I think by now the U.S. has a pretty good idea of how the Soviets intercepted that aircraft. They're just not telling Congress."

Eleanor closed her eyes, giving her head a little shake as if to clear it. "Will we ever know why Powers didn't destroy the plane? Why he didn't follow orders?"

"Maybe he wanted to live. When the moment came, he wanted to live," Talbot said. "Or, it happened so fast, he couldn't reach the destruct lever. Either way, he'll be back in the U.S. to grapple with the consequences of all of it."

"Could have been me crossing that bridge today. How in the world did it work out that I'm still here—that I'm out of it, finally?"

Talbot swirled the bourbon in his glass, thinking. "I could answer that a number of ways. You're still here because George is a terrific lawyer. You're still here because you turned. Took you a while, but you cooperated, told the truth, knowing you could go to prison—or worse. But to the broader question of why you're here—living with me, in this house—well, Ellie, that's because of a little entanglement in Florence many years ago."

"An entanglement." She gave a low laugh and looked him in the eye. "Is that what you call this? You still here because you can't get un-entangled?"

He rose and went to the shelves that held the art pieces she loved, several things having been added, recently, to the collection. There was the tie clasp that commemorated his honorable discharge from the service. It had arrived in the mail some months back, the return address an apartment in Virginia Beach where it seemed Helen had decided to restart her life. There was a photograph of Tal and Eleanor, taken the day of their second wedding ceremony, both of them smiling, their joy effusive, genuine, and mutual. George had handled the paperwork that finally, legally, gave her the name Eleanor but this time, the marriage license correctly listed her birthplace as Kirov, USSR. The little art deco box from Florence now held the Minox, a symbol of both Talbot's best work and his worst mistake. Chamberlain had disabled the mechanism and presented it to Talbot, suggesting it serve as a reminder of how badly and quickly lies send life off the rails. The other addition came via Chamberlain as well—a print of the photograph of fifteen year-old Mishie, which Talbot had placed, incongruously, in a gilded, Florentine frame. Talbot took it from the shelf and carried it with him to sit next to Eleanor.

"I stayed for her. So she'd have a chance at a life that wasn't orchestrated by somebody else. I want her to have that. I want you to have that."

"Not sure I deserve it."

"None of us deserves it. Not a one. It's called grace, Eleanor. And now that we've reached this point, maybe we can exhale. Live our lives. Plan a future."

She reached for his face, moved a dark lock of hair off his forehead and looked into the eyes of a person she'd first met sixteen years earlier but only recently had come to know. Who'd only recently come to know her.

"We could do that?" she asked, tears gathering in her eyes. "I'm not sure I know what it's like to imagine a life wide-open, without secrets."

"Yeah. We could. We will. Do stuff again. Go places." Talbot thought a moment. "Maybe you can take me through the Renaissance sculptures at the National Gallery like you used to."

Eleanor looked alarmed. "Not that. I've seen enough of that to last a lifetime. But maybe the Renwick Gallery? American arts and crafts."

"American," echoed Talbot. "Yes. I'll show you around."

U-2 Vulnerability Tests

Vulnerability of the U-2 was tested against the F-102 and F-104 fighters at
Eglin AFB in December 1958. The tests were conducted under optimum
controlled ground and air environment for the attacking pilot (i. e. , outstanding pilots, isolated air space, ideal weather, pre-selected intercept
point, etc.). The F-104 cannot cruise at altitudes over 60,000 feet, but
it possesses a capability to convert speed to altitude and attain co-altitude
of the U-2 for a period of less than 30 seconds. The F-104 was equipped
with air-to-air missiles of the infra-red seeking variety and airborne radar
that locates the aircraft and allows the pilot to visually acquire the target
to complete the attack. The F-104 radar malfunctioned at high altitudes.
The pilot of this fighter could not visually acquire the target in sufficient
time to solve the fire control problem. The F-102 all weather fighter con-
sistently acquired the target and was able to solve the fire control problem
for launching air-to-air missiles. To be successful, the missiles require
outstanding high altitude performance and a slant range in excess of five
miles.

The performance of both aircraft exceeded the present capability of operational Soviet fighters. The standard operational Soviet fighters cannot
attain co-altitude of the U-2. A new fighter, the Fitter, of which an estim-
ated 120 have been produced, is considered capable of co-altitude for a period
of several seconds. It is not, however, presently considered operational.
The standard Soviet all weather fighter, YAK-25/Flashlight, is considered
capable of acquiring the U-2 on airborne radar. However, to complete a
successful intercept would require an air-to-air missile with a slant range
in excess of seven miles. The USSR is considered to have air-to-air missiles,
however, there is no intelligence source that indicates that the missiles are
operational.

Conclusions

1. The F-104 can attain co-altitude, but the difficulty in visually acquiring
the target makes any single attack a low probability of successful intercept.

2. The F-102 with its radar can acquire the U-2 and possesses the performance to solve the fire control problem, however, air-to-air missiles of
outstanding performance and long range are required to accomplish airborne
intercept. There is no known operational deployment of air-to-air missiles
by the Soviets.

3. Successful intercept of the U-2 by the Soviet defensive fighters for the
next few months is unlikely.

AUTHOR'S NOTE

Even today, questions remain regarding the U-2 Incident—how the Soviets brought down this particular flight on May 1, 1960 and how American pilot Francis Gary Powers survived the crash landing of a plane he had promised to destroy. Until Powers' fateful flight, the Soviets had ignored years of overflights without public acknowledgment or protest. I worked within these gray areas to write *The Florentine Entanglement*, imagining how Eleanor's work might have furnished just enough data to allow the Soviets to zero in on this U-2 zipping through Soviet airspace on this particular day.

Aides assured President Eisenhower the U-2 could fly unimpeded because Soviet technology could not reach it as it cruised 70,000 feet above the earth. Beginning in the mid-1950s, U-2s began photographing sensitive Soviet installations, returning safely to bases in Turkey and Pakistan. The intelligence yield was so rich—you could count the parking spaces at Soviet military bases—Eisenhower and his staff found it hard to relinquish opportunities to gather more images. Popular political columnists of the day, unaware the administration had unequivocal photographic evidence of Soviet military strength, accused Eisenhower, the former Supreme Allied Commander who'd helped win World War Two, of going soft on the Communists. There were rumors of a widening missile gap with the Soviets and the fear they'd built a long-range bomber that could cross the ocean. Eisenhower knew there was zero evidence of this but could not refute it without giving away the spy plane program. But surely, as reporters accused him of ignoring the Soviet threat, he must have been tempted.

So how, on that May Day 1960, was Powers' plane taken down? Some believe a MIG flying at a lower altitude fired up at him. Alternatively, a MIG might have been hit by a surface-to-air missile (SAM), and ricocheting debris from the MIG hit the U-2. Or perhaps, a Soviet SAM hit Powers' plane directly. In response to the repeated U-2 incursions, the Soviets had made rapid and significant improvements that extended their SAM range. Given the uncrowded skies on this May Day holiday, Powers might have been easier to spot. As to how and why Powers survived the crash, accounts say his plane went into a flat spin, which likely slowed his descent and lessened the crash impact. This disorienting spin could have also prevented Powers from reaching both the destruct lever, and the poison he was meant to take to keep himself out of Soviet hands.

Michael Beschloss's excellent book *May Day* provides deep insight into Eisenhower and Khrushchev during the U-2 crisis, while Monte Reel's *A Brotherhood of Spies* describes how a vast collection of thinkers were brought together in secret to create the U-2 program, the CIA's first large-scale technological operation. Liza Mundy's *The Sisterhood* affirms not only how tough it was for women to advance beyond the clerical ranks within CIA, but that serial affairs were once the habit of men in the case officer and agent ranks. Married men, most notably founding Director Allen Dulles, were referred to as "geographic bachelors," men who seemed to forget commitments they'd made to wives when they traveled, in favor of women within reach. It would not have been unusual for his superiors to overlook Talbot's extracurriculars, until, of course, it appeared to threaten national security.

For additional book and movie recommendations about this incident and this era, visit PamelaNorsworthywrites.com

ACKNOWLEDGEMENTS

To the gracious readers of *War Bonds*—how to thank you for your many kindnesses as I set out on this writing journey? Your emails and reviews, along with conversations at book events, provided just the right oomph to bring this second book to life. While even *more* morally conflicted than their *War Bonds* brethren, I hope you rooted for the *Florentine* characters all the same and that above all, they kept you guessing.

I extend wholehearted thanks to the members of the many book clubs I've been privileged to attend—for the hours of lively, thoughtful, enriching discussions. It's been a gift to see history through the prisms of your family stories.

Huge thanks to my family—all of them smart and lyrical writers themselves—who asked important questions that made this story better. My brother, Jeff Mason, shared his legal expertise, helping me hash out how a scandal like this might play out publicly, and nudging me to include important context. My sister, Melanie Fraser, has a special talent for encouragement on top of her ability to sniff out typos and less-than-clear sentences. Her input improved this manuscript immensely. I'm grateful to my children and their SO's for their love and interest and the piles of books they find for me that deepen my understanding of historical context. Thanks to Margarita Rogers who has championed my writing to all within her reach. And to friends and family whose names I borrowed (purloined?) to fill out this rather long cast of characters: know I pictured your sweet, earnest faces and as I tapped away on my Mac.

To Reagan Rothe and his wonderfully efficient team at Black Rose Writing and to Atlanta's Hot Olive Agency led by the fearless Raven Wilson: thank you for helping get my work into the universe.

Finally to Gray, my husband, live-in publicist, and consultant on aircraft and aeronautics, who's always willing to sort out plot lines and technological considerations with me, who kindly ignores me when I'm heads-down in my writing, and who never complains when we spend the whole day at a literary event. The good guys in my novels? They're all based on Gray.

ABOUT THE AUTHOR

Pamela Norsworthy earned a 2025 Georgia Author of the Year nomination for her debut novel, *War Bonds*, which drew heavily on her father's experiences in World War Two. A former journalist, Pam began writing fiction to explore the vast, unforeseen reverberations when world events collide with the peaceable lives of average people. A lifelong singer, Pam enjoys making music and performing with her guitar-playing husband, rooting for the Atlanta Braves and her alma mater, the University of Virginia, and lingering over spirited dinners with friends to chew over ideas from every angle. She and her husband live in Atlanta, Georgia, where Pam's writing is interrupted every day at noon by their two barking dogs, taken by surprise once again by the arrival of the mail carrier.

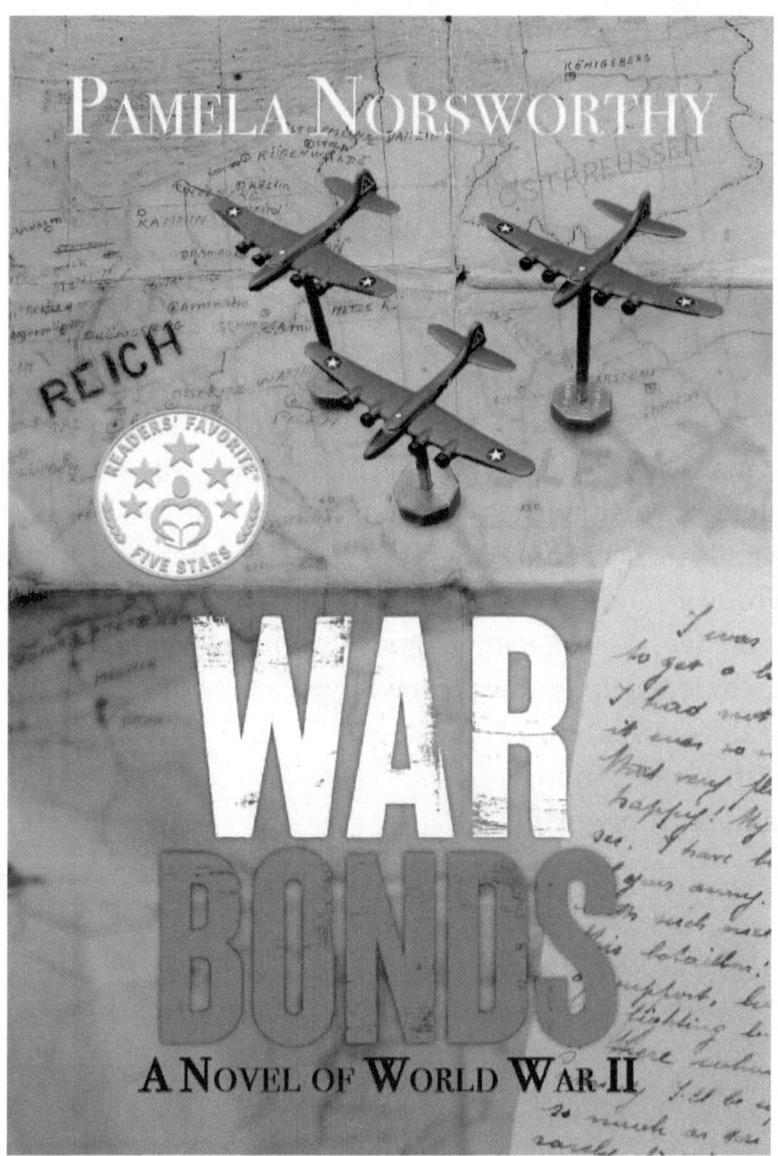
PAMELA NORSWORTHY
REICH
READERS' FAVORITE
FIVE STARS
WAR BONDS
A NOVEL OF WORLD WAR II

NOTE FROM PAMELA NORSWORTHY

Many thanks for reading *The Florentine Entanglement*. Please visit pamelanorsworthywrites.com to find book club questions, blogs that add historical context, and to sign-up for my newsletter.

Word-of-mouth is crucial in helping a book find its audience. If you enjoyed *The Florentine Entanglement*, please share on social media, or leave an online review. Even a sentence or two makes all the difference.

With appreciation,
Pamela Norsworthy

We hope you enjoyed reading this title from:

www.blackrosewriting.com

Subscribe to our mailing list – *The Rosevine* – and receive **FREE** books, daily deals, and stay current with news about upcoming releases and our hottest authors.
Scan the QR code below to sign up.

Already a subscriber? Please accept a sincere thank you for being a fan of Black Rose Writing authors.

View other Black Rose Writing titles at
www.blackrosewriting.com/books and use promo code
PRINT to receive a **20% discount** when purchasing.